Advance Praise for F

"So very charming . . . brought to life b
She weaves the perfect blend of fact and fiction in this '50s tale of five brides who shared something rather uncommon, a wedding dress. I found myself smiling, cheering for the young women who sought what we all seek, happiness and love."

RACHEL HAUCK, bestselling author of *The Wedding Dress*

"One dress, five lives deftly stitched together. In *Five Brides*, Eva Marie Everson tells the stories of resilient young women navigating a time of personal and cultural change. Chasing their dreams, they arrive at different futures, each wrapped in one unforgettable wedding dress."

LISA WINGATE, bestselling author of *The Prayer Box* and *The Story Keeper*

"Whether you're about to say 'I do' or simply want to reminisce on your own marriage journey, *Five Brides* is just the novel for you. I can't wait to read more from this creative author, who seamlessly interweaves five very different women's stories into one pleasurable experience, so rich with sensory detail—clothing, food, etiquette—I felt I was transported to the 1950s. Place this gem at the top of your reading list."

JOLINA PETERSHEIM, bestselling author of *The Midwife* and *The Outcast*

"*Five Brides* made me fall in love again . . . and again . . . and again. Eva Marie Everson's richly drawn characters are skillfully woven together like the dress that binds them all. This story deeply touched the romantic in me."

NICOLE SEITZ, author of *Beyond Molasses Creek*, *The Inheritance of Beauty*, and *A Hundred Years of Happiness*

"*Five Brides* is a beautifully written, moving portrayal of five women finding themselves and love in a time of cultural obligation. Eva Marie Everson has penned an enchanting and emotionally satisfying story that will no doubt capture readers' hearts."

KELLIE COATES GILBERT, author of *Where Rivers Part* (a Texas Gold novel)

"In the tale of *Five Brides*, Eva Marie Everson brings us the stirring story of five young women whose lives intersect in their quests to love and be loved without losing themselves to the expectations of others."

SHELLIE RUSHING TOMLINSON, the Belle of All Things Southern and author of *Heart Wide Open*

Five Brides

FIVE BRIDES

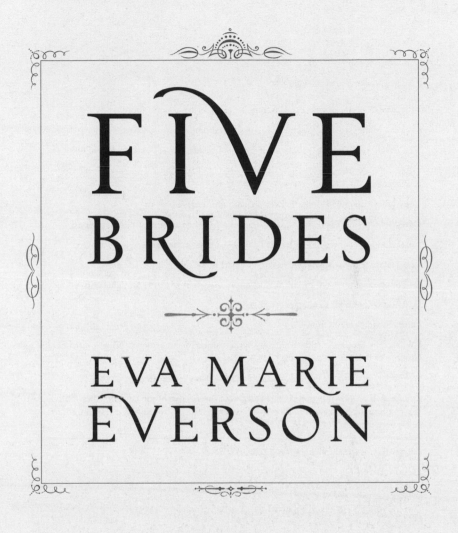

EVA MARIE EVERSON

Tyndale House Publishers, Inc.
Carol Stream, Illinois

Visit Tyndale online at www.tyndale.com.

Visit Eva Marie Everson at www.evamarieeversonauthor.com.

TYNDALE and Tyndale's quill logo are registered trademarks of Tyndale House Publishers, Inc.

Five Brides

Designed by Dean H. Renninger

Edited by Kathryn S. Olson

Published in association with the literary agency of Jonathan Clements, Wheelhouse Literary Group, PO Box 110909, Nashville, TN 37222.

Scripture quotations are taken from the *Holy Bible*, King James Version.

Library of Congress Cataloging-in-Publication Data

Everson, Eva Marie.
Five brides / Eva Marie Everson.
pages ; cm
ISBN 978-1-4143-9744-3 (sc)
I. Title.
PS3605.V47F58 2015
813'.6—dc23 2015001358

Printed in the United States of America

21 20 19 18 17 16 15
7 6 5 4 3 2

To Robert and Joan Hunt Zimmerman.

Your generosity inspires me . . .

Your hospitality amazes me . . .

Your love captivates me . . .

And knowing you has made me a better person.

Thank you.

Acknowledgments

Allow me to begin by giving my utmost thanks to my dear friend Sharon Allred Decker, who gave me the idea for this story. To Joan and Robert Zimmerman for allowing me to tell, with creative license, *their* story. To my agent, Jonathan Clements, for his unwavering belief in me as a writer and author. To Jan Stob . . . Finally! We work together. And to Kathy Olson for trusting me to "do it all over again."

To all the fine folks at Tyndale . . . I appreciate you already more than I have words to say. Working with you has been a long-held dream of mine. (Did you know my eleven-times-great-grandparents hired a young William Tyndale to serve as a tutor for their sons at Little Sodbury, and that once after he was jailed, they bailed him out? Well, it's true.)

To Sandie Bricker, who worked alongside me start to finish (and start to finish again) as a critique partner . . . I thank you! And thank you for allowing me the privilege of working with you on your excellent manuscript as well.

To Word Weavers International, my wonderful champions.

A great big *danke schön* to Kirstin Shafer and a *merci beaucoup* to Rose Chandler Johnson.

Thank you, thank you, thank you to my beta-readers-slash-critique-mavens-of-all-good-fiction: Deb Haggerty, Shellie Arnold, and Jessica R. Everson.

To my family—my husband, children, grandchildren . . . I love you!

And above all, to my Lord and Savior (my bridegroom) Jesus Christ and to His Father God and to the Holy Spirit . . . I am humbled.

Ani ohevet otcha.

PROLOGUE

June 2015
London, England

The phone on the hotel's bedside table rang, startling Julie Boland from her near-nap. She jerked upright, placed her feet on the plush carpet between the two beds, and reached for the handset. "Hello?" she said, her voice shaking. Glancing at the Fossil watch her husband had given her on her last birthday, Julie groaned before speaking, this time her voice steady. "Hello?"

"Mrs. Boland?" the crisp British voice inquired.

"Yes, this is Mrs. Boland."

"We have the rather large package you've been expecting at the front desk, if you'd like to make your way down."

The door to the bedroom opened, and her daughter Rachel all but flew over the threshold. Light from the living room streamed in past the height of her, brightening the room without the assistance of electricity, bringing a sheen to the room's burgundy and gold accent colors. "Is it here, Mama?"

Julie waved a hand, hoping her daughter would get the hint and shut the door. "I'll be down in a moment," she told the caller.

Julie replaced the handset, then reached for the sleeveless linen shift she'd slipped out of only fifteen minutes earlier. "Yes, my darling, it's here," she said, standing. She straightened her dress as she turned to shove her feet into the pair of Antonio Melani sandals at the foot of the bed. "Zip me up, hon."

Rachel rushed to her mother and tugged at the hidden zipper. "Oh, Mama, I could just burst from the excitement of it all. To think, in five days I'm going to be Mrs. Jeremy Sullivan, and *today* I *finally* get to see MiMi's wedding dress. Well, *yours* and MiMi's."

"It was Miss Evelyn's long before it was mine." Julie turned and pressed her hands on both sides of her daughter's face. "Miss Evelyn's and Miss Joan's—"

"And the sisters and Betty," Rachel finished for her. "*Hurry*, Mama."

Julie tapped her daughter's upturned nose. "Don't get sassy," she teased, smiling. "Oh, darlin', just wait till you see it in person," she said. "A Carson's original." Julie started for the living room, running her fingers through shoulder-length chestnut hair. She stopped at one of the room's several wall mirrors. "What is it with this hotel and mirrors?" she asked rhetorically, tugging lightly at faint crow's-feet.

Rachel practically skipped beside her, forcing another smile out of Julie even as she said, "I wish Edwin hadn't insisted on taking in a tour this afternoon. But your daddy's going to do what your daddy's going to do." She exhaled in the fashion of every Southern woman she'd ever known from childhood on.

"You know what I wish," Rachel said, putting her arm through her mother's as they crossed the room to the outer door, her voice suddenly quiet and reflective. "I wish MiMi had lived long enough to see this. She'd have thought it something that I'm marrying an Englishman."

Julie stopped to look at her daughter. "You look so much like

Miss Evelyn, you do. Same soft features. Same eyes." She tousled Rachel's bangs. "Same light hair." She sighed again. "Miss Evelyn never saw herself as beautiful, although I don't know why. I always thought she was quite something, just by the way she carried herself." Julie cupped her daughter's chin. "You, however, should have *never* doubted *your* beauty. You won enough beauty pageants to fill our house with ribbons and trophies, and your grandmother's besides."

"Mama," Rachel laughed, nudging her mother out the door. "Hurry *on* now." She looked at her bare feet. "I'm not dressed to go down, or I'd have gone and been back ten times already."

"In those shorts and that tee you look more like you should be the junior bridesmaid than the bride." Julie pointed to the middle of the room. "Park it over there on the sofa, young lady. Your mama will be back in a minute with your grandmother's wedding gown."

She'd made it halfway out the door when Rachel called out to her again. "Mama?"

Julie turned.

"You'll tell me the story then? As *soon* as you get back? You always said you'd tell me the whole story—start to finish—the day I was fitted for my own wedding."

Julie smiled. "I will tell you exactly what Miss Evelyn told me the week before I married her son. Start to finish. How they all met in Chicago, how they saw the dress for the first time, and about the days each of them wore it."

Rachel beamed. "Who will you start with? Which one of the brides?"

Julie pondered a moment, her fingertips touching lightly on the doorknob. "I believe I'll tell you the story the same way Miss Evelyn told me. Starting with Miss Joan, her English pen pal . . ."

CHAPTER 1

October 1951
Chicago

An early morning wind whipped around the right-front corner of the medieval and French Renaissance building on Chicago's south side. Once the splendid home of one of the city's most respected doctors, it now served as a temporary home for young women in transit. Women like nineteen-year-old Joan Hunt.

She stretched under the weight of a starched sheet and a thick blanket that smelled of mothballs and time, then pulled her left arm out from under the light weight. The chill in the air drove gooseflesh up and down its length. With the fingertips of her right hand, which only peeked out of the covers, she turned the Timex double-mesh banded watch to view the face, then blinked. She'd slept over ten hours.

"Well, no wonder," she mumbled, returning the covers to her chin. Squeezing her eyes shut, she whispered, "Good morning, Lord. We've a lot to do today, now, don't we?" Then, as though her life depended on it, in one movement she threw the covers to her feet and sat upright.

Up and out of bed, Joan opened the battered trunk at the end of the twin cot in the narrow room she'd been assigned the evening before. Her clothes—neatly folded in short stacks, skirts on one side, blouses on the other, lingerie in a satin case beneath them all—smelled of home, of lavender and England, and a long but exciting week on the *Mauretania II*.

She removed the cedar cubby shelf filled with a collection of framed photos, two of her favorite Agatha Christie novels, a small leather address book, and the paper she'd written for a contest in which the young ladies of Leigh, Lancashire, England, were to write an essay titled, "The Man of Your Dreams." It had been simple enough for her to pen. Even at sixteen.

"The man of my dreams will be able to do things," she'd written. "Lots of things. And be creative. And," she'd added, "it would be nice if he were six foot two, had blue eyes, and lots of dark hair."

Joan smiled now at the reaction her mother had given her. "I'm so sure, Joan. God is going to create some man out of clay just for you."

Joan now lowered the shelf to the industrial-white tile floor, then slipped her hand behind the skirts and withdrew a stack of correspondence bound by a wide pink ribbon. The swirl of her name in Evelyn Alexander's penmanship brought comfort, welcoming her to Chicago and her temporary home. It also helped her to know she'd done the right thing in journeying here.

"Just come," Evelyn had written from her home, which Joan had always pictured as having a wide wraparound porch dotted with wicker furniture and surrounded by lush lawns.

> *Come to Chicago. If your father says this is the best place to find a job here in the States, then it must be true. If you dare to board a ship and cross the Atlantic, I'll dare to take the train up the Eastern Seaboard.*

Joan had dared, all right, the scariest part of her journey having been the announcement to her mother—the truest of all

Brits—that she wanted to return to America, the land of her birth. She had endured Mum's shock and calmly said, "I know, Mum," after she'd reminded her that "dual citizenship is not possible, you know. You cannot belong to both the king *and* the president."

And Joan endured it again when her mum stoically cried, "I don't know if I can bear this."

Difficult as it was to hear Mum cry, the idea of remaining in war-ravaged England—of merely enduring her days until some poor bloke asked her to marry him—was more than *she* could bear. While she wanted her future groom to be able to do things, first *she* wanted to experience life. Then, she wanted bride and groom to do so many wonderful things *together*.

Joan pulled the top letter from the stack, returned the rest, and placed the shelf over her clothes. Her fingertips brushed across a photo of her family, all eleven, clustered together in their Sunday best, wide-eyed and smiling. Her index finger rested over the place where her mother's heart beat, and she closed her eyes and breathed in deeply, remembering the cries that pierced the halls of the American offices in Manchester when she boldly repeated, "I denounce the king and all his rights, and swear my allegiance to the United States of America."

She exhaled as she stood, shaking away the memory as she laid the last letter from Evelyn at the foot of the bed. She grabbed her robe from the lone black spindle-back Windsor chair and shoved her arms into the sleeves, tied the belt around her too-thin waist, stepped into slippers, and darted out the door toward the bath and showers down the hall.

Minutes later, with her teeth brushed and hair combed, she returned to her assigned room, closed the door behind her, and walked to the window.

The previous night, after a week on the ship and another

twenty-four hours on a train, she'd been too tired to eat. But now, as she pulled the muslin curtains away from the room's single window, her stomach rumbled.

"There's a restaurant just down the block," the man behind the desk had said when she arrived, and she wondered how he'd known she stood there praying she wouldn't collapse in the lobby. "They're open until nine."

"I'm afraid I'm just too worn out to walk there and back." She chuckled with all the energy of a turtle at the end of his race. "Pathetic, isn't it?"

The young man—tall and lanky with a full head of dark curls—scratched along his temple before holding up a finger and saying, "Tell you what." He ambled over to the desk behind him, piled high with papers and files of all sorts. He pulled out a drawer and dipped his hand in, retrieving a candy bar. "Do you like Baby Ruths?"

She honestly didn't know, but nodded anyway. "Thank you," she'd said as he handed her what would be dinner.

"Be back down before eight in the morning and get yourself some coffee and a nice hot breakfast. We start serving at six."

Now, with her nose pressed to the cool glass and peering at the street below where cars already rolled past, her stomach declared that the meal of peanuts, caramel, and chocolate had officially worn off.

Joan dined alone in the expansive cafeteria of the YMCA. Fine by her; she wanted to read Evelyn's last letter again before the first order of business—embarking on her job search.

If you arrive on the 16th of October, you'll have to go it alone for a few days. I cannot possibly be there until the 20th. Perhaps not until a couple of weeks after that. I'd hoped to meet you in New York and we could take the train together, but I have had to handle Mama with kid gloves.

Joan understood. All too well. Though their situations were similar, they were also vastly different. Joan had to denounce the king and travel to a country she hadn't seen for years, not since the Great Depression. Her father, a fun-loving Irishman, and her mother, a gentle Englishwoman, had packed up all their belongings and their brood of children and returned to the United Kingdom from their Chicago home. Evelyn, on the other hand, had never been to the "Windy City." She'd been to Atlanta once, she'd said, but that was as far "north" as she'd traveled.

Still, if I don't do this very brave thing . . . if I don't square my shoulders and tell Daddy how desperately I want to leave on this great adventure . . . I just know, Joanie, that I'll regret it for the rest of my life. I can feel it in the marrow of my bones. Every morning I wake with one thought: You must do this, Evelyn. This is your one opportunity.

Indeed, Joan thought, swallowing the last of her tea and toast. *Mine as well.* Being the middle child of nine, she'd felt she had to come to America. Create her own adventure. Write her own story. Or simply burst from the need. For something . . . something more than England could offer.

Something. Although she couldn't say quite what. And if she didn't find it here, she reasoned she would have to return across the Atlantic to seek it elsewhere.

Joan stood resolutely and brushed a few crumbs from her

skirt. The time had come for her to find a job. And find it quickly. Today. She had only thirty-seven dollars to her name, and, as comfortable as her room at the Y seemed to be, it was only a room.

It wasn't home.

For her first day in Chicago, she chose a simple blue over-the-knee pencil skirt and a white shirtwaist. Her only accessories were a strand of pearls, a small hat with a net that she pulled back, and a pair of gloves the color of midnight. She'd taken stock of herself as best she could in the small mirror in her room, but now, in front of one of the wide front windows of a four-story office building, she had a better view. And, if she said so herself, she made a rather smashing reflection.

Joan adjusted the clutch she carried under her arm. It held Evelyn's letter with suggestions for employment, and her cash for safekeeping. The building she stood in front of appeared squatty in comparison to those around it. But the brass address plate indicated it contained a number of businesses within, including Hertz, which she had heard of. Seemed a good place to start.

And if you land a job, Joanie, promise me you'll save a spot for me.

No "if" about it. She *would* land a job.

Joan entered the lobby off of South Wabash, which was austere by every definition of the word. Only a few ordinary chairs flanked the perimeter between office doors. A receptionist's desk sat smack in the center.

"Hallo," she said to the young blonde on the other side of it.

The woman looked up from her work with wide blue eyes made bluer by the dark liner that curled from the ends of the lids. "May I help you?"

Yes, she absolutely could. Joan straightened her shoulders and smiled. "I'm here for a job."

CHAPTER 2

The receptionist smiled, although Joan didn't read any kindness in it. "Any particular one of the businesses here?"

She only knew of one, so she stuck with it. "Hertz."

"Second floor. You can take the stairs," she said, pointing with a pencil to a far corner. "Or the elevator, which is just over here." She moved the pencil a few inches, indicating doors several yards closer to where Joan stood.

"Thank you," Joan said, then made her way to the elevator. She pressed the small black Up button and waited for the faux-wood double doors to open.

Less than a minute later, she stepped onto the second floor, which seemed to be an exact replica of the one below. Chairs near the elevator clustered around a coffee table strewn with Hertz fliers and the *Chicago Tribune*.

Joan adjusted her shirtwaist, straightened her shoulders, and marched to the receptionist, a well-groomed woman who appeared to be in her thirties.

"Hello," she said. "How may I help you?"

"I'm here for a job."

The woman—Mrs. Michaelson, according to the nameplate—smiled. "What kind of job?"

Joan said the first thing that came to mind. "I'm a very good secretary." Which was true. She'd been working in some capacity or another since before her tenth birthday, and she'd graduated from business college before her seventeenth.

Mrs. Michaelson tilted her head apologetically to the left. "I'm sorry. We don't have any secretarial jobs open at the moment."

"Oh. Well, then," Joan said, suddenly aware of the clip of her brogue against this woman's American accent, "what kind of jobs *do* you have?"

Again, the head tilted. "Why don't you tell me what you are trained to do."

Joan took in a breath. "I should tell you that I graduated from business college when I was sixteen. I've worked steadily since then."

"And how old are you now, dear?"

She wished Mrs. Michaelson would stop talking to her as though she were twelve. "Nineteen," she answered. Clearing her throat, she added, "May I speak with your manager, please?"

Joan was certain she could do better with him. Tell him about her excellent grades in school. About her work habits and integrity while on the job.

"Mr. Ferguson?"

"Is that his name? Your manager?"

Mrs. Michaelson folded her hands together, fingers interlocking. "The head of human resources. Yes."

"Then yes. Mr. Ferguson."

With a slight shake of her head, Mrs. Michaelson picked up the handset of a phone, dialed a couple of numbers, and waited. "Mr. Ferguson," she said, "there's a young woman here who'd like to see you . . . Yes, sir . . . Yes, she—yes, sir." She returned the handset. "He'll be right with you."

"Shall I wait over there?" Joan asked, looking toward the chairs.

Mrs. Michaelson picked up a pencil as though she were about to take a note. Before she could answer, a door to her left opened and a man approached.

"I'm Mr. Ferguson," he said, adjusting his suit jacket at the button. His breath smelled of coffee and peppermint.

Joan extended her hand, which he took. "Joan Hunt." She smiled, hoping he would return the gesture.

He did.

Mr. Ferguson was a handsome man. Midforties, she suspected. Angular face, tanned complexion, eyes the color of a French silk pie, their centers twinkling with merriment. She immediately warmed to him. "Joan," he said, as he released her hand. "Why don't you come with me?"

Joan breathed a sigh of relief and flashed a smile at Mrs. Michaelson. She mouthed, "Thank you." Following the head of human resources, she offered up another prayer, asking God for favor. *I don't have to run the company,* she prayed silently. *I only want to work for it.*

They stepped through the door Mr. Ferguson had exited earlier and into an ordinary office with a metal desk, neatly arranged with stacks of files, a typewriter, telephone, and a single rose budding from a narrow vase. "My secretary's desk," he said, indicating that Joan should continue toward the inner office. "She's running an errand for me presently but should be back soon."

As Joan sat in one of two vinyl-covered chairs in his office, Mr. Ferguson said, "Tell me, where are you from?" He sat in the imposing black chair behind his desk.

"I was born here in the States," she said. "But my family returned to England when I was nine."

He folded his hands in the same manner as Mrs. Michaelson,

placing them over white papers fanned across his desk. "What kind of work experience do you have, Joan?"

"As soon as we arrived in England, I began working for Mr. Higginbottom, the local pig man."

Mr. Ferguson appeared amused at the story. "And what did you do, at nine years of age, for Mr. Higginbottom?"

"I collected leftover food scraps from the neighbors. For his pigs, of course. Then, between ten and twelve I picked potatoes, as did all the schoolchildren in England."

Mr. Ferguson's brow furrowed. "And why was that?"

"The men were at war and it was necessary." Joan pressed her ankles together as she remembered the weeks of harvesting alongside her school chums as well as her brothers and sisters.

"Ah, yes."

"At twelve I took a job collecting past-due accounts for the newsagent." She suppressed a giggle. "I'm sure most people don't think a twelve-year-old can be intimidating, but believe me, sir, I was."

Mr. Ferguson grinned, sending parenthetical lines up both sides of his face. "I have no doubt."

"Then, at thirteen, I won a scholarship to junior business college. My first *adult* job was at sixteen, working in a textile manufacturing factory . . ." She knew she could continue, but thought to let Mr. Ferguson ask, should he have further questions.

"Tell me, Joan, what do you think you work best at? Because we have no pigs to feed or potatoes to pick here in Chicago."

Joan thought for a moment. Whatever they placed in front of her, she knew she could do, and do well. So she said, "What openings do you *have*?"

"We have an opening in accounting . . ."

"I'm a *very* good accountant." *Of course, I'm accustomed only to pounds, shillings, and pence . . .*

His dark eyes fixed on hers. She took a deep breath and held it until he blinked. "You know, Joan, I have a daughter your age. You remind me a lot of her, actually." He waited for a reaction, but she gave none. "If she were in England, I'd want to know that someone gave her a job." Then he smiled. "When can you start?"

Joan could hardly believe it, though she whispered a prayer of thanks anyway. "Why, today, of course."

One side of his mouth curled upward. "How about tomorrow?"

She stood, extending her hand again. "Tomorrow it is."

Mr. Ferguson took it. She squeezed, feeling nothing short of confidence. Released. "Come straight to my office. Introduce yourself to Betty . . ." He nodded toward his secretary's office with a mischievous smile. "She should be back by then."

Joan rolled the name over in her mind. *Betty, Betty, Betty . . .* "What time then?"

"Be here at eight." His eyes met hers in a most fatherly way. "Don't be late."

"Of course not."

She turned toward the door, which she reached in three long strides.

"And Joan?"

She peered over her shoulder with a smile. "Yes, Mr. Ferguson?"

"Welcome home."

CHAPTER 3

Portal, Georgia

Night had settled around the old farmhouse in quaking shadows, pungent with the scent of burning autumn leaves. Evelyn Alexander, more used to her quiet surroundings than she wanted to be, stood at the open kitchen window drying the last of the pots and pans from supper. She returned them to the lower cabinet where they belonged and whisked the dishrag over the white Formica countertop.

She pressed her hands against the small of her back and stretched, then jumped when her mother spoke behind her. "Don't forget to close the winda."

Evelyn spun around. Her mother had already dressed for bed—her hair had been set in pin curls, and the scent of talcum powder drifted across the room. "Yes, ma'am," Evelyn said. "I won't."

Her mother turned away, shoulders slumped against the weariness of life.

"Mama?"

Mama stopped, turned back. "What?"

"Where's Daddy?"

"Out yonder. On the front porch, I 'spect. That man loves the smell of those leaves more'n anyone I know." She shook her head, and for a moment Evelyn thought she saw her mother smile. But before she could know for sure, her mother shuffled down the hall. "Don't forget the winda."

"I won't," Evelyn muttered. She returned to the sink and leaned over, pushed the raised window toward the sill, then pulled the curtains shut.

A minute later she stepped over her younger brother, Sol, who lay on the living room rug reading another Hardy Boys mystery. "It's about time for bed," she said to him.

"I'm almost done with this chapter," he answered without looking away from the book.

Evelyn smiled at him, at the red in his cropped hair and the way he'd managed to kick off only one shoe while the other stayed secure on his foot.

She walked out onto the front porch, where, sure enough, she found her daddy sitting in one of the rockers, pipe stem clutched between his teeth. The scent of it mixed with that of the leaves, and Evelyn inhaled deeply. "Hey, sugar dumplin'," he said without turning his head.

Evelyn walked past him to the nearby swing hanging by two half-rusty chains. "Hey, Daddy."

She pulled a postcard out of one of the side pockets of her skirt as she pushed her saddle oxfords against the narrow gray-painted boards, making the swing squeak. She made an effort to read the words on the back, but without the porch light on and with no moon to speak of, her endeavor went unrewarded. She sighed dramatically, hoping her father would take notice.

He did. "Whatcha got there?"

"A postcard from Joan." Evelyn pressed her lips together as she waved it in his direction.

"She make it to the States all right?"

"Yes, sir. She mailed this from New York before she boarded the train. I reckon she's made it to Chicago by now."

Her father pulled on the pipe, causing the tobacco to glow. "Chicago, Illinois," he said as though he were talking about heaven itself.

"Daddy—"

"I know," he said before she could say much else. "You aim to go."

"I do, Daddy, but—"

"Your Mama's go'n be heartbroken, you know."

"Even more than she is already. I know."

Daddy pulled on the pipe again. "What about Hank?"

"I don't love Hank, Daddy." Evelyn struggled to keep her voice low enough that if Mama hovered near an open window upstairs, she wouldn't hear. "Mama practically has my trousseau laid out, but . . . Daddy, Hank's a good boy and all, but . . ." The rest was difficult to say. Hank Shute had been her boyfriend for all of their high school years. And he was a fine young man. Strong in his faith. Strong in body. He had to be to work his daddy's farmland, which he intended to own himself one day. Hank was also strong in his love for her. And, as plain and homely as Evelyn had grown up to be, she shouldn't look a gift horse in the mouth. Still . . .

"But he doesn't turn your skin to gooseflesh."

Evelyn giggled. "What?"

Daddy laughed lightly. "When the right one comes along, you'll feel your skin turn to gooseflesh every time you get around him. Hank doesn't do that for you?"

"Did you? When you were dating Mama?"

Now he turned to look at her. "Yes'm. And I still do."

Evelyn bit her bottom lip to keep from grinning. "Well, I haven't had those feelings yet. Not with Hank. Not with any boy."

Her daddy raised the toes of his work boots, which set the chair to rocking as he faced forward again. "Whatcha think you want to do once you get to Chicago, Evie-girl?"

Evelyn allowed her imagination to take flight. "I want to get an apartment—*not* live in a boardinghouse—and I want to get a job in a big company. I want to get dressed up every day to go work in one of those tall buildings downtown in the Loop."

"The what?" He peered at her again.

"The Loop. It's like the business area of Chicago." Evelyn drew an imaginary circle in the air. "It's kind of round so they call it the Loop."

"Do you know where you'll live?"

"Joanie is taking care of that for me." At least she hoped so.

"What about money?"

"I've got some saved from my job at Mrs. Bryant's Kitchen."

Daddy remained silent for a moment. "When do you figure on going?"

Evelyn raised her brow. "Soon?"

For a few moments more, they swung and rocked in silence. "Tell you what let's do," her father finally said. "Give it a month."

"Daddy—" The air in Evelyn's lungs rushed out and hung in the air between them like an old sheet on the line. "Then you'll say it's too close to Thanksgiving . . ."

But her father's eyes held firm, locking with hers as best they could in the dark night. "Listen to me now."

"Yes, sir."

"One month. If you still feel like you want to go, I'll give you the money you'll need to get set up and put you on the train myself." He pointed the stem of his pipe in her direction. "Not a word to your mama, now. We don't need to go borrowing no trouble."

Evelyn's heart raced, but she managed to stay calm. "Yes, sir."

Then she smiled so wide her cheeks hurt. She hoped her father didn't see. "I mean, no, sir."

"Chicago, Illinois," he said again, whispering the city's name like a prayer. "You always were one step ahead of us here, sugar bear. I 'spect you'll do all right amongst those city people. Still . . ." He turned the pipe upside down and knocked the tobacco into his calloused hand. "If you ever want to come back, this is always home."

CHAPTER 4

Highland Park, Illinois

Betty Estes sat with her legs crossed at the ankles as she'd been both taught and scolded to do, whether by her mother or by the nuns or during her time at finishing school. She stared down the long linen-draped dining room table where her father sat regally at the head, sliding his spoon into the broth that had been served as their first course.

"So, work is going well?" he asked her, peering beneath thick brows.

Betty suppressed the urge to run, knowing full well where this conversation was headed. The same place as always. She glanced at her mother, sitting at the other end. While Mother reminded her of an older Lauren Bacall, Father looked more like Ernest Hemingway, leaving Betty to feel nothing short of gratitude that she'd grown into more of her mother's features.

She looked again at her father as she glided her own soup spoon through dark broth and inhaled the fragrance of beef and onion. "It's going very well, actually, Father."

"I still don't understand—"

"Harrison, please," Chloe Estes said as she nestled her spoon between the bone china bowl and matching plate beneath it. She picked up a tiny silver dinner bell and rang it, summoning Adela to bring the next course and save them all.

The rotund colored woman with silver streaks in her hair, the one who had cared for the family as though they were her own since as far back as Betty could remember, entered through the swinging door separating the butler's pantry from the dining room. She carried an ornate silver tray and, as was her custom, went immediately to Chloe. "Miz Estes, you haven't hardly touched your soup," she scolded. "Was it all right?"

Betty detected concern in Adela's voice, though she couldn't tell whether it was about the soup or Betty's mother's health.

"It was fine, Adela." Chloe Estes smiled up at her as she swallowed hard. "I'm just ready for the next course, and I don't want to spoil my appetite."

"Not sure how that could happen with a little soup," Adela mumbled as she gathered up the dishes, then moved to the other end of the table. "How about you, Mr. Estes? Are you done?"

Betty's father took another hurried spoonful before adding, "I am."

Betty took a final spoonful as well. Best to do so while she could. These weekly dinners—plus the ones after Mass on Sunday—were sometimes the best food she ate. Not that she would admit that to her parents. And not to mention that no food anywhere in the state of Illinois could come close to Adela's cuisine.

"Thank you, Adela," she whispered before the housekeeper whisked the dishes away to another room. Then she looked at her father. "You might be interested to know that I recently received a raise from Mr. Ferguson."

Her hopes that her father might be impressed were dashed by reality. Instead, he pointed a manicured finger at her. "You should be running that department, not working as a secretary. When I think of the money I spent sending you to college and the diploma collecting dust in my office—"

"It's doing no such thing," Betty said before Adela returned with the next course. "Adela would never hear of dust collecting on anything in this house." She smiled, hoping to get her parents to do the same. But a quick look at her father and then her mother told her they weren't in the mood to play.

"Betty," her mother said, pressing her fingertips against the edge of the table and making a show of pressing the linen, "have you heard from George?"

Betty's stomach clenched. "You mean since he and his family were here on Sunday for brunch?" Her wheat-colored hair tossed as she shook her head. "No. Mother, we're *not* a couple. We're friends."

"You're twenty-six years old," her father all but barked.

"I know how old I am," Betty snapped back. "You reminded me on my last birthday by making sure the cake looked like a house on fire once the candles were lit."

"At twenty-six, your mother was married with a child running underfoot. She was climbing her way to the top of social clubs, doing charity work . . ."

Betty blinked. "You act like I'm turning forty on my next birthday. Twenty-six is *not* an old maid. At least, not anymore." She took a breath. "And Mother *never* had a child running underfoot." Perhaps *Adela* had, but not Chloe Estes.

Her mother sighed so deeply Betty wondered if she'd forgotten herself. Ladies, she had often told Betty, do not show signs of emotion at the table. "The least you could do is *entertain* George's affection toward you." She brushed imaginary strands of hair from her brow, as if her locks would dare fall out of place. "When I think of that splendid ring he gifted you with last Christmas . . ." Her voice trailed as Adela returned with the serving cart loaded with plates of steaming food.

"Saved by the serving cart," Betty said.

"Are they picking on my girl again?" Adela asked as she rolled the cart between Betty and her mother.

"Aren't they always?" Betty asked.

Adela set a plate in front of Betty's mother before picking up another and walking it around to her father. In the interim, Betty grasped the opportunity to change the subject. "Mother, the new painting over the sideboard is amazing." The artwork—a late-nineteenth-century piece depicting a French farm scene—had been recently snagged from a Chicago gallery for more money than Betty's annual food bill. At some point between Sunday afternoon and this evening, her mother managed to get it to the house by courier and professionally hung.

How *did* she do it all?

"You like it?" her mother beamed, her eyes taking it in.

"Very much so." At the very least, it brought a smidgen of color to an otherwise-pale room. What with the taupe drapes and seat cushions and the sand-colored carpet, even the crystal chandelier overhead couldn't find enough color to cast rainbow prisms in the middle of a sunny day.

"She's changing the subject," her father said. "And doing a fine job of it. She knows good and well that if she brings up art, you'll forget about George."

Adela set Betty's plate—filled with roast beef, asparagus, and julienned potatoes—before her. "Hold your own," she mumbled.

Betty held her laughter as she glanced at her watch. "Can we please eat in peace? I have to catch the train back to Greenleaf soon."

"Why don't you spend the night here? In your old room?" her mother asked. "Leave early enough in the morning so that you're not late to work."

The suggestion was tempting, but Betty shook her head. "That's okay, Mother. As much as I dread the train ride back, I'd really best be getting home."

CHAPTER 5

Joan stood at the front door of the Y, staring out at the rain-drenched sidewalk and street.

The one thing she should have packed without so much as a second thought—an umbrella—she'd left in the tiny closet she shared with her sisters. Although she wore an all-weather coat, it would do little to protect her from the deluge she now witnessed.

Joan squeezed her eyes shut; with the weather like this, she would be late on her first day at Hertz.

Her first and *last* day if the rain delayed her any longer.

A tap on the shoulder caused her to turn toward the dark eyes of the day manager, a middle-aged man named Samson. He smiled down at her, the white of his teeth a stark contrast to the ebony of his skin. "Could you use one of these, Miss Joan Hunt from England?" he asked, holding an umbrella by its curved handle.

She sighed in relief. "I could very much use one of those."

He nodded once. "You look like the kind of girl who'd bring it back at the end of the day," he teased.

Joan raised her hand as though taking a solemn oath. "On my word."

They stepped outside where he opened the umbrella straight

out, then swept it up and over her head. "Here you go. If I'm not here when you get back, just leave it behind the counter over there."

She placed her hand on his arm. "Thank you so much. I don't know what I'd do—"

"No need for all that. Just go on to wherever you were heading. And the good Lord be with you."

Joan hurried along with a stream of others, the rain dancing around her, dripping off the tipped ends of a stranger's gift. Water sprang from the tops of her open-toed black pumps, soaking her feet and pooling in the tips of her nylons. She could hardly walk fast enough to reach the train.

By the time she'd reached the Loop, and then the Hertz office building, a chill had penetrated to her bones. Determined, she ducked under the awning, lowered the umbrella and shook it, then brushed moisture from the shoulders of her coat. With a shiver, she opened the front door and stepped into the already-busy first-floor reception area.

She smiled at the same receptionist she'd seen the day before and walked purposefully to the elevator where she hoped not to leave a puddle on the floor. She waited with several others—three suited men and one finely dressed woman, her raincoat slung over her arm. She appeared to be a few years older than Joan and carried an air of sophistication Joan didn't possess.

"Good morning," Joan said.

The other young woman gave a wide smile in response. "Hello." She shifted her wet umbrella from one hand to the other.

"Quite a storm out there." Joan looked to the front. "I'm afraid I'm quite wet from walking in it."

"Oh, dear. Where do you live?"

"Lancashire. England." Joan chuckled at the error of answering by habit. "Sorry. I'm *from* Lancashire. I'm *staying* temporarily at the Y."

The woman's expression brightened; a splash of blue burst across her green eyes. "And would your name happen to be Joan? Joan Hunt?" When the elevator door slid open, and the three men stepped aside to allow the women to enter ahead of them, the woman made eye contact with each of them. "Thank you, gents."

"Miss Estes," one replied, tipping the brim of his fedora glistening with rainwater.

The others copied his action, dipping their hats first to Miss Estes and then to Joan. The man closest to the doors pushed a series of numbers. As the elevator doors closed, the woman turned to Joan. "I'm Betty Estes. Mr. Ferguson told me you'd be coming in this morning."

"Betty." Joan pointed to her. "*You're* Betty?"

She nodded with a laugh. The elevator doors opened again, this time to the nondescript Hertz offices.

"See you fellas around," Betty said as she stepped onto the floor, and Joan fell in behind her.

"How about a cup of coffee, Joan?" she asked when they reached her office. "Or do you prefer tea? Being British and all."

"Coffee is good." Joan hadn't even bothered with breakfast that morning. Drenched and cold, coffee would do more than just fill the emptiness in her stomach; it would heat her bones.

Betty hooked her coat on the metal tree by the door. "Get out of that wet coat and maybe you'll warm up," she said while opening a bottom drawer in her desk. "And you can put your purse in with mine for now."

Joan did, nearly ashamed at how shabby it appeared next to what looked to be something straight off a showroom floor. In fact, Joan reasoned, *she* looked completely out of place next to the woman who appeared somewhere between five and ten years her senior. She didn't feel inferior, but Joan could see that Betty Estes would be someone she'd look up to during her time at Hertz.

"Let me show you to the break room," Betty said. "Then we'll come back, I'll get your paperwork started, and then I'll show you to your desk." She eased out of the office, a light floral scent trailing behind her, and toward a door near the back of the building. "We've got coffee, a few pastries. Doughnuts, that kind of thing. Do you like doughnuts?"

"I'm not a big eater," Joan answered.

Betty laughed lightly. "I can look at you and see that."

They entered the break room—empty except for one other woman—to the rich fragrance of fresh-brewed coffee. "Oh, hey, Pegs," Betty said. "This is Joan." She motioned to Joan. "Joan, Peggy."

Joan nodded at the older woman stirring cream into her coffee.

"Peggy is also in accounting, so you'll be working together."

"So you're the new hire," Peggy said. She took a sip of her drink. "Good to have you, Joan." She walked toward the door. "I guess I'll see you soon."

Betty pointed to a cabinet where a few coffee cups had been placed in stacks of two and three. "A few employees brought some mix-and-match cups from home. If you have one you'd like to bring—"

"I'm afraid I didn't bring anything like that with me."

"From Lancashire or from the Y?" Betty asked, smiling broadly.

Joan returned the kindness. "Both. Or . . . neither. However it should be said."

Betty waved her words away. "Well, of course not. Don't worry about it." She pulled two cups from the cupboard. "Someone always manages to get here early enough to start the coffee. Some days that'll be you," she said. "We all pitch in—" she peered around the bleakness of the room—"to keep our break room clean."

"Got it."

She opened a small fridge. "Peggy left the milk out for us, but it usually goes here." She closed the door, then pointed to a small table where a sugar bowl and a box of pastries were the only centerpieces. "Sugar and doughnuts."

Joan poured two cups of coffee. "I drink mine black."

Betty shook her head. "I've never understood how anyone could do that. But to each his own." She prepared her coffee, grabbed a cocktail napkin from inside a drawer, and laid a doughnut on it. "Sure you don't want one?"

"I'm sure."

She took a bite and continued speaking around it. "So, you're staying at the Y."

Joan wrapped her hands around the warm cup, which sent a shiver through her. "Yes. Temporarily, of course."

"Are you looking for a room to rent then?"

"I will be." She smiled before taking a drink. "Once I have a paycheck."

"I ask because I have a room coming up for rent. Some girls and I share a small place on Greenleaf. Two of the roommates are leaving in a couple of weeks if you're interested in one of their beds."

Joan immediately thought of Evelyn. "That would be great. I mean, if you have two." She tossed her hair with a shake of her head. "I have a friend who is joining me here soon."

"From England?"

"No. From Georgia actually. Portal. It's a small farming community near Savannah."

Betty placed the milk in the fridge. "A Southern girl? Well, I don't see why not." She took another sip of her coffee, then rinsed the cup and placed it upside down in a nearby drainer. "Won't we make quite the fivesome?"

Joan was both unsure what Betty meant and too elated at the notion of having a place to live to ask. "Will you need to talk to your other flatmates first?"

"Talk? Oh, heavens no." She waved her hand again. "Say, let's get you started, and we'll talk about moving into the apartment in a week or so. How does that sound?"

Joan finished her coffee, rinsed and turned the cup upside down as Betty had done. "It sounds perfect."

CHAPTER 6

Hundreds of voices echoed in the cavernous waiting room of Chicago's Union Station—some from new arrivals exiting trains and others from those relaxed or perched on the benches scattered throughout. Sunlight burst through the iron grating over the high window above massive doors leading to the tracks, directly across from where Joan sat, waiting. The brilliance was such that she could not see things clearly; they seemed, rather, shrouded in dust and smoke. People moved like apparitions through the beams of light—starting as shadows, then fully illuminated, and finally appearing human again.

Joan glanced at her watch, then up to the round face of the large clock for confirmation. Evelyn's train would arrive at any moment. When it did, years of correspondence would give way to a new chapter in their friendship. And Joan would be able to tell Evelyn the secret she'd kept from her for more than a month.

From overhead, the announcement she'd waited for penetrated the cacophony of chatter and shoes clomping on the polished floor. She stood, wrung her gloves in her hands like a dishcloth, and walked toward the center of the Great Hall.

"Find the information desk," she'd told Evelyn in her last letter.

I'll be there waiting for you. I'll be wearing a black pencil skirt with a white long-sleeved blouse. It's quite cold here in Chicago, so I may be wearing a coat. But surely, after years of letter writing and picture exchange, we will recognize each other.

Who would have guessed that when our teachers matched us to each other as international pen pals, we would arrive at this day?

Within minutes, a sea of hats and suits moved toward her, and she realized how difficult finding Evelyn might be. The onslaught of passengers pushed and shoved, asking questions of the attendants behind the desk. Enveloped by the throng, Joan twisted her gloves again, repositioned the coat she'd thrown over her arm, and adjusted her hat. After what seemed an eternity, the crowd thinned and scattered, leaving only one person standing several yards away. Hatless, she wore a camel-colored wool coat with wide cuffs and a look of sheer panic in blue eyes that darted behind cat-eye specs. A worn suitcase rested at her feet.

Joan pulled herself upright. "Evelyn," she called.

Evelyn's face found hers. "Joanie!" She picked up the luggage and hurried toward her.

"You made it." Joan wrapped her in a hug before holding her at arm's length. "You look wonderful."

Evelyn ran a hand over the mousy brown hair she'd always complained about in her letters. "I'm a mess." Her eyes closed. "And so tired." They opened again as she sighed. "I want a hot bath and a bed more than I've ever wanted anything in my life."

Joan linked their arms. "Do you have any other luggage?"

Evelyn held up the small suitcase. "I'm afraid not. This was all I could pack that my mother wasn't unpacking. To be honest with you, Joan, I . . . I finally told her that I wouldn't leave, but then . . . I slipped out in the night. With Daddy's blood money in my pocket, no less."

Joan pulled her close. "Oh, Evelyn. You didn't."

Evelyn blinked back tears. "Daddy said that even with Christmas only a few weeks away, it was the right thing to do. But like I told you before, Mama can only see life as it affects her. And her plans for me." She sighed. "Daddy told her that I was destined for greater things than a husband whose idea of excitement was watching corn grow. But she wouldn't listen."

Joan suppressed a giggle. "Come on." She tugged Evelyn toward the exit. "Let's get you home."

"Home?" Evelyn asked. "You think of the Y as 'home' now?"

Joan squeezed her arm. "That's my surprise. I have a place for us to live *and* a job waiting for you."

Evelyn stopped. "Are you serious?"

Joan held up a hand. "I am. And you'll adore our flatmates. There's Betty," she said as they started walking again. "I wrote to you about her. Evelyn, I tell you she's the most amazing person I've ever known. You'll see. And then there are the sisters—Inga and Magda Christenson. They're from Minnesota originally."

"Twins?"

"Oh, no. They're sisters, all right, but quite different." They stopped at the outer doors where Joan slipped into her coat and gloves. "Did you bring gloves?" she asked.

Evelyn nodded. "They're in my luggage. Will I need them already?"

"We've had bitter cold days lately." She glanced through the glass doors to the buildings across the street where Christmas displays brought a festive air to the season. "But you should be fine between here and there."

They stepped out into the crisp air. Evelyn glanced toward the cabs lined up on the street. "No taxi?"

"No, no. We can make it on our own two feet to the Loop. From there, we'll take a train out to where we live."

Evelyn sighed. "How far is it? I'm pretty tired, Joanie."

Joan squeezed her arm again. "Come on. It's not far. Lean on me and I'll tell you all about the girls and your new job."

"And I want to know more about this place where I'll be living."

"Oh, that," Joan said with a laugh. "Wait till you see. We live in a basement apartment on Greenleaf. Two bedrooms with double beds and one little box room with a twin. That's where Magda sleeps."

"She doesn't sleep with her sister?"

Joan shook her head. "No. Not sure why, though. I think maybe they shared a room when they were children and didn't quite fancy it any longer, if you know what I mean."

"Do they work with you and Betty? At Hertz?"

"No. Magda works as a secretary for Olson Publishing." Joan threw up a hand. "At least I think that's the name. Honestly, Evelyn, we don't make a lot of small talk. I can tell you she works for a magazine and I *think* it's at Olson. But Inga is a stewardess. She's not home too often." She pressed her hand on Evelyn's arm. "Betty and Inga share a room, and you and I will share a room. We have a small kitchen—barely big enough to turn around in—but a fairly nice-sized living room with comfortable furniture, which is ideal for those times when friends or coworkers might want to come by." Not that it happened too often. At least, not since she'd moved in.

They stopped at the end of a city block and waited for traffic to clear. Around them, the sounds of the city swirled—a symphony Joan had grown deliciously accustomed to. She looked at Evelyn, who appeared almost frightened. "Are you okay?"

A burst of air escaped her lungs. "I've tried to imagine what this would be like, you know. From the movies I've seen and all." Her eyes climbed the height of the buildings as they continued onward. "But the noise. Is it always like this?"

Joan laughed. "Welcome to Chicago!"

They squeezed each other's arms, walking in time until they came to the train station. "Joanie," Evelyn said after she'd been helped with getting a ticket. "I should call Daddy when we get there. Will that be okay?"

"Of course. But you'll have to use the phone in the hallway because there's not one in the flat."

"Oh?"

"Not to worry, though, Evelyn. We stay so busy. I promise you . . . there's hardly time for phone calls."

CHAPTER 7

Evelyn shook hands briefly with Betty, nearly rattled by just how elegant she really was. "Thank you so much," she said, "for allowing me to stay here. To *live* here, I guess." She laughed lightly, her laughter sounding—even to her own ears—like tiny bells chiming as one walks through a door. "I simply can't believe I'm *in* Chicago." She glanced up at the two narrow windows that peered out to Greenleaf. "Look at that," she commented after a short pause. "Feet, walking by."

Betty crossed her arms. "That's what you get when you live in a basement apartment." She swung around, a whiff of her cologne lingering in the air. "At least we aren't like the poor gals who live in the apartment behind us. I don't think they have a window in the entire place."

Evelyn frowned. "I wouldn't like that so much. Especially since I come from a house with multiple windows in every room."

"Come on," Joan said with a tap on her elbow. "Let me show you our room."

"Oh. Okay. Nice to meet you," Evelyn said to Betty. "Are the others here?" she asked Joan.

Joan looked at Betty, who'd picked up a magazine from the coffee table.

"I haven't seen Magda since earlier this morning. Inga hasn't been here in two days, so . . . I expect she'll be back today at some point. Tomorrow at the latest, what with this being Saturday." Betty dropped the magazine as though nothing about it interested her.

Joan picked up Evelyn's suitcase. "Inga's the stewardess," she said.

Evelyn nodded as she mouthed, "Oh."

Together they started toward the narrow hallway that led to the bedrooms and bath. "Like I told you before, we really don't spend a lot of time together. Well, Betty and I . . . and *you*, now . . . because we work in the same building. Take the same train to the Loop. Walk the same sidewalks, so to speak." Joan stopped talking as she opened the door. "This is it, Evelyn. This is our room."

Evelyn stepped in slowly. She held her breath. The sleeping quarters weren't much to write home about, but the room offered everything she needed for the little bit of time she'd spend here.

Joan dropped the suitcase near the foot of the double bed. "It's not much, but at least *this* mattress doesn't cave in the middle like the one I used to share with one of my sisters back home."

Evelyn smiled, although she knew that once she found herself alone, tears would spill down her cheeks. The bedroom walls, as those in every room of the apartment, had been painted hospital white; boring, but in a windowless room, white walls made for a happier existence. The floors were hardwood and, even through her shoes, Evelyn could feel the chill coming off them. The only artwork in the room was a cheap painting of a lake with mountains rising behind it, all painted in various shades of green. When her eyes froze on it, Joan pointed to it. "If you want to add anything—paintings, wall hangings—by all means, be my guest."

Evelyn swallowed. "Is that . . . yours?"

"That awful thing?" Joan asked with a smile. "No. Betty said it came with the place."

Evelyn reached for her suitcase and laid it on the bed. "I should unpack." Weariness hung on every word. If her daddy asked, she wondered, would she tell him her new room was half the size of the one she'd left back home? That she'd traded white lace and eyelet for quilts that looked like they'd come from a five-and-dime?

Joan reached for her coat and said, "Let me hang this in the front closet for you."

Evelyn swiped at tears that pooled behind her glasses.

"Oh, Evelyn," Joan said, patting her shoulder. "It'll be okay."

"I know."

She held up the coat. "While I take care of this, *you* are going to go right to bed. As my mum always says, everything will look better after a good nap."

Evelyn nodded, speechless, as Joan closed the door behind her.

Joan's heart ached for the things she'd hadn't yet considered when it came to Evelyn. While Joan's mum had been heartsick at Joan's denouncing the king, she'd also understood that Joan had come to the States to better her life and to help the family. Evelyn had come to Chicago in *defiance* of her mother. Suddenly, her arrival felt different.

With a quiet breath, Joan tiptoed back up the hallway.

Betty met her in the living room, holding up an envelope Joan immediately recognized as being from England. "Mail call," Betty said.

"Let me hang Evelyn's coat up first." Joan opened the closet door and found a wooden hanger with *Pick-Congress Hotel* printed across it. She draped Evelyn's wrap over the words and hung it on the rod. "Don't you wonder how it is that when you moved here so many wooden hangers with hotel advertisements were left behind?"

Betty laughed. "No. And I don't want to know. They're sturdy and that's all that matters to me." She handed Joan her letter before looking down the hallway. "Your friend all right in there?"

Joan nodded. "She's just tired." She walked to the unadorned six-cushioned sofa and sat with her back against a tufted pillow. "Can we turn the radiator up a little?" she asked while ripping the side of the envelope. She puffed it open with a sharp breath and pulled out a letter written in her mother's hand, caped in the smell of home.

Betty walked to the ornate cast-iron radiator near the windows and turned a knob. "I read somewhere that these old beauts are soon to be replaced by a newer version made of steel."

Joan looked up from her letter. "Really?"

"Paint it and hide it, the article said." Betty crossed her arms, tilted her head back, and peered out the window as though the feet and calves passing by were of the utmost interest. "If you ask me, with every change we make in this country, we lose something special along the way." She tossed her curls as though clearing her head, looked at Joan, and blinked. "Everything fine back home?"

Joan glanced at the unlined paper in her hand. "I haven't really gotten into it yet." She read a few lines. "It's tough back there. The war . . . trying to rebuild . . ." She fought tears that rode a wave of remembrances of a different England, the England of her childhood.

Betty walked a few steps toward the kitchen. "I think we could both use a cup of coffee." She smiled weakly. "Finish your letter and I'll perk us up a pot."

Joan nodded, waiting until after Betty had left the room to

go back to her mum's updates about her brothers and sisters, her father, and the townspeople of Leigh. By the time Betty returned, she'd folded the letter and returned it to the envelope. She curled her feet under her backside, sitting sideways to better watch the frost gather on the outside window. "Thank you," she said, reaching for the matching rose-and-ivy cup and saucer Betty extended.

"Want to talk about it?" Betty sat in a nearby squooshy chair. She crossed her legs before delicately swinging the one on top.

"Talk about what?" Joan asked, taking a sip.

"Whatever was in that letter that has gloom and doom all over your sweet face."

Joan held the cup to her lips but didn't drink. Instead, she took a moment to just breathe in the comforting aroma of the fresh-brewed beans, her focus on Betty's shoe—a fur-lined moccasin-style house slipper—as it bounced up and down . . . up and down. Even in house shoes, she managed to look like a magazine cover. "Betty?" Betty brought her eyes to Joan's. "Do you know of anyone who's hiring?"

The bobbing of her foot stopped. "As in a job?"

Joan nodded.

"For who? You?"

She nodded again. "Mmm-hmm."

"Is something wrong with your job at Hertz? Something I need to know about?"

Joan eased the cup and saucer to the low coffee table. "Gracious no. But as you know, I've been sending some money to my family. To help out. And . . ." She held the letter up. "Mum says it's been a help, but I can tell by the tone of her words that more would be appreciated. Plus, with Christmas right around the corner . . ."

Betty stood and placed her cup and saucer next to Joan's. "Hold that thought," she said before disappearing down the hall. Within a minute, she returned, her handbag dangling from her fingers. She flipped the clasp, reached into the brown satin-lined interior, and brought out a card. "A friend of mine—her name is Delores—is the private-showing manager at David & DuRand."

Joan took the card, read the name and the address.

"On Michigan Avenue," she said.

"Not too far from the office. So, if you get some evening hours, you won't have far to walk." Betty returned to her seat with her cup of coffee.

Joan waved the card. "And you just happened to have a business card?"

Betty swallowed the sip of coffee she'd just taken, the sound of it echoing in the room. "I went in yesterday to pick up a dress for Mother. Ran into Delores and she gave me her card." Betty smiled. "She told me she was hiring and that if I knew of someone at Hertz who might need some extra cash . . . Consider it serendipity." She cocked a penciled brow. "It's part-time, mind you."

"I only need part-time." Joan stared at the card again. "A *fine apparel* department store. I don't believe I've ever *been* in a *fine apparel* department store." A sudden thought pressed a frown to her face. "Or *own* anything appropriate for an interview, I'm afraid."

Betty placed her coffee on the butler's tray next to her chair. "Not to worry. Between your closet and mine, we'll pull something together." Her eyes widened and sparkled with an idea. "Why don't I give her a call and let her know you'll come by Monday on your lunch break."

Joan pondered the possibility for a moment. Working behind a desk was one thing, but in a fine apparel store? Sure, Betty had something she could borrow for the interview, but what would she wear all the other days—or evenings—she worked there? Certainly not the same dress over and over. And Betty's offer to raid her closet wouldn't mean—or *shouldn't* mean—helping herself every other day, even though some of the prettiest clothes she'd ever seen hung there.

Then again, she held the card of a woman who could give her part-time work without her having to put her feet on the pavements of Chicago in the frigid cold.

"Okay," Joan finally said. "Call her and let her know." She sighed in both contentment and apprehension. "Thanks, Betts."

"More coffee?" Betty asked, standing and reaching for her cup and saucer.

Just like Betty. When she did something nice for you, she didn't expect anything in return. She didn't gloat over what she'd just done—or might possibly *be doing* for you. This was simply her nature. She was a giver and as much of a friend as Joan could have asked for in such a short time in the States.

Joan stood with her, picking up her own cup and saucer. "I'll join you." After they'd poured another cup for themselves, Joan turned to Betty. "You know? I only hope I can do something special for you one day, Betts."

Betty pretended to pick at the pink cashmere sweater hugging her frame. When she looked up again, she smiled in the easy way she had. "Who knows, Joan," she said, her words not really forming a question. "Maybe one day you will."

CHAPTER 8

Betty's mother's idea of the perfect ending to Sunday Mass was going home to a brunch of eggs Benedict, served with fresh fruit and mimosas.

Somehow, Betty found it rather odd, although she wasn't sure if the problem fell on her mother's need to have someone serve her an uptown drink or that she appeared completely incapable of a Sunday without the Volbrechts. She recognized, of course, that the Volbrechts were her parents' oldest and dearest friends. But she also knew their desperation for marrying the two families. Literally.

"Make an effort," Mother hissed as they came through the front door. She pulled off her gloves and shirked out of the full-length mink Betty's father had recently given her for absolutely no reason at all, he said, except that he loved his wife and the coat made her happy.

"What does that mean?" Betty reached for the mink before slipping out of her cashmere coat. "Give me your gloves. I'll put everything away," she added, not waiting for an answer.

"Where's Adela?" her father barked, coming in behind them and closing the door. *"Adela!"*

Betty took her mother's gloves and clutch as she somehow

managed to drape the fur and cashmere over her arm. "I've got it, Father," she said.

"Adela!" her father barked anyway.

Betty was halfway up the stairs when the front door opened again. She turned to look over her shoulder, all the while keeping one hand on the banister. Gracefully, just as she'd been taught.

"A vision of loveliness gliding up the staircase," George Volbrecht called up to her. He smiled, his perfect white teeth made all the whiter against his suntanned skin. She returned the gesture, then turned to face forward and suppressed a snarl. By the time she returned downstairs, the family had gathered in the Florida room, which—like the rest of the house—was entirely too froufrou for Betty's taste. George, who lounged like a cat in sunshine on an occasional chair, stood immediately.

"A drink, Betty?"

"Orange juice is fine," she said, walking toward the wet bar. She waved a hand at him. "I can get it myself."

But George joined her anyway, standing so close that she could smell his aftershave.

Betty poured the juice into a Tom Collins glass—one that came from her mother's extraordinary collection of crystal. She held it up to the light coming through the window and studied it, weighed the heaviness of it.

"What are you thinking?" George whispered.

She peered up at him. Undeniably, he was one of the most handsome men she'd ever met, which was a big part of the problem she had with him. "Too handsome," Adela had said to her once. "I don't trust a man prettier than me."

Betty grinned at the memory.

"What?" George said. "What's so funny?"

Betty shook her head. "Nothing. As for what I was thinking . . ."

She took a sip of juice. "I was thinking that I'm as much at home holding a glass that cost a month of my salary as I am holding a tumbler I bought at the A&P." She watched the features of his chiseled face grow rigid, then soften.

"You like being the rebel, don't you?" He chuckled.

She took another sip. "I like being myself."

He turned and leaned his elbows against the edge of the bar, then crossed his legs at the ankles. "I've got a secret," he said, keeping his voice low enough that their parents—all of whom chattered away like hens and roosters—couldn't hear.

She turned her back on the four older adults. "If you think for one second," she mumbled, "that they can't hear you or read your lips, you're sadly mistaken. All that chitchat over there is nothing more than a ruse."

He smiled at her and winked before leaning over and whispering in her ear, "Play along, Betts."

She drew back. "All right. What's your secret?" She set the glass back on the bar.

George stood straight and grabbed her by the elbow, ushering her with slight force to the wide French doors leading out to the veranda. "We're going to step outside for a second," he called over his shoulder.

The gossip from the other side of the room came to a halt. "You'll freeze to death, Betty," her mother said. "Where's your coat?"

"Only for a moment," George countered. "I want to show Betty something. It'll only take a minute, I promise." He grinned. "And if she gets too cold, I'll wrap her in my arms and hold her close, Mrs. Estes."

"Oh, George, go on," Chloe gushed.

"Yes, George," Betty mumbled. "*Do* go on . . ."

George turned the ornate knob and pushed the door wide

enough for them to walk through. A gust of cold air hit, forcing Betty to cross her arms over herself. "This had better be good," she said after he'd closed the door behind them.

"This way," George said, walking her to the end of the flagstones beneath their feet. He pointed toward a cluster of bare-limbed trees and naked bushes surrounding a rambling ranch-style house at the end of a cul-de-sac. "Pretend I'm showing you something and that you're in awe."

Betty sighed. "I can't imagine what. Or why."

"I'm pointing to a house."

"I see that."

"A house I just bought, Miss Estes."

Betty swung around to search his eyes, to see if he told the truth or something to keep her guessing at his silly game. "What? Why?"

"Right now," he continued, his eyes twinkling, "your parents and my parents are thinking that I'm telling you about the house. And that I'm asking you, once again, to marry me."

Betty gritted her teeth. "George . . ."

"Bear with me, Betts."

She hated it when he called her that. If anyone else did—Joan, Evelyn, the sisters—she didn't mind in the least. But *George* saying her name in such a way was far too . . . intimate. "I'm freezing to death," she said instead, squeezing herself tighter.

"Just listen." He looked toward her parents' house and smiled.

"Are you giving them some sort of signal?"

"Are you listening?"

"Hurry. Up."

"Your father has this idea, Betty. He's going to cut you off if you don't stop all this running around in the city and come back home."

"And do what?" Her arms squeezed again.

"*Marry* me, Betts. Become Mrs. George Volbrecht. My gracious, woman, don't you ever get tired of working the old nine-to-five?" He grinned. "Besides, I'm a catch. You can't do much better than this, you know."

"Ugh," Betty said with a stomp of her foot. She swung around and headed back inside.

"Betty, wait. I was only kidding about the last—"

She kept walking. When she got to the French doors, she jerked them open and stormed through. All four of the parents stood, looking expectant.

"Well, darling. What do you think?" her mother asked.

But she didn't answer. She crossed the room, heading for the long hallway leading to the foyer.

"Betty, where are you going?" her father called.

"Betty!" George's voice echoed, his sounding more like a plea than a demand.

Betty took the stairs purposefully, stomping up each one, then strode down the hall until she reached her old bedroom, the one her mother had redecorated not five minutes after she'd moved to the apartment on Greenleaf. One act of defiance deserved another, she supposed, not that she cared.

She picked up the coat she'd laid across the foot of the bed earlier and slid her arms into the sleeves, then grabbed her purse. She had nearly made it out of the room when George walked in, bumping into her and grabbing her shoulders in both of his hands.

"Let go of me," she demanded, though she kept her voice controlled. "And get out of my bedroom. You know perfectly well it's not appropriate."

"You'd really better hear me out."

Betty jerked free. "I'm going home," she said. A second later, she dashed back down the stairs where her parents and the Volbrechts waited. She read their faces as easily as she read Mr. Ferguson's morning reports. Her mother's eyes begged; her father's stormed. And as for George's parents—theirs held confusion. How could any woman in her right mind turn down their son?

Well, maybe that was it. Maybe she wasn't in her right mind. Maybe she—

"Young lady," her father said, "don't you dare leave this house."

Betty kissed her mother's soft cheek and drew in the scent of Shalimar that lingered from her morning bath. "I'm sorry," she whispered. George's footsteps could be heard coming down the upstairs hall. She looked at his parents. "Mr. Volbrecht. Mrs. Volbrecht. You must excuse me."

And with that, Betty ran out of the house. Against the wishes of her parents.

Inga and Magda Christenson sat shoulder to shoulder on the train rushing along the tracks toward Evanston. Magda licked her right index finger absentmindedly and turned the page of the novel she'd begun the night before, while Inga sat next to the window, her eyes fixed on the gray and dying landscape.

"Christmas will be here sooner than we can blink," she said to her sister, though she wasn't sure Magda heard her.

Surprisingly, her sister dropped the book, holding her place with her left thumb. "What are your plans? Are we going back to Minnesota?"

Inga shook her head. "I've already told the airline I'd work." She removed her hat and touched the knot of blonde hair she'd pulled into a tight chignon earlier that morning. A tiny headache throbbed behind her left ear.

Magda shifted. "But why? You know Mor and Far will want us to come home. They'll be counting on it."

Inga returned the hat, then patted her sister's thigh. "You go."

Magda's brow furrowed and her blue eyes grew lightning fierce. "But I don't want to go alone. You know what it will be like. They'll grill me like a steak. Especially Far."

Inga smiled, though she knew it didn't quite reach her eyes. "Just tell them what they want to hear."

"You mean lie?"

She looked back out the window. They were nearing their stop. Inga picked up the purse she'd wedged between herself and the arm of the seat, then hugged it to her middle. "I mean," she said slowly, "tell them what they want to hear. I don't care if you lie or not."

"After spending this morning in church, I cannot believe you'd suggest such a thing, Inga."

Inga laughed as the train screeched to a halt. She and her sister were such opposites; she often didn't know what to make of their relationship. "I'm kidding you, Magda. Why do you always have to be so serious?"

Magda closed her book fully and reached for her own purse. "I never can tell with you." They stood together once the train came to a complete stop. "Besides, we haven't been home since you took the job with the airline. I can't imagine what the air will be like with Far."

They walked the aisle together, then exited onto the platform. "If it's anything like the letter I received from him after I took the job, perhaps it's just as well I *don't* go home this Christmas season. He practically called me a—"

"Inga."

Again, Inga laughed.

They began their walk toward home, Inga more grateful now than before that she'd met Betty Estes at a dinner party given by a mutual acquaintance. Six months earlier, she and Magda had come to Chicago to work for their aunt and uncle, who owned a mom-and-pop grocery on the outskirts of the city. She'd thought—they both had—that leaving Minnesota meant leaving behind the strict upbringing they'd been subjected to by their parents. Instead, Aunt Greta and Uncle Casper proved to be ten times—no, a hundred times—more controlling.

The restrictions of Inga and Magda's father, a professor at Lutheran Bible College, couldn't hold a candle to the religious shackles Uncle Casper wanted to lock around their ankles. For months, they'd endured the constant pressures as they worked alongside their uncle and aunt in their fledgling business. And when they could almost take it no more, Inga had done something she'd heard about but never done for herself. She'd prayed.

God answered her prayers in the form of Betty Estes. "What do *you* want to do with your life?" she'd asked Inga that evening over plates of apple pie.

Inga thought a moment before answering. "I want to *go* places. *See* things."

"What about your sister?"

"Magda? The only adventuring Magda has done is through the pages of all those books she reads. They're all she talks about. Sometimes I think she thinks the characters are more real than the flesh-and-blood people around her."

Betty paused before responding. And when she did, her words were so brilliant, they changed everything for Inga. "Well, I'd say, if you want to *go places*, fly there."

Within days Betty had the sisters moved in to her apartment on Greenleaf, and the day after that she made a phone call to someone she knew at Trans World Airlines. Then she placed another call to a friend at Olson Publishing and landed Magda a job.

"I wonder if Betty has made it home yet," Magda now said as they rounded the sidewalk in front of their street. The scent of burning firewood filled the air as it hung between the leafless branches of the few scrawny trees lining the street.

Inga glanced at her watch. "I doubt it. She probably won't be home until later."

"Maybe the other two are there. Joan usually gets home early after church on Sunday."

"Because she—they—don't have family here. There's nowhere to go after service."

They arrived at their building, and Inga drew out her key before Magda had a chance to even open her purse.

"Yes, they do," Magda said.

They headed down the stairs leading to the basement apartments. "Yes, they do what?" Inga asked.

"Have family," she answered quietly. "Here, I mean." She opened the outside door.

"How do you see that?"

Magda smiled. "They have *us*."

Inga chuckled as they hurried in. "Us? We see each other five minutes a week. I'd hardly call us *friends*, much less *family*."

CHAPTER 9

Joan punched out at precisely noon on Monday. After grabbing her coat, gloves, and hat, she made a beeline for Betty's office, where she found her pulling her purse out of her desk's bottom drawer. "Are you leaving now for the interview?" Betty asked.

"I am. But I wanted to ask . . . Did Evelyn do all right this morning?"

Betty closed the drawer. "So far so good. She filled out the paperwork and starts in the morning. She said to tell you she'd see you this evening."

They made their way to the elevator. "I hope she got home okay." The thought of Evelyn—who had appeared scared mindless during the morning's commute to the Loop—taking the train alone back to the apartment on Greenleaf was frightening in and of itself. Joan imagined Evelyn wandering around the city, her eyes filled with tears as they scanned the massive height of the buildings.

Betty pushed the Down button next to the elevator. "Not to worry. I walked her to the Loop and put her on the train myself."

The elevator doors opened and the two women—along with several of their workmates—stepped in. "But did you tell her where to get off?" Joan asked with a smile.

Betty shoved her left hand into a black glove and wiggled the fingers. "I repeat: Don't worry." She slanted her eyes playfully toward Joan.

Joan giggled as the elevator car came to a stop. Their shoes clomped along the polished flooring, echoing with the shuffling of men's shoes. Joan slipped into her coat and gloves, and finished by pinning her hat into place. Outside the front doors, the chill of Chicago slapped her face as though she'd said or done something to offend it.

"How do I look?" she asked, turning toward Betty.

Betty reached up and adjusted the hat. "This hat looks better on you than it does on me, quite frankly." She finished with her fiddling and took a step back. "Okay. Smile pretty and make me proud," she teased. "Now, off you go . . ."

Joan pushed through the revolving door of David & DuRand with a sense of trepidation that heightened as she stood inside the store. Classical music floated overhead, hovering between chandeliers dripping with crystals and glittering in a rainbow of colors. Salesclerks stood behind various display cases while women draped in fine coats, hair perfectly coiffed and rhinestone bracelets glimmering on their wrists, stood on the other side.

And all this before one o'clock on a weekday.

A deep yet feminine voice interrupted her plan of escape. "May I help you, dear?"

Joan turned, mouth gaping, to an older woman, stocky in build but as authoritative as a schoolmarm. Her chest jutted forward, nearly matched in distance by her chin. She smelled of talcum powder and didn't smile, but Joan did, and as quickly as she knew how.

"I'm here to see . . . Delores . . ." The last name escaped her, but only momentarily. "Delores King."

"*Mrs.* King?"

"Yes."

"Of course. This way please." Joan followed her for several feet before the woman turned and spoke. "You have an appointment?"

"Yes."

They wove through the departments—accessories, shoes, costume jewelry—until finally arriving at shiny gold double elevator doors. The woman who smelled of talcum pushed the call button and stepped back. "This will take you to the private showing room on the fifth floor, where you'll find Mrs. King."

"The private—" Her words were interrupted by the swoosh of the elevator doors as they opened. Joan glanced inside, and back to the woman who had already walked away, leaving her to scurry inside and push the gold-etched *5*.

As the elevator glided upward, she read the brass plates next to the floor numbers.

Infants and Children.

Ladies.

Men.

Formal and Bridal Wear.

And next to the *5—Private Showing Room.*

Locating Mrs. King didn't prove difficult; she was the only person on the entire floor of velvet-covered settees, French Provincial armchairs, and low tables. The scents of fresh-brewed coffee and tea roses permeated the air, clinging to the spaces between massive Monet replicas.

At least Joan *assumed* they were replicas.

"Mrs. King?"

Delores King was nothing if not exquisite. And tall and

willowy in a form-fitting crepe dress. The color of her shoes perfectly matched the navy blue of the dress. Her hair—dark and luxurious—had been combed back and held in place by her hat. Though she stood on a round platform-type stage rearranging a vase of long-stemmed roses, she wore wrist gloves. Rhinestones winked from her ears, throat, and wrists.

She finished placement of the last rose, stepped from the platform, and extended her hand with all the refinement of Grace Kelly. "You must be Joan Hunt."

Joan took her hand and released it quickly, unable to keep her eyes from the woman's—the perfectly shaped brows, the intensity with which she drank her in. Joan felt undressed, as though she might have to turn around and walk back to Hertz, defeated. In spite of Betty's efforts to "doll her up," she stood like a poor child without twopence to her name, peering into a window showcasing elegance. "Nice to meet you," Joan said, her voice cracking.

Mrs. King smiled—white, even teeth behind full red lips. "You'll have to excuse me. I'm getting ready for a show."

"A show?"

"For a private client." She glided to a blond wood desk accented with gold trim. A French-style phone stood on one side, an ornate lamp on the other. In the center, an appointment book lay open wide with a fountain pen poised on top. Matching chairs sat angled just so on both sides. "She'll be here momentarily, but I hoped we could at least talk for a minute." Mrs. King turned, waiting for Joan to join her, and Joan quickly made her way to one of the chairs on the opposite side of the desk. After Mrs. King sat, Joan followed. "What did Betty tell you about the job?"

"Only that it's part-time."

"And that you'd be working for me? Here?"

Joan glanced around the room. Behind the carpeted stage stood three massive gilded mirrors where a client—she now understood—could see the form of a model dressed in any number of outfits and imagine herself looking as fashionable as the figure before her. "Here?" she asked, returning her attention to Mrs. King.

"As a model. Evenings mostly, with the occasional Saturday."

"And I'll—" she could hardly imagine it—"model for society women?"

"Mostly men. They come in, wanting to buy that special something for their wives. Mothers. Sisters." The arched brows rose. "Whomever. We don't ask and they don't tell."

Joan had managed to work in a number of capacities in her young life. Standing and turning in fine apparel couldn't possibly be any more difficult than collecting scraps of food for a man's pigs. "When do I start?"

"We'll want to train you first." Mrs. King flipped a page on the calendar. "Tomorrow evening. I'll set an appointment for you with Mrs. Blue. She'll teach you all you need to know about walking, standing, turning . . ."

"Modeling," Joan said, feeling a sudden sense of adventure.

Mrs. King nodded as she wrote Joan's name on a page of the calendar. "You get off from Hertz at five?"

"I do."

"You can be here by five thirty?"

"I can be here by five fifteen," Joan said, feeling assured.

Mrs. King opened the right-hand drawer, removed a small pad of paper, scrawled her pen across it, and then tore the top sheet away. "Here you go," she said. "When you arrive tomorrow, let anyone downstairs know that you are here to see Mrs. Blue. You'll be taken to her straightaway."

Joan took the paper. Read it. "Thank you, Mrs. King," she said.

Delores King pulled the hem of her glove away to reveal a thin watch around a dainty wrist. "I'm sorry, Joan, but I must say good-bye now. The client will be here soon."

Joan stood, opening her purse as she did, and dropped the now-folded piece of paper into it. "Thank you again," she said.

Mrs. King glanced toward the elevator. "The dressing room for our models is to the right here," she said, pointing her fountain pen in that direction. "Go through it, look around, and you'll find a door that leads to a stairwell." She smiled. "That's the best way for you to leave." Again her eye went to the elevator.

"I understand," Joan said, and she did. "I'll see you again soon, Mrs. King."

Joan was trained in a matter of afternoons, ready to begin her new part-time position by the start of the following week. The job suited her as well as any she could have hoped for. She spent her days at Hertz, typing on forms and adding up sums, and her evenings draped in the finest ball gowns, party dresses, and furs.

Mrs. King had been correct in saying that most of the clients were men. And, as she'd assumed the day of her interview, the models were expected to be discreet. Whether the customers purchased for their wives or their sweethearts was not the concern of the models. *They* and *their satisfaction*, Mrs. King said time and again, were the primary concern.

"And no flirting," she admonished before each show. "Not with your eyes. Not with your lips. And certainly not with the rest of you."

Mrs. King had nothing to worry about from Joan. The last thing on her list of many things to do was find a man. Especially one considering which lovely or luxurious item to purchase for another woman.

"The man of my dreams has specifications I have yet to find in Chicago," she told Evelyn on the first Saturday evening in December as they sat cross-legged on their bed, dressed in thick robes and warm pajamas and signing Christmas cards.

Evelyn licked a three-cent stamp and affixed it to the envelope. "Which are?" She pulled another card from the stack. "Do you think I should send Hank a card?" she asked, not waiting for Joan to answer.

"Why wouldn't you?"

Evelyn frowned. "I don't want to lead him on."

"It's a Christmas card, Evelyn, not an invitation to come to Chicago."

"I know, but . . . you don't know Hank. He'll think for certain that I've changed my mind about marrying him."

"Then don't send him one. *Really*, Evelyn."

Evelyn bit her lip. "But if I don't, he'll think I don't care at *all*." She grabbed Joan's hand as she reached for another card. "And I *do* care, Joan. Just not . . . in *that* way."

Joan picked up a card from her stack with her free hand and waved it between them. "Then send him a card and sign it *Your friend, Evelyn*."

Evelyn sighed as though the idea was beyond brilliant. "Excellent idea, Joanie." She took the card and opened it. "So?"

"So?" Joan asked, signing her name to another card.

"The man of your dreams?"

Joan looked up. "Oh. Him. Six-two. Blue eyes. And lots of dark hair."

Evelyn grinned, her pen ready to sign the card to Hank. "Oh, is *that* all?" She signed, then peered up. "Do you think you'll find him anytime soon, Joan?" she asked, her voice whisper-soft.

"No. But I'm not looking either. There's a lot to do before I even think about settling down." She chuckled at the thought. "So, what's been going on around here at night while I'm away?"

Evelyn's shoulders slouched. "I really wish you weren't working two jobs, Joanie. It gets lonely around here without you."

"Magda and Betty are here most nights though, right?"

"Well . . . yeah . . . but . . ."

Joan studied her friend. "But?"

Evelyn shook her head. "Magda is always in her room reading and Betty is so . . ."

Joan couldn't imagine the end of Evelyn's sentence. "Betty is so . . . what?"

Evelyn picked up another card. "She's so sophisticated, Joan. She must think I'm a complete dunce."

Joan started to laugh, then caught herself. "Betty's not like that. She doesn't think she's better than anyone else." Joan placed a hand over Evelyn's. "Just talk to her sometime. And stop hiding out in here thinking you're not worthy of Betty Estes." She squeezed Evelyn's hand. "Oh, Evelyn. You're so much more than you realize."

CHAPTER 10

Betty looked up from the late-afternoon cup of coffee she had treated herself to as Evelyn meandered into the tiny kitchen of their shared apartment. She jumped, rattling the pages of the newspaper she skimmed. "You're as quiet as a Christmas mouse, Evelyn. I didn't hear you walking down the hall."

Evelyn held up a slippered foot. "My old bedroom shoes," she said. "They make for soft footsteps."

Betty glanced at the foot and frowned. "Were they . . . *blue* . . . at one time?" Then she laughed to show Evelyn she meant no harm. "I made us some coffee."

"Good," Evelyn said. "I never knew I could be this cold." She sauntered over to the counter where Betty had left out a cup and saucer for her. "I think my bones actually ache."

"The cold is made colder because of Lake Michigan."

"We have cold weather in Portal," Evelyn said, sitting at one end of the table, "but nothing like this."

Betty folded the newspaper and adjusted her posture for a better view of the timid woman-child she shared a home with. "Tell me something, Evelyn." She reached over and touched Evelyn's hair. "Have you ever thought of having your hair professionally styled?"

Evelyn blushed furiously as she swallowed her first sip of coffee. "My mama always cut my hair."

"With *what*?" Betty locked eyes with Evelyn. "I'm not trying to embarrass you, but sweetheart, you've got such lovely hair color, it's a shame not to . . ." She allowed the idea to trail off.

Evelyn shook her head. "You mean, I have practically *no* hair color."

"I would call it the color of honey." Betty turned her coffee cup 360 degrees before looping her index finger into the handle. "Do you know how many women pay the big bucks to have hair that color?" Her mother, for one . . .

Evelyn smiled in appreciation. "I don't have the kind of money to do anything fancy. I'm barely making ends meet now."

Betty sighed as she stood. "Stay right there."

She walked into the living room, grabbed the latest copy of *Vogue* she'd purchased at the drugstore on Saturday, and returned to the kitchen, stopping at the Philco long enough to flip it on. "Fools Rush In" played tenderly from the big band station out of Indiana. The station came in clear only after five o'clock in the evenings, and became all the more clear after nine.

Betty dropped the magazine on the table. "Study this, Evelyn. I'll bet we can figure out the best hairstyle for you, and I'd be willing to bet we can pull together the right look for you from the clothes you already have in your closet."

But Evelyn shook her head, already in defeat. "No, I—"

The front door opened and Magda called, "Anyone here?"

"In the kitchen," Betty sang out, sitting in her chair again.

Magda pulled a scarf from her rich auburn hair as she entered. "Do I smell coffee?"

Betty jutted her thumb in the direction of the counter. "Knock yourself out. I'll get up in a little bit and see if I can't rustle us up something to call dinner."

Magda smiled as she reached into the cabinet and pulled out

a cup and saucer, one that matched the pattern Betty and Evelyn drank from. One of the eight-piece set Betty had talked her mother into buying her when she first moved into the apartment.

Betty couldn't help but notice the expression; Magda rarely showed happiness. "Is that a smile I see on your face?"

Magda practically twirled as she turned and sat at the opposite end of the table from Evelyn. Her full skirt fanned out around her petite frame, and once her coffee had been placed on the table, she dropped her chin into the cup of her hand.

Betty looked at Evelyn. "She's met someone. Dollars to doughnuts, she's met someone." Then, to Magda, "Dish it out, sister."

"Maybe," Magda said.

Evelyn slapped her hands down on the table, rattling the dishes and sloshing a little of the coffee into the saucers. "Tell us!"

"He's a writer, but he hasn't even remotely noticed *me* yet."

"Name please," Betty said.

Magda sighed. "Harlan." She waved a hand in the air. "Harlan Procter. It's an odd name, I know, but, girls . . . he has an absolutely *brilliant* way with words."

Evelyn leaned over. "What's he said?"

Magda rested her fingertips over the cup as though allowing it to warm her hands. "Well, nothing to *me*. Not really, anyway. What I mean to say is that he writes short stories for one of our magazines and I've always enjoyed them. And then *today* I met him face-to-face. He had a meeting with my boss." Again, she sighed. "So, other than 'Harlan Procter for Mr. Cole,' he hasn't said a peep to me. I doubt he could even tell you what I look like."

Betty took a long swallow of coffee. "Well, then. Let's not go out and buy a wedding dress *tomorrow*, shall we?"

The three looked at each other and giggled. A knock sounded from the door as Evelyn stood to pour another cup of coffee. "I'll get it," she said, then disappeared into the shadows of the living room.

Betty patted Magda's hand. "Seriously. If this Harlan is as big a writer as you are a reader, you may have met your match."

Magda grinned as Evelyn reentered the kitchen. "Betty," she whispered, approaching the table. "A man who looks an awful lot like a movie star is out there wanting to see you. He says it's important."

Betty frowned. Only one person she knew fit that description.

George.

If Inga Christenson had hoped to see the world by taking a job at Trans World Airlines, the most she'd managed so far was Chicago to Los Angeles. Not that it was a bad route. Quite the contrary. What could be better than those three-day layovers in Hollywood like the one she was currently enjoying, after all? Strolling along the Walk of Fame . . . taking in the sights on Hollywood Boulevard—such as Grauman's Chinese Theatre—and dining at The Brown Derby on Wilshire.

But so far, she'd only managed to do this with some of the other stewardesses. And even then, not so often.

Where was the glamour the airline employment ads had promised? Where was the thrill of the flight? And where were the all the single, good-looking pilots she'd thought she'd have met by now?

She only needed one, for pity's sake. One who'd say, "Fly with me, Inga. I'll take you anywhere you want to go."

"Oh yeah? Where?" she asked her reflection in the gilded wall mirror in front of her. She stood in the center of her hotel bathroom and carefully removed her cap, making sure to fasten the bobby pins to the loop on the inside front.

"Hey, Inga." Her coworker and friend, stewardess Henrietta Swift, tapped on the bathroom door. Henrietta was also her roommate for the night. "I could sure use five minutes in there."

Inga opened the door. "Sorry." They passed each other as Inga walked out, closing the door behind her. "I'm thinking of going out for a bite tonight," she said. "Not to the hotel's restaurant. I'm in the mood to walk around a little."

The toilet flushed, and after a moment of water running, Henrietta, a willowy green-eyed redhead, opened the door. She dried her hands on one of the hotel's towels, marked with a giant blue *HH* in the center, lest someone thought to steal one. "I know it's only four o'clock, but I'm too tired to go out," she said. "I think I may just order up a sandwich later." Her brow wrinkled. "Do you mind finding one of the other girls?"

"Sure, or I'm good with going out alone. Especially considering how nice the weather is tonight."

Henrietta tossed the towel back into the bathroom. "Sure beats Chicago, doesn't it?"

Inga laughed easily. "That it does."

She set about changing from her uniform into an emerald-green pencil-skirt dress, but slipped her feet back into the same shoes she wore in flight. She frowned at herself in the bedroom mirror.

"What's wrong?" Henrietta asked. She'd changed into her pajamas and had stretched out on the bed, the pillows at her back and a book in her hand. Henrietta, like Magda, loved a good book.

"Last year's dress," Inga said. "I thought when I came to Chicago and went to work for my uncle, I'd have scads of money for clothes. Instead, I'm working to pay for an apartment I'm hardly ever at and have little money left over for a new dress, or new shoes, or—" she turned to face Henrietta instead of speaking to her reflection—"even a new hat."

Henrietta dropped the book, leaned forward, and crossed her legs in a single movement. "My dear, you could walk out in a gunnysack and you'd look like a million. Don't you have any idea how the men turn and ogle you wherever you go? Why do you think all the others want to make sure that where *you* go, they go too?"

Inga pressed her hands into her tiny waist and stretched. "Really? Tell me something, Retta. Where are all the men then?"

Henrietta returned to her original position. "Look behind you in the storefront windows. They're *behind* you, following the caboose, if you get my drift."

Inga got it all right. "Okay. I'm out of here."

She rode the elevator to the expansive lobby, which boasted one of the largest Christmas trees she'd ever seen. After taking a moment to get her bearings, Inga walked to the concierge station, which stood empty. She started to tap the silver call bell, but a well-groomed man with dark hair and thick dark brows arching perfectly over clear blue eyes stepped behind the counter.

"Hallo," he said, the brows rising.

"Hello." She paused, startled by the man's accent. "You're English?"

"British," he corrected her, his accent clipped and dreamy.

She pointed at him playfully and smiled. "Sorry . . . I have a roommate who is . . . *British*."

"Do say." He leaned forward, resting his forearms on the edge of the counter. "And where do you and this *British* roommate live?" He glanced around as though he were searching to see if ticker tape would fall from the garland-laced ceiling.

She looked up and around too. Then, turning back, she answered, "Chicago."

"Chicago. The Windy City. I hear it's cold there."

"*Cold* doesn't begin to describe it."

His eyes searched hers and she held her own, matching him blink for blink. Finally, he whispered, "So, how can I help you this evening?"

"I wondered if you might suggest a place for dinner."

He grinned, sending a deep dimple into his left cheek. "For you only?" He looked over her shoulder. "Or will your husband be joining you?"

Inga decided that the game had become fun and she wanted to continue playing. "No. Just me. All alone." She pictured her father and mother frowning at her forwardness, then dismissed the notion.

He glanced at his watch. "I'm done with my shift in ten minutes." He straightened. "You could wait right over there—" he pointed—"and I'll show you personally one of my favorite spots. *Or,* I can hand you a map of Hollywood, which I conveniently have right here, and point out a few places."

Maybe, just maybe, her heart told her, meeting and marrying a pilot wasn't what God had in mind for her. *Maybe* she had come from Plymouth to Chicago and from Chicago to Los Angeles to meet this charming, dapper Brit standing before her. For sure there was only one way to find out. "I'll wait," she said, then turned gracefully, as the airline had taught her, and sashayed to the cluster of chairs nearby. Minutes passed before she realized the young man she'd just accepted a dinner date with had failed to give her his name or to inquire as to hers.

CHAPTER 11

Somehow—and she wasn't quite sure *how*—Evelyn found herself sitting across from the most handsome man she'd ever laid her eyes on. They were in a restaurant filled with string quartet music, linen-draped tablecloths, and flickering candles, the likes of which she'd never seen before.

Like Dorothy in Oz, Evelyn wasn't in Kansas anymore. And certainly not in Portal, Georgia.

"Tell me again," the man who'd introduced himself as George Volbrecht said over a sip of hot coffee. "*Exactly* what did she say?"

Evelyn swallowed hard as she pressed her palms against the plain skirt she'd donned earlier that morning. At least, she surmised, she'd managed to slip her feet back into her pair of cast-off shoes after Mr. Volbrecht surprised her by asking her to "have a bite with" him. "She said that she didn't want to see you. Didn't want to speak to you. And if you didn't get out of her apartment, she would call the police." Evelyn reached a shaky hand toward her cup of coffee, then placed it back into her lap. "Although I don't know how. I mean, we don't even have a . . . phone . . ." Her voice trailed. Maybe she'd said too much. She took a deep breath, and in her best effort to be as worldly and glamorous as Betty, she squared her shoulders. With one finger, she turned the coffee cup all the way around as she'd seen Betty do earlier. But unlike Betty's smooth move, she nearly knocked the delicate cup off its saucer. "How do you know Betty, Mr. Volbrecht?" she asked, hoping to keep the conversation flowing.

The man's jaw flexed and his eyes flashed in the candlelight. "George." He smiled so briefly, Evelyn wondered if she'd imagined it. "Please call me George."

"Okay. George." The name sounded strange on her lips, even though she had an uncle named George. Still . . .

Their waiter appeared then, carrying two plates of steaming food George had ordered, most of which Evelyn had never heard of and felt sure she'd never be able to pronounce. As soon as they were served, Evelyn bowed her head and said a silent prayer of gratitude, although whether it was for the food or the dinner companion, she wasn't sure. When she opened her eyes, George stared at her from across the table.

"Is something wrong?" he asked.

"No. Why?" She slid the folded powder-blue napkin into her lap, picked up the fork that had been beside it, and stabbed at what she thought might be some type of potato.

George was midway through a mouthful. He waved his fork over his plate and said, "I thought perhaps you'd gone to sleep."

"Oh. I just said the bless—I was just thanking God for the food." She took a small bite, chewing slowly. Yes. Most definitely a potato. "Um, how do you know Betty?"

"We've been friends all our lives." He took a long drink of water from a goblet so delicate Evelyn was almost afraid to pick hers up. Even her mama's wedding crystal didn't come close to the intricacy. "Our fathers have known each other since *they* were in diapers, I believe. They both tell stories of rolling around on the carpets, wrestling over a toy. Today my father is the attorney for her father's company. We're not sure who's wrestling who anymore." He smiled at his own wit.

Evelyn smiled with him, hoping the response would relax her. "I've only just met her." She pushed her glasses up her nose. Not that they had slipped, but it gave her hand something to do, and her stomach had tightened to the point where she wasn't sure she could eat. "Why did you—did you want me to tell her something for you, maybe?"

George sliced into his meat with his knife. "What do you mean?"

"I mean, why did you ask me to come out with you? Did you want me to give her a message?"

He chuckled. "Yeah . . . yeah. Ah, no. I thought . . ." He paused as if gathering his thoughts. "I hoped to take my old friend out to dinner, and since she obviously wasn't biting—pardon the pun—I thought perhaps you'd like to go. Out to dinner with me." He pointed to her plate with the knife. "Eat up before it gets cold. Excellent filet mignon, by the way."

She watched the way he held the knife and fork. The way he used them, together, to cut the meat. Not the way she'd always done, almost as if she were attacking it, hoping that if it were not already dead, she'd kill it. The way George did it held an air of such sophistication. Fork held in the left hand. Upside down . . . *then* slice . . . slice . . . slice.

She did it. Evelyn smiled, then looked up at George, who looked back at her. "What?" he asked.

She giggled, feeling heat rise to her cheeks. "Nothing."

George leaned over the table and she did the same. "There is something you can tell Betty for me, if you will."

"Okay." She hoped she didn't sound too anxious.

"Tell her that I tried to warn her, but she didn't . . . hear me."

Evelyn dropped her silverware onto her plate, making an awful racket. "Warn her?"

"Her father," George said, bringing his eyes from her plate back to her face. "He's not happy, you tell her. He's *going* to cut off her allowance. He means it this time."

"Cut it off?" Evelyn wasn't aware of an allowance. Well, sir. No wonder Betty had such beautiful clothes. And shoes and hats to match.

"That's right. No more party dresses. No more extras for whatever it is she thinks she needs. Her fine perfumes and talcum powders. He's going to give her an ultimatum and she'd better prepare herself. Tell her . . ." He made a show of cutting more meat. "Tell her I tried to warn her." He looked up again. "Because we are, after all, such longtime friends. Got it?"

"Got it," Evelyn whispered.

He wiped his mouth with the linen napkin before asking, "How about a little dessert? Tiramisu?"

"What brought you to America?" Inga asked the man she now knew as Frank Martindale. They were an hour into the most exciting dinner she'd ever eaten and the liveliest conversation she'd ever had.

"A plane," he said.

She laughed heartily, not worried in the least if it sounded more like a guffaw than a bell ringing. Her grandmother would say there could be nothing worse than a woman laughing like a moose, but at that moment, Inga didn't care. "My roommate, the one I told you about, came over on a ship. Then took the train to Chicago."

Frank nodded as he twirled his fork into the tangle of spaghetti on his plate. "Seriously, I flew to New York, then took a train to Chicago, then a plane to LA."

Inga raised her hands. "But why LA? Weren't New York and Chicago exciting enough for you?"

They sat in a booth with plush semicircular seating, as close as they could while still facing each other. He smiled at her. "Hollywood. I can sing. I can dance." He turned his face toward the dim overhead light. "On the whole, I think I'm pretty good-looking."

She playfully patted the side of his face. "You're adorable."

"So, back in London, I see this movie with Gene Kelly—"

"Which one?"

"*Summer Stock*."

"With Judy Garland."

"You know it?"

"Know it? I went to the picture show three times to see it."

"Only three?" he teased. "I went four."

"You know," she said, leaning back, pretending to take him in. "You sort of look like Gene Kelly."

"Nothing doing. Besides, my real friends tell me I look more like Montgomery Clift."

She made a game of studying his face. "Mmm . . . no. They're obviously not your real friends."

He leaned over and stole a kiss so quickly Inga hadn't a moment to prepare for it. "Are you, then?"

"Yes," she whispered. "Absolutely the best."

"Then what do you say? Honestly. Who do I really remind you of?"

She had to think, if she could. She had to be clever. "I think . . . you look like a man from London destined to be a star."

The hour hand on her watch had passed nine when Joan finally returned to the apartment. As always, a small table lamp burned dimly in the living room while the rest of the place stood dark and quiet. She kicked out of her shoes and dropped her house key into the purse dangling from her arm. And, as always, Joan slipped into the kitchen, turned on the light, and padded over to the fridge where she pulled out a bottle of milk. Just enough for half a glass rested near the bottom. She poured herself all that was left, drank it, rinsed the glass and the bottle, and set the glass in the sink. She then returned to the living room, placed the empty bottle next to the door, picked up her shoes, and walked wearily to her bedroom.

A sliver of light peeked out from beneath the closed door. Joan paused at the unusualness. She opened the door slowly and peered in to find Evelyn propped up in bed, her knees drawn up to her chin and her arms wrapped around her legs. Her glasses lay cross-armed on the bedside table, and her face appeared streaked with tears.

"Evelyn," Joan whispered. "What—"

"Close the door," Evelyn whispered back.

Joan did, then walked to the bed and sat on her side, looking at Evelyn over her shoulder. "Are you okay? Is it your mum?" She eased her shoes to the floor.

Evelyn shook her head. "No. Not my mama. And it's not my daddy or my brother. It's Betty." She hiccupped softly. "She's so mad at me . . ." The gentle flow of tears became a silent flood.

Joan scooted closer. "Betty? No. Betty doesn't get angry."

"You don't know," Evelyn said. "You weren't here." She looked at her accusingly. "You're *never* here."

Joan sighed. As much as she hated leaving Evelyn alone so often, she knew she'd hate even more telling her she'd just taken another job at the Museum of Science and Industry. Saturdays only—and only for a few hours—but . . . "Tell me what happened."

"George came over, before dinner."

"George? Who is George?" Joan opened her purse and pulled out a handkerchief, then handed it to Evelyn.

"They're old friends. He said so."

"When? When did he say so?"

"At dinner."

"He came for dinner?"

Again, Evelyn shook her head. "No, no," she said, her voice continuing to whisper. "He came to see Betty—to take *her* out to dinner—but she wouldn't go with him. So he asked me if I would like to go and . . ." She drew in a shaky breath as she pressed her hand against her chest. "I've never seen a man so good-looking, Joanie. He's like one of those men you see in the movies."

"And he's Betty's friend? And you went out with him?" Joan tried to remember if Betty had ever mentioned a George. Or even a boyfriend. None came to mind. Then again, she was tired and hadn't had anything to eat since lunch.

"Only to dinner." Evelyn blew her nose into the handkerchief before handing it back to Joan.

Joan waved it away. "Keep it."

"He's asked me out again, Joan."

Evelyn's face glowed and, Joan determined, not from tear tracks. "He has?"

"For Friday night. He's really nice and I said yes because . . . Oh, Joanie, no one who looks like George Volbrecht has *ever* asked me out on a date, much less two of them."

Joan patted Evelyn's hand. "I see. What happened when you told Betty?"

"She started huffing around, telling me that George Volbrecht is a cad. A womanizer. That he was up to something and she'd get to the bottom of it, no matter what. The worst of it is that George wanted me to tell her that her father is issuing some kind of ultimatum—I don't know over what—and that he's cutting off her allowance."

"Her allowance?" Joan had no idea Betty received an allowance. Here Joan worked two-soon-to-be-three jobs to help her family, and Betty's income had been supplemented by her father? "Did you then? Did you let her know?"

"No."

"Why not?"

The tears began again. "With all the huffing going on, I'm afraid I just forgot."

CHAPTER 12

Betty stood rather than sat across from George's expansive oak desk. "George Volbrecht, what are you up to? And don't tell me nothing," she said, shoving her fists into her sides, which caused the coat she refused to remove to bunch up. "Because I know you, and you're most definitely up to something."

George swiveled in the tufted leather chair, his elbows resting on the arms, a pencil twirling between his index fingers. "What makes you think I'm up to anything?" The swiveling stopped. "You're the one, Betts. You're the one playing games."

Betty turned and paced the finely decorated room with its rows of built-in shelves lined with volumes of law books, exquisite reproductions of Renoir paintings—*Dance at Le Moulin de la Galette*, *The Theatre Box*, and *Two Sisters*—the expensive, dark furniture. When she had collected her thoughts, she stopped and said, "George, if you have a shred of decency in you, you'll listen to me. That girl you took out last night—"

"Evelyn," he said, his voice like the snow-white pappus of a dandelion, caught up by a breeze. "Lovely name—Evelyn."

Betty felt her spine tingle. "*Evelyn* is an innocent girl from a small town in Georgia. She's a farmer's daughter—"

"I know. She told me." George dropped the pencil onto his

desk and sat straight. "What are you trying to say, Betty? You don't want to marry me but you want me to take on the role of a priest? Am I never to marry then?"

Betty knew she had to take a better tack. She walked around the chair where earlier she'd deposited her handbag and sank slowly into its soft leather. "George," she said, leaning over and resting her forearm against her crossed knee. "You are *not* interested in marrying someone like Evelyn Alexander."

His eyes met hers. "I find her charming."

"And what do you think will happen here? You'll take her home to meet your parents on Christmas Day? Your mother will eat her for lunch and spit out the seeds."

George stood, came around to the front of his desk, and took Betty by the hand, helping her to stand. "Come this way, Betty," he said, reaching for her purse and leading her to the paneled door.

Betty slipped her hand from his, which only resulted in his placing the hand at the small of her back, which arched under his touch.

When they'd made it to the door, he turned her around, slid her purse over her wrist, and cupped both hands under her elbows. "Listen to me, Betts. I get it. *You* don't want to marry me. Although *why not* I can't comprehend. *No one* can."

Betty searched his face, remembering the years they'd played together as children. The talks they'd had under the canopy of low tree branches in her backyard as they'd neared adolescence. She'd told him everything. Trusted him with all her secrets, as he trusted her with his. But then . . . puberty hit and he had gone from a cute little boy to an entirely too good-looking young man. A fact neither he nor any girl in their school had missed. His attentions, however, had always stayed on her. Maybe, Betty surmised, he *did* love her. Or at least he thought he did, or did as much as he was capable. And maybe he saw their marriage as the perfect union between their families—as did their parents. But she knew his faithfulness wouldn't last a year. Six months, tops. George Volbrecht needed beautiful women like every other human needed air.

And love.

Real love. That's what she wanted. *Needed.* A man who adored her *not* for her father's social status and business position, but for herself. A strong woman. Independent. *Somewhat* independent. But a woman who knew her own mind and what she wanted. Superficiality had no place in her life. She wanted the real deal.

She released a sigh. "George." She rested her hands on the hard muscles of his upper arms. "George, if you are playing some kind of game . . ."

His eyes stayed on hers. "I'm not. She's a sweet kid and I'm really hoping to get to know her better."

"A kid. She's a full-grown woman, George. With feelings. And dreams." She applied pressure to his muscles with her thumbs and felt them flex beneath her fingertips. "If you hurt her, I am telling you now, I'll call her daddy," she said, accentuating the words in her best Blanche DuBois voice, "and I'll tell him to load his gun full of buckshot and run you from one end of this city to the other."

George chuckled. "Cute." He turned her as he opened the door. "By the way, did Evelyn tell you what I told her to tell you?"

Betty paused, unsure, not wanting to admit she'd spent more time stomping around the apartment than speaking to Evelyn after she'd returned home. "Of course she did. We're roommates, after all."

George's brow shot up. "And you're okay with it, still? Not changing your mind?"

Changing her mind could only mean one thing. "I'm not marrying you, George Volbrecht. Get that through your head." She glanced at her watch. "Now, I have to go. I told Mr. Ferguson I'd be late, but I didn't count on *this* late." With that, she walked past George's entirely too-gorgeous secretary, whose eyes she felt following her. With all the dignity she'd learned in charm school, she stepped into the hall, closing the outer door behind her. There she quickly removed her gloves from her purse and shoved her fingers into them as she approached the elevator. When its doors finally opened, she stepped in and turned. Only then did she realize George had followed her halfway and that he now stood in the office doorway, watching her every move.

Inga could barely keep her mind on her work as the plane careened across the clear blue December sky toward Chicago. She stood at her station in the back galley, getting trays of food together for the passengers in her rows, watching her hands do their job automatically. But her thoughts were elsewhere. They lingered in the restaurant where she and Frank had eaten the night before. Eaten and talked . . . and talked and kissed . . . until the candles were all blown out and the management begged them to leave.

"Young lovers," the manager had said as he opened the door for their exit. "Such a nice thing to see, but I have my own love to go home to tonight." Then he chuckled, and they'd laughed with him.

They walked together back to the hotel, their arms linked around each other's waists, holding one another close, commenting on the Christmas lights twinkling from lampposts. They both agreed that cold weather around the holidays made the season seem more festive, but they weren't complaining either.

When they neared the hotel, Frank had scooted her into an alley where he'd been so ardent and yet so tender that she'd thought her knees would buckle had he not held her so tightly against him.

When he finally released her, he whispered in her ear. "I can't believe we've just met and you have to leave tomorrow."

The warmth of his breath sent chills down her spine and she shuddered as she promised, "But we'll be back. Soon. We don't always stay overnight, but sometimes we stay for longer than a day." She buried her face in his neck, breathed in his scent, setting it to memory. "I'll call you." She planted her lips against the most tender spot on his throat, then broke away and dashed into the hotel lobby as quickly as she could.

"Bet I know what you're daydreaming about," Henrietta now said, coming up beside her.

Inga felt the temperature rise in her cheeks. "What makes you think I'm daydreaming?"

Henrietta pointed to one of the trays. "You just put two desserts on this tray and two breads on another one."

Inga laughed, correcting her error. "Oh, Retta. He's so amazing." She looked into the face of the auburn-haired beauty. "Did I mention that already?"

"About ten times after you came in and woke me so I could watch you gush all night. It's a miracle I'm standing upright at all, I'm so tired."

"I'm sorry."

"No, you aren't," Henrietta teased. "And I'm not sorry either." She studied Inga's face. "By golly, he's put more pink in those cheeks than God already blessed you with." She glanced up the aisle. "Now, you'd better put Mr. Hollywood on a back burner before Mrs. Bricker comes back here and finds you mixing up the meal orders."

Inga nodded. "Thanks, Retta. You're a true friend."

"Merry Christmas, Adela," Betty said, pressing her cheek against the colored woman's. "Doesn't Mother *ever* give you a day off?"

Adela helped Betty out of the fur-lined cashmere coat she only wore on special occasions, then draped it over her arm. "I wanted to be here," Adela confirmed with a sure nod when they faced each other again. "I told her I'd be here this morning and for your Christmas lunch, and then I'd be with my own."

Betty clasped Adela's hands in her own, noting the perfectly shaped nails, tinted red with polish. "Did you make it to church last night?"

"You know I did. I'm not missing the Christmas Eve service, not for no one or no*body*. Your mama and daddy went to Mass. Did you?"

Betty nodded. "In the city. Mother wanted me to come here and go with them. Spend the night. But . . ." She allowed her words to drop off, unsure how to explain how she'd felt the night before. The need to be alone with God instead of alone with God and her parents. The recent chasm between them had left a wound, one she hoped might heal sooner rather than later. But one she didn't know how to treat. And so came the need to be alone where she could listen, undisturbed.

"But you're a big girl now," Adela finished for her.

Betty grinned, then peered down at the large shopping bag resting on the floor by her feet. "I've got a surprise for you."

"And I've got one for you too. Made your favorite pie for dessert."

Betty gasped in delight. "Banana cream?"

"My own mama's recipe. Baked two of 'em. One for here and one for you to take home."

Betty started to thank Adela, but her mother's voice coming from the top of the stairs cut her off. "Darling, is that you?"

Betty squeezed Adela's hands once more before looking up. "Hello, Mother. Merry Christmas."

Adela patted her hand before her heels clipped down the hall toward the back of the house, and Chloe Estes descended the staircase, one hand lightly trailing the banister. Her elegant red velvet wraparound gown cascaded around and behind her, displaying a chic picture of sophistication. Betty met her at the base of the staircase, kissing her cheek as soon as her mother made it to the final step. "Mmm, Mother. You smell delicious."

Chloe's fingertips traveled the length of her swan-like throat. "Your father gave me the scent last night as a surprise."

"Hurray for Father," Betty said, determined to keep the day festive and fun. "Where is Romeo? Upstairs still?"

Chloe looked over her shoulder. "He'll be down soon." Then, glancing at the shopping bag filled with wrapped packages, she said, "For under the tree?"

Betty nodded as she turned and reached for the bag's handles. "Let's put them there before Father comes down."

Mother and daughter linked arms as they stepped into the living room, where the scent of pine reigned. A massive tree nearly reached the twelve-foot ceiling and dripped with silvery icicles and both large and small red, green, and blue ornaments. As much as Betty desired her independence, on Christmas Day she couldn't imagine another place in the world she wanted to be than right here, among the sleek French-inspired pale-pink furnishings, offset by evergreen boughs on the hearth and brass baskets of cinnamon- and clove-laced pinecones. The parlor reflected her mother's unusual and extravagant taste. Nothing about it appealed to Betty's personal sense of style, yet *this room* beckoned her on this most holy of days.

Betty squatted before the tree and pulled three packages out of the bag, one at a time. When she had stacked them just so, she reached for a large box wrapped in blue foil paper and tied with a silver bow.

"Touch it and I'll send you home immediately," her father's voice boomed from the open doorway.

Betty turned, duly scolded, but noting the joy on his face. "Oh, Daddy," she said, using the term of endearment she saved for moments such as these. She stood, crossed the room, and wrapped her arms around him. His strong, beefy arms came around her, enveloping her in security and love. She kissed his cheek, taking in the scent of a morning cigar blended with aftershave. "Merry Christmas, Father."

He kissed her cheek as well. "And to you, my child." Then, releasing her, he barked over his shoulder, "Adela!"

Betty pinched his elbow. "Do you *have* to do that?"

Harrison's eyes filled with mischief. "If she wants to be a part of the gift giving, I do."

Betty turned to her mother, who'd draped herself over one of the sofas. "I thought we'd eat brunch first. Isn't that what we usually do?"

"Not this time." When Betty cocked a brow in question, Chloe continued, "This way Adela can go home early."

"Oh," Betty said as the sound of Adela's footsteps neared the doorway. "Brilliant," she added. Because it was.

Adela entered, bringing with her a tray of small crystal cups filled with eggnog, which she placed on the coffee table. After making certain everyone had a cup, she sat in one of the revered Hitchcock chairs, crossing her ankles and tucking her feet underneath the chair. With her hands holding her serving of eggnog and resting in her lap, she declared, "I'm now ready, Mr. Estes."

Harrison Estes played Santa, passing out the gifts to everyone until neat little piles surrounded each of them. Betty, who had the largest number of presents, began the family's tradition of opening one gift at a time so that everyone could see . . . and ooh and aah over the bounty. When an hour had passed and the room had been littered by torn paper and satiny bows, and when treasures had been returned to boxes for carrying upstairs or to their respective homes, Adela stood. She gathered the paper as she said, "Once again, I thank you all for your kindness. For making me a part of your family."

Betty jumped up to help. "Oh, Adela. Whatever would we do without you?" Then, coming close enough for only Adela to hear, she said, "I truly hope you like the fruit bowl. I thought it one of the most beautiful I've ever seen."

Adela nudged her with an elbow. "I'll treasure it the rest of my life. The earrings too. But I'm thinking you spent too much on me."

Betty smiled, hoping Adela knew the clusters of pearls were real and not cheap imitations. "You are worth every penny."

It seemed to Betty that her parents waited now, waited for Adela to finish her straightening and to leave the room. Adela felt it too; Betty knew by the way the woman's lovely dark eyes met hers, almost in empathy. Betty felt her brow furrow.

As soon as Adela had gone, Chloe brushed imaginary lint from her gown and spoke around a sigh. "So, what are your roommates doing today, Betty? Did they go home to their families?"

Betty perched on the edge of the nearest chair. "No. Inga and Magda spent yesterday and today with their aunt and uncle. Christmas Eve is nearly as important in Sweden as Christmas Day, you know," she said. "Joan has begged for quiet to sleep—she works three jobs—and there's absolutely no doubt in my mind that you know where Evelyn is."

"Evelyn?" her father asked his wife. "Which one is she?"

"The mousy one Betty told us about," Chloe answered.

"I never once said she was mousy."

"Where did I hear that then?"

Betty crossed her legs and leaned into the chair as though she had not one care in the world, as though the joy of Christmas had not suddenly come to a halt. "I cannot imagine, Mother. Where *did* you hear that?"

Chloe's eyes—older versions of Betty's own—met hers. "I suppose Vivian Volbrecht said it."

Betty couldn't help but wonder where Vivian would have gleaned such a description, if not from George. "It's Christmas, Mother," Betty said, offering a silent prayer for her friend who would, soon enough, face the wolves known as the Volbrechts for the first time. "Can't you just be nice?"

CHAPTER 13

Evelyn sat on the passenger side of George's 1951 Lincoln Cosmopolitan, her eyes struggling to take in the neighborhood he drove her through. She adjusted the cat-eye glasses for the fifth time in as many minutes and turned to George—who looked fine with his hand draped lazily at the top of the steering wheel. "These sure are some nice houses."

He smiled at her. "You've said that already. Better said, 'These houses are nice.'"

She blinked and looked out the windshield. "These houses are nice."

George reached for her gloved hand, which she willingly gave to him. "Don't worry, Evelyn. You'll do fine."

Evelyn searched his eyes for what might be going on behind them. For what he meant by his words. "Do you think . . ." She took a deep breath. "Do you think your mama and them will like me?"

"My *mother* and *father* will like you because I like you. They like what I like. I've told you that."

Evelyn felt the sting in his voice. "And your baby sister will be there too?"

"Sandra, yes. With her husband and her baby."

Evelyn shifted in the seat. "So you're an uncle."

His grin brought a shimmer of love into his eyes. "I am. His name is Martin and he's everything and then some."

"You love him."

This time, when he looked at her, she didn't have to try to read the expression. "Very much so." He returned his attention to the road. "One day . . . when I marry . . ."

Evelyn felt the squeeze of his hand. Or had it merely flinched?

"I want a houseful of children," he finished. "Mother and Dad only had the two of us, but I think deep down my father always wanted more."

Evelyn's heart pounded; he had just confided something about himself and about his family to her. And for the first time. "But your mama—your *mother*—didn't?"

He seemed to calculate his answer. "Those are not the kinds of things we talk about in my family." Then he smiled and the dimple returned, sending whatever reprimand Evelyn might have felt into oblivion.

She glanced out the window again. "And Betty comes from this neighborhood?"

George nodded. "A couple of streets over."

"My goodness," she whispered, just as he turned the car into a long driveway leading to a box-style, two-story house. "This is it? This is where *you* come from?"

George released her hand and shifted the car into park. "No, Evelyn," he said, turning to face her. "This is not where I 'come from.' This is where I grew up." He touched the tip of her nose with his finger. "Remember what I told you. Try not to sound too much like a hick, okay?"

Evelyn bristled under the reminder, but only for as long as it took for George to say the words. He brought her hand to his lips and kissed the bend in her finger. "I'll try," she said.

"That's a good girl."

He got out of the car and she waited until he came around for her. After helping her out, he folded the passenger-side seat forward, reached into the back, and produced a large bag full of gifts. "Remember what else I said," he told her, closing the door. "You and I will exchange gifts later."

She nodded happily. "I remember." She looked toward the house and released a breath she hadn't realized she'd kept pent up. "I'm ready, George," she said, peering up at him. "And I promise you won't be ashamed of me when this day is over."

Betty alternated her stares between the opposite ends of the table where her parents sat. Christmas lunch—their version of Christmas dinner—had been served. Eaten. Enjoyed. Conversation had stayed clear of Evelyn and George and the Volbrechts and veered toward topics like work—both hers and her father's—and some of the social events her mother had ahead of her in January.

And then . . .

With dessert nothing more than a memory of banana cream pie and hot, sweet coffee, Betty's father cleared his throat and announced that they needed to have a talk. "Maybe today is not the day for this," he said, "but I want to start the New Year off right."

"Sounds like an ultimatum is about to be handed down," Betty said, keeping her voice steady.

"Call it what you will, but I'm going to say this plain and simple."

"Get on with it, Father."

"Accept George Volbrecht's proposal or lose your allowance."

Betty sat in stunned silence for what seemed an eternity, but could have only been half a minute. "I cannot believe this," she finally breathed out.

"And I have no doubt you cannot live without my monthly gift to you, Elizabeth."

Her mother leaned forward. "I believe those were real pearls you gave to Adela. *Really*, Betty."

Betty waved away the shifting of subjects. "Mother. Father . . ." She chuckled at the nonsense in the conversation. "George and I are friends, yes." Her thoughts landed on the trump card. "But George has been dating Evelyn for nearly a month now. You know that." She threw her hands up. "I would never come between two young lovers."

"Nonsense," Harrison said. "That boy is only seeing the girl to make you stand up and take notice. Anyone with half a brain could see that."

Betty placed the red linen napkin accented with tiny holly leaves on the table next to her dessert dish. "Well, fortunately, Father, I have a *whole* brain. And all my faculties. I'm well aware that George thinks he can sway me with this . . . *whatever* . . . he has going with Evelyn. But the truth is, I have spoken with him about it and I think—I *know*—he may have the spark of feelings for her."

Her father brought his fist down on the table, clattering the dishes. "You will do whatever you need to do to reinstate your relationship with George Volbrecht or, at the very least, someone of his caliber, or you'll not see another penny from me. It's time you stopped this working nonsense, moved back to Highland Park, and made a respectable woman out of yourself."

Betty stood, her legs feeling more like gelatin than muscle. "Someone of his caliber?" She looked at her mother, hoping for evidence of shock. Instead, Chloe's face held the same resolve as her husband's. "What about love? Mother, you have told me more than a dozen times how much you loved Father. Almost as soon as you met him."

Chloe blushed as she smiled. "With all my heart," she said, looking down the length of the table.

"And did his *caliber* have anything to do with that emotion?"

Her brow cocked. "Absolutely it did. And your father felt the same."

"Cut from the same cloth," her father countered. "Which is why we've had such a successful marriage."

"And we want the same for you," her mother finished. "Wouldn't any parent?"

"George is perfect for you. He loves *you*, Betty. Not this little girl he is carrying over to his parents' home today."

"A lamb to the slaughter," Chloe whispered, sending Betty back to her seat.

She grasped her napkin, squeezing it for strength, and swallowed. Her eyes rested on the crumbs left behind from her serving of Adela's pie.

Adela. Now she understood the look the woman had given her. Adela knew. Had probably overheard her parents plotting out the path of the bombshell they would drop after dessert had been eaten.

"If George," Betty began slowly, "is the type of man who would lead a lamb to its death, then why in the name of all that is good and decent would you want me to marry him?" She stood again, raising her chin before she could do the same with her eyes. When she did, they went first to her father, then to her mother. "Thank you for the gifts." She made a show of studying her watch. "I must be going."

As she stepped away from the table—and it seemed lately that she always left this way—her mother grabbed her hand. "Just think about it, darling. *Think* about the life George could give you. The love. The adoration. Our little allowance is nothing compared to what he could lavish on you."

Betty closed her eyes. "Or someone of his caliber?"

"Exactly," Chloe exclaimed, as if Betty now understood.

"Thank you, Mother," Betty said, then slipped out of the room.

Evelyn copied every move George's sister made at the expansive table that sat in the middle of an equally expansive dining room. Even her grandmother's home in Savannah—the one where her Aunt Dovalou still lived—paled in the shadow of this one. Until today, she'd thought it the grandest house ever with its family heirloom table, hutch and cabinet filled with crystal and china, wool carpets warming the heart-pine floorboards. But this—

"Evelyn," George said, drawing her away from the memory.

"Hmm?" She turned to the man sitting to her left.

He looked at her as if she'd lost her mind, then gave her a tender smile. "Mother asked you a question, dear. Did you not hear her?"

Evelyn clasped her hand into a fist, her bare nails digging into the pad. "I'm sorry, no." She glanced down the table to where the dark-haired beauty George called Mother sat in a velvet-covered seat, much like her own but with high, stately arms. "I apologize." Her hand relaxed; she felt proud of her choice of words. George had previously taught her the inappropriateness of "I'm sorry."

"I asked, dear, if you went to Christmas Eve Mass with George."

"Ah—no. I'm—ah—Methodist. I went to the Methodist church near where I live." Evelyn noted the disapproval on Vivian Volbrecht's face. "Where I live with Betty Estes," she added, hoping to ease her displeasure.

"I see."

Sandra, who insisted Evelyn call her Sandie, laughed lightly from her place directly across from George. "Mother, the entire world is not Catholic, despite what you might think."

"Perhaps they should be," Mr. Volbrecht said, smiling.

Evelyn smiled back at him, which wasn't difficult. Lawrence Volbrecht's looks were soothing. Inviting. And it wasn't difficult to see where George—and Sandie—had received their good looks. Both parents reminded Evelyn of a couple inside the pages of a glossy movie magazine. Or like something she'd only witnessed on the silver screen at the Lucas Theatre.

"I've been Methodist all my life," Evelyn told him. "My parents were. My grandparents." She looked from one family member to another, including Sandie's husband, Philip, whose handsomeness didn't quite match George's but wasn't far behind. "My great-grandpa Doyle was a Methodist preacher, as a matter of fact."

George cleared his throat as he brought the linen napkin to his lips and wiped them. "Mother, please let Katherine know how delicious this dinner is."

"Doyle," his mother said. "Is that Irish?"

Evelyn pushed her glasses up her nose. "It is."

"The Volbrecht name is German," his father added.

"My grandma—my grandmother's family—my father's mother—was of German descent."

"Tell me," Vivian spoke up from her end of the table, "what it is your father does."

Evelyn glanced at George, hoping she didn't embarrass him. His father worked day in and day out as a fancy lawyer in a swanky office, just as George did. Not that she had seen his office, but she'd *imagined* it dozens of times.

"My father is . . ." She struggled.

"A farmer" sounded dirt-poor. Growing up, she'd seen him in overalls more than in any other form of dress. For church, of course, he wore his Sunday best. But even at night, after a hard day in the heat, working often-unyielding earth, he changed from one pair of overalls into another. She pictured him sitting in the front-porch rocker, talking to her, his words filled with gentleness. Kindness. Godliness. She thought of him slipping money into her hand, money she knew he could hardly spare, and then sending her on her way to Chicago. To this land of tall buildings and fancy houses and people who spoke strangely.

Evelyn swallowed the fear of answering and said, "My father is a farmer." She glanced at George, who turned red as his jaw muscles flexed. He picked up both fork and knife, holding them the way she'd learned to do, and made a show of cutting the meat on his plate.

"Agriculture," Lawrence Volbrecht said, bringing everyone's attention to him. Evelyn mentally kicked herself for not using that term. "What would we have done without those who made their living in agriculture during the war years?"

"Indeed," Philip added. He raised his glass in a toast. "I say, 'To the farmer.'"

Evelyn looked at George again. His face had softened and he smiled, reaching for his glass. She quickly did the same, raising hers as she saw the others do, including George's mother. Although she also noted she was the last one to do so.

Bing Crosby's "White Christmas" greeted Betty as she entered the apartment on Greenleaf. Her arms ached from carrying the same bag she'd used to transport the few gifts out to her parents'. It now overflowed with unwrapped packages, throbbing reminders of the cost associated with being the daughter of Harrison and Chloe Estes.

The Christenson sisters sat together on the sofa, their feet tucked under them and the skirts of their housedresses covering their legs. Joan, who sat in one of the occasional chairs, still wore her pajamas along with a thick quilted robe and Japanese-inspired slippers. The three were in midconversation, their hands wrapped around mugs. The unmistakable aroma of hot cocoa lingered in the air and Betty's stomach rumbled.

"Don't let me interrupt you," she said, so happy to be home that she could hardly keep herself from smiling.

Joan leapt to her feet, helping Betty with the bag. "Someone made out well," she said, and Betty laughed.

"Looks that way, doesn't it?" she said, not wanting to talk of the truth behind it all. She glanced at the sisters. "How did it go at your aunt and uncle's?"

The girls were even more resplendent than usual. They both wore their hair brushed away from their faces, and it appeared the chill of the day and the warmth of the cocoa had left a glow on their cheeks.

"Like Christmas in Sweden," Inga said. She tossed her blonde hair and said, "*God jul*, Betty."

"Where shall I put these?" Joan asked her, lifting the bag.

"My room. Thank you. Oh, and there's a pie at the bottom of the bag." Then to Inga, "What is 'God . . . God . . .' what?"

"*God jul*," Magda answered with a laugh. "Merry Christmas." She looked to her sister and then back to Betty, who held on to the back of Joan's chair to balance herself as she removed her rubbers. "We really did have a good time last night and today. Sometimes I forget how important our traditions are. And all the scrumptious food on the *julbord*."

Betty raised her eyes without lifting her head. "Sounds heavenly. Any cocoa left?"

"Plenty," Joan said, padding back into the living room and carrying the pie. "I'll pour some for you. Maybe we can slice into this later?"

"Absolutely."

"Sit, then," Joan told her.

Betty didn't have to be asked twice. She took the chair near Joan's, then called over her shoulder, "What about you, Joan? What did you do all day?"

Joan returned within a minute, carrying a steaming cup of cocoa topped with three giant marshmallows. "Here you go."

Betty took it, inhaled the aroma of sugar and chocolate, thinking it almost enough to stop there without taking a sip.

"How was your day?" Joan asked, picking up the mug she had placed on the coffee table. "Looks like your parents were generous."

Betty pushed a smile upward. "A typical day at the Estes home." She blew into the cocoa, watched as the melting thick mounds of white shimmied to the other side.

"Did Adela appreciate the pearls?"

Betty swallowed her first delicious sip, felt it traveling past her throat, slipping down her esophagus, burning on the way to her stomach. "She did. They looked quite pretty on her." She looked down the hall. "I take it Evelyn's not back yet."

Magda stole a glance at her watch. "Should be soon."

Joan shook her head. "I don't know. She told me that after eating over at George's they were going to go out for coffee and dessert and exchange their gifts to each other." Joan chuckled. "She's quite beside herself wondering what he will give her."

Betty nodded. "I hope he's generous then," she whispered, but added nothing more.

CHAPTER 14

On a Wednesday in the middle of January, Inga hurried through LAX as quickly as her uniform heels allowed. Her calves ached, not only from standing so much during the day—and most especially on this last flight—but from the speed she now tried to accomplish. The speed that strained against the pencil-skirt uniform she wore.

Henrietta walked beside her, both of them weighed down by overnight luggage in one hand and a cosmetics case in the other. "Do you realize," she said, huffing, "we've traveled the entire country in one day? O'Hare to LaGuardia. LaGuardia back to O'Hare. O'Hare to LAX." She laughed lightly. "But I daresay you're matching the time for most of the jets I've been in. *Slow down.*"

Inga tried to pace herself, but thoughts of seeing Frank again that evening were almost more than she could bear. "Do you know how long it's been since we've seen each other? Two weeks. Nearly three." They came to an escalator and stepped upon two of the steps, one behind the other, for the trip downward. Inga glanced over her shoulder at Henrietta. "Since before Christmas. I think TWA did this on purpose, switching our flights the way they did. I thought I'd never see LA again."

Henrietta laughed. "And now we have two glorious days here."

They stepped onto the floor and strode toward the outer doors and the yellow cabs waiting like ducks in a row beyond the sidewalk's curb. "I don't know what you have in mind," she continued, "but I'm going to soak up as many sunrays as I can by the pool. Nothing like LA weather to make you forget about Chicago's blizzards."

The two women found a cab and, as soon as their luggage had been tucked securely in the trunk, slid into the backseat. "Does he know you're coming?" Henrietta asked, opening her purse and pulling out her compact.

Inga did the same. "Yes. I phoned him last night." She peered at herself in the tiny mirror, then dabbed at her chin and nose with the small puff. She couldn't help but smile. "He said he couldn't wait to see me." The compact closed with a snap. "Oh, Retta. I really do believe this is it. He's the one. I just know it."

The cab driver pulled away from the curb as Henrietta said, "How? How do you know?"

Inga shuddered. "I can't explain it. I'm all giddy when I'm around him. I feel . . . I feel like I've known him my whole life and that I'll know him until I die. We're—" She gazed out the window to the familiar landscape of Los Angeles. "We're like a hand and a glove. Or—what is it Evelyn says?—peas and carrots." She giggled. "I can say this for sure—if he asked me to marry him tonight, I'd say yes."

"After, what? Two dates?"

Inga waved away the notion. "We talk once a week and he's written me the most wonderful letters." She opened her purse again to pull out a small stack tied with ribbon. "I'd share but they might make you blush."

Henrietta raised her chin. "Then they should make *you* blush." Her eyes met Inga's. "Be careful, Inga. You say he's special, but he's still a man."

Inga looked out the window again, determined to be somewhat cautious but not so restricted she couldn't breathe. If she'd wanted that kind of existence, she would have married some nice man her father had found for her.

As the first generation born in America, she and Magda had heard countless stories of arranged marriages. Of fathers and mothers knowing what was best for their children, especially their daughters. The men of her father's dreams for her and Magda were both Swedish and Lutheran. They were proud men. Fervent. The kind of men who wouldn't be caught dead having fun just for the enjoyment of it. They were not the kind of men who laughed easily, like Frank, but instead kept their chins high, their jaws firm, and their chests bowed. Her father called that conviction.

Inga just called it boring.

At five till six that evening, Inga stood dressed to the nines in an elevator that descended all too slowly to the lobby of the hotel. The last time she'd been there, a Christmas tree had dominated the room. Today when she came in, she noted it had been replaced by luxury as far as the eye could see.

Frank stood near the elevator doors, waiting for her arrival. His face lit up when they saw each other, and she felt hers do the same. She'd hardly had time to step onto the lobby floor before he slipped his arm around her waist and whisked her toward the revolving doors leading outside.

"Where are you taking me?" she asked him as soon as they stopped on the sidewalk.

His hand squeezed her to him and he mumbled, "I know where I'd like to take you. Back to my place."

She looked over her shoulder, then straight into his eyes. "I thought you lived in the hotel."

"I do," he said, smiling. "If I had any sense I would have told you to come straight to my room."

She put her fingertip against his chin. "Oh, but as it turns out, *I* have sense."

He smiled. "Meaning?"

"Meaning I would never walk into a man's apartment. Alone." The disapproving face of her father rushed toward her, and just as quickly, she pushed it away.

Frank released her, then took a step forward and called out to the valet. "Hey, Charlie. Get us a cab?"

Charlie—a pimply-faced young man she'd previously met—whistled, and within seconds, a cab slid up to the curb.

"Your chariot, milady," Frank said, his accent adding authenticity to the choice of words.

She listened as he told the cab driver the address of their destination, but waited until he had nestled beside her to ask, "Again, where are you taking me?"

"A great little place on Fairfax called Tom Bergin's. Actually, it's Tom Bergin's Old Horseshoe Tavern and Thoroughbred Club, but most people around here call it simply Tom Bergin's."

Inga opened her purse and pulled out her gloves, which she then slid her hands into as if putting on a show. "What kind of place is it?"

She couldn't help but note the way his eyes watched as she wiggled her fingers into the soft fabric of the gloves. She could almost hear Magda's voice whisper in her ear, "Playing with fire." But she didn't care. They no longer lived in the 1940s world of their mother and father; they were free, independent women of the '50s. Able to work even with the men home from the war. Able to have their own apartments outside of boardinghouses. Able to run and play with the big boys.

She gave the hem of her skirt a deliberate tug. "Did you hear me?" she asked.

He swallowed. Hard. "Irish. An Irish pub." He forced his eyes to hers. "Ever been to one?"

"Are you kidding me?" She laughed. "I live in Chicago, remember?"

Frank chuckled, his face so close she could smell the lingering sweetness of a mint he must have popped before she'd come to the lobby. "Tom Bergin's is hailed as one of the best. You'll have to let me know what you think about—"

She didn't allow him to finish; instead she cut his words off with a kiss, one he leaned into with passion. Brazen, she knew, but she'd waited too many days for this. Weeks. Perhaps her whole life.

And she wasn't wasting another moment. By this time next year, she vowed as her hand gripped the nape of his neck, she would no longer fly from Chicago to LA to see him. This time next year, she would be Mrs. Frank Martindale.

Early the next morning, Magda exited the mail room with a bin full of manila envelopes, the kind she'd come to recognize as holding unsolicited manuscripts and folded self-addressed, stamped envelopes. SASEs, her boss, Barry Cole, called them.

Moments later, she entered her office and stopped at her desk, positioned to the left of the door and facing a wall of windows overlooking a street of city buildings directly across from the Olson offices. She dropped her purse and the bin onto the walnut surface, removed her coat, and hung it on the tree by the door. She then hoisted the bin from her desk, resting it against her hip to free a hand for opening Mr. Cole's faux-wood door, rich in imaginary grain.

As was her custom each morning, Magda deposited the mail onto his organized desk, walked to the two walls of windows, and pulled open the short floral drapes. She then turned his calendar to today's date. After starting a pot of coffee at the wet bar, she pulled a clean cup and saucer from beneath the counter and placed them near the percolator.

Magda walked into her office, picked up her own daily calendar and a pencil, and returned to compare entries. Every line read exactly the same, but one. When she'd left the day before, Barry Cole had a free lunch hour after a meeting with one of the bigwigs upstairs. Now the name *Harlan Procter* stared up at her in Mr. Cole's bold handwriting.

Her heart slammed against her chest and her hand quivered as she scribbled *HP* onto her calendar. Magda turned suddenly, bumping her boss's oversize black leather chair. It rolled toward the bookshelf behind it. She grabbed for it, dropping the calendar onto her foot. Her left hand flew upward, knocking the silver-framed Cole family photo from its place next to several of Mr. Cole's awards. She fumbled with it, but managed to keep it from crashing to the floor next to the calendar.

When the moment had passed and her foot throbbed only mildly, she gripped the photo, staring at the four people. Mrs. Cole, whom she'd never met or even spoken to, looked back at her with large eyes and blonde hair styled in a fashion Magda hadn't seen in a few years. The children—a boy and a girl—both resembled their father. She'd been curious about the ages of his children. Mr. Cole appeared much younger in the photo, leaving her to wonder—

"Good morning, Miss Christenson." Barry Cole's baritone voice spoke from behind her.

Again she fumbled with the photo, but managed to get it back to the shelf. She turned. "A little accident, sir," she said.

He blinked and she couldn't help but note the jet-black lashes as they swept over almond-colored eyes. "Is everything okay?" he asked, placing his briefcase on the edge of the desktop.

Magda reached for the calendar still on the floor. "Oh, yes. I bumped the—and then the—this—" she held up the calendar—"dropped." She inhaled deeply, keeping her eyes on him. "I see you are having lunch with Mr. Procter today, sir."

His smile encouraged her to relax, reminding her she wasn't on trial. "I am." He looked over his shoulder to the wet bar as the percolator coughed and sighed. "Sounds like the coffee is ready." He shrugged off his coat and loosened his tie, common movements she'd witnessed since her first day on the job. She reached for the coat, hung it on the nearby chrome tree, and promptly walked across the room to prepare his coffee. By the time she returned, he stood behind the desk and had started flipping through the envelopes.

"Miss Christenson," he said without looking up, "I want you to do something for me."

She placed the coffee in a clear area next to the Bible that always seemed to be nearby. Mr. Cole was not only a family man, she reasoned, but also a man of faith.

She stood upright. "Yes, sir."

He sighed and raised his eyes. "Do you like to read, by any great chance?"

She chuckled. "More than I like to breathe, sir."

He smiled. "Do you think you know a good story when you read one?"

"I do."

He pushed the mail bin toward her as his attention went to

a file lying nearby. "We're going to see how good you are then. I believe you know our standards here, do you not?"

"I'd like to think so—"

"A new part of your job, starting today, is to weed through all these and find *one* good one." He opened the file and studied the top page.

Something that felt like success coursed through her, and she reached for the bin. "And if I should find two, sir?"

For a moment, time hung suspended between them. "You'll have the unenviable job of picking the best between them."

Fifteen minutes before noon, Magda slipped into Mr. Cole's empty office to powder the sheen from her nose and to freshen her lipstick. Ten minutes later, she'd rubbed her lips together so hard that she needed to apply the deep-red color again. When the office door opened, she looked up, all but gasping in anticipation, to see Harlan standing there in a heavy coat flaked with snow. He removed his hat and said, "Hello."

When she said nothing in return, he shrugged out of his coat and hung it on the tree next to hers. The implied intimacy took her by surprise, and she exhaled loudly.

"Are you all right?" he asked her.

She blinked rapidly. "What? Oh, yes."

Harlan Procter approached her desk, peering at her through his black horn-rimmed glasses, making her feel as if she were a specimen in a petri dish. "Do you have something in your eye?"

Magda brought her fingertips to her eyes. "Oh. No. Sorry." She swallowed to gain composure. "I'm afraid I was so into my work you scared me."

He looked at her desk, noting the stack of manila envelopes she'd already begun to read through. "Submissions?"

"Yes." Then, jarred by her lack of professionalism, she stood. "Oh, please. Would you like to have a seat? Or a cup of coffee?"

His pale-green eyes narrowed. "No." He looked around the room and pointed to one of the two armless chairs. "To the coffee. I'll wait here, though." He folded into the chair, and she surmised he had to be at least six feet tall. He crossed one leg over the other easily. Without looking up, he reached for a nearby magazine, opened it, closed it, and then brought his attention back to her. "I take it Barry is not in."

Magda returned to her seat, tucking her skirt beneath her. "No, sir. He'll be back soon, though."

He exhaled as though he'd reached the end of exhaustion. "I see." He clasped his hands together, lacing the fingers, which Magda saw were long. Slender. Better for typing, she mused. "I suppose I'll have to wait then."

"I'm happy to get you a cup of coffee. Or . . ." Her desk phone rang and she jumped, recovered quickly, and answered it. "Barry Cole's office. Magda Christenson speaking. How may I help you?"

"Miss Christenson . . ."

"Yes, Mr. Cole."

"Has Mr. Procter arrived?"

"Yes, sir. Only moments ago, sir."

"I'm leaving to return now. Please make sure he's comfortable."

"Of course."

"And offer my apologies."

"Yes, sir." She returned the handset to the phone. When she looked up, Harlan Procter stared back at her.

"I take it he's going to be late."

"Only by a few minutes."

"Editors," he mumbled, sending an unhappy wave of disappointment through her.

"I—"

He stood, walked toward her, perched one hip on the edge of her desk, and reached for one of the envelopes. "Anything any good?"

She grimaced. "Not so far, I'm afraid."

"Good news for me, though, huh?" he added with a chuckle.

She smiled. "I suppose so." Her heartbeat fluttered; were they having a conversation?

He crossed his arms and hunched his shoulders. "Tell me, Miss—" He reached for her nameplate. "Christenson." He looked up, and for the briefest of moments, she found herself drowning in the cleft of his chin, which rested beneath full lips and a prominent nose. "Do you fancy yourself more a writer or an editor?"

Stunned by the question, she wished against all she knew that she were Betty. Or, at the very least, more like her. "I—I suppose I can only fancy myself a secretary, Mr. Procter."

"Harlan," he corrected her. "Mr. Procter is my father, and not a very good one."

"I see." She worried what Mr. Cole would think if he walked in and found one of their writers poised on her desk. "I'm not sure—"

"So which is it?" He straightened his shoulders. "Writer or editor?"

"What makes you think either one?"

He laughed so loudly she wondered if the secretary in the office next door might hear. "You have that hungry look about you."

"Hungry?"

Barry Cole's voice boomed from the hallway as he called out to someone.

"Mr. Procter," Magda warned quickly.

Harlan spun off the desk and to his feet, facing the door when it opened. "Harlan," Barry Cole said, extending his hand. "I'm so sorry to have kept you."

"No problem. Shall we go then?" He motioned to the door.

"Yes, yes."

Magda hurried into her boss's office, grabbed his coat and hat, and returned to dutifully hand it to him. "Thank you, Miss Christenson." He escorted Harlan Procter out of the office, closing the door behind him as she dropped into her chair, willing herself to breathe.

Seconds later, the door reopened and Harlan strolled back in. "Hold the elevator for me," he said over his shoulder, then pointed to the coat tree where his forgotten coat and hat hung next to hers.

Magda smiled in understanding.

But instead of walking back out the door, he ambled to her desk, pulled a piece of paper from the notepaper tray, and said, "Your address, please."

"What?"

"You're having dinner with me tonight. I'd like to talk to you further."

Were there rules about this? "But I'm not sure I—"

"Of course you're sure." He tapped on the paper with his middle finger. "Hurry now."

She did as she was told, caught somewhere between concern over ethics and sheer joy.

"I'll see you at six thirty," he said, folding the paper and slipping it into his pants pocket.

CHAPTER 15

Only three months had passed since Joan had arrived in the States, but she felt she'd packed in a lifetime of experiences. Most of it at work. Monday through Friday, she put in her time at Hertz during the day, and every weekday evening, she left the office on Wabash and headed for David & DuRand on Michigan. On Saturdays, she led tours into the coal mine at the museum. And somewhere in between it all, she'd managed to accept a part-time job with Manpower.

"So," Betty said, glancing at her watch as she and Joan walked across the lobby at the end of their workday, "what time do you think you'll be done tonight?"

Joan shrugged. "Not sure, really. Mrs. King mentioned last night that a *big client* is coming in this evening and she'll need all of us there and ready to go."

Betty nudged Joan with her shoulder. "You're getting along well there, aren't you?"

"I enjoy it, Betts. I do. Besides, what other opportunities would a girl from Leigh, Lancashire, have to dress in some of the clothes I've modeled?" Joan cut her eyes toward Betty. "I only wish I could bring a dress home now and then."

Joan laughed, and Betty laughed with her—even though Joan

knew that, with Betty's father's money and her mother's social standing, Betty'd had plenty of opportunities to wear formal gowns and fashionable clothes.

"Maybe one day," Betty said matter-of-factly, "when you are no longer sending money back home, you can afford a new dress."

Joan could hardly imagine it. To be able to buy a dress *just because*. She had two pairs of shoes in her closet—three if one counted the galoshes she'd been forced to purchase to keep her feet high and dry during the winter months. Betty, on the other hand, had enough to start her own shoe store. To think Joan might one day have a pair for every outfit was almost too much to consider.

They arrived at the point where they'd separate. Joan turned to Betty, then glanced back at where they'd come from. "I'm sorry Evelyn has to work late tonight."

Betty frowned. "Evelyn shouldn't have taken such a long lunch, but I suspect George had something to do with that." She placed her hand on Joan's shoulder. "Never mind that now. Vegetable soup when you get home. And Evelyn has promised to make corn bread."

Joan's stomach rumbled. Unlike Evelyn, she'd used her lunch hour to work on a Manpower project, skipping the meal entirely. Breakfast had been nothing more than a cup of coffee and a Danish. The night before, she hadn't had enough energy to complete the extra work she'd brought home *and* chew her food, so she chose the work over the meal.

"I'll see you later then," Joan said, and she turned and walked down the sidewalk, moving between the men and women either heading home at their workday's end or slipping into the storefront doors of the shops and cafés along Michigan. In the midst of the crowd, she had a sudden thought of home. Of her parents, her brothers and sisters. She missed them. And sometimes, even in the excitement of Chicago, she missed Leigh. She missed her people, the sounds of their voices. But she'd grown to love the States as well and to appreciate the part of her heritage that had begun here.

Mrs. King gathered the young women together after they clocked in. One of Chicago's most prestigious businessmen, Mr. Guy Reeves, would arrive at precisely seven o'clock, she told them, intent on purchasing formal gowns for his wife, his three young-adult daughters, and his sister-in-law. "For a most important event," Mrs. King said. "The social event of the season."

"Black tie?" Helen, one of the other models, asked.

"And everything that implies," Mrs. King answered, her voice collected. She looked directly at Joan. "Joan."

"Yes?"

"You are the exact size of Mr. Reeves's oldest daughter. When you go into the dressing room, you'll find a black gown hanging on the door of your closet. But it needs a bridal petticoat."

Joan nodded, waiting for the remainder of her instructions.

Mrs. King leaned in and said, "Go downstairs first to bridal and get one. Be quick now."

"I won't be five minutes."

"And be sure to use the stairs," she called after her.

Joan did as instructed, then took the stairwell back up to the fifth floor. Her descent had been much faster than her ascent, and her legs now shook; her mind felt fuzzy. She needed to eat. But when she returned to the dressing room and saw the dress intended for her, all thoughts of food fled.

The floor-length gown—an Adrian Original with cascading rows of sheer black nylon ruffles over a full aqua tulle skirt—boasted spaghetti straps and a scooped neckline. Beneath the skirt lay an additional layer of aqua tulle and a pale dusty-rose taffeta lining that felt cold against her skin as she slipped the dress over her head and shoulders.

With the waist of the gown resting just above her hips, Joan turned her head to Helen, who had already dressed in an elegant black gown. The young beauty leaned over one of the dressing tables toward a lighted mirror and applied red lipstick to her full lips.

"Helen?"

Helen looked past her face in the reflection of the mirror to Joan's. "Mmm?"

"Would you mind zipping me?"

Helen smiled, turned, and slipped the zipper up along her spine. Joan's stomach growled as Helen slid the top hook into place. Joan splayed her hand over her stomach. "Sorry," she said.

Helen chuckled. "Hungry?"

Joan only nodded.

The show did well; the distinguished Mr. Reeves purchased a formal gown from David & DuRand for every member of his female entourage. Mrs. King could not have been happier. She congratulated each of the models, reminding them of the bonus they had earned.

Joan said her good-byes and left the store, thinking only of hot vegetable soup and corn bread. She made her way toward the train station; all the while the sounds of the city at night seemed to come at her through a thin veil of gauze. The lights from the storefronts and the streetlamps formed halos. The remaining Chicagoans who, like her, headed for the train, looked like the figures in the Monet paintings on the fifth floor of David & DuRand.

Her head felt fuzzy, her thoughts scrambled. She walked to the train by instinct, but as she neared one of the restaurants along the way and the aroma of cooked food reached her, she felt her legs buckle. The semidarkness of the evening became a blanket, growing heavier as her body crumpled to the sidewalk.

Joan awoke in the sterile environment of a hospital, still dressed in her clothes but covered with a crisp white sheet. The room was cold, permeated with the smell of alcohol and Betadine, and the light over the bed shone bright. Too bright.

"Hallo?" she called out.

A nurse padded into the room almost immediately. "Ah. Good. Let me get the doctor," she said as soon as she stepped over the threshold. "Please lie still."

Joan complied, waiting only a few moments before a doctor—middle-aged, balding, and wearing half-glasses low on his nose—stood over her. "Hello," he said, gripping a metal chart cover and flipping the top. "I'm Dr. Kauffman."

At the risk of sounding cliché, she asked, "Where am I?"

"Do you know what happened to you?" he asked, without answering her question.

"Well, I assume I passed out."

"Do you know your name?"

"Of course I know my name." What kind of fool question was that? "Joan. Joan Hunt."

"Miss Hunt? Mrs.?"

"Miss."

"I see." He jotted a few notes in the chart. "*Miss* Hunt, is it possible you are pregnant? Are you with child?"

Joan's head jerked toward him. The way he towered over her was reminiscent of Father O'Malley when he'd caught Joan and her sister running through the halls at school, which was strictly forbidden. "I don't believe so," she answered. "Not unless, that is, Jesus is coming the second time in the same way he did the first."

The doctor peered over his glasses. He forced a smile as her stomach growled again. "Miss Hunt, tell me; when was the last time you ate?"

She laid her hand over her stomach. "I had a pastry for breakfast."

"And before that?"

"Lunch, I think. Yesterday."

The doctor closed the chart. "Is there a reason you have not eaten in so long?"

Joan explained about her work. Her family back in England. He shook his head, turned toward the door, and called out, "Nurse James?"

The nurse who had gotten the doctor stood at the doorway. "Yes, Doctor?"

"Get Miss Hunt some food, would you? There's nothing wrong with this girl." He winked, genuine and fatherly. "She's just overworked and underfed."

Joan called home as soon as she was allowed, thankful that Betty was the one to hear the phone in the hall and answer. "You have to eat, Joan," she admonished after Joan recounted the details.

"I know," she said. "They brought me a hot meal."

"I don't mean just tonight."

"Yes, of course. I know. I will."

"And maybe you need to not work so many jobs."

"I've already thought about it, Betts. I'm going to look for another job. One that pays more than Hertz. Enough so that I can make in one job what I'm making in three or four."

Her comment was met with silence. "You'll leave Hertz?"

"If need be. For now, I'll drop the Manpower job and ask to not work *every* night at David & DuRand."

"When do you think you will be home?"

"In the morning," Joan said. "The doctor wants me to stay overnight. I'll be at work, though, first thing."

Betty paused. "Get a good night's rest, Joan. I'll let Evelyn know you won't be home tonight, and we'll explain to Mr. Ferguson tomorrow if it turns out you're late."

"Evelyn made it home all right then?"

"Yes."

Joan felt more than heard the tension. "Don't be mad at her, Betts. She's never known anyone like George. She'll figure it out soon enough."

"It's not that."

"What then?"

Betty paused again before answering. "Nothing for you to concern yourself with tonight. Now be a good girl and get some sleep."

Joan giggled. "Yes, Mummy."

Harlan Procter was everything and more that Magda had dreamed a writer—a real writer—could be. *Should* be. Dark. Moody. Mysterious. Wonderfully brilliant and authoritative. In an underground café she'd never be able to find in the light of day, he'd ordered for them like she'd seen men do for their dates in the movies.

What few movies she'd seen, anyway.

They sat in a corner booth, where the flicker of a candle jammed into a squatty wax-dripped wine bottle provided scant light. Harlan did most of the talking. Mostly about himself. Although, if Magda really thought about it, he'd revealed little. With the meal complete and nothing left but two half-consumed demitasse cups of coffee before them, Magda offered him a notebook filled with her writings.

He held it on the other side of the candle, his eyes shooting back and forth like a tennis ball at Wimbledon. Magda remained quiet, keeping her eyes on him and her ears tuned to a woman standing next to a grand piano at the front of the restaurant. Her sultry voice crooned "I Only Have Eyes For You."

When Harlan finished scanning several pages, he closed the notebook and handed it back to her with a slight smile. Try hard as she could, there was no reading the expression, so she waited.

Finally, "What are your thoughts, Magda? What are your dreams? Your aspirations?"

"To write books like Madeleine L'Engle." She leaned forward. "Have you read any of her work?"

Harlan stared as though he'd gone into a catatonic state. Then, "No. Tell me about her."

"She's only written a few titles, but . . . I think she's marvelous. She'll be a household name one day."

He rested his elbow on the small, linen-draped table, and his chin on the pad of his palm. "Is that what you desire? To be a household name?"

She felt herself blush, her cheeks grow warm. "Is that wrong? To want to be more than just an average writer or . . . or a secretary at a publishing company?"

He laughed. "Not at all." He tapped the notebook between them with his middle finger. "Your characters are one-dimensional. You've not gotten to know them well enough for them to be fleshed out properly."

She shifted, turning fully toward him. "Tell me what to do. I mean, if you don't mind."

His hand, the one he wasn't using to prop up his head, came

up suddenly, brushing the hair away from her face. He studied her, the contours of her face and, tilting her head back, the length of her throat. "You're very pretty; did you know that?"

Magda pulled away and looked to the stage. To the piano player and the singer who now sang Doris Day's "It's Magic." "My sister . . . Inga . . . She's the pretty one."

His fingertips caught her chin and turned her face back to his. The candlelight cast new shadows, giving him a softer look and a harder appearance, all at once. Magda exhaled sharply. She wanted to run.

And she wanted to throw her arms around his shoulders and beg him to teach her. To hold on tight and plead with him to make her the most remarkable writer of all time.

But before she could do either, his fingertips became a memory and he said, "Write in your notebook a letter that your character—your Jenny—might write to her sainted mother. Then another that she would write to her father, who left the family when she was only three to marry this other woman, this . . . Constance. Then to the man she loves, but who doesn't know the depth of her true feelings. Her fears of losing him as she lost her father." He paused. "Do that and we'll have dinner again so I may check on your progress."

The thumping of her heart began again and she wondered if he could hear it as well. She barely managed to push out, "When?"

"Let's see," he said, drumming his fingers on the table. "Tonight is Wednesday. I'd say Saturday evening should give you enough time."

Saturday? She'd have to endure three days before she saw him again?

"I can do that," she said.

"Good. I don't have to tell you, do I, that our meetings should not be shared with Barry?"

"Of course not."

CHAPTER 16

On Friday afternoon, Inga wearily slipped her key into the apartment door's keyhole and turned it. Before she could push the door, it opened from the other side.

"Magda," she said, reaching for the cosmetics case she'd set next to her feet. "What are you doing home from work so early?"

"Come in," she said, her face grim. After she shut the door behind her sister, Magda turned and clasped her hands together. "Our mother and father are here."

"Mor and Far? *Here?*" She looked around the tiny living room, then peered into the kitchen.

"Not *here*," Magda clarified, her voice a panicked whisper. "At Uncle Casper's and Aunt Greta's."

Inga handed the smaller of her two cases to her sister. "Here. Help me take this into my room." She started down the hall with Magda behind her.

"They called me at work, Inga. *At work.* Fortunately, Mr. Cole goes easy on these sorts of things. They—"

Inga opened the door to the bedroom she shared with Betty. Together they dropped the luggage onto the bed, which squeaked in protest. "They what?"

"They want us to have dinner with them tonight."

Inga pulled the regulation cap from her head and kicked off

her shoes. "Tonight?" She placed the hat on the dresser, pulled off her gloves, and unbuttoned her uniform jacket. "I'm exhausted. Why not tomorrow night?"

"No." Magda grabbed her sister's hands. "Tomorrow night, I'm going out to dinner with Harlan."

"Who or what is a Harlan?" She stepped out of her skirt, tossing both the jacket and the skirt over the back of a chair before unbuttoning her blouse.

"Harlan Procter, Inga."

Inga stopped in the unbuttoning and smiled. "Well, don't be so frustrated. A man, Magda?"

Her sister crossed her arms and huffed. "Yes, a man." She stared at Inga for a moment before the arms dropped and she collapsed onto the bed, grasping the wrought-iron footboard. "But more than a man. He's a *brilliant* writer."

Inga stood in her slip and nylons and giggled. "Oh, Magda." She sat in the chair, crossed her legs, and worked one stocking down her leg, then the other. "Can't you find a man who is just . . . *a man*?"

"That's not very nice."

Inga looked up. Magda wore her temper as she always did—red hot and between her ears. She laughed again.

Magda stood. "We're having dinner with Mor and Far tonight at Uncle Casper's. Take a bath and get dressed." She crossed the room to the door. "We need to leave in an hour. I'll meet you in the living room." With that, she slammed out.

Inga stared after her for nearly a full minute before laughter overtook her.

"Hello, George," Evelyn said as she approached the restaurant table. "I'm sorry I'm late."

"What took you so long?" He kissed her cheek as he always did when he greeted her.

And when he said good-bye. As long as they'd been going out, not once had he *really* kissed her. The way she imagined he might one day. The way she dreamed it.

"I got caught up in a project at work." He held her chair out for her and she sat, tucking her full skirt under her. "I'm so sorry. I know you don't like to be kept waiting."

"Well," he said, returning to his seat, "you're here now. I've ordered for us. Pork chops. Our meals should be here soon."

Evelyn pushed her glasses up her nose. "Thank you. I'm sure whatever you ordered will be wonderful."

"Evelyn," George said, leaning his forearms against the edge of the table. "While we have a minute, I want to talk to you about your glasses."

Evelyn blinked. "What about them?"

"There's something new—relatively new. They're called corneal lenses. They're—" he brought his thumb and index finger together—"little. Not like old contact lenses. These you wear just on the cornea of your eye." He circled his right eye with an index finger. "You know, instead of glasses."

Evelyn blinked to keep from crying. She'd worn glasses since the age of thirteen, when her body had decided to turn against her, making her into a young woman, albeit a nearsighted one. *Men don't make passes at girls in glasses,* she'd heard more times than she could count. And it hurt.

"What are they made of?" she asked, deciding that, in this case, to keep George happy meant having an intelligent conversation about something he found of interest.

"I'm not sure exactly, but I've done some reading up on them and you can wear them, instead of those glasses of yours, for up to sixteen hours a day."

Evelyn felt her brow furrow. "Do they hurt?"

"Does it matter, sweetheart? Think of how much better it will be for you."

For her, she wondered, or for him? She reached for the water-filled crystal stemware at her place. "I—"

"You—"

They both chuckled. "You first," she said.

"No, no," he insisted, his eyes lighting up with merriment, which sent shivers down Evelyn's arms. First he had called her sweetheart and now . . . gallantry. "Ladies first. I insist."

"All right then. I—" But again Evelyn stopped when she saw their server approach with two plates of food. She looked at George. "Oh, my. This smells wonderful."

He beamed across the table at her. "It does, doesn't it?"

Quickly, before George could see her or comment on her custom, Evelyn closed her eyes and blessed her food. When she looked up, George's eyes had followed the waiter to another table, then back to her. "Now," he said, reaching for his fork, "tell me again what you were about to say."

Evelyn shrugged as she, too, picked up her fork. "Only that the lenses must be very expensive." She stabbed a snap bean with the fork.

George frowned. "This is no time to think of money, Evelyn."

She brought the bean to her mouth and chewed, giving herself time to think. Then she frowned.

"What's wrong?"

"This snap bean tastes funny." She peered at him. "Like wax."

He shook his head ever so slightly. "What is a snap bean?"

She pointed to the pile of green "snaps" lying one atop another like a haystack. "These."

"*Those* are green beans."

She chuckled. "We've always called them snaps."

"Well," he said, reaching for his knife, "now you know better."

Evelyn sighed. Yes, now she knew better. She laid her fork on her plate as he had shown her to do when still eating so that the waiter would not think her done with the meal. "George, Betty has been talking to me about getting my hair done differently."

"Marvelous," he said, not looking up from slicing into the pork chop on his plate.

"She says she knows a stylist and she'll help me—"

His face shot up. "Help you what?"

"Help me. You know. If it's too much to spare on my salary."

George rested an elbow on the table—something Evelyn knew he'd chastise her for had she done so. His fork waggled as he pointed it toward her. "You know . . . That *is* marvelous. Betty knows all the best hairdressers." He bounced a little in his chair. "Tell her . . . tell her for me to take you to David & DuRand."

"Where Joan works?"

"Who?"

"*Joanie.*" How could he have forgotten?

He waved the fork in the air again. "Oh, yes. Yes. Tell her to take you there. They have a counter where the women will help you with your cosmetics too. If you're afraid of the lenses, the least you can do is find out how to wear your makeup to accent your eyes."

Evelyn sat still, unable to move. The dichotomy of his words had both cut her and made her feel as though she might soar on eagle's wings any moment. Perhaps he didn't mean to be so cruel. Perhaps he didn't understand that to speak to a woman about such things was hurtful . . . Then again, that he seemed to care at all made her ecstatic. Hopeful.

She reached for the water glass. *Goblet.* "I will," she said, her eyes meeting his. She took a sip. "I bet when Betty and I are done you won't even recognize me."

Magda and her sister made it to their uncle's store just as a hand reached under the front door blind to flip the sign from Open to Closed. Magda hurried to knock on the glass, which rattled beneath her knuckles. The edge of the blind peeled away, exposing an eye and part of a woman's cheek.

"Aunt Greta," Magda said. "It's us. We're here."

The lock flipped and the door opened. "You're late," she said. "Your poor *mor* and *far* have been worried you wouldn't come."

In spite of her testiness, Magda grabbed her aunt by the shoulders, squeezed, and kissed her cheek. "Sorry, Aunt Greta. I had to wait for Inga to get ready."

Inga walked in behind her. "Inga just flew back from Los Angeles," she said, announcing herself in third person.

Aunt Greta's frown turned deeper as she closed the door behind them. "I don't know why you insist on this way of life, Inga. A pretty girl like you . . ."

Magda waited, hoping to hear something similar, but the words didn't come. She looked at Inga, who smiled at her sympathetically. She'd grown somewhat accustomed to the differences between them. Her hair, in spite of being technically blonde, looked more like dishwater in comparison to Inga's, which sparkled in sunlight. Even their eyes—both blue—made them opposites in spite of their color. Magda's had always been described as "clear blue," while Inga's were "sparkling blue."

"Like the sea shimmers on a summer's day," their father had once said.

A voice came from the door between the store and the living quarters. "Where are they?"

Magda turned. "Mor," she said, nearly running down the aisle between the canned vegetables and baking goods. She felt more than heard Inga's careful footsteps behind her. Magda wrapped her mother in a hug. "I can't believe you are here again."

Mor, a lovely petite woman with hair the same shade as her own and eyes the color of Inga's, kissed her daughter's cheek multiple times before releasing her. "I missed my girls," she said, reaching for Inga.

Inga hugged her mother dutifully. "Still," she said, "it's only been a few weeks."

"Your father," Mor said, lowering her voice. "He had business here."

Inga gave a half grin. "The truth comes out."

Mor playfully swatted Inga's backside. "Now, now. None of that from you, little girl. I can still take you over my knee." But she laughed at her own words, showing no real threat.

"If they were my daughters . . . ," Aunt Greta said from behind them.

Before another word could be said, Mor interrupted her older sister. "But they are not, Greta."

Childless Aunt Greta turned a deep shade of blush before moving on with, "Dinner will be ready soon. Let's go into the back, shall we? I need to check on my potatoes."

Mor slipped her arms around the waists of both daughters, turned her lips to Magda's ear, and said, "I should not have said that."

Magda kissed her mother's cheek. "She had it coming."

Mor squeezed her.

They stepped through the kitchen where the unmistakable and telltale aromas of dinner permeated the room: Meatballs with cream sauce. Boiling potatoes. And *ohhh!* Rose hip soup. Magda's stomach danced in anticipation. While independence had its benefits, moments like this made her salivate for the benefits of her mother's home.

"I'll be back soon," Mor said to Aunt Greta, who stood at the stove where several pots and pans gave off aromatic steam. Then, to her daughters, "Your father is with Uncle Casper, already talking politics."

Inga laid her head on Mor's shoulder. "Save me," she said, her words dramatic.

They pushed through the swinging door leading to the small but bright living room/dining room combination of their aunt and uncle's living quarters. Their father, dressed to the nines as always, sat relaxed on the low-backed sofa against the wall. He stood as soon as they entered. "There they are." When he opened his arms to them, Mor released her hold before returning to the kitchen, and they walked ahead of her. He hugged them simultaneously as they kissed his cheeks. "You both look good enough to eat, and you both look hungry."

Magda laughed, noting that Inga did not. Instead, she slipped out of their father's embrace, walked over to their uncle, and gave him a quick peck. "Hello, Uncle."

"Inga," Uncle Casper said. "You look tired."

She swung into the nearest chair and crossed her legs. "I am tired. I just flew back from Los Angeles. Even after a two-day layover, I'm exhausted."

Magda frowned at her sister as she took a seat in another chair—a new one, she noted, rubbing her hands over the blond wood of the arms.

"Why you would want to spend half your life in the air flying back and forth, back and forth is anyone's guess," Uncle Casper said, sounding exactly like his wife. "Surely you don't intend to do this forever."

"Heavens no," Inga balked. "I've got bigger fish to fry, I promise you." Her eyes held mischief.

"I would hope so," their father said, returning to his place on the sofa.

Magda studied him—his full lips, the prominence of his nose, much like Harlan's. He also wore glasses, although his were rimless spectacles. Far's expressions, also like Harlan's, were always studious. The look of intelligence beyond simply being smart.

"I've come to appreciate LA," Inga continued, drawing Magda's attention back to her sister. "I wouldn't be at all surprised if by this time next year I will have made my home there."

"*Inga!* You've never said."

She smiled so brightly she reminded Magda of a movie star whose loveliness had been captured on an oversize poster for a Hollywood premiere. "I only just decided." She looked back to their father. "What do you think, Far? Would you be proud of me if I—say—moved to California and became a famous actress?"

Controlled fury burned in their father's eyes.

"What you need, Daughter, is to come back to Minnesota, enroll in school, and meet a fine young man so you can marry and settle down."

Inga sobered. "Far, why would I need to go to college to meet a fine young man? Can't I meet a man without walking the hallowed halls of education?"

"There's a young man soon to graduate," Far continued as if

Inga had not spoken. "He's a seminary student and I have no doubt he'll make a fine man of the cloth. He'll also be a good husband and father one day."

Magda held her breath—this couldn't be happening. Surely their father had not come all the way to Chicago to tell Inga of a man he'd found suitable for her. She opened her mouth to say something—anything—to change the subject when Mor burst through the door. "Dinner is nearly ready," she said. "I'm going to step upstairs for a moment."

Magda dashed after her, offering her apologies to the others as she went up the stairs. "Mor?"

Her mother stood at the landing, surprise painted across her face. "Yes, Magda?"

Magda grabbed her mother's hands and drew them up, close to her heart. "Can I ask you a question, between us?" she said, keeping her voice low.

"Of course. You know that."

"Mor," Magda said again, drawing in a breath, "how did you know?"

"Know what, darling?"

"How did you know that Far was the one for you?" Joy spread through her as she asked the question.

Her mother gasped as she placed her palms against her daughter's cheeks. "You?"

"I'm not sure. Not yet, anyway." She took her mother's hands in hers again. "How did you know?"

Mor seemed to draw on a memory. "He was everything I wanted. Handsome, in his way."

Magda nodded in understanding.

"So, so bright. So smart. What a mind."

This time, Magda exhaled sharply, smiling.

"And a good Lutheran. He loved God more than he loved me, and that made me love him more."

Magda's eyes met her mother's. She felt herself begging her mother for the right answer to her next question, even before she asked it. "Mor," she barely whispered, "would you have felt the same had he not been?"

"Been what, dear?"

She took another breath. "Lutheran."

CHAPTER 17

Evelyn was in a near panic, what with Valentine's Day only a week away. While Betty had promised the month before to help with her hair and cosmetics, so far they hadn't been able to adjust their schedules. Still, determination forced her from her bedroom and across the hall to Betty's. Otherwise she knew she wouldn't sleep.

She tapped on the door. After hearing Betty's faint "Come in," she cracked the door and stuck her head in. "Got a minute?"

Betty, who wore red satiny pajamas, sat propped up in bed, under a mound of thick blankets and quilts, reading a book. "Sure." She closed the book and placed it on the bed beside her, then threw back the covers on the other side. "Come on in. It's cold."

Evelyn shivered as she clutched her own arms and scurried across the room, her slippers shuffling over the hardwood floor and throw rugs. When she had made herself comfortable next to Betty, she turned her face toward her. "I declare, you and I spend more time alone in our bedrooms than with our roommates."

Betty smiled broadly, bringing light to an already-beautiful face, which reminded Evelyn why she'd crossed the hall in the first place. "Betty, you said you'd help me with my hair. Can you—*will* you—tell me the *best* place to go to have my hair styled?"

Betty looked at her almost sympathetically. "That would be the Bobby Pin over on North State near Randolph. I've gone there since moving to the city."

"Is it expensive?"

Betty sighed deeply. "Very." Then she smiled again, this time briefly. "But let me put in a call for you. I think I can pull a few strings."

Evelyn twisted in the bed to see her roommate better. "Can you?"

"Sure."

"Oh, Betty, that would be wonder—" She stopped at the sound of the front door opening, then closing with a quiet click. "That's probably Magda."

Betty looked at her bedside clock, then showed its face to Evelyn. "Nine o'clock. Looks like her date with the writer ended early tonight."

Evelyn shook her head. "According to Magda, they aren't *dating*. She told me he's only helping her with her writing, and sometimes he helps her choose manuscripts from what she calls a slush pile."

Betty chuckled. "I have no idea what that is, but it sounds awful, like something that piles up on the sidewalks of Chicago in February and March."

Evelyn laughed with her, then said, "One more thing, Betty, if you don't mind. George . . ." She paused, still uncomfortable talking about him with Betty.

But Betty took it in stride. "Go on. George . . . ?"

"George wanted me to ask you about going to David & DuRand to see some cosmetics clerk. He says if I insist on wearing glasses I should learn how to wear eye makeup."

Betty scoffed. "Oh, he did, did he? Now, why do you think George didn't have you ask *Joan* about that?"

Evelyn slid back until she was flush against the upturned pillows. "I don't know," she mumbled, fiddling with her torn cuticles. "I guess because he knows you."

Betty patted the covers over Evelyn's leg. "Listen up, hon. I've known George for a long time and I'm telling you, no matter what he's said, I still don't trust him."

Evelyn kept her face down. "But he's been real nice, Betts. And he's teaching me things I would have never known about had I not met him." She sounded pathetic, even to her own hearing.

"Evelyn, look at me." She did. "Is he *really*? Nice, I mean. Does he treat you like you deserve to be treated?"

"Sometimes . . . sometimes he gets a little short with me, but I think that's only because I'm not a fast learner."

"I beg to differ. I've seen you at work. You're smart. You're a quick learner. A capable student."

"Me?" Evelyn laughed.

Betty poked her in the arm. "Yes, you. You deserve—you *deserve* to be *loved*, Evelyn. Not for the person your boyfriend is trying to make you into, but for who you *are*. Without the hairdo and the cosmetics and the fancy-schmancy ways."

Evelyn's chin shot up. "That's easier to say when you're already beautiful and adept at the finer things in life . . . like . . . like proper etiquette."

Betty shook her head. "Touché. I'll call the Bobby Pin for you tomorrow. You talk to Joan when she comes home—which should be any minute—about where to go at D&D." She smiled weakly. "Should I assume you and George have a date for Valentine's?"

Evelyn nodded.

"Well, then. When we are done with you, you'll have him eating out of your hand."

"Thanks, Betts," she said, turning toward the door, hoping

Betty didn't see her frown. She didn't want George eating out of her hand. She only wanted him to be proud of her. To want her more than he ever wanted—or still wanted—Betty.

And she wanted him to kiss her, even if only once.

Because, she knew, one kiss from George Volbrecht would be more than enough to last her a lifetime.

Betty stood under the platform awning next to Joan. Nearby, Evelyn and Magda carried on a quiet conversation, no doubt discussing their plans for the great lovers' holiday coming up the following week. She nudged Joan with her elbow. "Advice for the lovelorn?"

"What?" Joan asked. She wore her usual coat, gloves, and hat, her arms crossed over her small frame against the cold. "Oh. You mean . . . you?"

"I mean us."

"Us? I'm not looking for love, Betty."

"Me either." She waved her gloved hand as if she were swatting at an insect. "Well, not anytime soon. But let's face it: you and I are the only two in the apartment without sweethearts for the fourteenth. Want to go out on the town with me?"

Joan narrowed her eyes in contemplation. "What about Inga?"

"Inga has a certain someone out in Los Angeles. I'm sure she'll be with him if her schedule allows."

Joan tilted her head toward Betty. "Really? Are you sure? I mean, about the beau."

"I'd be willing to bet a month's salary. Wait. I take that back. These days I can't afford to bet a month's salary."

"What do you mean?"

Both women turned toward the sound of the train screeching

along the tracks. "Train's here," Betty said. "And what I mean is, my parents have cut me off."

"Your allowance, you mean?"

"You knew?" The train halted in front of them with a piercing cry and exhausted cough.

Joan's eyes widened and she dipped her chin. "Evelyn."

"Oh, sure. And she heard from George. How quickly I forget."

The doors opened. "What are you going to do?" Joan asked over her shoulder as they stepped onto the train.

Betty waited until they had settled to answer. "I'm going to learn to live without new dresses and shoes and perfumes and all the other little luxuries I've had my whole life."

Joan laughed. "Welcome to my world, Betts." She looked out the window as the train pulled away from the station, then turned back and said, "Of course, I've never had it to know what it feels like to lose it. In fact, I can't imagine, quite honestly."

Betty shrugged. "Well, Joan, I suppose we're about to find out just how strong and independent I really am, aren't we?"

As soon as Betty arrived in her office and had performed the daily preliminaries, she tapped on the opaque window of Mr. Ferguson's door.

"Come in, Miss Estes," he said.

She opened the door only enough to stick her head in. "Mr. Ferguson, I need to make a short personal phone call. Would now be a good time or do you need me for anything?"

He looked around his desk as if waiting for something to pop up from the paperwork scattered here and there. "I think it's all good here." He looked at her more directly. "Is everything okay?"

"It is. I only need to make a call before the day gets too busy."

She smiled. "Thank you, Mr. Ferguson." She closed the door and returned to her desk, picked up the handset of the phone, and dialed an outside operator. A minute later, she heard the voice she'd hoped would answer at the Bobby Pin.

"Bobby," she said. "Betty Estes."

"Hello, beautiful lady. What can I do for you today? Cut? Perm?"

"No," she chuckled. "Not today. Look. No questions, you hear?"

"Sounds ominous."

"Remember my mink coat? The one you practically frothed over?"

"My wife would love that coat," he said, keeping his voice low.

"She must be nearby."

He answered with a laugh.

"I need to sell it, Bobby." Pain shot through her chest. A twinge really, but she felt it nonetheless. "I've only worn it a handful of times and I still have the paperwork on it, of course. The box it came in."

"How much?"

She gave him the price a furrier had told her would be fair. "Plus," she added quickly, "I have a friend I want you to give the full treatment. Hair, nails, facial."

Bobby didn't answer right away. Then, "When can you have it to me?" he whispered. "Marigold's birthday is next month."

"I can meet you on Saturday. Just name the time and place."

"Done," he said. "I'll call you later with details. What's your friend's name?"

"Evelyn Alexander."

"Next week is crazy, what with Valentine's Day."

"How about Monday afternoon? After five?"

Betty heard the phone drop away from Bobby's chin. "Mari,"

he called out to his wife, "what openings do we have after five on Monday?" Marigold's soft, muffled voice spoke from a short distance away. Then, "Tell her to be here at five thirty. If she's late, I can't see her."

"She'll be there," Betty said with a smile. She started to hang up, then brought the phone back to her ear. "And Bobby?"

"Yeah."

"Thanks."

"Thank *you*, doll. You just saved me a bundle."

Inga couldn't believe her luck. Valentine's Day and she had a layover in Los Angeles.

As soon as she got her schedule, she called Frank to let him know. He stalled at first, probably from pure shock, then recovered with, "I'm going to wine and dine you like you've never been wined and dined before, baby."

She felt her entire body grow warm, especially at his British clip on the endearment "baby."

"Since I've never been wined *and* dined before, you won't have to try too hard," she said, keeping her voice as sultry as she dared . . .

As always, she nearly left Henrietta in her dust. When their cab arrived in front of the hotel, she grabbed her overnight bag and skipped to the revolving door, pushing it with all her strength. When she entered the lobby, she turned right toward the concierge desk, expecting to see the man of her dreams standing behind it, waiting only for her. Instead, he was leaning intimately close to a tall brunette, who looked to be about the same age as she, dressed in a form-fitting cocktail dress.

Fury rose up in her like bile, but she squared her shoulders and walked purposefully to the edge of the desk, placing her hand lightly upon it. "Hello, darling," she cooed.

Frank turned, pinked, and then gathered himself and said, "Hello. Be right with you." He continued then with his instructions to the hotel's guest, who gave Inga a look of contempt. A look that said, *Who do you think you are?*

Inga stepped away from the desk and joined Henrietta as she arrived. "It just dawned on me, Retta, that my future husband's job requires him to talk to far too many beautiful women."

Henrietta threw back her head and laughed. "Oh, sweetie," she said, bringing her twinkling eyes back to Inga's. "He could say the same about your job, you know. Only, in your case, you spend too much time talking to good-looking passengers."

The woman said thank you to Frank loudly enough to get her point across, then spun on her high heels and walked past Henrietta and Inga as though they weren't there, her shoes tap-tapping on the polished tiles.

"Retta," Inga said. "Go get our keys for us, will you?"

"Happy to."

Inga turned her attention to Frank, cocking a brow as her coworker walked to the registration desk. "Well, well," she said after she'd crossed the floor again to stand near him. "I suppose you have women all over you, all the time. I shouldn't be so shocked."

He winked. "You look delicious."

Her eyes narrowed. "I look like I've been on a plane for the last several hours."

"And powdered your nose in the cab." His thick eyelashes cast a veil around his eyes as they traveled to the tip of her nose and lingered there. "I'd kiss you right now if my boss weren't six feet away, watching me. Wondering who the leggy blonde is." He smiled and she melted. "It's my job, pet."

Inga pouted once more for effect, mainly because she understood all too well. "What time should I meet you down here?"

"Seven."

"And where are you taking me . . . so I know how to dress."

He slipped his hands into his pockets. "Well, that's the thing. I couldn't get a reservation on such short notice. Not in this town and not with a premiere tonight." He must have read the anxiety building up in her. The disappointment. They couldn't possibly spend their first Valentine's Day sitting in some out-of-the-way café. "Don't worry, sweetheart. I have a plan. Dress casually." He looked toward the revolving door. "And be sure to bring a sweater. Nights get chilly in the hills."

CHAPTER 18

Evelyn looked to the mirror's reflection of Betty and Joan standing behind her. For over an hour, she'd stood there primping, fluffing, and puffing. Dreaming and hoping.

"You'll answer the door, won't you, Betty?"

Betty smiled back. "Absolutely. And I promise to be nice."

"And Joanie," Evelyn said while turning to face them, "you really think this dress is all right?" She ran her fingertips over tiny freshwater pearls and rhinestones encrusted along the V-neck and bodice of the seafoam-green gown, then adjusted the full, floor-length skirt. "The color, I mean? And me in it?"

Joan laughed. "Don't worry, Evelyn. Betty wouldn't steer you wrong. After all, she suggested Bobby for your do-over and, my gracious, just *look at you*."

Betty picked up a pair of opera-length gloves from the dresser. "Enough of that. Final touch." She handed the seafoam gloves to her. "And I promise you, Evelyn, George never saw me in this gown. Not once."

Evelyn took the gloves, turning again to the mirror. She blinked behind the glasses she now wished she didn't need. Leaning over, she inspected the dark kohl outlining her eyes, the sweep of her lashes, and the arch of each perfectly tweezed brow. Her cheeks blushed pink and her lips looked almost pouty beneath dark-red lipstick as she tried to prevent herself from nibbling the bottom corner. "All right, then," she said with a rumbling sigh. "I guess I'm ready for when George—"

The knock on the apartment door caused her to suck in her breath with such velocity she nearly choked. Joan and Betty giggled.

"Betty," Evelyn gasped, shoving her hands into the gloves.

Betty waved a hand at her. "Remember, Evelyn. A lady never panics."

"Then I'm not much of a lady, am I?"

Another knock on the door and Betty said, "I'm going. I'm going."

Joan picked up the tiny perfume bottle Betty had brought in earlier and, with her fingertip, dabbed droplets behind Evelyn's ear, at her temples, and along the length of her throat. "You now smell as wonderful as you look."

Hearing George and Betty's muffled exchange, Evelyn gave a final tug of the gloves. "I'm nervous as a cat."

"Go have fun," Joan said, pressing their cheeks together.

Evelyn lifted her skirt like she'd rehearsed a dozen times already only to take shaky steps to the door. She looked over her shoulder. *"These heels."*

Joan smiled. "Square your shoulders the way Betty showed you . . . There you go. Now, walk."

Evelyn turned the corner and stepped down the hall, waiting for the moment George saw her. She'd imagined it for days. The look in his eyes. The slight upturn of his mouth as he tried not to gape. She'd dreamed it over and over, reveling in her own imagination.

"She's beautiful. She's—"

"Do you ever get tired of hearing yourself say that, Magda?" His eyes held something akin to anger. Or maybe frustration.

"Saying what?"

"That your sister is beautiful and you are somehow insufficient in that department."

She shook her head slowly, calculating her answer. "I suppose . . . I suppose I just don't like living in her shadow."

Harlan blew smoke from between his lips before returning the cigarette to the ashtray. "Then don't," he stated simply. Before she had time to ask how she should accomplish that, he cupped the back of her head with his left hand, lacing his fingertips between the strands of her hair and drawing her lips to his.

They were soft. Tender. Almost caring, she thought. Magda tilted her head, laying it against his shoulder, breathing in the scent of aftershave and old smoke. She moaned, or at least imagined she did. Women being kissed for the first time by a man of such literary intrigue *should* moan, she decided. So she moaned again, in case she had only dreamed the first one.

When he released her, she looked at him through her lashes, studying his eyes, hoping to find something there. Something like love. Or adoration. Or . . . *something.*

But he only seemed to study her in return. "That was nice," he said. Then, after looking out on the dance floor, he asked, "So what do you think? Would it make you happy if I asked you to dance, Magda?"

As much as Evelyn had dreamed of George Volbrecht taking her into his arms and kissing her for the first time, nothing compared to the intensity of the actual moment. Hank Shute, in all

When she turned the corner she received all she'd hoped for. "Evelyn," he breathed.

Her eyes went to Betty, who smiled and nodded, then back to George. "Good evening, George."

"I—uh—I have . . ." He extended a small white box. "This is for you," he said, then blew a breath from his lungs and collected himself. "Your corsage."

Betty took a step back so that she stood behind George. She pointed to her wrist, then to him.

Evelyn understood. "Would you put it on for me, please?"

"I'm happy to." He removed the bunch of tiny pink carnations from its package and slipped it over her wrist. He handed the empty box to Betty, mumbling something Evelyn couldn't understand. When he turned back, he ran a hand down the front of his tuxedo, then extended his arm. "Shall we?"

Evelyn slipped her hand into the warm place between his arm and his heartbeat. "We shall," she said, smiling up at him. Then, looking over her shoulder to Betty and Joan, she whispered, "See you later."

Joan closed the door behind Evelyn and George, waiting until she heard the outside door open and close before turning to look at Betty, who stood grim-faced, holding the empty white box.

Joan leaned against the door and crossed her arms. "If he hurts her, Betts, I'll—"

"You don't have to say another word." Betty walked to the window, lifted the hem of the ruffled Dutch curtains, and peered beyond the frosty glass to the snow-lined sidewalk and street.

Joan crossed the room. "What did George say to you? Just then, when he turned his back?"

Betty flattened the box so it became only a sheet of white cardboard. "He said, 'This has *you* written all over it.'"

"What does that mean? Is he playing her?"

"Like a fiddle."

"Betty," Joan groaned past the anger building inside. "Are you sure?"

"I couldn't be more sure." She cut her eyes to Joan, who read the absolute certainty within them. "We'll never convince Evelyn, though."

Joan took the disassembled box from Betty and folded it in two, preparing it for the trash. "What do we do then?"

"Only one thing to do, Joan—give Evelyn all the skills she needs to overcome that rascal. Because when this whole thing comes crashing down on her, she's going to need all that and then some."

Magda didn't care that Harlan Procter's idea of a date on Valentine's Day was to go to the same club they always went to. It only mildly bothered her that he seemed more interested in talking about point of view than listening to the sultry music coming from the stage. And she tried not to think about the fact that while couples swayed on the dance floor, woven so tightly together they appeared to be one, she and Harlan sat two feet apart having what amounted to a business meeting.

But what had her nearly beside herself was the realization that this—whatever she and Harlan had together—wasn't enough. She wanted Harlan, yes, but she also wanted more than coffee and shoptalk. More than hearing his voice reading her own written words out loud so she could hear the "inflection of voice." She wanted . . .

"You have this scene in the point of view of the weaker character," Harlan said, pointing to the paper resting between them on the table.

"Hmm?" Magda tore her eyes away from his face to the page.

"Are you even listening to what I'm trying to tell you, Magda?"

"It's not easy, Harlan," she said, glancing at the woman standing behind a microphone. The now-familiar singer cupped her hands around the mic's chrome head as she purred "Tennessee Waltz."

"I suppose you are one of those romantics who wants to sit and listen to every ballad of perfect love on Valentine's Day." He leaned into the booth's back and reached for his coffee.

Magda rested her left shoulder against the tufted, velvety cushion. "Not really. *I'm* not one of those girls who thinks life is a movie script." She smiled, hoping to draw the same from him.

It didn't work.

"What makes you so sure you're not?" he probed.

She thought before answering, knowing him well enough by now to realize he was trying to bait her to dig deeper into herself. "My sister, Inga . . . She's the romantic. I look at her and then at myself and see such a difference."

Harlan pulled a Pall Mall pack from the inside pocket of his jacket. He popped the bottom, sending one cigarette straight out. She watched him, frowning. Even though smoke hung like a cloud in every office and restaurant in the city, she'd never much cared for the odor. Harlan had told her if she wanted to be a real writer she needed to do three things: write, smoke cigarettes, and drink coffee.

Magda told him she'd stick to numbers one and three and leav number two to more sophisticated writers. He'd only laughed at he

"What other differences do you see? Between your sister ar yourself?" he asked after blowing out the first intake of smoke.

his countrified sweetness and with all the kisses he'd bestowed on her, had an awful lot to learn from this city boy. "George," she whispered, her body wanting nothing more than to drop like a noodle at his feet.

He kissed her again, this time quickly. A peck, the way her mother kissed her father before he walked out to work the farm and when he returned at the end of the day. Not that she minded the brevity. Kissing George Volbrecht, no matter how ordinary or passionate, had just become the best part of her life. One day she'd tell her daughters—hers and George's—about the great and magical love their parents shared. Maybe even their granddaughters. "The night your grandfather kissed me for the first time . . . ," she'd begin.

George slipped her glasses back onto her face. "Now all we have to do, Evelyn, is take care of these—" he kissed her again, gently—"for more of these."

She nodded. "I know. I'll see what I can do."

"Tell me," he said, extending a hand for her key. "How do you really think Betty is doing with all this?"

Evelyn dug into her clutch until her fingertips found the key. She handed it to George before answering, "I think she's happy for us. Betty is one of the most selfless people I've ever known. She seems intent on making sure other people are blessed, rather than herself."

"Blessed . . . ," George repeated as he inserted the key without turning the lock. "Where did you come up with that word?"

"*Blessed* is an important word in my vocabulary, George," she whispered, unsure as to whether one of her roommates might be close to the other side of the door. "I would think it would be in yours as well."

George leaned against the doorframe. "In what way? In what way is it important to you?"

"I think . . . ," she began, closing the clutch fully and staring at its shiny handle, "I think that . . ." Evelyn's eyes found his. "I'm more than just a person who goes to church every Sunday, George. I love God. I believe in him. In what my faith stands for. I think . . ." She drew in another shaky breath, struggling to find the right words. "I think God has *blessed* me, first with having Joan as a pen pal, then with meeting her here in Chicago. Because of that I met Betty and because of meeting Betty, I'm now standing in front of my door with you."

"Is that what you *think*? Or is that what you *know*?"

Evelyn raised her chin to the question. "Is there a difference?"

George crossed his arms and sighed. "Yes, there is. If I tell you I *think* the sun will rise in the east tomorrow, you *assume* I know what I'm talking about. But if I tell you that I *know* the sun will rise in the east tomorrow, I have then spoken with authority. You can take my words to the bank, so to speak."

He reached over and turned the key. The lock clicked open, telling Evelyn their date—their magical, wonderful date—had come to an end. George pressed his lips to hers again, whispered, "Good night," and stepped away. "I'll call you soon. Sleep tight."

Los Angeles sparkled like a million diamonds under a bright light.

Frank wrapped his arms around Inga from their place on the blanket he'd laid earlier. She leaned against him and he kissed the lobe of her ear, then twirled the bracelet he'd gifted her with—a simple strand of pearls that shone in the moonlight. "You really like?" he asked.

"They're exquisite."

He nuzzled her neck, sending shivers up her spine and down her arms.

She allowed a light moan to escape, then said, "You were so right . . ."

"About the bracelet?"

"No, silly," she said with a giggle. "About coming *here*. No city restaurant could compare to this."

"I'm always right," he teased. "There's nothing like looking down over Los Angeles at night."

She turned enough to kiss him, then shifted again to face the glory of the sparkling landscape laid out beneath them.

"Every time I'm up here," he said, "I can't help but wonder what stories lie within each of those lights."

"Now you sound like my sister."

He squeezed her. "Maybe I'm out with the wrong sister, then."

Inga pinched his arm and he pretended injury. She took in a breath of satisfaction in their evening, thinking she couldn't wait to share the details with Retta. To tell her of driving up to the hills, of finding the perfect out-of-the-way spot, of laying the blanket on the ground near the car and then eating a picnic dinner with a man so utterly romantic she thought her head would spin off just being near him. She'd tell her how the car's radio played one love song after the other and how Frank had sung along with several of them, as though they'd been written for her alone.

He squeezed her again and she snuggled deeper into his arms, feeling their warmth against the chill of the night.

Then it hit her. She pulled herself free of him and shifted until she rested on her knees, facing him. "And just how many times *have* you been up here?"

He chuckled. "A few."

Inga crossed her arms. "With whom, might I ask?"

Frank didn't answer right away. Instead he pulled her closer until they stretched out side by side on the blanket with only black sky and brilliant stars to cover them. "No one you should worry about," he spoke against her lips. "Right here, right now, there is only you and me."

Inga allowed the kiss to take over, to melt her like butter on a hot plate, and to turn her mind into mush. Frank eased her onto her back, looming over her. "I want to love you," he said.

Tiny moments passed before Inga understood what he'd said, the words playing like a song inside her. Here she was, exactly where she wanted to be, looking into the eyes of the man she planned to spend the rest of her life with. What could be more natural? What could be more right?

She opened her mouth to say yes. To give him permission to take all of her love and to give all of his in return. But as she did, her mother's teachings on virtue and purity rose from somewhere deep inside, and became louder than the music from the car radio.

Her muscles tightened at the cacophony. At the dream of one and the logic of the other. She'd hate herself in the morning, she knew. She'd hate herself and Frank, too. But breaking the magic would be so difficult . . .

Inga moved out from under him and sat up straight. "Frank," she said, keeping her voice as firm as she could against its quiver. "I think it's time to take me back now."

CHAPTER 19

A Saturday morning in March broke with a cool breeze passing through the open window and beyond the draperies of the bedroom. The wafting air tickled Joan awake, inviting her to rise early and start the day.

After a stretch, Evelyn turned and asked, "Do you work at the museum today, Joanie?"

Joan shook her head and sat upright, slipping her feet into her house slippers before reaching for her robe. "Hard to believe, isn't it? To tell you the truth, Evelyn," she said, shoving her arms into her robe, "I'm looking for one job that will pay enough to help eliminate working so *many* jobs."

Evelyn reached for her glasses on the bedside table. "Do you ever . . ." She adjusted the glasses on the bridge of her nose. "Do you ever *think* about anything more than working?"

Joan shrugged. "I enjoy working. Prefer it, really, to parties or sitting around doing nothing."

"But what about finding someone special? I have George, and Magda has Harlan, and Inga has someone out in California." She shrugged. "I worry about you and Betty."

"Worry about us?" Joan stood and grinned at her friend. "Don't be silly. Finding a man is low on my list, Evelyn."

"But if you found the *right* man—you know, one with lots of money—you wouldn't have to work so hard."

Joan sighed. Sometimes when she looked into the eyes of someone like Evelyn, it felt as if a needle had screeched across the record of her life, reminding her how truly different she was from most every other single woman. Like an alien in a foreign land of hopeful brides-to-be, Joan saw "once upon a time" and "happily ever after" through a different lens.

"Trust me, Evelyn. If I found the most wonderful man in the world and he came with more money than Rockefeller, I'd still want to work." She pointed to the closed bedroom door. "Let's make some coffee and see what's what for breakfast. I'm starving."

They made their way down the hall, where the aroma of brewed coffee met them, and into the kitchen to see their other roommates gathered around the table.

"Well, this is highly unusual," Joan said.

Betty smiled at her. "I was just saying the same thing. And that *someone* should go get some pastries from the bakery."

"I'll go," Evelyn said. "Give me a few secs to get dressed."

Minutes later, as Joan sipped on a cup of coffee with the others, Evelyn returned from her room wearing a blue-and-white gingham blouse with pedal pushers, a pair of sneakers, and a scarf tied around her hair. "I won't be long."

"I almost can't believe this," Joan said, when Evelyn had returned with a box of delectable treats. "Both sisters. Betty. Evelyn. And me. Sipping coffee and nibbling on warm delights. All of us here together." Joan set her cup on its saucer. "We should *do* something. Together."

Magda leaned her elbows on the table. "A movie perhaps?"

Inga glared at her sister. "Do you have a fever or something? I've never known you to want to go to a movie."

Magda frowned across the table. "I like a good movie every now and then. It's story."

Inga, her blonde hair already styled and her face put together, shrugged. "I only thought that, knowing you, you'd want to lie in bed and read all day."

Betty chuckled. "You two really don't know much about each other at all, do you?" She raised a hand. "Don't bother answering. Tell you what—I'll run over to Mrs. Cline's next door and borrow her newspaper. See what's playing for the matinee."

"Mrs. Cline?" Magda asked. "Since when is Mrs. Cline ever up at this hour?"

Betty winked. "She won't be. I'll simply borrow the paper and we'll have it back before she stumbles out of bed."

They all laughed her on her way.

A few moments later, the front door opened and closed again. "Who's up for *Singin' in the Rain*?" Betty called as she walked through the living room and into the kitchen.

Joan frowned; she preferred substance in her movies to frolic. But, she decided, spending the afternoon with her flatmates made watching a movie she wouldn't have otherwise chosen worth the time and effort. "When is it showing?"

"Starts at two." Betty leaned against the door, the paper folded back, revealing an advertisement of Gene Kelly, Debbie Reynolds, and Donald O'Connor, draped in raincoats and sporting opened umbrellas.

"Hey," Inga said, standing and clearing her dishes. "Let's get dressed and go into the city. Find a drugstore counter where we can order greasy burgers and cheese fries. After that, we'll go to the movie and then . . . Well, the day is still young, isn't it? Who says we have to act like old *hemmafruar*?"

"Housewives," Magda interpreted for the others.

Chairs pushed back from the table and dishes quickly found themselves stacked neatly in the sink. "I'll do these when we get back," Joan offered.

"And I'll return this to its rightful owner," Betty said, refolding the paper and swinging back into the living room.

"Meet at the front door in one hour," Inga declared, holding up one finger.

"Synchronize your watches," Evelyn chimed in, holding the face of hers between two fingers and staring down at it.

The roommates laughed before departing to their own rooms.

Joan stepped out of McVickers Theater on West Madison and blinked, trying to bring the real world back into focus and wishing she could reenter the make-believe one in the cinema, if only for a few more minutes.

Adjusting her gloves, she turned under the massive marquee near the box office, where a thick line of folks waited to see the same movie Joan and the others—who'd all made a mad dash for the ladies' room afterward—had just enjoyed.

"I'll be outside," Joan had said to them after applying a light touch of lipstick and repositioning her hat.

She shook her head now as she made a final tug on the gloves. Sensing a sudden onslaught of moviegoers about to enter through the dark-glass doors, she shuffled to the right just as her flatmates exited.

"There you are." Evelyn adjusted the frames of her cat-eye specs and squinted into the sunlight.

"Ice cream soda, anyone?" Inga asked, pointing across the street to a malt shop.

Betty linked her arm through Inga's and pulled her eastward. "Wasn't all that popcorn and soda enough for you?"

The rest followed. "My sister," Magda called out, "should be worried about her figure or risk TWA firing her."

"But we're talking *ice cream*," Inga called over her shoulder.

"Girls," Magda continued, "steer her away from temptation."

Evelyn turned her face toward Joan with a pout. "I guess we're heading home."

Joan shrugged. "I suppose we are."

"But to *what*?" Magda asked. "I have no plans." With a jut of her chin, she added, "Look at them. Somehow they've managed to get a good half a block ahead of us."

Joan smiled at the words. "Oh look . . ." Betty and Inga had begun a shuffle-ball-step. "They think they're dancing with Gene Kelly now."

"I wish I had a date tonight," Evelyn drawled. "But . . ."

"A date?" Magda all but barked. "I wish I had a *boyfriend*."

"But I thought—" Evelyn began.

"I mean a *real* boyfriend," Magda said, growing more solemn. "Not like . . ." Her voice trailed.

"Oh, yes," Joan said, determined to lighten the mood again. She pretended to take a note on the palm of her hand. "I can practically read the letter now. Dear Mum and Dad—"

"Mor and Far," Magda corrected.

Joan cleared her throat. "Dear Mor and Far . . . As it turns out, I can't marry Hans, whom I'm sure you think a perfect match for me. I have met the man of my dreams right here in Chicago."

"And that's not the bad news," Evelyn added, also taking up the pretense of writing a letter. "The bad news is . . . he's . . ."

Magda smiled then, adding, "He's *Baptist*."

The three laughed easily, sobering only when they came to

where Betty and Inga had stopped in front of one of the colossal, architecturally framed storefront windows of Carson Pirie Scott & Co.

"Would you look at that," Evelyn breathed.

"I have to say," Betty said, "that is the prettiest wedding dress I've ever seen in my entire life."

"I'd give my eyeteeth to have a gown like that." Evelyn's eyes scanned the dress as though she already did.

The young women remained silent for a moment, lost in the folds of the dress, the long, lacy sleeves, and the sweetheart neckline.

"I've never seen so much lace in my entire life." Betty continued in her ogling.

"What do you think?" Joan asked, feeling the eastbound crowd brush against her. She stumbled slightly but managed not to fall as her eyes roamed the cathedral-length veil floating from a headband of pearls crowning the mannequin's brunette hair. "Two fifty?"

"Two fifty?" Betty cast a glance that inquired if she'd quite possibly lost her mind. "For all that elegance and enchantment? You must still be thinking in quid, Joan. I'd say more like four hundred. *Dollars.*"

"If I wore that dress on *my* wedding day," Evelyn said, once again adjusting her glasses, "I'd feel like Cinderella on her way to the ball."

Betty crossed her arms as a look of genius settled on her face. "I say let's do it."

"Do what?" Joan asked.

"Go in." She tipped her head toward the front doors. "Try it on."

"Are you serious?" Magda asked, turning to stare at the dress once again.

"Why not? We're not doing anything else the rest of the day."

She smiled, the fire-engine-red lipstick making her pearly whites look all the more so. "Unless someone wants to go home and dust something . . . or *cook* something . . ."

"But," Joan said, "we . . ." She looked around at the faces of her flatmates. "None of us has so much as an engagement ring."

"So?" Betty asked, her eyes shining with the excitement of it all.

Inga bounced on the balls of her feet. "I'm with Betty. Let's do it."

Joan looked to Evelyn. Behind the specs, her blue eyes had grown wide and anxious with anticipation.

Joan nodded. "Okay. Let's do it," she said, making a dash toward the door. "Last one in has to clean the loo for the rest of the month."

Betty pushed through the heavy, bay-shaped revolving doors on the northwest corner of the imposing department store. She looked over her shoulder at the others. Inga stood closest to her heels, Evelyn only steps behind her. Joan and Magda pulled up the rear. She watched their faces as they stood just inside the door. Each of them looked up, then turned slowly, mouths gaping at the splendor and architectural genius of the glittery interior. Their eyes scanned the gold capitals encircling thick supporting columns that stood like Buckingham Palace guards and the chandeliers, as big as boats, hanging from the ceiling, dripping crystal, light, and color.

"Come, come, come," Betty said. "Bridal wear is on one of the upper levels. Four, I think."

Opting against the elevator, they darted up stairs with banisters that matched the ornate decor of the store itself, the tap-tapping of their shoes announcing their excitement to the fourth floor, where the plaster ceilings hung much lower than those on the first.

Again, they all stopped, clustered together and breathing heavily as they absorbed the grandeur and elegance of the department.

A middle-aged salesclerk with perfectly coiffed hair approached, and she nodded as Betty described the dress in the showcase window along Madison.

"I know the one you mean," the clerk replied, and she smiled at the cluster of young women wearing their Saturday-go-into-the-city clothes and wide-eyed expressions. "And, if I may inquire, which one of you is the lucky girl?"

Evelyn grabbed Joan's hand as though they were about to be hauled off to jail for impersonating blushing brides-to-be.

"That would be me," Betty piped up.

Joan shot Betty her best are-you-joshing? look.

"You're in luck," the clerk said. "I believe we have it in your size." Again, she smiled. "And would these lovely ladies be your bridesmaids?"

Betty smiled knowingly. "Perhaps. For now, we're interested only in that *one* dress."

The woman arched a brow. "Please have a seat and I'll be right back."

Velvet settees encircled the bridal showroom's marble-topped platform. The women perched like real ladies on the edges of five individual sofas, straight-backed with legs crossed at the ankles, lips pressed together. Betty couldn't help noticing that no one dared to look at the others for fear of breaking into laughter at their own courage to do something so daring.

The salesclerk returned, holding a plump satin-covered hanger high above her head. The dress draped from her right hand over her left arm, sweeping the air in front of her as she walked. "Here we are," she sang, looking at Betty.

Betty rose from her seat, heart pounding as she glided toward the clerk as though stepping down a wedding aisle. In the window, clothing the inanimate mannequin, the dress had appeared nothing short of lovely. But here, so close to her twitching hands, it became the gown of fairy tales. The kind of dress a girl could only hope to wear on her wedding day. The kind she had always dreamed of . . .

"I don't believe," Joan whispered out of a sort of reverence, "that Her Majesty Elizabeth's dress was any more beautiful than this." She stood, and the others followed suit, each of them taking a step forward.

Evelyn leaned close to Betty's ear. "Maybe we shouldn't—"

Before Betty could shush her, the salesclerk interrupted. "Would you like to have one of our girls model this for you or would you prefer to try it on yourself?"

"Oh, no," Betty said. "I'll try it on." She turned to the others. "And then I want my friends to do the same."

"All of them?"

"Yes, please," Betty answered, scooping the dress from the clerk's arms and into her own. The material rustled, sending a shiver of anticipation through Betty that she hadn't known in months. Not since her father had cut off her allowance and her endless days of compulsive shopping had come to an end. "Point me to the dressing room, if you will be so kind," Betty said with the same flourish she'd heard in her mother's voice time and again.

Then to the others, she said, "Girls, I'll be back momentarily."

Inga cleared her throat as she returned to her seat. "I suppose we'll wait here."

Magda followed. "That Betty has some nerve. Some . . ."

"Moxie. It's called moxie," Joan added. She took Evelyn's hand

and squeezed, leaving Inga to wonder if it was for her sake or for the little mouse from Georgia. "And listen, girls. Marriage may be the last thing on my mind, but in its own way, this could actually be *fun*."

"I just hope we don't get in trouble," Evelyn countered.

Inga shot her a look. "What on earth for? Like Joan just said, we're only having fun."

"I'm with Evelyn," Magda added.

"Of course you are." Inga straightened her dress's skirt over her crossed knees. "As for me, this may be more than just window-shopping. This may be my first real try-on." She closed her eyes, aware of the instrumental music wafting from somewhere overhead. If her years sitting on Mrs. Dexter's brutal piano bench had taught her anything at all, it was to recognize the finer pieces of music. This was . . . Chopin . . . Nocturne in E flat major?

She waited, listening. Yes. Most definitely Chopin.

She allowed it to relax her. To drown out the strain between herself and her sister and the fear emanating from Evelyn. She imagined herself in the dress, walking down the aisle in her father's church—she'd give her parents that much. Frank, looking expectant and madly in love, dressed in a tux. No. A morning suit. She'd demand a late-morning wedding. The sooner they said "I do," the sooner the honeymoon could begin. And where to? She'd always wanted to go to Niagara Falls.

Was that too cliché? What of it. That's where they'd go. From one end of the country back to the other—Los Angeles, where life with Frank Martindale would finally begin. She sighed, opening her eyes as the name *Mrs. Frank Martindale* tiptoed through her thoughts.

"Well?" Betty stood on the nearby platform looking as radiant as Inga felt. The salesclerk fluffed the skirt behind her, and then drew the train to its full length. Light from overhead cast a shimmer along the folds of satin and Chantilly lace.

"Oh, Betts," Joan said, nearly breathless and pressing her hand against her chest. "Just look at you."

Inga knew she had stopped breathing, but figured she needed to in order to allow her heart to catch up with her head. She had only imagined herself in the dress. But there she stood—Betty Estes—looking more radiant and more bride-like than Inga had considered possible.

"Tell me," the salesclerk said, "what is the name of your fiancé?"

Betty blinked as if the magic of the moment had been broken. Her eyes shot to Evelyn's, and Evelyn's suddenly dropped to the floor.

"Evelyn," she said, ignoring the woman looking up at her. "Why don't you try the dress on next?"

CHAPTER 20

The salesclerk led Evelyn and Betty into the dressing area—one large round room with its own carpeted center platform and a massive tri-fold gold-leaf mirror against one wall. From there, several changing rooms jutted behind heavy gold-and-cream drapes hanging in deep folds, ceiling to floor, one of the rooms flanked by drapes drawn back with thick gold tasseled rope. Beyond them, Evelyn spotted Betty's clothes hanging from a hook.

"Miss Estes," the clerk said, "if you will return to your dressing room . . ." She extended her hand toward the room. Betty did as instructed, releasing the drapes as she passed, allowing them to envelop her and the dress, leaving only the gown's train behind. Within seconds, it too disappeared.

The clerk turned to Evelyn. "My name is Mrs. Marchman," she informed her. "And you are?"

Evelyn quivered, in spite of her resolve to hold herself together. "Evelyn," she barely whispered. "Evelyn Alexander."

"This way, Miss Alexander."

Evelyn followed Mrs. Marchman to another of the rooms, where the clerk threw back one panel of the curtains with a flourish. "If you will go ahead and remove your clothes, I'll return momentarily with the dress."

"Yes, ma'am."

Minutes later, as she stood with her arms crossed, shivering in her underthings—a pair of panties and a girdle, nylons, and a brassiere under a sleek white slip—Mrs. Marchman returned with the dress.

"I'm going to bring this over your head," she said. "So you may want to remove your spectacles."

Evelyn removed the glasses, folding the temples and laying them on a round corner table.

"Arms up," Mrs. Marchman ordered.

Evelyn shot her arms over her head as though she'd been commanded by a drill sergeant. With a rustle of fabric, cool silk taffeta slipped down her arms, over her head, and came to rest on her hips. Mrs. Marchman then held the bodice out. "Arms in," she said, and Evelyn slid her arms into tight lace sleeves that came to a V over the backs of her hands. She drew back her shoulders as the clerk walked behind her to adjust the sweetheart neckline. Then, starting below her hips, she buttoned the dress with skilled fingers, ending at the top of the illusion neckline.

"Come this way." She pushed both drapes aside, tying them with the tasseled rope. "Stand on the platform, if you will."

Evelyn lifted the gown's heavy skirt and, keeping her gaze on her toes peeking out, mounted the platform and dropped the skirt. Then—and only then—did she dare glance into the mirror.

A blur of white in the center of an array of color met her. "I can't . . . I can't see," she said. She turned her face back toward her dressing room. "My glasses."

Mrs. Marchman sighed. "Don't move. I'll get them."

Evelyn pressed her lips together, regret overpowering her. They were putting such added pressure on the woman to help five young women try on a dress without even making a sale.

"Here you are," Mrs. Marchman said upon her return.

Evelyn slid the glasses onto her face, looked up, and gasped. "It's quite—something. Isn't it?"

"One of the loveliest I've ever seen." Mrs. Marchman stepped back. "And Carson's is known for its wedding gowns, as I'm sure you know."

"Is it?" Evelyn asked without taking her eyes from her own reflection. She looked . . . *almost* . . . like a real bride. Like this was *her* fitting. All her own, and Mrs. Marchman stood next to her to make certain all her bridal needs were met.

"Do I detect a Southern accent, Miss Alexander?"

The question jarred Evelyn from her own reverie. She looked down at the clerk. "Yes, ma'am. I'm from Portal. Georgia."

Mrs. Marchman smiled. "What in the world brought you all the way up from Georgia, if I might ask?"

Evelyn smiled briefly, then returned her gaze to the mirror. "A need for change, I suppose." She shrugged. "You know, after the war and all."

"And have you found it? The change?" She reached for a small bouquet of artificial flowers placed on a nearby table that Evelyn hadn't noticed before. "Here," she said, not waiting for the answer to her question. "For the full effect."

Evelyn took the cluster of pink-and-white flowers. "Betty didn't have these."

"Miss Estes didn't *need* them." She crossed her arms. "In fact, I'm not so sure Miss Estes is in need of a wedding gown." Evelyn jerked her head toward the clerk, who laughed lightly. "I see women who are madly in love all the time, Miss Alexander. So, I can spot when one is *not*."

The observation brought a wave of comfort to Evelyn, and she sighed. *Betty isn't in love.* She had no worries, then, that Betty might want George back.

"You, on the other hand . . ."

"Me?" Evelyn felt herself blush. She looked again to the mirror, staring past the glasses and the nearly unadorned face. She could imagine that, with the right upsweep of her hair and the right amount of makeup, she'd make a proper bride walking down the aisle to meet George Volbrecht. She closed her eyes and pictured him. Handsomely dressed. Awestruck by the way she looked in this exquisite dress. Eyes twinkling as he watched her march the aisle toward him, her father beside her, dressed in his Sunday best.

A frown found her and her eyes shot open. Even in his nicest dark-blue suit, Daddy wouldn't hold a candle to the guests who'd sit on George's side of the church. And what about her mother? Would she wear some homespun dress or would she allow Evelyn to help her shop for something special in Chicago?

Chicago? Yes, Chicago. Certainly not Portal. But if the wedding was to be held in Chicago, would her mother even come? Or would she remain behind, pining away for the son who would never return from the war and the life she could never again have? Or for Hank, the man her mama would adamantly declare Evelyn *should* have married. Because if she *had* married Hank, her mother would say, there'd be no need to worry about tuxes and Sunday suits or trips to Chicago.

But Evelyn knew, if she married Hank, there would never have been such a lovely wedding gown. The most she could hope for was something her mother stitched on the old Singer . . .

"Would you like to show your friends now?" Mrs. Marchman asked, drawing her away from her imaginings.

"What? Oh. Yes," Evelyn whispered.

Mrs. Marchman held out her hand to assist Evelyn in stepping to the floor. "My guess is," she said, "you've met a certain someone here in Chicago."

Evelyn released a pent-up sigh and smiled. "Yes, ma'am."

"And from the look on your face, I'd say he must be something very special." She paused at the opening to the sales floor and raised her chin as though the statement were more question than fact.

"Yes," Evelyn said again. "Oh, yes."

And yet, she pondered, *still so far out of my league.*

Joan tried on the dress after all the others. Not that she minded. After all, it was Betty's moxie that had brought them in. And dear Evelyn's anxiety wouldn't have allowed her to be much more than third in the lineup. Then Inga had tried on the dress, declaring to them all that she'd most assuredly meet Frank Martindale at the altar in nothing shy of a gown like this one. And soon.

Magda had stood quietly as she modeled, but Joan had little trouble reading her thoughts. In spite of her resolve to be a modern woman of the fifties, Magda's heart remained trapped between her family's traditions and a moody writer named Harlan Procter. Out of all of them, Magda seemed the most tormented by the gown, and, for that, Joan's heart ached a little for the flatmate she hardly knew.

"This way." Mrs. Marchman now guided Joan through a set of draperies, and she entered into a smaller version of the round room, this one without mirrors, for which she felt grateful. "Go ahead and undress. I'll be right back."

Before they'd left for the city that morning, Joan had put on her first real purchase since moving to the States—a black bouclé suit she thought looked quite Katharine Hepburn-ish—and a simple sheath top beneath it. She pulled off the jacket and draped it over a provided hanger, followed by the skirt and top, leaving her to stand on the platform in her slip and a pair of nylons. She almost laughed at the silliness of the escapade; before she could, Mrs. Marchman swooped in with the dress sprawled over her arm as she'd done earlier.

"Arms up," she instructed in such a way as to make Joan wonder how many times a day she repeated the two simple words.

Minutes later, with the gown adjusted to Joan's frame, the clerk pushed back the panels of the drapes. "This way to the platform area."

Joan followed, stepped onto the platform, completely nonplussed by the adventure. After all, this was simply a day of fun, was it not? And she tried on gowns of equal beauty at David & DuRand each and every week. She'd grown accustomed to seeing herself clothed in elegance, whether she felt chic or not.

But when her eyes found her mirrored reflection, her heartbeat rolled with an avalanche of emotions. How was it possible that one frock of white lace, silk, and illusion—simply by being worn—could change a girl into a woman? And how could one dress change a poor miss from Leigh, Lancashire, into a princess fit for tea with Her Royal Highness, Elizabeth II?

Furthermore, how could it change a girl with a mind for business into a woman with thoughts of marriage?

"Hmm," Mrs. Marchman said, reaching for a bouquet of flowers and then returning them to the table. "No, I think not."

"What?"

"The flowers, dear. Not the dress. You look quite lovely, actually. As though the dress were made for you." She shook her head. "Amazing, don't you think, that all five of you are the same size? I understand from one of the Miss Christensons that you are all roommates."

Joan smiled briefly. "We are. Yes."

"Miss Alexander is from Georgia, she tells me. And you are from . . ."

"Leigh, Lancashire."

"Quite interesting, when you think about it, isn't it? Did you all know one another before—?"

Joan plucked at the fabric of the skirt, making it fuller. "No. Not really." She looked again at her reflection. She'd always been so practical, never dreaming of wearing such a dress as this. No doubt she'd marry in a suit, more like the one hanging in her dressing room. Nothing like this. Nothing so—

"Let's get you out to the others," Mrs. Marchman said with a sweep of her hand. "And then get you back in here to re-dress."

"I daresay," Joan admitted, stepping to the floor, "that you've had your fill of us."

Mrs. Marchman stopped short. "Obviously, there won't be any commission made off of this past hour and a half, but I do admit it's been rather charming watching the five of you."

Charming? Yes. Charming to watch. But more than that, the afternoon's adventure had been great fun and a wonderful diversion from what Joan usually did on a Saturday.

By the time Joan re-dressed and joined the others, a strange buzz vibrated between her flatmates. Hearing her, they turned. Evelyn pressed her lips together while Betty grinned like a cat. Magda linked the fingers of both hands, holding them up as though saying her prayers. Inga sat off to one side, legs crossed, the top one swinging lightly.

"What?" Joan asked. "What's going on?"

Betty took her hand and pulled her to one of the settees. "Joan . . ."

"Oh, dear . . ."

"Here's what we're thinking . . ."

"Please say yes, Joanie," Evelyn interrupted, sitting on the other side of her while Magda squatted in front of them.

Looking over to her sister, Magda said, "Inga?"

Inga raised her hands, palms upward. "I'm right here. I can hear every word." She shrugged. "Besides, I already said I'm in."

Joan looked from one anxious face to another. "In what?"

"Did you like the dress, Joan?" Magda interjected. "The wedding gown?"

"Wearing it was . . . *amazing*, really. Quite honestly, if I hadn't seen myself in a mirror, I'm not so sure I'd have recognized the little girl from Leigh."

Betty cut her eyes toward Inga, then back to Joan. "That dress," Betty whispered, "is three hundred dollars."

"Three hundred . . ." A near fortune.

"But," Evelyn said, now standing.

"But . . . ," Betty chimed in quickly, waving Evelyn back to her seat, "if we were to each put in sixty . . ."

"Sixty?"

"Quite inexpensive when you think about the cost of a wedding gown. *Any* gown."

"But for what possible *purpose*?"

"For our weddings," Betty said. "The deal is that we *all* wear the dress."

Evelyn quivered. "Betty has it all figured out."

Joan looked at the woman she'd known nearly since her first day in the States. Betty smiled slowly, as though she were about to give away the map to Frances Hodgson Burnett's secret garden.

Mrs. Marchman exited the dressing room, the dress now draped from its original hanger and ready to be returned to a rack of exclusivity. "Ladies, something tells me you've had a fun afternoon. If there's nothing else I can do for you—"

"Hold on," Betty said with a voice of authority. She eyed Joan again. "Your vote is the only one we need, kiddo."

Joan shook her head. "This is all quite mad. We're going to buy a dress for weddings we've not yet received proposals for? And what if one of us *never* marries? Or waits. A *long*, long time." She pressed her hand against her chest. "As I intend to do."

"What if . . . ," Inga began, and all faces turned to her. "Let's say we do this. What if, when the time comes, we are no longer rooming together?" She looked at each of them in turn. "That's a real possibility, you know. If Frank were to give me the slightest hint that he wants me to move to LA, I'm out of this blustery city on the next flight." She nodded toward her sister. "Magda could move back to Minnesota, Evelyn to Georgia, and Joan to England. We could completely lose touch."

Attention moved back to Betty. "Good questions, all of them. Let me think."

Mrs. Marchman cleared her throat. "While you *think*, I'm going to hang this dress up, if you don't mind."

Betty waved a hand, dismissing the salesclerk. Then, as though she thought better of her attitude, she added, "Thank you, Mrs. Marchman. Give us a few minutes. We may not have wasted your valuable time after all."

After the clerk shrugged and walked away, Joan said, "Well?"

"Here's what I'm thinking. I'm a Chicagoan. Always have been. Always will be. So, I'm not going anywhere. I'll be the 'keeper of the dress.' No matter where we are in this whole wide world—Chicago, Portal—" She looked at Joan. "England. You all stay in touch with me, and when you need it, I'll send the dress."

Evelyn's eyes grew wide at the thought. "Genius. Pure genius. That's what you are, Betty."

"The bride," Betty added, "will wear the dress, have it dry-cleaned once she's returned from her honeymoon, box it up, and send it back to me, ready to wear for the next bride."

"Okay, okay," Magda said. "But what happens after the fifth bride wears the dress?"

Betty nodded. "Another good question." She paused. "Fifth bride keeps the dress. Forever."

Joan burst into laughter. She couldn't help herself. "We're talking about ourselves as *brides* and yet—did I mention?—none of us has an engagement ring."

Evelyn's hands flew to her mouth. "But, Joan," she said, lowering her fingertips, "there's the *hope* of one." She held out her left hand. Her eyes misted over as they held a faraway gaze. "There's the dream of a certain someone who will slip a ring on this finger right here and say, Evelyn, will you do me the honor of—" her attention returned to the rest of them—"being my wife and the mother of my children."

Even Magda sighed. "Yes . . ."

Joan exchanged a look with Betty as Inga stood and took deliberate steps toward the others. "I think," she said, "that we should do it." She smiled. "And, to be perfectly honest, I imagine *I'll* be using it sooner rather than later."

Magda rolled her eyes. "Inga . . . if you think Far is going to allow you—"

"Allow? Do you really believe I need his . . . *allowance*?"

"Permission," Betty interrupted, standing. "I'm the one in need of an allowance." She looked each of them in the eye. "If we don't do something like *this* . . . well, quite frankly, I don't see my father ever paying for it."

Evelyn looked down. "Betty . . ."

"I'm not asking for pity, Evelyn. I've made my decision and I'm sticking to it." She patted Evelyn's hand. "And aren't you glad?"

Evelyn's eyes found Betty's. "Yes. I am," she whispered.

"All right then. Let's make a decision. Joan? You're the only one we need to cast a vote really, but I'll get us started anyway." She raised her right hand. "Who's in?"

Inga repeated the action. "Me."

Then Evelyn. "Me." She looked at Joan and bit her lip.

Magda raised her hand. "Me."

Attention settled on Joan, who laughed out loud. "I've always been such a sensible girl, you know."

"And?" Betty asked.

"I mean to say that the craziest thing I've ever done is step on a boat and cross the Atlantic with only a little more than thirty dollars in my purse."

"So then," Magda urged, "what's sixty?"

"And now you have a job, Joanie," Evelyn reminded her.

"More than one," Joan said, locking eyes with Evelyn, hoping she remembered her desire to somehow manage with *only* one.

Inga dropped her hand. "Just say yes, Joan."

Joan giggled.

"What's so funny?" Inga asked.

"Your accent," she admitted. "It becomes stronger when you're—"

"*My* accent?" she asked, attempting to sound like royalty.

All hands dropped and Betty cleared her throat. "Ladies." She lifted her hand again. "Me."

Evelyn followed. "Me."

"Me," Magda and Inga said together.

Joan sighed, raising her hand and then, teasingly, dropping it again before lifting it high. "Me."

And then, as though they'd known each other all their lives, they drew one another into a group embrace.

"I can't believe we're doing this," Joan said.

"Me neither," Evelyn whispered into her ear. "Thank you, Joanie."

Joan closed her eyes and chuckled. "You're welcome."

CHAPTER 21

Betty sashayed into George Volbrecht's secretary's office, closing the door behind herself in one fluid movement. "Is he in?"

Josephine reached for the phone.

"No, no," Betty said, waving her hand.

"Miss Estes, I must—" Josephine continued in her efforts to perform her secretarial duties, as Betty walked past her desk, where the unmistakable scent of Chanel swirled around her movements. "Mr. Volbrecht, Miss—"

Betty opened the door to George's office to find him sitting on the edge of his desk, a golf club resting against his knee and the phone in his hand. He smiled as she stepped in, locking eyes with hers. "That's okay, Jo. Miss Estes has a way of thinking she owns the world." He replaced the phone's handset. "To what do I owe this pleasure? And so close to the lunch hour. Hungry?"

Betty closed the door. "Stop it. Tell me, do you always call your secretary by a pet name?"

He shrugged, taking the putter in hand before closing the distance between them. He kissed her cheek, lingering long enough to say, "You smell delicious, Betts."

She pulled back. "Well, it's not Chanel, but for a poor working woman, I suppose English Lavender will do."

He touched the tip of her nose with his finger. "But not entirely your style." He returned to the game of office golf in the center of the room.

Betty crossed her arms as he rested the putter against the cratered white ball, gave it a gentle bop, and watched the ball head straight into a glass tumbler. She clapped lightly. "Bravo."

George tossed the club up and caught it. "Step aside, Ben Hogan." He pointed toward the wet bar. "Something to drink?"

Betty ignored him, choosing to sit on the long sofa, which she instantly regretted when George joined her. He leaned against the back, stretching his arms and resting them there. "So why are you here, Betts? Need an attorney?"

She shook her head as she removed her gloves and shoved them into her purse. "George, something has . . . happened. I'm sure Evelyn hasn't told you, but I feel you and I must talk." She looked at him then, noting the furrow in his brow.

He shifted, turning more toward her. "What? What has happened?"

"I can't say, really." How would she ever explain the purchase of one wedding dress by five women? Not only would it sound ridiculous—especially to a man—but she knew he'd waste no time telling his mother, who'd tell her mother, who'd report it to her father. "Not the details, anyway." She sighed. "George Volbrecht, what are your intentions toward Evelyn?"

George stood, crossing the room to the bar where he poured himself a glass of water. He took several sips before placing the glass on the counter and leaning against it. "Does there have to be a plan, Betts?"

Betty pushed her purse onto the sofa and stood. Walking to him, she said, "George. Please. Evelyn is—"

"Really becoming quite something, isn't she? I mean what with your influence and all."

She stopped. "The beauty that is Evelyn has always been in there . . ."

"Just hidden? Is that what you are saying?"

"George?"

"Hmm?" he taunted.

"If you don't think this is heading toward matrimony, please, by all that is sacred—"

"*Matrimony?* So what if it is?" He took another drink of water. "Well, why shouldn't it be? After all, she's single. I'm single. She loves me—don't tell me you haven't noticed—and, well, I myself am rather fond of me."

"George!" Betty stomped a foot, but before she could say another word, he grabbed her by her shoulders, brought her to himself, and kissed her. Hard at first, then more gently, holding her with such ardor she couldn't have broken away if she'd tried.

She raised her hand to slap him. Just as soon as—

"Betty, Betty," he whispered against her lips. "Just say the word. You know how I feel about you. Just say the word and I'll—"

The door to his office opened and they broke apart in time to see Evelyn standing there, her hand on the brass doorknob. She gasped. "I knew it," she cried. "I just knew it!"

"Evelyn!" Betty pushed George away, then darted after Evelyn.

Joan utilized her lunch hour to run down to the Automat with a handful of nickels and a copy of that day's want ads from the newspaper. In spite of the crowd inching its way along the vending machines, she managed to get a tray of meat loaf, mashed potatoes, and green beans over to a table in the corner. She had hoped to avoid Betty and Evelyn while she put in her search. Fortunately, Betty had left the office early, quite evasive about where she was off to. And Evelyn had a prearranged lunch date with George.

"What are you looking at so intently in the newspaper?"

Startled, Joan looked up to see the face of Magda. "Hallo," she said. Then, seeing that she held a tray, she added, "I didn't expect to see you here. Join me?"

"I don't mind if I do," Magda said, placing her tray opposite Joan's. "What are you looking at?"

"The want ads. By chance are there any jobs over at Olson?"

Magda shook her head. "Not that I know of. Excuse me," she said, bowing her head for a silent prayer, and Joan waited until Magda looked up. "Is something wrong with where you're at?"

Using her fork, Joan cut off a piece of meat loaf. "Nothing at all. I just need more money, and I'm a little overworked between Hertz and D&D and . . ." She slipped the fork between her lips.

Magda reached for the folded paper Joan had laid on the table between them. "Look at this," she said, pointing to an ad with her fork. "The Callahan Agency is looking for an executive secretary."

"The Callahan Agency?"

"I've heard of it. The home office is somewhere else, but I read an article about it. It's supposed to be quite the up-and-coming business."

Joan took the paper from Magda, her eyes wandering over the small advertisement. "Pat Callahan . . ."

"What?"

"The ad says to ask for a Pat Callahan."

"That's right," Magda said, brightening. "The Callahan Agency is owned by the Callahans out of Milwaukee, I think."

"What do they do? The Callahan Agency?" Joan looked at the ad again. "It doesn't really say here."

"They're an advertising agency." She wiggled her brows. "And, if I remember correctly, they're located on the second floor of the twenty-story high-rise next door to the Drake Hotel. You know, where all the *beautiful* people go and live."

"Perfect," Joan said, only half-feeling the sentiment.

"Joan," Magda said, her voice as authoritative as she'd ever heard it. "You're in financial over there at Hertz, right?"

"Mmm-hmm."

"What I mean to say is, you're not a secretary, much less an *executive* secretary. Do you think you could handle the change?"

Joan squared her shoulders. "Magda, you're looking at a girl who can do anything she puts her mind to." She shook her fist in mock salute. "I'll apply for that job. I'll interview for that job. And I'll *get* that job. And if you don't believe it, just watch."

Magda smiled over the rim of her coffee cup. "I like that about you, Joan. You're not afraid to try new things."

"What about you then, Magda? How's that book coming along?"

Magda placed her cup back on the table. "I'm not sure, to tell you the truth. I think I'm heading in the right direction and then I meet with Harlan and . . . he sort of . . . dashes all hope. He's told me my writing needs work, but he spends more time asking me about *me* than getting into the facts of my characters."

Joan speared a green bean. "Maybe by getting to know yourself better, you *can* create better characters."

"Now you sound like Harlan."

Joan reached across the table, clasping her hand around Magda's. "Just keep believing in yourself, Magda. You'll do just fine, I'm sure of it."

Betty had run to the end of the block before she realized two things: One, Evelyn was nowhere to be found; and two, her purse and gloves were still in George's office. Her shoulders dropped and she turned to make her way back when she spied the opened doors of a church—its facade massive and imposing—across the street.

Churches—especially Catholic churches—always had an open-door policy, she knew. But the doors of this one were literally wide open, and she took it as a sign.

Betty darted across the street and ran up the narrow cement steps, keeping her eyes on the Celtic cross silhouetted against the brilliance of the early afternoon sky. Until she stepped through the doors and into the chill of the narthex, at least; and then into the nave, where the scents of old furniture polish and melting wax met her.

She crossed herself, then walked down the center aisle under a canopy of angelic beings soaring so high she almost couldn't make them out. She continued toward the altar, taking a seat on one of the hard, finely polished benches, and folded her hands in her lap. "What a mess I've made of things," she whispered, hoping none of the others who had entered to pray could hear her. "What a mess all the way around."

Besides making a cataclysmic mess of her own life, she'd done even more to poor Evelyn's. She would surely never understand. And probably never forgive her. Not that she could forgive herself.

She felt more than saw the presence of another and looked to the end of the row, where a nun stared down at her.

Betty stood. "I'm sorry . . . This isn't my—"

The woman's face showed a great number of years and wrinkles. She shushed Betty as she batted her hands, palms down. "Sit, sit," she said.

Betty did, and the nun sat beside her, her rosary falling into the folds of her habit. "You seem greatly distressed, my child," she said, patting Betty's hand as she smiled. "I saw you when you came in and couldn't help but notice."

"Oh, Sister," Betty said, keeping her voice whisper-soft. "I'm afraid I've hurt someone I have come to care about." Betty poured out the story, leaving out almost no detail. When fifteen minutes had passed and she'd come to the story's conclusion, she took a breath and said, "Now I don't know what to do. I saw the opened doors and I felt that . . . *God* . . . I felt him direct me inside."

The nun patted her hand again. "Tell me your name, child," she said, her voice holding the lilt of an Irish brogue.

Betty laughed lightly. "Betty Estes. And you are?"

"Sister Brigit. Now then, let's see where I should begin." Her hazel eyes twinkled behind frameless, octagon-shaped glasses, made all the more prominent by the tight wimple. "If you want me to begin, that is."

"Please."

"You say you have not seen your parents since they cut you off."

Betty looked down, shaking her head. "I know I should have, but—I've hardly known what to say and I don't like arguing with them."

"Before you can go changing things in the lives of others, you must first change the messes in your own. So, first things first. The Bible tells us that we are to *honor* our father and mother."

Betty sat straight. "So I should marry George?"

The old nun looked up, rolling her eyes heavenward. "Good heavens, no." She chuckled. "But you should make amends with your father and mother." She pointed at Betty's chin. "Hold your ground, *but* be respectful."

"What about Evelyn? How am I ever going to fix this with her?"

"Tell her the truth." She peered at Betty, blinking once. Twice. "It's all you can do. But *you* must know the truth first."

"What do you mean?"

"*Did* you feel anything when this George fella kissed you?"

Betty smiled. "As kisses go, it was pretty nice. But . . . no. I'm not interested in marrying George." She sighed. "Sometimes I wonder if I'll ever find the right one."

"The Good Book says that 'a man's heart deviseth his way: but the Lord directeth his steps.'"

"Meaning?"

"Meaning that right now, even as you sit here with me, the Lord is at work—whether you know it or not—directing you to the right path. You only have to trust him with your steps."

Betty smiled, albeit briefly. "I do, Sister, but . . . but I think that what I'm more concerned about—even more than whether or not God has a special someone for me—is that George is leading Evelyn on terribly. She thinks *he* is her special someone and I . . . I know he'll never marry her." She captured the nun's eyes with her own. "I *really* don't want her to get hurt."

Sister Brigit nodded. "You can only tell her the truth. How she reacts is up to her, not you. She must make her own way down her own path. But when you speak to her, remember these words from Saint Paul: 'Let your speech be always with grace, seasoned with salt, that ye may know how ye ought to answer every man.'"

"That's good advice," Betty said, then looked down at her watch. "I have to go, Sister. I'm late as it is."

Sister Brigit stood with her. "I will pray for you, dear. And that your boss will be most understanding."

"Thank you, Sister." She stepped around the old nun, pausing at the end of the row. "Maybe I'll see you here at Mass sometime."

"That would be nice, child. Most pleasant indeed."

CHAPTER 22

The large-faced clock on the opposite side of Magda's office ticked loudly, its minute hand inching too slowly toward the twelve. Seven minutes more and she could clock out. Go home. Work on the story that had played itself out in her mind all afternoon. She knew now what needed to happen next. What her characters should say to each other.

They'd been talking in her head since lunch; the only way to silence them was to put their words on paper.

The door to Mr. Cole's office opened and he stepped through it. "Magda, good. You're still here."

She smiled appropriately—not so much as to seem forward, not so little as to seem annoyed. "Where else would I be, Mr. Cole?" She looked from the paperwork on her desk to her boss, who now stood over her. "Besides, don't I always say good-bye at the end of the day?"

He smiled, his face warm and kind. "You do. Sorry. I have a lot on my mind." He ducked his head to top it with his hat. "My daughter has a school function tonight, and she's a little upset already that I won't make it home in time." A fatherly grin slid across his face. "I'm leaving a little earlier than usual to make certain I don't lose my Father of the Year status."

Magda laughed. "I'm sure she'll appreciate it, Mr. Cole."

Barry Cole crossed the room for the door. "Well, wish me luck that the trains are all running on time and that Deanne will do well in her little play."

"Deanne? That's your daughter?"

His brow furrowed. "Yes, of course."

"I don't believe I've ever heard you say her name, sir."

"Hmm," he said, opening the door and looking over his shoulder at her. "I suppose I haven't. Well, I should rectify that. Deanne is my daughter. Douglas is my son."

"I see." She looked at the clock again. Another three minutes. She wondered if she should stand and call it a day herself, but she didn't dare. The last thing she wanted was for Mr. Cole to think of her as a slacker.

"Good-bye, then." He stepped out of the door, closing it behind him. The door reopened and his head peered around it. "By the way. You gave me work by a Clarissa Jones."

Magda straightened. Only a few days previously she'd read an article she thought held merit and had passed it along to her boss. "The article about the women behind the men of baseball?"

"That's the one." He winked. "Good job."

The door closed behind him. Only then did she smile, allowing it to evolve into a grin, then to form a chuckle.

"Good job," she repeated as she stood, shuffling the work in front of her into one pile. She set the paperwork in the to-do basket, then went about her end-of-the-day tasks—covering the typewriter, switching off the table lamp in the far corner, and righting any magazines that had been disturbed on the coffee table by those waiting for their appointments with her boss.

The door opened again as she returned to the desk to retrieve her purse. Magda looked up, expecting Mr. Cole's face, but seeing Harlan's instead.

"Harlan," she breathed out. "What are you doing here?"

He walked in and closed the door behind him, then removed his hat. "I was afraid I might have missed you."

She pointed to the door as an awkward twitch shimmied down her spine. She'd never been in such private quarters with him before—not without Mr. Cole nearby—and never with the door closed. "I was about to go home. Mr. Cole already—"

Harlan shuffled as though nervous. "I see." He waved a hand, beckoning her to him. "Come. Sit over here with me. I have something to talk to you about."

Magda sighed. "Perhaps we should open the door in case—"

"In case what?" His eyes widened. "Oh, I see." He looked over his shoulder at the door, then back to her. "Don't worry about that. Come." He waved again, then tossed the hat on the sofa and sat. "Here, next to me," he said, patting the seat beside him.

Magda walked over, then perched on the edge of the sofa.

Harlan looked at her as if she'd developed some strange disease that left her face scattered with green polka dots. "What is wrong with you, Magda? You act like you've never sat with me before."

She sighed and laughed at the same time, then slid back. He did the same, resting his arm along the back and drawing her into the crook of it. "There. Better."

Magda looked up into his face. "This feels strange, Harlan. It's one thing, sitting close at the club or necking at my front door." Her eyes swept over the room. "But this is my place of business and . . . I would be mortified if someone walked in right about—"

He cut off her words with his lips pressed against hers. She couldn't help herself; she sank into the kiss, wrapping her arm around his shoulder, twining her fingers through the curls at the nape of his neck. When he broke the magic and pulled away, his pale-green eyes traveled from her lips to her eyes, and back to her lips again. "I was hoping you'd react that way," he said, his voice smoky.

She slid away from him, but only an inch or so. "What way?"

Harlan took her hand, squeezing it, and then lacing their fingers. "I've come with a proposition."

Her heart pounded and for a fleeting moment she thought of the dress, covered and hanging in the closet her sister shared with Betty. "What kind of . . . *proposition*?"

"I have some intensive work on a short story I have to have finished by next Tuesday."

Magda blinked. "Do you need me to read it for you? Go over it before you turn it in?" The prospect of such a request gave her nearly as much pleasure as the thought of being the first to wear the wedding dress.

He smiled. "Yes, but more than that." He brought her hand up and kissed her fingers. "I've grown so fond of you, you know."

"And I, you."

Harlan's eyes met hers and held fast. "That's so good to know," he whispered. Then he cleared his throat, released her hand, and sat closer to the edge, resting his elbows on his knees. "I have a cabin up a ways on Lake Michigan."

"You've never talked about it—"

He looked at the floor. "It's where I go to write. Sometimes for a week. Sometimes for a month. Sometimes for a weekend." Harlan looked back at her. "I'm going this weekend—I'll leave Friday afternoon and return Sunday evening. I want you to go with me, of course. You can read. Take long walks. That sort of thing . . . while I write. Then read my work if you wish and tell me what you think."

Magda stood. "You mean . . . but who else would be there? Besides the two of us?"

Harlan stood as well. "Just the two of us." He reached for his hat and set it on his head. "Don't *you* become provincial on me, Magda," he said, studying her from under the rim. "Surely you knew this was the direction we were headed." He took her by the elbow and guided her to her desk. "Get your purse, my dear, and I'll walk you to the train. I've given you much to think about, I know. And I don't expect you to answer me right now. But by Thursday, shall we say? I'll meet you at Tillie's for lunch. You can give me your answer then."

Magda stood in the kitchen doorway, staring at her sister, who sat at the table with a half-consumed cup of coffee in front of her. "You look like I feel," she said, noting the worry lines forming along Inga's brow.

Inga glanced up, pushing the cup and saucer a couple of inches away from where it stood. "And how's that?"

"Like you've lost your last best friend." She walked to the percolator, still on the counter, and laid her fingertips against it, testing its warmth. "Can I warm your coffee?"

She reached into the cabinet and pulled out a cup and saucer.

"No." Then, more kindly, "No, thank you."

Magda joined her at the table where the sugar and creamer stood near Inga's now-ignored cup of coffee. "What's wrong?" she asked, preparing her drink. "Or do you want to talk about it?"

Inga sighed. "They've changed my route. I'm flying Chicago to New York now."

"New York?" Magda added a cube of sugar and stirred. "I've always wanted to see New York." She took a sip. "Maybe one day I will." When she became a famous author . . . When she went to the grand city for business meetings with her publisher. And surely a

New York house would want her books. More than one. They'd be in competition for her, especially knowing she'd been tutored by—

"Easy for you to say," Inga mumbled. "You don't have a boyfriend in Los Angeles."

"Oh," Magda breathed out. "I see." She took another sip. "How long will you have this new route?"

Inga shrugged. "I don't know." She picked up the cup and saucer and stood, then walked to the counter, where she added more of the hot coffee to what Magda assumed was stone cold. "All I know is, without the airline flying me there, I won't have time to go to Los Angeles." She returned to the table and plopped back into her seat.

"Have you talked to him? To this boyfriend?"

"Frank. Yes."

"I take it that didn't go well."

"He said he was upset, but . . . I worry that I . . ." Her words trailed and Magda waited.

When she said nothing more, Magda asked, "What? What are you worried about, Inga?" She heard the lilt in her own voice, sounding so much like Mor's.

Inga must have heard it too. She smiled, albeit weakly. "That voice," she said. "Do you think we'll ever get away from it?"

Magda shook her head. "I hope not."

Inga sighed again, drawing the cup and saucer closer to her. "That voice kept me from a night of what I imagine would have been the most intense passion ever experienced by any woman."

Magda sat straight. *"Inga . . ."*

Inga raked her long, polished fingernails through her hair. "I can't help it, Magda. I'm not like you."

"Like *me*?"

Inga remained quiet for a moment, her gaze on the still-untouched coffee in her cup. "Chaste."

"Inga . . . surely you haven't—"

"No. But . . . but I've thought about it." Her eyes met Magda's. "Valentine's night. Frank took me up into the hills and he . . . he practically begged."

Magda hugged herself as if the room had suddenly become too cold to bear. "And did you?"

"No. Mor's voice—her words of chastity and warnings from God's Word—kept me in line."

Magda choked out a bubble of laughter. She inhaled deeply. Released it. "But you wanted to."

"I'm in love with him. Of course I did." She picked up the cup and took a sip. "Wretched."

Magda took the cup, stood, and walked to the sink, where she washed it out. She then poured another cup and returned to the table with it, preparing it the way she knew her sister liked it. After she placed it back on the saucer, she said, "Harlan has asked me to go away with him this weekend."

Inga's eyes grew wide. "And will you?"

Magda shook her head. "No. Not that I didn't think about it all the way home on the train. Believe me, I did."

"But Mor's voice . . ."

"More than that, Inga. God's voice."

"God's? Don't tell me you're hearing the voice of God now."

Magda smiled. "No. Nothing like that. But I suppose it's more than Mor's words that have impacted my decision, though surely they have to some degree. We grew up—you and I—in the strictest of homes—"

"You can say that again."

"—but we knew our parents loved us. Cared for us and about us."

Inga only nodded.

"Truth is, we say their faith is theirs and we're only living a certain way out of obedience to them. But when Harlan asked me to go away with him, I felt so violated. So . . . disrespected. Not that I don't love him, but . . . I don't think he loves me in the same way. He has no faith tendencies . . . and . . . I asked Mor what she would have done had Far not been Lutheran."

"When? When did you do that?"

"At Uncle Casper and Aunt Greta's."

"And what did she say?"

Magda took a sip of her coffee. "You know Mor. She said, 'But he was.'"

Inga stared at her. "That's it?"

"Mmm-hmm."

"I call that blind faith."

"At least she knew what she wanted."

Inga stood, this time pushing the chair back into place under the table. "I know what I want, too, Magda. And what I want is Frank Martindale. Besides, I'm not that keen on religion. It's all an act, anyway."

"Inga . . ."

"Act this way. *Don't* act that way. If I ever see Frank again, it won't be with Mor's voice running around in my head. I'll exorcise it out if I have to."

"Inga!"

But before her sister could respond, the front door opened and closed and—a second later—Betty and Joan stood in the doorway, anxiety covering their faces and Evelyn's lightweight coat draped across Joan's arm.

"What?" Magda asked. "What is it?"

Joan pushed out a breath, her chest heaving. "Have either of you seen Evelyn?"

CHAPTER 23

Evelyn sat in a sleek orange chair in the corner of the building that housed George's office five floors up. The chill from outside crept through, making her wish she'd worn her coat. But at noon, when she'd left Hertz to come here, the sun had shone so brightly. So warmly.

There'd been no need, then.

Now, everything was different. The weather. The world. Herself. Now she understood things she hadn't before, and she'd had all day to consider them.

It had only been a few weeks since the salesclerk at Carson's told her Betty was not a woman in love. That much she knew for sure. Betty wasn't the type of girl to *toy* with a man or his affections. As Joan had said time and again, Betty was one of the most selfless women she'd ever come to know.

George, on the other hand . . .

Evelyn crossed her legs in an attempt to stay warm, then wrapped her arms around her middle. She looked at her dress, attractive enough by most standards, but shabby compared to those Betty owned. Even with her new hairstyle and the use of cosmetics, she knew she paled next to her roommate. Betty had

had a lifetime of practice at being sophisticated; Evelyn had only recently begun to scratch the surface.

Perhaps that had only been a facade. Now, after an afternoon of contemplation, she knew what she had to do.

She looked up in time to see George's beautiful secretary walk across the lobby floor toward the front door. No, she didn't walk. She sashayed, like that actress . . . that blonde one . . . What was her name?

Marilyn. Yes.

Evelyn stood, straightened her skirt, and walked toward the elevators, attempting to do the same. *Heel in front of toes . . . heel in front of toes . . . wiggle, wiggle, wiggle like Marilyn Monroe.*

She felt ridiculous, but it seemed such a proper way for a lady to walk.

A minute later, she repeated the action from the fifth-floor elevator to George's office. She opened the outer door without making a sound, pausing long enough to hear George's voice from the other side of another closed door. He laughed. So heartily, so easily. She wondered what it must be like to be so carefree in the face of such a day as this one had been.

Evelyn crossed the outer office, breathing in the lingering scent of his secretary's perfume. She paused, drawing it deep within her lungs, then continued forward, stopping at George's office door.

". . . at ten o'clock in the morning," he stated, then remained quiet for a moment. "I can schedule the depositions then or I can wait a week, whichever works best for you . . . All right then. We'll wait." George laughed again and Evelyn turned the doorknob slowly, opening the door with such ease, she wondered if George would even hear her.

When she peeked her head in, she saw that he had his back to her. He leaned in his chair, feet up on the desk and crossed at the ankles. He wore only his suit pants and a crisp white shirt, the sleeves cuffed halfway to the elbow. His coat hung from the small brass hook on the bookcase. Even from this angle, and only half put together, he looked so handsome, so perfectly at ease, Evelyn wondered if she could go through with what she'd decided to do.

She stepped all the way in, her footsteps muffled on the carpet. She waited just inside until he said good-bye and dropped his feet to the floor, swinging around to replace the handset.

"Hi," she breathed out.

"Evelyn—what on earth are you—?"

She raised a hand. "I need to talk with you."

George stood, shoved his hands into his pockets, and looked down. "I know I must be the—"

"Stop," she said, and he did. "I get to talk first."

He looked up—with his eyes only at first, followed by the lift of his chin and the tilt of his head. She tried to read his expression; George Volbrecht didn't like to be interrupted and he surely didn't like to be ordered about. But for once, she had something on him.

Even if only for a moment.

She turned to the sofa and said, "Can we sit?"

"Of course," he said, as if all his gallantry training came back in a whoosh. He extended a hand. "Please." He pushed the sleeves of his shirt down and grabbed for his coat.

Evelyn swallowed hard as she sat, then watched him until he sat next to her.

She spied it then, Betty's purse, perched on George's desk . . . waiting.

"Betty left without her purse," she commented.

He glanced over his shoulder, then back to her. "Do you blame her? She went running after you, you know."

Evelyn folded her hands in her lap and looked at them, waiting for the courage to continue. "She never found me, I'm afraid." She lifted her eyes to his. "I took the rest of the afternoon off . . . to think."

"Look, Evelyn, I—"

She placed her hand on his. "Wait. I told you. I go first. After today, you can go first, but right now, it's my turn." She swallowed again, never wanting her eyes to leave his and settling finally on the cleft in his chin. She would speak to it, she decided. That would be easier.

"My father is a farmer," she began. "So was his father and his father before him. I come from a long line of men who work the land—sometimes. Mostly, the land works them. It works them until they have nothing left to give . . . until they're old before their time. I also come from a line of strong Southern women." She laughed lightly. "I know how the movies often portray us . . . swooning and fanning ourselves out on verandas with a hundred acres of oak trees in the background and a black mammy standing close by with a glass of lemonade." George smiled and she did, too. "Truth is we're more like Scarlett in the middle of *Gone with the Wind* than at the beginning *or* the end." She paused. Licked her lips. "But my mother and her mother, well they married for love, George. When they said, 'for richer, for poorer,' what they really meant was 'for poorer.' Not every Southern farmer is a plantation owner. Not all of them have fields white with cotton as far as the eye can behold, either.

"I made my mind up a long time ago that I wanted something more. Now Mama had her mind set that I would marry a boy named Hank Shute. And Hank's not a bad fella, but his father is a farmer, and he's already working his daddy's land and I'm sure—one day when Hank has a son of his own—his boy will farm too." Evelyn raised her eyes to George's, to gauge what he might be thinking. But his eyes were unreadable, like those of her daddy when they used to play a hand of cards.

"Hank wanted to marry me as much as my mama wanted me to marry him. But like I said . . ."

"You wanted more."

"Yes. Now, I've had all day to study this thing and I know I'm not Betty Estes. I know I don't have her sophistication or her clothes, and I know I wear these awful glasses and that I don't know half of what you order at these restaurants you take me to. And . . ." She took another deep breath, allowing her gaze to drop back to the cleft. "I know you are in love with her."

"Evelyn—"

Evelyn brought her hand up to his lips, touching them lightly with her fingertips, shushing him. "I also know she is *not* in love with you, George Volbrecht."

Her hand returned to her lap, slowly, the way she'd imagined it would as she'd rehearsed these words earlier in the afternoon. She tried not to look at George too closely for fear of his radiant light sidetracking her, confusing her thoughts.

"But I am," she continued. "In love with you, that is. And I don't care that you don't love me, George. What I *do* care about is becoming everything you want me to be. I want to know what you know. I want you to teach me what only you can teach me. And, more than anything in this whole wide world, I want to be the kind of girl you are not ashamed of anymore. So, then." She squeezed her hands together. "If you're willing to be my teacher, I'm willing to be your student." Again her eyes found his, and she nearly drowned in the sea of blue. She gulped a bubble of air. "No strings. No conditions."

He studied her, she felt sure to ascertain whether or not she was kidding. "A sort of *Pygmalion*," he finally said.

"Yes."

His eyes twinkled. "You know what I mean when I say *Pygmalion*?"

"Of course, George. I'm from the country, but it's still *this* country. I went to high school." She crossed her eyes. "I even graduated."

He laughed, taking her hand in his. "Look at me," he said when he sobered. "Do you know what these last few months have been about? You and me?"

"Yes. You've been working very hard at making Betty jealous. You thought she'd come running back to you when she saw that you'd moved on." Evelyn raised her brow. "You see? I'm not so dumb."

"No," George said. "But that makes me a very not-so-nice person."

"Indeed it does."

He chuckled, and this time she laughed with him. "Evelyn," he said with a toss of his sandy-blond waves. "The door is right behind me." His voice was low. Somber. "I warn you now. Run. Run and don't look back."

"Would you say the same to Betty? If she were sitting here instead of me?"

"If I weren't such a cad, yes. Truth is, I'm no good for her *or you*."

Evelyn pulled her glasses from her face before placing her hands on both sides of his. "I'll be the judge of that."

The deep blue sea of his gaze turned to cloudy gray smoke. "You're bound to get hurt."

She didn't care. She didn't. If Evelyn had come to understand one thing that afternoon, it was that she had no desire to go backward. Only forward.

Wherever that took her.

She kissed him. Soundly. And he kissed her back, the same way she'd seen him kissing Betty earlier in the day. When their lips parted, she smiled at him and he smiled in return. "I think—" she whispered—"excuse me, I *know* it's time for you to take me to dinner. I didn't have lunch and I'm about to starve to death."

George stood, taking her hand to help her up. "You're hungry."

"That's what I said."

"Then learn to say it correctly. 'I'm hungry' or 'I'm famished.' A true lady is never 'about to starve to death.'" He threw in an over-exaggerated Southern accent.

Evelyn raised her chin. "George," she said, trying her best to sound like Betty. "I'm famished."

He winked. "Good girl." He walked to his desk and picked up Betty's purse. "I expect you'll want to return this for me, then?"

She took it from him as gently as her emotions would allow. "I shall be happy to."

George chuckled once more. "Good girl," he said. "Very good girl."

Joan stood at the doorway of Betty and Inga's bedroom. "I've got a problem," she told Betty, who stood at her dresser, methodically removing her pearl earrings and dropping them into a heart-shaped glass bowl.

Betty turned only her face. "What's that?"

"I've got an interview with the Callahan Agency tomorrow during my lunch hour."

Betty gasped, turning fully. "You're kidding."

Joan shook her head. "With a man named Pat Callahan."

"With *Pat*?"

Joan nodded.

"Pat Callahan." She spoke the name not as a question but more as if she didn't believe Joan had said the name correctly.

"Is that good?" Her stomach turned as queasy as it had been the day of her hospital stay. Only this time, she'd eaten. "Do you know him?"

Betty shook her head. "Only *of* him. He's a vice president at the agency, I believe. His father being president."

Joan ran a hand over her hair, which needed a trim and a perm. "How do you know?"

"He knows Mr. Ferguson. They had lunch a few weeks back."

Joan leaned against the doorjamb. "Did you meet him? Is he nice?"

Betty went to the bed and sat on the edge, hiking up her dress to unhook her nylons. "Oh, no. I didn't actually meet him. Mr. Ferguson met him out somewhere." She pulled one stocking from her leg and went to work on the other. "I can't believe you want to leave Hertz."

Joan sighed. "Time to move up in the world, Betts. I need to make more money and work fewer hours."

Betty stood, turning her back. "Unzip me, will you?"

Joan complied.

"So, what's the problem?" she asked, turning again. "You said you had a problem."

"Would you have *anything* I could borrow for the interview? To wear, I mean?"

Betty's lips turned up at the corners. "Again you need to snag an outfit from my closet."

"Mmm . . ."

"I have the perfect thing," she said, rushing toward the closet. "Simple. Creamy white. Very professional look." She carefully opened the door and fumbled around until she pulled a coat hanger from the wooden rod. "Here ya go." She extended the suit. "Need the shoes to match?"

Shoes. Of course. Fortunately, they wore the same size. "Do you mind?"

Betty pulled a pair from the shoe rack stretched along the closet floor. "If you get the job, I'll miss you," she said, extending the pumps. "But I'll celebrate every second with you."

Joan held the treasures close to her chest. "If I get the job," she told her, "I promise that, one day, I'll do something wonderful for you."

"For me?"

Joan held the suit and shoes up a little. "For this . . ."

"Think nothing of it." Betty blinked a few times. "Joan . . . how's Evelyn? I mean, really? Other than an offhanded remark about moving out, she's hardly said two words to me in two days."

Joan shook her head. "Evelyn is convinced she knows what she's doing. I told her I don't think George is good for her, but she begs to differ."

Betty sighed. "She loves him, then."

"Absolutely. And she knows he doesn't love her, but says she's willing to continue onward." Joan waved a hand. "She even said something about *Pygmalion*."

"*Pygmalion*?"

"Mmm."

"Good heavens."

Joan shrugged. "She's a big girl, Betty. We have to let her have her way with this."

Betty looked at the floor, planted her hands on her hips, and shook her head. "Poor Evelyn. She thinks she knows how to fight the bull, but this is a ring unlike any she's ever seen before." She crossed her arms and looked up. "Speaking of the bull's ring, I'm going to see my parents for the first time in a while this weekend. Care to go with me?"

"When?"

"Sunday."

"After church?"

Betty nodded. "I can let Adela know we'll be there for afternoon coffee and dessert."

"I'd like that. It's a date."

CHAPTER 24

Pat Callahan—a handsome-beyond-words bloke of Irish descent—turned out to be as vivacious in personality as anyone Joan had ever met. Unlike Mr. Ferguson and Mrs. King, who'd been on the other side of their desks during her job interviews, Mr. Callahan (who insisted she call him Pat) sat in one of the two occasional chairs—both golden yellow and boxy—in the midst of a true workingman's office.

The man she hoped would be her next employer wore dress slacks and a white shirt, its long sleeves cuffed, exposing tanned arms with thick red-blond hair. He also sported a shiny gold watch, which she suspected was more than just *toned*. Pat Callahan seemed the kind of man who'd wear only the real deal or nothing at all.

Joan kept her legs crossed at the ankles and her back straight as an ironing board, gripping the lifeline—her purse, the one thing on her that didn't belong to Betty. Pat leaned over, resting his elbows on his knees. He held her résumé loosely between the index and middle fingers of both hands. A hi-fi phonograph in the corner of the office played a Dean Martin tune, and his right toe tapped in time.

"So," he said, glancing up at Joan. "Tell me a little about yourself."

"Do you want the short version or the long version?"

He chuckled. "Let's stick with the short version. You're currently with Hertz?"

"I am."

"Working in finance."

"A secretarial position wasn't available," she told him. "At the time." Then she smiled. "But I'm a *very* good secretary."

"And everything before this? You're from England, this says."

As if her accent wouldn't give it away. "Leigh, Lancashire."

Pat straightened as he folded her résumé. "That's near Manchester, isn't it?"

"It *is*," she said.

"I spent a little time in England." He winked. "What made you decide to come to the States?"

"Actually, I was born here."

"You don't say?"

"But my father is from Ireland and my mother from Leigh, and in the midst of the Depression, they decided it best to move closer to family. So, when I was a little girl, they packed up the whole lot of us and we returned."

Pat batted his lips with an index finger. "Interesting." He opened the résumé again. "And you say you're a good secretary?"

"*Very* good."

Again, he leaned over, resting his elbows on his knees. "Well, Joan Hunt, let me be honest."

"By all means."

"You aren't the most qualified or the most experienced, but . . ." He cocked his head. Light streaming through the windows caught on the red in his blond hair and made his green eyes seem all the greener, like the ocean at midday. "I learned a long time ago to go on my gut. It's the only way to do business, Joan." He stood and cast the résumé over to his desk. It slid across the rest of the papers and files like an airplane gliding onto a landing strip.

Joan gripped her purse all the tighter, instinct telling her she had a new job.

"You'll want to put in a two-week notice, of course."

Her breath caught in her throat. "Of course. Mr. Ferguson has been kind to me. Like a father, really."

"I know Jim Ferguson. He's a good man." He folded his arms in front of him and rested against his desk. "So? Meet me right here," he said, pointing to the floor as though it would be the exact spot where they would reconvene, "in two Mondays. Can you do that?"

Joan stood and extended her hand in one movement. "I can do that."

Pat Callahan laughed. "Something tells me, Joan Hunt, that you can do just about anything you put your mind to." He took her hand and squeezed.

"I like to think so." She turned and walked to the door. As she reached it, Pat said, "By the way . . ."

Joan looked over her shoulder at him. "Yes?"

"I really like that suit. Sharp. Real class."

On Thursday morning, the same clock Magda had watched a few days earlier taunted her as the noon hour drew near. She wished—no, she prayed—that Mr. Cole would call her into his office and tell her that he had some important project to take care of and would she mind skipping lunch. Just this one time.

Not that he had ever done such a thing in the past, but there was a first for everything. Only, not today. Today, as the hour and minute hands came together to announce the noon hour, she covered her typewriter, put the few papers and files she had on her desk into order, and retrieved her purse from the desk drawer that kept it safe during the day. She opened the catch, removed her gloves, and put them on. Slowly, working each finger into them, lacing the fingers of both hands for a final shove.

Barry Cole's office door opened and she turned in time to see him sliding his arms into his suit-coat sleeves. "Ah, Miss Christenson," he said. "I'm on my way out to lunch too. Glad I caught you."

Magda brightened. "Do you need something, sir?"

"Yes," he said before stepping back into his office. When he returned he held a stack of manila interoffice envelopes. "I apologize that I didn't get these to you sooner." He laid them on her desk. "When you return from lunch, would you get right on this? The one to Mr. Freeman needs to reach him sooner rather than later." He moved toward the outer door.

"Should I take care of that now for you, sir?" Magda asked, hopeful.

"No, Miss Christenson. It can wait until you've had your lunch." He smiled at her and her heart hammered.

Could she possibly have a heart attack at such a young age? "How . . . how was your daughter's show the other night?" The words shot from her mouth.

He turned fully. "Deanne had a solo. Did I tell you that?"

"No, sir."

Pride washed over his face and he looked away, as though reliving the moments of his daughter's performance. "Never could a father have been prouder. She has quite a singing voice. Much like her mother."

"Mrs. Cole has a lovely singing voice, does she?"

Barry Cole blinked a few times before looking at her again. "Like an angel."

"She's very pretty." When he said nothing in return, she pointed toward his office door. "The photo."

"Ah," he said. "Yes. That was a few years back. I think the kids were six and eight."

"Oh? How old are your children now?"

"Douglas is twelve. Dee is ten." His brow furrowed and then he chuckled. "That would be correct, wouldn't it?"

Magda smiled. "I would imagine so, sir. If they were two years apart then, they'd be two years apart now."

Barry Cole laughed. "All right, Miss Christenson. Have a nice lunch." With that, he opened the door and walked out, leaving it ajar.

Magda blew out a breath, her cheeks puffing in the process. "Oh, well. I may as well get this over with."

At twenty after, she walked into Tillie's Café, spotting Harlan immediately in one of the booths running along the left wall of the restaurant. When he saw her, he nodded and slid from the seat to wait for her.

She crossed the room as well as she could on legs made of gelatin. "I was beginning to wonder," he said, kissing her cheek.

Magda took the bench seat across from his. "Mr. Cole had some things he needed to talk to me about," she said, wondering if her excuse was a half-lie or half truth.

"Ah," Harlan said, returning to his seat. He held up a finger for a waitress standing nearby and said, "We're ready now." Then, to Magda, he said, "I've ordered for us. Coke and grilled cheese for you. Burger and coffee for me."

She smiled. He knew her, Harlan did. He was also, she decided, looking at him, incredibly good-looking in an offbeat sort of way. Handsome? No. But there was something about him, especially right now with the sunlight coming in from the storefront window, casting highlights on his dark-blond hair. And she adored that special something in him, something so deeply intellectual within his eyes that she felt she could drown in them and be happy for the dying.

He reached across the table and took her hand. "I cannot tell you how excited I am about this weekend." He reached for a pack of cigarettes sitting next to the rolled silverware at his elbow, then dropped them back on the table. "You know, I've never asked a woman—not any woman—to come to the cabin with me," he said, as if the revelation had just come to him.

"Why is that?"

He shrugged. "I've never met anyone I wanted to take there with me. It's a sort of . . ." His eyes wandered around the room, then back to her. "I suppose you could say that when I'm out there, I'm in my sanctuary."

"Like a church?"

He reached for the cigarettes again, this time pulling one from the pack. "I suppose you could say that."

"I did say that." She waited for him to respond, but he only lit the cigarette in silence. "Harlan, do you go to church?"

A stream of gray smoke shot upward from his lips. "Whatever for? 'Religion is the sigh of the oppressed creature, the heart of a heartless world, and the soul of soulless conditions. It is the opium of the people.'"

"Karl Marx?"

Harlan chuckled. "You know the quote. That's refreshing." He seemed both genuinely pleased and fully shocked.

"Yes, I know it—" Magda stopped speaking as the waitress dropped two plates in front of them.

"Be right back with your drinks," she said.

Magda chose to wait until after she'd returned to finish her thought, even as the aroma of butter and cheese wafted upward, enticing her to forget her decision and dig right in. But then, in her mind's eye, she saw Far standing behind the pulpit, preaching to his flock about the hunger the Lord Jesus endured during his forty days of testing in the wilderness.

Perhaps *this* was her test. Such temptation . . . A handsome, brilliant man who wanted her to go away with him . . . and her favorite lunch, all at one table. She closed her eyes, praying the moment would pass.

"Are you all right?" he asked her.

She looked at him. "Yes. I'm just waiting for—" The waitress returned and placed a cold glass with a bobbing straw in front of her and a steaming cup of coffee next to Harlan's plate.

"Anything else?" she asked Harlan.

"No," he said. "Thank you."

Magda waited a moment before speaking. "To some degree, Harlan, I agree that religion is the opium of the people. Opium is a drug, after all. It alters the way those who take it feel about things or look at life. But opium is a killer—or, it can be. And so, in that respect, I disagree." She took a long swig of her drink, watching as he bit into his burger and chewed thoughtfully. Listening to her words—truly listening. For a moment, she wondered if perhaps she'd been too quick to judge his invitation so harshly. Maybe he intended them to have separate bedrooms. Perhaps his intents were purely platonic in nature—

"And?" he said after swallowing.

"Oh," she said. "Um—I know religion has gotten a bad name of late. The things we've heard about and learned in the last five or six years are . . ." She stopped, unsure if she could go on, but deciding she must.

"I'm not talking about *religion*, Harlan," she said. "I'm talking about *faith*."

He swallowed. "Whose?"

"Mine."

"You have faith?"

"Yes, don't you?"

He sat back and crossed his arms. "I don't think I've ever really thought about it. I didn't grow up in a very religious household, Magda. My father was a drunk and my mother worked more hours than most men on the block. If God exists, he certainly didn't bother showing up on my street. What you see here," he said, extending his hands, "is all self-made. I clawed my way up and out and never looked back."

"I didn't know that," she whispered.

"It's nothing to talk about," he said, sliding up to the table and taking the burger back in his hands. "My father is dead, my mother is dead, and I'm still here. Alone."

She reached across the table, palm up, encouraging him to take her hand. He placed the sandwich back on the plate before sliding his hand on top of hers, twisting them until they became like a fist. "You don't have to be."

"Don't have to be what?"

"Alone. God is—"

He squeezed her hand and she stopped. "Magda," he said, his eyes focused on hers. "Are we going to talk this nonsense for an entire lunch hour? And, more importantly, are you or are you not coming away with me this weekend? That's why we're here, remember? To make our plans."

She pulled her hand from his. "I don't see talking about God as nonsense, Harlan. And, no. I'm not going away with you. That's against my *beliefs*." She pursed her lips, waiting for him to say something. Anything. But he did not. He only stared at her, the green in his eyes churning, dark and stormy for a moment before turning back to their original pale state. "I'm sorry," she said, finally. "I believe in . . . *that* . . . belonging only in the marriage bed."

"My gosh," he breathed out at last. "You *have* become provincial."

"No," Magda said with a toss of her hair. "I *always* was. I'm just now realizing it, is all." She reached for her purse and slid out of the booth. "Good-bye, Harlan. And thank you, sincerely. For everything."

CHAPTER 25

Spring released herself to summer, and summer inched to autumn during that first full year of Joan's return to the States. Life had settled down for her in many ways. She continued to work at David & DuRand—though only a few nights a week—and her job with the Callahan Agency had been more fulfilling than she'd imagined it could be. She'd been able to send money back to England on a regular basis and still build a small savings fund for herself while adding an outfit or two to her closet. With shoes.

She rarely saw the others, it seemed. When Evelyn—whose new personality she hardly recognized at times—wasn't working, she was with George. George, who had taught her the proper way to sit, to talk, and to walk. George, who had instructed her on the finer points of theater and music and books. Books Joan knew Evelyn hated, but books she read nonetheless. What burdened Joan the most, however, was that Evelyn had expressed her joy that God had answered her prayers through George. That she would not live out her days as a farmer's wife, struggling. Always struggling. Or forever sad, as her mother had become.

Over the months, Betty had managed to reestablish a fairly decent relationship with her parents. Although she didn't take the train to Highland Park *every* weekend, she managed *most* of them.

She and her mother had even gone out for dinner and a movie a few times in the middle of the workweek. Missing her own mother the way she did, Joan felt a certain satisfaction on Betty's behalf regarding the relationship mend.

Magda had mainly returned to her room. When she wasn't working for Olson during the day, she worked diligently on her own manuscript, privately, at night. Sometimes, when only she and Joan were at the apartment, Joan managed to cajole her into reading a few pages aloud. When Magda finished, Joan praised her appropriately. "I've loved to read my whole life," she told her once. "And I don't believe I've ever read anything quite as good as your work, Magda."

She meant every word of it too.

Inga, on the other hand, continued to sulk and bemoan her new route with the airline, threatening on a weekly basis to quit, but never carrying through. From April until the end of October, when the air turned chilly and the scent of home fires burning wafted through the evening air, Inga carried with her a dark cloud of misery.

One brisk November evening, however, the tide turned. While Joan and Magda sat in the living room, listening to music on the Philco and talking about Magda's next literary move, which was to show her manuscript to her boss, Barry Cole, Inga burst through the front door—nearly scaring Joan half to death.

Inga dropped her luggage at her feet and sang out, "I'm returning to LA! Frank Martindale, here I come!"

Betty interrupted her scramble around the kitchen to throw a simple dinner together and ran out to join them after the announcement. She ran the palms of her hands along the frilly bib apron she wore. "Well, thank the good Lord. Maybe now you'll stop being such a gloomy Gloria."

Inga grabbed Betty by the shoulders and drew her close for a dramatic hug, and Joan laughed as she did. "Oh, Betty. You'd be gloomy too if you loved someone like Frank only to not see him for months on end. To only hear his voice from the long wire of a telephone, never knowing for certain if he's alone or with another woman."

Joan crossed her arms. "If I had to worry as to whether or not he's with another woman, I'm not sure I'd *want* to talk to him on the phone."

Inga straightened, angling her chin toward Joan and her sister. "This, coming from someone who doesn't even date."

Joan chose to remain silent, waiting until Inga had walked down the hall to the bedroom she shared with Betty. The truth was she'd rather remain dateless than to worry about a man who might date other women simultaneously.

Betty pointed to her watch. "Dinner in ten," she said and returned to the kitchen.

"I wonder when she flies back west again," Joan asked Magda.

"Can't be too soon for me," Magda remarked with a toss of her hair. She reached for the manuscript she'd laid between them when Inga had walked in. "So you *really* think I should show this to Mr. Cole?"

"Absolutely," Joan said, nodding. "First thing. Tomorrow."

Magda went about her usual early morning duties, readying Mr. Cole's office for his arrival and striving to keep her nerves at bay. When she sat at her desk and Mr. Cole hadn't yet come in, she closed her eyes and offered up a prayer. "I believe you gave me this talent," she whispered, "not to hide under a basket but to use appropriately. I only ask that you give me a chance, if that is your will."

The door opened and she jerked. Barry Cole stood there, looking nearly as startled as she felt. "Did I scare you, Miss Christenson?" he asked with a smile. "Were you sleeping on the job already?"

"Oh, no, sir. I was just pra—I, um—" She straightened her shoulders. "Mr. Cole?"

Her boss closed the door behind him. "What is it, Miss Christenson? You look positively petrified."

She tried to laugh, but it only came as a cough. "I have . . . a little something I . . . I wrote, Mr. Cole." She drew in a deep breath and said the rest quickly before she could change her mind: "And-I'm-wondering-if-you-would-mind-looking-at-it." She blinked. "Sir."

He chuckled. "Why, Miss Christenson. I had no idea." He moved to the front of her desk, his hat still on his head and his briefcase hanging from his right hand. "Of course. I'd be happy to." He grinned down at her.

Magda reached into the bottom drawer, where she'd hidden her purse and the manila envelope holding evidence of her months of hard work. She brought it out, extending it to him. "Only if you have time, Mr. Cole."

He took it. "I look forward to it, Miss Christenson." He started toward his office door. "Well, then. I suppose I should get my day started."

"Yes, sir," she said. "You have a nine o'clock with Mr. Van-Michaels."

"His office or mine?" Mr. Cole asked.

"His, sir."

"Ah." He smiled again, calming her nerves. "Then I'd best get to it."

Inga could hardly believe her good fortune. Just the day before she'd been told she'd return to the Chicago-to-LA route, and that morning her supervisor called instructing her to pack her bags and be ready for an early afternoon flight. She hadn't even minded being awakened by the neighbor pounding on the door to tell her she had a call waiting for her in the building's hallway.

As soon as she'd hung up, she placed a long-distance call to California to let Frank know she'd arrive that evening. That they could have dinner together. And that another picnic in the hills could be marvelous.

The phone rang several times before his roommate mumbled a sleepy hello.

She looked at her watch. It was not quite nine o'clock in Chicago, which meant the seven o'clock chime had yet to ring in LA. "Oh. Sorry," she said. "Mitch, this is Inga Christenson calling for Frank."

"What time is it?" She pictured him, dark hair tussled, eyes barely open, standing in his pajamas in the small living room of their apartment.

"Not quite seven. Again, I'm sorry, but can you please call Frank to the phone?"

A slow exhale met her ear. "He's not here, for crying out loud. Call later. He should be back before work." With that, he ended the call.

Inga hung up, both puzzled and startled. If it wasn't quite seven in California, where on earth would Frank be? A sudden, sickening feeling came over her, and she tightened her robe as she padded back to her apartment only a few feet away. Closing the door, she laid her forehead against it, pressing in, trying not to think about the obvious. Frank . . . *Frank with another woman.*

Their night overlooking the city came back to her, the way he had laid her on the blanket. The tenderness with which he had kissed her. The words he used to tell her that he wanted more. So much more.

And she'd said no.

She turned, resting her shoulders against the door and squeezing her eyes shut. "Well, no more," she said. If a real woman of the world was what Frank wanted, then a real woman of the world she'd become.

"Tonight," she said decidedly, then started toward the bedroom . . . her uniform . . . and an empty suitcase to pack. "Tonight," she said again, her hand gripping the doorframe to the empty bedroom. "I won't lose you to another woman, Frank Martindale," she spoke into the room as if he could hear her from wherever he now lay. *With whomever.* "Not to my mother's silly rules of chastity, least of all. I'm not losing my future. Not like *this*."

Excitement reigned at the Callahan Agency that late October day as the company prepared to roll out the new campaign for Supreme Soups. The company's president, Mr. Clinton, was expected to arrive in the building's boardroom at any moment along with a number of his high-ranking executives. Joan had prepared the room to look more like an intimate restaurant. For the better part of the last half hour, while Joan made sure their hired waitstaff readied themselves, Pat Callahan had worked feverishly on getting the presentation board ready. Joan glanced to the front of the room and watched him fidget for a few moments before she stepped forward to help in any way she could.

"Nothing like a million-dollar account to drive a man crazy, is there, Joan?" Pat asked her with a laugh.

She shooed him away from the giant easel. "Why don't you go back to the office for any last-minute details and I'll finish up here."

He sighed as he gave her his best little-boy-lost look. "Thank you, Joan. You're a godsend."

He was halfway out of the room when she called his name and he turned back to look at her.

"My roommate Betty is coming by tonight after work. She and I are going to do the most unusual thing of having dinner out on a Friday night. Would you care to join us?"

His eyes flashed with mirth. "Are you fixing me up, Joan?"

Joan crossed her arms. "Actually, I am." She walked toward him. "You and Betty would be quite perfect for each other. You have similar backgrounds. You're both from prominent families. And you're both a lot of fun. I can't imagine two people being more perfect for each other, actually."

He paused, appearing to ponder the idea. "Well, I'm not seeing anyone," he said with a wink. "And I'm assuming she isn't seeing anyone either."

"In the entire time I've known Betty, she hasn't had a single *serious* date. Which I don't quite understand. She's *beautiful*."

He nodded, took one step away, then looked at Joan again. "Then you've got yourself a date." He started to walk away, stopped, and raised an index finger. "Does *she* know about this?"

Joan shook her head. "Not even a hint. Let's just say you wormed your way into an invitation after our soup du jour presentation went so well."

Pat roared with laughter. "Deal," he said, and he glanced at his watch. "All right. I'll be back in fifteen minutes, ready to roll."

Joan waited until he was well out of sight before dashing to the conference room phone and dialing the number for Hertz. The switchboard had picked up the call, and she asked for Betty Estes, then waited until Betty's voice came through the line. "Mr. Ferguson's office. Betty Estes speaking. How may I help you?"

"The question is," Joan teased, "how I may help *you*."

"Joanie. What are you up to? Isn't your big 'The only thing

better is a night out on the town' presentation supposed to start any minute?"

"It is. Pat is on his way upstairs for last-minute details and—I was thinking—why don't you and I celebrate tonight at Pollywog? Dinner's on me."

"Goodness. You are in a celebratory mood if you're volunteering to pay. What time?"

"Five thirty?"

"See you then," she said.

Joan hung up the phone with a smile, knowing she'd finally come up with the perfect way to pay her flatmate back for the use of her cream-colored suit.

CHAPTER 26

Betty said good-bye to Evelyn at the office before heading to the downtown restaurant Joan had suggested for dinner. When she didn't spot Joan, Betty turned to the host and said, "I'll take a seat at one of the tables, if you don't mind."

"Certainly, miss," he told her, then led the way to one of the many vacant white-linen-draped tables near the back of the room.

Betty pulled off her gloves and placed them in her pocketbook before setting it at her feet. She looked up just as the front door opened and Joan stepped in. Directly behind her, a decidedly tall and incredibly handsome man allowed the door to close against his back. Betty waggled her fingers Joan's way and Joan did the same.

Betty watched her friend speak to the stranger before the two indicated to the host that they were Betty's dining companions. It only took a moment as they strolled toward her for realization to shower over Betty. *Pat Callahan.*

"Well, for the love of pete," she said under her breath. She smiled broadly as they reached the table.

"Betty," Joan said immediately, her voice laced with hope. "I'd like to introduce you to my—to Mr. Pat Callahan." She looked at Pat, her face practically glowing with anticipation. "Pat, *this* is

Betty Estes, whom I'm sure you've heard me talk about dozens of times."

When Betty extended her hand for a shake Pat took it, squeezing gently. "I've looked forward to this, Miss Estes."

Betty squeezed back. "Please. Call me Betty." She waited until the host helped Joan to her chair and announced that their waiter would be with them shortly. She turned then to Pat, sitting at her left. "So, Pat, *exactly* how many times has my good friend Joanie talked about me?" She pulled a breadstick from a short glass in the center of the table and waved it around. "Ballpark."

"Oh, dear," Joan said, looking about as though trying to find an exit.

Pat laughed heartily. "Well, let's see . . . She mentioned you around eleven this morning. Maybe eleven thirty. Again at—" he looked at his watch, which brought a smile to Betty's lips—"I'd say around three. And she pretty much talked about you nonstop from the office to the restaurant. All totaled, I'd give the Betty references a total of more than five and less than ten."

Joan covered her mouth with a gloved hand, then dropped it. "I've been had."

Betty eyed Pat playfully. "I'd say *we* have, wouldn't you?"

The three laughed together as their waiter arrived to fill their water goblets and to take their drink orders. He handed each of them a menu and rattled off the evening's specials before leaving the conversation to pick up where Betty had left it.

Pat spoke first. "Well, maybe *we* have," he said, "but I'll tell you this much, Betty. Everything Joan said about your beauty was exact and honest."

Heat rose to her face. "Why thank you, Mr. Callahan. And you are every bit as gallant as Joan has previously indicated."

Again they laughed. Joan pulled off her gloves as her eyes

danced between the two of them. "Okay, you two. Have your fun, but quite honestly, I can't imagine two people getting along more famously than you. In fact—" she dropped both gloves into one hand and waved toward the front of the room—"I don't know why I don't just leave you here to dine alone. I'll practically be a fifth wheel at this meal."

Pat pointed to her. "Leave and you're fired," he said, adding a wink. Then he smiled at Betty. "Not that I find dining with you alone—just the two of us—to be burdensome, Miss Estes."

Warmth ran through Betty's veins, pulsating all the way to where her heart beat inside her chest. "Why, I believe that's one of the nicest things anyone has said to me in some time," she said, meaning every word. She looked from Pat to Joan, who beamed in the chair to the right of her.

A second later, their waiter returned with their drinks, and as Pat gave the toast to new friendships, Betty knew that a page in the book of her life had been unexpectedly turned.

Joan could hardly wait for the weekend to come to an end and for Betty to return home. She had hardly been there since early Saturday morning. Evidence of her late-night arrival on Saturday remained in the kitchen sink on Sunday morning, but other than that, neither Joan, Evelyn, nor Magda had seen or heard from her.

By Sunday evening, as the three flatmates gathered in the living room to listen to *The Big Show*, Joan's frazzled nerves caused her to wonder if she'd made the right decision, putting the two of them together.

"So, what do you think, Joan?" Magda asked as she tuned the radio to the right station. "Do you think Mr. Cole will have looked at my manuscript by tomorrow morning?"

Joan had forgotten all about Magda's manuscript. "When did you give it to him?" she asked, sitting on the sofa and tucking her legs under her.

Evelyn, dressed in a fashionable pair of pink matador pants and matching sweater, sat in the chair across from her. She carried the latest fashion magazine she'd purchased from the local five-and-dime—one, no doubt, George had insisted she study. "What manuscript?" she asked.

The radio crackled to life as *The Big Show*'s announcer said, *"And here is your hostess . . . the glamorous . . . the always unpredictable . . . Tallulah Bankhead."*

"Tell you later," Magda said, hurrying to sit next to Joan.

"You know there are weeks when we have the most handsome, the most divine men on this show," Tallulah Bankhead began, *"and then again there's* this *week."* The studio audience laughed and the three roommates chuckled with them. *"This week we have a real meatball, Jack Carter."*

As Jack and Tallulah began their shtick, Joan glanced at Evelyn, who flipped quietly through the magazine. *Double duty,* she thought. Poor lamb couldn't even enjoy the show without trying to please a man who hadn't bothered to take her to dinner that evening. Joan looked at Magda, who frowned in unison as Jack Carter started the opening lyrics to "Peg o' My Heart."

The front door opened and all three turned toward it.

Betty stepped in, smiling contentedly. "Hello, girls."

Joan jumped from her seat to turn the radio's volume down as Miss Bankhead introduced James Mason and his wife, Pamela. She swung around to face Betty. *"Well?"*

"He's to die for," she said with a smile, closing the door behind her. "A dream in every sense of the word." She sighed. "I can't say I'm in love—not yet—but I will tell you all that I'm so fully in . . .

something . . . I can hardly imagine what tomorrow will be like. Not seeing him." She sat on the arm of Evelyn's chair and pulled the magazine from between her fingers. "George have you reading this?"

"Stop it, Betty," Evelyn answered with a pout. "Concentrate on your own romance, why don't you?"

Betty cupped Evelyn's chin in her hand. "You're right. You are absolutely right." She stood, casting her attention on Joan. "I want a full report tomorrow night. Every word—every single word—he tells you. Leave nothing out."

Joan felt her grin draw her cheeks taut. "I promise, Betts. Every word." She clapped her hands. "Yay," she exclaimed.

"Well," Betty said with another sigh. "I'm exhausted." She pointed to the radio. "Enjoy the show without me tonight. I'm going to bed."

She'd hardly made it halfway down the hall when the front door opened again and Joan turned to see a somewhat haggard-looking Inga step inside.

Magda leapt up. "What happened to you?" she asked, then crossed the room and took her sister's suitcase from her hand.

"Nothing. Don't ask me anything."

Betty reentered the room. "You look like you've lost your last nickel, kiddo."

"I lost something, all right," Inga mumbled, then waved her staring roommates away. "I need sleep."

"Inga," Magda whispered. *"What happened?"*

Inga gave her sister a harsh look, one that cut into Joan's heart. Never had any of her sisters treated her as poorly as Inga often did Magda. "Nothing for you to concern yourself with." She looked at Betty. "I'm going to bed."

"I'm right behind you," Betty said, taking the luggage from Magda.

Joan waited until Inga had closed the bedroom door behind her before she smiled weakly at Magda. "Don't worry, little sis. She'll be all right. Whatever it is."

Magda arrived at work earlier than usual the next morning, her nerves heightened. She'd hardly slept, imagining every scenario that might come her way when Mr. Cole entered the office. Would he look her directly in the eye and declare her the most amazing writer he'd ever had the pleasure of reading? Or would he avert his eyes, a sure indication that he'd hated every word? Every jot and tittle?

She had gotten halfway through sorting the morning mail when he strolled in. He removed his hat and smiled at her, bringing a wave of relief.

"I daresay," he began. He stopped as she looked into his eyes, knowing full well they begged him for anything that might quench her discomfort. Even if it was bad news.

He cleared his throat, shutting the door behind him and then walking to her desk. "I daresay that your work is beyond what I imagined it would be." He smiled.

A rush of air blew from her lungs. "Really?" she asked, pressing her hand against her chest.

"Miss Christenson . . ." He paused, looking over to his office door, which she'd left open not five minutes earlier. "Can you come into my office, please? Let's talk for a moment about . . . well, what I see as your future."

Magda stood so quickly she almost stumbled, then—at Mr. Cole's insistence—walked ahead of him into the room, already bright with sunlight and permeated by the rich aroma of brewed coffee.

"Please sit in one of the chairs," he said, indicating one of the two across from his desk.

She pointed to the wet bar. "Can I get you a cup of coffee?" she asked. "It's ready."

He dropped his briefcase onto the desk. "I'd like that. Make one for yourself as well."

She bit back a smile, forcing herself to take on a wholly professional stance, even as she placed his cup of coffee in front of him.

Magda took her seat, her cup rattling in its saucer. She took a deep breath followed by a slow sip of coffee, then sighed. "So, you liked it, Mr. Cole?"

He took a sip of his own coffee as he raised an index finger. "First," he said after swallowing, "can we drop the 'Mr. Cole' business? I know it's professional, and I appreciate it. I do, but—" he took a moment to pull the manila envelope holding her manuscript from his briefcase—"I think you and I are about to become more than just boss and secretary." He blushed at his own words. "I don't mean that disrespectfully."

Magda smiled, hoping it looked natural. "Mr.—Barry. I have spent a lot of time on that manuscript, and . . ." She gulped back a giggle. "Hearing that you like it means so much to me. More than I can say."

"What do you hope to do with this, Magda? And may I call you by your given name?"

Magda blinked back tears. Everything she had hoped for . . . everything she had dreamed of . . . right here, coming from the mouth of a man she admired and respected. "Yes, sir. Of course you may."

He opened his mouth to say something, but as he did the phone on Magda's desk rang. "Oh, dear," she said. She stood, placing her cup of coffee on his desk. "I'll be right back." She dashed into her office to answer the call. Thirty seconds later, she had placed the caller on hold and poked her head into Barry's office. "It's Mr. VanMichaels."

Barry sighed in obvious disappointment. He stood, reaching for the phone, but without pressing the line button. "Magda?" he asked as she turned to leave.

"Yes, sir?"

"Ahhh—tell you what. This day isn't going to get any better, I'm afraid."

She'd looked at his calendar earlier. He spoke the truth; that much was for sure. "Yes, sir."

"How about if you and I grab something to eat? Tonight after work? I'd suggest lunch but . . ." He pointed to the desk calendar. "I'm already booked."

The joy she'd felt not sixty seconds earlier dissipated at the sound of his words. A married man, asking her to dinner? Were they all like this? Every man in publishing? Like Harlan had been? *I'll help you, baby, but first let's have dinner and* . . . And what? A casting aside of all virtue and goodness?

"Mr. VanMichaels is waiting, Mr. Cole," she said as professionally as her quaking voice allowed.

Barry Cole appeared genuinely puzzled. "Miss Christenson?"

She closed the door on his question, turning instead to stare at the red blinking light of line one until it stopped.

He'd taken the call.

She opened the desk's bottom drawer, retrieved her purse, and walked out the door, closing it gently behind her.

CHAPTER 27

The instant Joan walked into the office on Monday morning, Pat Callahan astonished her by leaping onto his desk and shouting, "Top of the morning to you, Joan Hunt!" He flung out his arms and jumped back down, landing in front of his desk. "Is it a grand day or isn't it?"

Falling back on her father's Irish brogue, she said, "'Tis, Mr. Callahan. 'Tis."

"Ha-ha-ha." Pat encircled her with his powerful arms and swung her around. When he finally stopped, he looked into her upturned face. "I could kiss you, I could. In fact, I think I will." He planted wet kisses on both cheeks and Joan swerved. "We Callahan men have that effect on women," he teased.

She pointed to the sofa. "I think I'll sit for a moment, if you don't mind."

Pat Callahan was nothing if not vivacious. Full of life and vigor. But she'd never seen him quite so . . . animated. He led her to the cushioned security of the leather couch before darting over to the wet bar. "I'll get you something to drink."

"But that's *my* job," she said, resting her fingertips against the hollow of her throat.

Pat laughed again, loud and raucous. "Consider it my thank-you."

Joan placed her head in her hands. The sound of coffee sloshing into café-style mugs traveled across the room. She peered through splayed fingers as Pat walked over carrying two cups, curls of steam rising above them. She straightened and smiled, taking the proffered mug from him. "I take it you had a good weekend."

Pat sat in the same chair he'd occupied during her interview. "Betty didn't tell you?" For the briefest of moments, a look of concern skipped over his face, then retreated. "Of course she did. You gals have a way of sticking together. Telling each other everything."

She shook her head. "Not this time."

Her boss leaned back in his chair, stretching his long legs out and crossing them at the ankles. He stared at the ceiling. "My *gosh*, Joan, but she's a keeper." He intensified his gaze. "Don't you think she's a keeper?"

Joan nodded.

Pat bolted up. Then he laughed. "I sound like a high school boy, Joanie. Do you hear me? A high school boy."

She had to laugh with him. "I suppose that's what . . . *liking* someone a lot . . . does to you."

"Liking? No, no, Joan. I'm in love. Didn't she tell you?" He placed his mug on the coffee table as he stood, then stepped behind his chair. "Thank you, thank you," he shouted, raising his hands to God before planting them on his hips. "God is good, lassie," he said, drawing on his own Irish heritage. "God is good."

"Yes, he is."

Pat gripped the back of the chair with his long fingers and squeezed. "Ever been in love, Joan?"

She nearly choked on the swig of coffee she'd just taken. "Who, me?" She shook her head. "No. And not planning on it. At least, no time soon."

Pat leaned over. "You just haven't met the right man yet." He winked. "No broken hearts back in England?"

"Goodness, no," she said. "Who had time for such frivolity? I've kept my focus on work since I was old enough to gather scraps for Mr. Higginbottom's pigs."

Pat's laughter filled the room to all eight of its corners. "Mr. *Who*?"

"That was part of the long version of my story," she reminded him. "You know, the one you said to skip the day you hired me?" She pointed to the door leading to her outer office. "Speaking of which, I've got work waiting for me. . . ."

Pat's face sobered. He stepped to his desk and, leaning his backside against the front of it, crossed his arms. "Wait. You and Betty both. Such unique women, Joan. Modern. You enjoy working, don't you?"

"I'm not going to tell you I *don't* want the husband and the children and the suburban house. But . . ." She sighed, feeling the weight of the times on her shoulders.

"But?"

"You're right when you say that I *like* working." She laughed lightly. "Would you want Betty to work? If it went that far, I mean?"

He shook his head. "I can't say I would. I'd like to think I can provide for my wife and the kids, once there are kids."

Knowing Betty as well—or as little—as she did, Joan wondered how she'd feel about such a statement. She'd worked hard to reach her position at Hertz. Would she be willing to give it up for love and marriage, even to the charismatic Pat Callahan? "Well," she said, choosing her words carefully, "I guess we'll have to wait and see what life brings." She shifted again to her father's brogue. "Won't we, laddie?"

Pat Callahan roared with laughter again. "We will, lassie. We will."

Inga had the whole long day ahead of her to sleep. Eat. Listen to music or read a book. A whole long day. Alone.

As soon as quiet had settled in the apartment, she slipped out of bed, slid her feet into her moccasin-style house slippers, and padded into the kitchen wearing only her baby-blue cotton pajamas. The house held a chill, she decided. An unusual chill she didn't feel when the others were there. Or perhaps Betty had turned the heat down. The first part of November meant that the outside temperatures had dropped drastically from even a couple of weeks before. She crossed her arms tightly as she stepped into the kitchen to make a fresh pot of coffee. Once she'd gotten it started, she'd return to the bedroom for her robe.

She had no intention of dressing that day. The whole day she'd spend in her nightclothes. She'd nap and listen to the radio and flip through magazines, but she wouldn't dress.

Inga ran water into the percolator, then scooped coffee into the basket before pushing the top down and plugging it in. It sighed instantly. Within seconds, the gurgling began. Like clockwork.

She trekked back into the bedroom, pulled her robe from the end of the bed, and shoved her arms into it. She caught sight of herself in the dresser's mirror and frowned, stepping closer to the reflection.

Did she look different? She raked her hair with her nails—painted strawberry red, the way her supervisor demanded. Look the part, act the part, *be* the part . . .

Her fist came down on the dresser, rattling the crystals in the small lamps. The trinket boxes shifted. "Oh," she moaned. "What have I done? What have I done?"

It had been so easy. Too easy. And she'd been such a fool, thinking that Frank would feel for her the way she felt for him. That the "morning after" would hold tender kisses and promises of forever after. Instead, he'd acted like what they'd done the night before was the most casual thing in the world. Another night, another conquest. And instead of talking about their tomorrows—their *years* of happily ever after—he'd scoffed when she mentioned their future.

"What are you talking about?" he'd asked her. "You think *that* was the seal to the deal? Blimey, no. Not out here, sweetheart. If that's what you thought . . ." And then he'd brightened. "But hey," he said, throwing his arms wide. "What a ride, huh? We had some fun, didn't we? Well, didn't we?"

Inga tied the sash of her robe tight around her waist—tighter than necessary—then returned to the kitchen, where the aroma of fresh-brewed coffee filled the air. Almost warming it. She removed a cup and saucer from the sink's drainer and poured a cup, nearly to overflowing, then walked into the living room.

Two weeks, she figured. Three at the most. Two weeks and she'd know if her foolishness of one night would cost her a lifetime of regret. She took a long sip of the coffee, nearly spilling it as the door behind her opened.

Inga turned to see her sister marching into the room. "What are you doing home?" she asked.

"I quit my job," Magda said, her voice filled with defiance. "And I'm never going back."

Joan decided to take a long walk around the Loop during her lunch hour, nibbling on a sandwich and sipping a soft drink from the Automat. She glanced into shop windows, taking in the displays. Around her, Chicago hummed its usual lunchtime tune. Traffic, both pedestrian and automotive, buzzed by, the noise of it rising around the buildings, rattling the windows, and knocking on the doors.

She stopped in front of one and then another until nearly time to turn around and return to the Callahan Agency. She crossed the street with a parade of others, turned left, and started back down the sidewalk in front of a different set of windows. She merely glanced at these—her time now short—until one in particular caught her eye. The placard posted in the far-bottom corner read:

Do You Want to Work in Europe?
Tests to qualify for overseas positions
with the U.S. government
will be held at 9:00 a.m. this Saturday.
Come inside to register.

An unexpected wave of nostalgia and longing for England washed over her. For her mother's cooking, her father's laughter, and the constant "picking at" between her siblings and herself. She missed being close enough to visit them whenever she wanted. She missed their voices. And this sign, Joan realized, could be a ticket. A way not necessarily to Leigh, but closer to England.

Joan stepped to an outside trash can wrapped in fluted wrought-iron bars, depositing the wax paper that had covered her sandwich and the now-empty Dixie cup decorated with funny-looking leaves. Squaring her shoulders, she walked to the storefront door, opened it with purpose, and entered.

The room was plainer than that of the first floor at the Hertz building, something she would have found hard to imagine without actually seeing it firsthand. Government-issue desks and filing cabinets, bulky phones, and gray-metal Royal typewriters were the only items visible by way of office decor. If one could call it "decor."

A young, uniformed man—baby-faced and scrubbed clean—sat behind the desk just inside. "May I help you?" he asked, looking up.

Joan pointed to the sign. "I'm here to register."

His eyes followed the path of her finger. "You're interested in going overseas? To Europe?" He opened the top-right drawer and removed a form, then slid it across the uncluttered desk toward Joan.

"I am." She looked at the form, then back to the young man.

"You're from . . ."

"Chicago. I live on Greenleaf out in the . . ." *Oh.* "You mean originally?"

He smiled, his hazel eyes twinkling. "Yes, ma'am."

"Leigh, Lancashire, England."

An easy wince crossed his face, then fled. "And you're sure you want to go to Germany?"

"Why wouldn't I be?"

"You're British, ma'am. You'd be considered . . ." His voice trailed.

"More of an enemy than the Americans?" Joan finished for him.

"Well, yeah." He cleared his throat. "Yes, ma'am."

She pressed her lips together and looked back at the sign.

Do You Want to Work in Europe?

Even reversed, the words stirred something inside, like a God whisper in her ear.

Joan returned her gaze to the young uniformed officer and picked up the form. "Do I just fill this out?"

"Yes, ma'am. But you can take it with you. Bring it back on Saturday."

Joan started for the door, but not before getting the final word. "And just so you know . . ." She focused her eyes on his. "I'm an American."

What would have been Magda's lunch hour had nearly come and gone, and so far, Barry Cole hadn't bothered to even call the number on her résumé. The one that corresponded to the phone in the hallway.

She'd listened for the ring since returning home, hardly moving from the living room chair nearest the door. But the phone never rang.

"You're crazy," Inga said before huffing down the hall to her room.

"What's wrong with *you*?" Magda hollered back, just as a knock came at the front door.

She whirled out of the chair, stumbling over her slippered feet, then grabbed the handle and jerked the door open. Barry Cole stood there facing her, framed by the door and draped in his overcoat.

"Mr. Cole," she breathed out.

"Magda—Miss Christenson."

"What are you doing here?" She took a step forward, forcing him to take one back, then another until they stood in the center of the narrow hallway.

"Can I talk to you?" he asked.

She pointed to the outside door. "Let's go stand on the sidewalk," she said.

"Can you tell me," he began when they were halfway up the

steps, then paused until they reached the open sidewalk. "Can you tell me *why* you left? Did I say something to offend you?"

She crossed her arms against the chill in the air. He immediately removed his coat and draped it around her. "Mr. Cole," she said, shivering in spite of the warmth from his body within the fabric. "You're a married man. Why would you ask me to dinner? Even to discuss my manuscript, which is something I dearly want to see published, but not . . . not with *that* price tag."

His eyes widened as he looked around, as though an answer to their dilemma might come dashing down the street and leap into his arms. "Married? Is that what you think? You think I was asking you out for ulterior motives?"

"Well, you *are* married."

"No—I—" He looked down at his hand, to the band of gold gleaming in the post-noonday sunlight, filtered by the cold. "This," he said, flashing it at her. "I never . . . I never told you?"

"Told me what?"

"Miss Christenson, my wife . . . my wife has been . . . my wife *died* some years back. She contracted meningitis when Deanne was seven and Douglas was nine. She died within a week."

Magda's hand flew to her mouth as she gasped. "Oh, Mr. Cole. I'm so—I didn't know. I—" She thought over the things he'd said about his wife several months ago. That she sang like an angel. That the photo of them and the children had been taken years previous. "When I asked you about the photo . . . Why didn't you tell me then?"

"I suppose I thought you knew," he said. He placed his hat back on his head. "Miss Christenson, please forgive me for not telling you. It's not a conversation that comes easily, as you can imagine. I've not ever taken my ring off because . . . well, partly because I'm trying not to rush things with the children and partly because

I don't want any wrong ideas in the office. Most of the people at Olson know, but I *do* have to meet with women from time to time—even at dinner parties and the like—and I try to keep everything aboveboard."

"Of course you do." Regret for questioning him welled up inside her. "I'm so, so sorry."

"Then you'll come back to work? Today?"

Magda darted down the steps, then back up again, removing his coat as she did. "Here, Mr. Cole. Um—Barry. I'll go grab my coat and purse and . . . we'll take the train back into the city together." She placed her hands on his arm. "Again, I'm so sorry." She started back down the stairs, turning halfway. "And, Barry? I'd love to have dinner with you tonight."

CHAPTER 28

Evelyn counted the minutes until Joan came home from her work at David & DuRand. The official-looking letter propped against her roommate's pillow mocked her, tempting her to rip it open. To see what lay inside the large manila envelope, packed thick and mysterious.

She was alone that evening, and as such, the torture had become nearly too great. If Betty had been there instead of off on another date with Pat Callahan, they could stare at it together. Then, when the temptation became too great, Betty would place her hand on Evelyn's and say, "Now, now. A lady never reads another lady's correspondence."

Or perhaps if Magda had been home instead of working *again* with Mr. Cole on her manuscript . . . No. Lately, Magda's nights were spent holed up in her room, typing on the portable typewriter he'd sent her home with. She would be no help at all.

Inga, of course, had become less agreeable over the past few weeks than anyone Evelyn had ever known. Even if Inga *were* at the apartment, Evelyn wasn't sure she'd want to share the agony of not knowing the contents of the envelope. Or share anything else with her, really.

That left only her, then, to bring in the mail that afternoon and to occasionally glance up from her French lesson book to eyeball it.

She sat up straight on the bed, legs crisscrossed, and wore thick pajamas and wool socks in an effort to ward off the cold. Her book lay open on the bed in front of her and she bent over it. "*Un*, *deux*, *trois*, *quatre*—" The front door opened before she could get to *cinq*, and she scrambled off the bed. "Joanie?"

"Yes?" Joan called back.

Evelyn met her in the entryway. "Oh, good." She helped Joan out of her coat.

"Where is everyone?" Joan asked, opening the closet door and pulling out a wooden hanger. She took the coat from Evelyn and hung it up, then draped her purse on one of the hooks inside the door.

"Betty is out with Pat."

Joan raised a finger as she closed the closet door. "*That* I knew."

"And Magda is with her boss."

Joan linked her arm with Evelyn's and proceeded to walk down toward their room. "I think a budding romance may be in the works, Evelyn."

"Do you?"

Joan nodded. "I think her excitement is becoming more about Barry Cole than whatever short story they are working on together."

Evelyn squeezed her arm as they entered their bedroom. "You have a letter on the bed there," she said, nodding toward it. "Very official looking. Something from the US government."

She tried to act nonchalant about it but knew she had failed by the look on Joan's face.

"Oh." Joan stared across the room to the letter.

"What is it, Joanie?" She returned to the bed, closing her French book.

"Are you done for the night?" Joan asked her, moving slowly to the dresser to remove her hat and gloves.

Evelyn shook her head. "No. Before class tomorrow night I'm supposed to be able to count to twenty. I've only gotten as far as fifteen."

Joan shrugged. "That's only five more numbers. You'll get it." She sat in the chair to work her nylons from her legs. "Evelyn, are you *sure* about this? I mean, taking French just to please George."

"Oui, oui," she answered, giggling. "George's mother says I'll never learn—I can tell she doesn't like me anyway—but I'm determined," she said, holding up a finger, "that, by Christmas, I'll be able to carry on a conversation with their cousin who is coming all the way from Paris for the holiday."

"Well," Joan said with a wink, "at least you'll be able to count with her."

Evelyn grabbed the envelope. "Ha-ha, Joan." She waved it in the air. "Come on. I'm dying to know what's in here."

Joan stood to take it, staring at it as if it held top-secret information. She tapped her other hand with it a couple of times before sighing. "It's either a letter of acceptance or a letter of rejection," she said. "From the weight of it, I'd say it's a letter of acceptance."

Evelyn sat up straighter. "Acceptance to what?"

"To work in Germany for the next two years. With the US Forces."

Evelyn wilted. "What? You're leaving?"

"If this is what I think it is, then . . . yes." She sat on the bed beside Evelyn. "Don't you see, Evelyn? It'll get me closer to my family, even if only for two years."

"But . . . but what about me? You'd leave me here?"

Joan patted her shoulder. "You'll be in good hands."

"You mean George's?"

Joan coughed out laughter. "I mean Betty's."

They stared at each other for a moment until Evelyn said, "Open it, Joanie." She watched, hardly blinking, as Joan tore into the envelope, pulled out a thick stack of papers, and read the top page. "Well?"

Joan looked up with a half smile. "Looks like come January I'm heading to Germany."

Magda treasured every moment she spent with Barry Cole, especially the extra ones that came after hours. In spite of her resolve not to do so, she'd become quite fond of him, his ability to get her published notwithstanding.

At least twice a week he'd asked her to dinner to talk and he always managed to keep it on course. But occasionally—blessedly—he broke from their conversation about characters and plot to mention something about his family. Or to ask about hers.

This time, unlike with Harlan, she managed to keep her thoughts and opinions about Inga to herself, mentioning only that she had a sister and that her sister worked for an airline.

And then, with Thanksgiving only a few days away and as he walked her to the train station, he mentioned his daughter's program at their church, asking if Magda would like to accompany the family to see it. "Sunday night. Seven o'clock." He held his hat in his hand, not having bothered to put it on yet, and twirled it on its side as though he were anxious to get her answer.

"I'd love to come. Do you—" She stopped as they neared the platform, not wanting the evening to end. "Do you think they will be okay with it? Another woman, I mean—even your secretary—needling in on a family event?"

He placed the hat on his head, tugging at the brim. "I think,

Magda, that you know I'm beginning to feel that you are more than a secretary."

Her heart skipped inside her chest, nearly keeping time with the clackety-clack of one of the trains as it sped by, then screeched to a stop. "As a writer, then . . . ," she mumbled, hoping he could hear her over the noises around them—the train, the other travelers, the wind blowing in from Lake Michigan.

She pulled her coat tighter around her and he cupped her elbows with both gloved hands. "Magda," he said. "Look at me."

Magda raised her eyes slowly. Carefully. She didn't want to overstep her bounds, but she wanted—more than anything, she wanted . . .

Barry tipped his head as one index finger reached up to push the hat away from his forehead. He moved close to her face, beautifully close. She held her breath, closed her eyes, and waited . . . for hours . . . days. When their lips finally touched, sparks ignited like those under the El cars. He wrapped his arms around her, deepening the kiss as her hands gripped the sleeves of his coat and held on.

When the kiss ended, he crooked his fingers and tipped her chin, forcing her to look at him. "We'll have to do something about this, I know. I don't think company policy will allow us to work in the same office much longer. But until we can figure it all out—" he kissed her lightly again—"we'll just have to make do."

This time she nodded.

He looked toward the platform. "I've got to get you on your train," he said. "And get myself home before the kids' grandmother thinks I've abandoned them for good."

Magda laughed. His children. His mother-in-law. These people would be in her life soon. And she would be in theirs.

"I'll comc get you Sunday afternoon. Say four o'clock. We'll go out to dinner—all of us—to give you a chance to get to know everyone, and everyone to know you."

She smiled up at him. "Okay."

The light from the streetlamps illuminated his face. She searched his dark eyes. His handsome face. Everything about Barry Cole was gentle. Kind. Genuine.

"Where . . . where do you go to church?" she asked, mostly because she couldn't think of anything else to say, and she didn't want to say nothing at all.

"Lutheran Church of the Trinity," he said.

She grabbed his coat lapels. "You're Lutheran?"

His hands cupped her face, chilled by the wind. The aroma of leather and aftershave reached her nostrils and she breathed in deep, savoring it.

"I am," he said. "Is that a problem?"

Somehow—mostly with Henrietta's help—Inga had managed to steer clear of Frank during their overnights in LA. And somehow—maybe by her earnest prayer or just a stroke of luck—she'd been booked to work Thanksgiving Day. Spending the holiday at Uncle Casper and Aunt Greta's with Mor and Far and Magda hardly seemed . . . *festive*. Especially now, what with Magda beaming like a lighthouse and pirouetting from room to room, going completely gaga over her boss's *love* of her literary work. The way she carried on, one would think she had suddenly become the next best publication great since Jane Austen.

Then again, *if* she found herself forced to go—even for only an hour during the weekend—at least Magda's joy would divert their attention from her. *If* she had to go, with her sister beside her, they wouldn't notice the look in her eyes. Or the puffiness beneath them. And perhaps they wouldn't notice her lack of appetite.

Or that she was officially five excruciating days late in her menstrual cycle. If such a thing were possible to notice.

"When are you going to tell him?" Retta asked her as they jetted toward Los Angeles early that Thursday morning. They stood in the back galley, preparing snack trays for the passengers.

"Not until I know for sure," Inga answered. "And keep your voice down."

"Trust me, sweetie," Retta said with a smile, "no one can hear over these engines."

When *would* she tell Frank? Well, certainly not until she knew for sure. She'd made an appointment with a doctor downtown—one sure not to know that her real name wasn't Henrietta Swift—for the middle of December. A few days later, she'd know. And, within a few days after that, she'd have a plan. Something practical. Something doable. Something that involved wearing that white dress from Carson's.

Inga shook her head as she set a filled coffee carafe on a tray. Was the dress really all that important at a time like this?

If what she feared was true, Frank would surely do the honorable thing and marry her. Quietly, of course, even with her in a three-hundred-dollar dress. And, with her realizing the state of things so soon, they could pass off the early pregnancy as a blessing from God. Far and Uncle Casper would pat Frank on the back the way men do, acting like he'd done something macho. "Attaboy," they'd say, laughing.

She would blush appropriately. And she'd allow her mother and aunt to cluck about and send her maternity clothes and little baby booties sewn and knitted with love. She and Frank would live in California, of course, so when the baby came early—just a tad early—they'd pretend concern over its health and declare God's goodness again that the little tyke had managed to come into the world at a strong weight.

She gripped the tray and hoisted it to one arm.

What burdened her about the only scenario she'd been able to come up with as yet was the fact that she didn't *want* to marry Frank Martindale. Not now. Not after his flamboyant and ungentlemanly behavior. Like Retta said after the whole sordid affair, "You obviously weren't his first, sweetheart, and you won't be his last. With or without the gold ring."

Marriage to Frank would mean a lifetime of wondering. Watching. She'd question every appointment. Every phone call. Every late night at the office. It would be her penance, not only to her parents—whether they knew it or not—but to God. She'd acted like Ava Gardner, sultry and sexy, throwing herself at a playboy, when all she had ever really been was a simple girl from Minnesota. A girl who reached for the stars, and caught hold of nothing but a handful of sand.

CHAPTER 29

Thanksgiving Day had never spun Betty into such a tizzy before. Then again, she'd always spent the holiday with her mother and father. And Adela. Spending the day with the family of the most amazing man in the world was completely foreign to her.

And Betty didn't necessarily *like* "foreign."

"*Très agréable de vous rencontrer,*" Evelyn hammered out from across the hall.

Betty crossed the hall between the bedroom she shared with Inga and the one Evelyn shared with Joan, her heels click-clicking on the hardwood floor. "Oh for pity's sake, Evelyn," she said, leaning against the doorframe, twirling the back of a pearl earring into place.

Evelyn sat cross-legged in the chair between the bed and the dresser. She looked up and smiled. "That means 'Very happy to meet you.'"

Betty shook her head. "Only if you're in French class. Try this on for size—*enchantée.*"

"On-what?"

"That's how you say, 'Nice to meet you.' It means . . ." She waved her hand in the air and smiled. "Enchanted."

"Enchantée," Evelyn repeated, then pointed to the book in her lap. "But I *do* have to know how to say this for class." She switched gears and smiled. "You look pretty."

Betty turned once in the champagne-colored suit she'd somehow managed to save twelve dollars for. She tugged at the black velvet collar highlighted with rhinestones and imitation pearls with her thumbs and index fingers. "Sharp, no?"

"Magnifique."

"Très bien." She looked down the hall. "Where's Joan?"

Evelyn shrugged. "Bathroom, I think."

Betty crossed her arms. "Are you sure she'll be okay here alone today?"

Evelyn closed the book and tossed it to the sofa. "She says she will." She glanced at her watch. "I've got to get ready myself. George will be here in an hour."

Betty sighed. "So, how's that going?" She pointed to the book. "Besides your French classes."

Evelyn shoved her glasses up her nose. "He's paying me more attention these days."

"More attention than *what*?"

Evelyn frowned. "I know you don't think I know what I'm doing—"

"I *know* you don't know what you're doing. Evelyn—"

"But if everything goes as planned, Betty, I *believe* George *will* propose on Christmas Day, which is practically our anniversary, so it'll be perfect."

"Propose *what*?" Betty asked.

Evelyn giggled. "Oh, Betty," she said as Joan sidestepped Betty to enter the room.

"Oh, Betty, what?" Joan asked.

Betty shook her head with a groan. "Never mind. Hey, Joan, are you *sure* you're going to be okay alone here today? Pat *insisted* I bring you along if not."

Joan shook her head. "He did no such thing." She paused long enough for Evelyn to excuse herself and leave the room. "Besides," she continued, "you're meeting Pat's family for the first time. I'm not about to cut in on that."

Betty pressed her lips together. "Maybe you *should* come along. I might need the moral support."

"Don't be silly. If the family is *anything* like Pat, you'll be in the best possible hands."

As she'd done on every trip to George's childhood home, Evelyn sat in the passenger seat of George's car and gazed with wide eyes at the lawns and houses along the way. Especially the one she knew he lived in, the one he'd purchased a little over a year earlier "for a steal at fifteen thousand." The one he'd believed Betty would occupy as "lady of the house."

But Betty had turned him down. *Betty's loss,* Evelyn thought now, *became my gain.*

Evelyn tried to imagine herself in such a role, living with George . . . as his wife, of course. She'd never been inside the house—that wouldn't be proper—but she'd envisioned the various rooms. The nooks and crannies, the high ceilings, the spacious closets, the sun streaming through wide windows. She'd pictured their children running from room to room—toddlers to teenagers—as she and their father grew old together. Gray and happy. Until death did them part.

She sighed. "Such *joie de vivre,*" she whispered.

"What's that?" George asked from the driver's seat.

She looked at him with a smile, which he returned. Deeply. Genuinely.

Oh, Betty. You're so, so wrong about him. I just know you are.

"Nothing," she answered. Then she giggled. "Actually, I said *joie de vivre* without thinking about it." She laced her fingers together, then flexed them beneath the tan shortie gloves.

Evelyn frowned at the remembrance of how George had drilled her on glove etiquette. Her whole life she'd worn gloves and no one had ever told her there were rules. When to wear them, how to wear them, when to remove them, how to remove them.

Of course, until coming to Chicago and meeting George, she'd never been around anyone who would care whether she took her gloves off *before* sitting for dinner or *after* being seated. No one. So perhaps, she now reasoned, his instruction had been for a good cause.

"I guess the French classes are paying off," George said, "if you're speaking in French without thinking about it."

"Are you proud of me?" she asked, hope rising in her voice.

He didn't answer. Instead he concentrated on turning into his parents' driveway.

"George?"

He turned the key in the ignition to Off. "Hmm?"

"I asked if you were proud of me."

George turned to look at her, taking long seconds to answer. He ran a hand over his perfectly coiffed hair, then leaned toward her. "Yes, sweetheart. I'm proud of you." He rested his right arm along the back of the seat. "Come. Give me a kiss."

She complied. She always did whenever he asked . . . the few times he asked. And, as always, she felt sparks, and prayed he felt them as well.

"Let's go inside," he said after pulling away. He looked out the windshield and up the driveway. "Looks like Sandie and her family haven't gotten here yet."

Evelyn sighed, torn somewhere between frustration and contentment. "I look forward to seeing them again," she said. And she meant it. After all, this time next year, they'd be family.

She just *knew* it.

"You're awfully quiet," Pat said as they left his family home in Lake Forest, a near-one-hundred-year-old city located along the Lake Michigan shore just a few miles north of Betty's family home in Highland Park. "How about a penny for your thoughts?"

Betty adjusted her coat around her knees, tucking the hem under her to keep her legs warm. "I was just thinking that I had no idea you had such a large family."

Pat laughed easily. "You knew there were six of us kids." He released the steering wheel to point at her playfully. "And by the way, I want no less than that when my turn to be a father rolls around."

"Six, huh?" She forced a smile. "Be sure to let your wife know of your intentions *before* you propose."

He gripped the steering wheel at ten and two, his fingers flexing. Betty allowed her gaze to travel up the sleeve of the black wool overcoat until it reached his face. His green eyes held hers for the briefest of seconds before turning their attention back to the highway. "I just did."

Betty heard the words, but chose to ignore him. "I had no idea so *many* of your family would be there. Aunts. Uncles. Cousins." She threw up her hands. "You even had a set of grandparents on board."

"I take it you don't have a big family," he said.

Betty shifted to relieve the crick forming in her neck. "You know I'm an only child."

"What about your mother and father? Were they only children?"

"No, but there's not a lot to tell in that department either. I have a few aunts and uncles, but we don't gather together on holidays, I'm afraid."

"You don't?" Pat asked, as though the notion of absence during special days seemed nothing short of ludicrous.

"No," Betty said plainly, and she stared out the window. They neared home . . . and the end of what had proven to be a day of both gratitude and a troubling in her spirit. She'd appreciated the way Pat's family welcomed her into their home, but had felt ill at ease with how easily they'd drawn her into their family. "By the way," she said, tilting her chin, "your family home is lovely."

"I know," Pat said, winking. "You told my mother about a half-dozen times."

Betty shoved her arms together. "I did not."

"Sure you did. The first thing you said to my mother in our foyer was how *lovely* her home was. And then, throughout the day, you had something to say about *this* painting and *that* piece of furniture." He shook his head. "Quite frankly, lassie," he said, sounding—now she knew—exactly like his paternal grandfather, "I had no idea you knew of such things."

She chuckled. "That's because you don't know *my* mother."

He reached across the seat for her hand, squeezing it. "I'd like to change that, if you don't mind. With both your mother *and* your father."

Betty slid closer to him, resting her head on his shoulder. "I'd like that too." She sighed. "But first I'd better tell them about you."

The car bounced and rattled as Pat shifted it to the side of the road, where he slipped the gearshift to Park. Betty sat straight as he turned to her. "You haven't told them about me? But Betts, we've been exclusive for the last several weeks."

Betty laid her hand against Pat's cheek. Even with her glove on, she could feel the light, masculine stubble. "Weeks, darling. Not *months*."

He kissed her. "I knew after a *day*."

She rubbed her nose against his. "Knew what?" she asked, keeping her eyes down.

"That you were it for me, Betty Estes. You're the girl I've been waiting on—*gracious*. My whole life, I'd be willing to say."

Betty slid her arms around his broad shoulders and felt his strong ones as they embraced her as well. "I feel the same way, Pat. I do. But . . ."

He drew his face back, his neck forming an extra chin. "But?"

She slipped back into his arms. "But I think it might be time to tell you about a certain man named George Volbrecht."

Magda had tried on no fewer than six outfits before she settled on a simple, three-quarter-sleeved dress with a belted waist, light-flare skirt, and bow-shaped buttons from midbodice to the top of the V-neck. Upon inspection in the mirror, she thought the gentle green color gave her less of a vixen look and more of one that reflected maternal instinct.

She sighed. Perhaps that wasn't wise either.

A tap on her open bedroom door caused her to swirl in its direction. "Inga," she said, genuinely surprised by her sister's presence. She held her arms out at forty-five-degree angles from her body. "How do I look?"

Inga stepped in as though she were a chief inspector—arms

crossed, eyes set on their subject. "Mmm-hmm-mmm-hmm," she said, then looked to Magda's face. "Not too sexy. Not too matronly. I'd say you've made the right choice."

Magda released a pent-up breath. "Oh, good." She took Inga by the hands. "You're so much better at this than me."

A look of sadness—or was it regret?—crossed Inga's face, but only for the briefest moment. "I've had more practice," she said, her words gentle.

"Inga, are you all right?"

Tears shimmered in her eyes, but she nodded in spite of them. "Just tired from all the traveling I've done lately." She breathed in deeply and exhaled as though cleansing her body of something distasteful. "So nice to have a Sunday off."

Magda turned back to her dresser and reached into the trinket box in the center for the only pair of elegant earrings she owned—clip-on drop rhinestones shaped like daisies losing their first petal.

He loves me, she thought, remembering the childhood game she and Inga had played growing up. Their mother had called it "The Decision of the Flower" and had taught them to change "He loves me not" to "He loves me lots."

"That way," she'd said, smiling down at her cherub-faced daughters, "you are never without love."

Magda sighed as she slipped on her gloves.

"I have something for you," Inga said from behind her.

Magda half turned to see a simple one-strand pearl bracelet. Inga clasped it around her wrist, allowing it to fall beneath the glove's hemline. "So when you take off the gloves, you'll have something pretty to show off."

"Where'd you get this?" Magda breathed. "It's lovely."

Inga shrugged. "It was just a gift. No biggie."

Magda kissed her sister's cheek. "I'll be sure to get it back to you," she said as a knock at the front door reverberated through the apartment. Magda pressed a hand against her stomach. "Oh, dear." Her eyes locked with a pair that looked exactly like hers. "I so want them to like me, Inga."

Inga wrapped her in a hug. "They won't have any other choice," she said. "Just wait and see."

CHAPTER 30

Apparently, Magda thought as she sat with Barry and his family at one of the fanciest restaurants she'd ever dined in, waiting for their salads to be served, his children and mother-in-law had not gotten the memo about liking her.

Or, more precisely, his mother-in-law and *one* of his children had not received the notice.

Deanne shifted her gilded chair closer to her father's, and stared across the blue-and-gold linen-covered table with dark, mistrusting eyes. A few times, Magda caught the ten-year-old glaring with such intensity, her eyes had narrowed to near slits.

Magda tried all the tricks she could come up with, telling the child that she liked her hair—pulled back with a white ribbon, curls kissing her shoulders—and how much she looked forward to hearing her later that evening. "Your father says you sing like an angel," Magda said through a shaky smile.

But the child's idea of expressing gratitude came back as, "I sing like my mother, who *is* singing with the angels."

"Deanne," Barry muttered under his breath.

"Well, she is," Deanne insisted, her eyes perfectly focused on her father's.

"Your father," Magda interjected, "has already told me that

your mother had a lovely singing voice." When no one responded, least of all Deanne, Magda concluded her attempt at reaching the little girl with, "You've chosen a pretty dress for your show," to which Deanne only poofed it over her knees and said, "Thank you very much, Miss Christenson. It was a gift from my nana." She then looked at the refined woman sitting next to Magda. Her "nana"—who'd been introduced as Harriet Nielson—a woman who appeared to be in her early to mid-sixties, despite the henna rinse in her hair. Her mouth—a thin line accentuated by blood-red lipstick—hardly smiled, and, Magda suspected, the laugh lines around her eyes hadn't formed from giggles, but from scowls. Especially at those she found distasteful. Like Magda.

Barry placed his left hand on his daughter's right at the same time as the singer near the front of the room crooned the opening lyrics to "I'm in Love" from *Romance on the High Seas*.

Magda swallowed past the irony as Barry spoke calmly to his daughter. "Sweetheart, you can call her Magda, if you'd like." Magda stared across the table, suddenly noting the band of gold wrapped around Barry's ring finger.

Magda brought her eyes to the child's face, watching her lips form a fine pout before she said, "But I *don't* like, Daddy. In fact, I'm not even sure what she's doing here."

As if on scripted cue, Douglas, in dramatic fashion, dropped his elbow onto the table followed by lowering his head into his hand. "Oh, come on," he moaned. "Are we gonna listen to *this* all night?" He glared at his sister. "Well, *are* we? She looks like a nice enough lady, Dee. Besides, Dad wouldn't bring some bimbo along to church, would he?"

"Douglas Cole," his grandmother admonished as Magda sucked in her breath in an effort to keep from laughing.

"Son," Barry said, biting back a smile of his own, which only served to endear him to Magda more. "We don't use words like *bimbo* in mixed company." He swallowed, his Adam's apple bobbing up and down as though it had grown larger in the last few seconds. "In fact, we don't use the word *at all*."

Magda sat quietly, squeezing the linen napkin in her lap. Earlier, she'd thought it most elegant; now it felt heavy and rough. She looked down at the pearl bracelet, hoping it would bring her strength. The kind Inga always seemed to possess.

"Young man, where did you hear such a horrid word?" Mrs. Nielson asked.

Douglas huffed as he crossed his arms. "Some kid at school. I wasn't even sure it was bad until I got a look at your face, Nana." He finished off the explanation with a chuckle.

Mrs. Nielson directed a pointed look at her son-in-law. "You pay good money to have the children in that school. Perhaps you should curb your *extracurricular* activities and have a talk with the headmaster."

"Nana—" Barry said, just as the waiter swept in carrying an oval tray filled with salad bowls. "Ah," he added. "Saved by the lettuce."

"Then *lettuce* pray," Douglas said, laughing at his own joke. "Get it, Dad?"

"Yeah," Barry said, shaking his head in disbelief. "I get it." He looked across the table at Magda and, with the deepest conviction, offered an apology with his eyes.

Later, after the blessedly short Thanksgiving concert, Barry drove her home while Nana drove the children back to their residence. Magda looked across the front seat and said, "That didn't go so well."

Barry released hearty laughter. "No. No, ma'am, it didn't. Not at all like I'd imagined it would."

"Perhaps this was too soon, Barry. Their mother has only been gone three years."

"Three years is long enough," he said, his voice tight. Then he smiled at her, his dark eyes shining in the flickering lights brought into the car by the streetlamps along the drive. "I've never once brought a woman to meet my children, Magda. To be honest, I haven't dated since my wife—" He sucked in his breath. "Since Barbara died."

"You've never said her name." She watched his face, searching for telltale signs of love and adoration for the woman he'd once pledged his life to. The woman who had given him two beautiful children, both of whom looked for all the world like their father. The woman he'd watched die and whose casket he'd stood next to as they eased it into the ground.

"Haven't I?" he asked, slowing the car to parallel park in front of her apartment. He placed the car in park but left the engine running, then slid closer to her, drawing her into his arms.

It seemed he held her for hours. Magda listened to his breathing—slow and steady—until she wondered if he'd fallen asleep, lulled by the warmth blowing from the vents or the barely audible sounds of Glenn Miller on the radio.

But then he pulled away. "I want you to do something for me," he said, his eyes looking into hers with such tenderness she thought she might melt into them.

"What?" she whispered.

He inched back, pulling his left glove from his hand to expose the wedding ring that had mocked her earlier in the evening. "I want *you* to be the one to remove this."

Magda rested her fingertips against the hollow of her throat. "Barry, *no*. I—"

"It's the way it should be," he said. "Barbara put it on and *you* should be the one to remove it." He cupped her chin with his right hand, forcing her to look at him. "*I* want you to do this, Magda." His lips met hers briefly. "Please," he said against them when the kiss had ended.

She nodded, then reached for the ring, grasping it with her thumb and index finger. A gentle tug brought it to the knuckle where it stopped, leaving Magda to ponder whether Barbara's love held it in place from the afterlife.

If she believed in such . . .

She twisted the ring, forcing it over the first knuckle, then slid it to the tip of his finger. It dropped into the cupped palm of her hand, which she stretched out, extending the token to the man her heart now belonged to so fully.

He took it. "Thank you," he said before slipping it into the side pocket of his overcoat.

Magda shivered. Tucked away, yet it still existed. And it always would, its life perpetual in the faces of two children.

Would he—*could* he—ever love her as he'd loved his first wife?

"Are you cold?" he asked her.

"No," she said, then thought better of it. "Maybe a little."

He brought her close again, kissing her fully, drawing a tiny whimper from her. "I love you, Magda Christenson," he finally said.

"I love you, too, Barry Cole," she answered back. "But at some point we *have* to talk about your mother-in-law and—" He kissed her again as the music on the radio changed from purely instrumental to Fred Astaire's "Cheek to Cheek."

The lyrics played through her head. *"Heaven, I'm in heaven . . ."*

But when the kiss ended, she managed to finish her sentence. "—Deanne."

"Don't worry, sweetheart," he said, straightening. "I've already planned a nice little speech for two very bad girls." He tapped the tip of her nose with his bare finger. "They're *my* problem, not yours."

"Go easy," she said. "Promise me."

He smiled, then chuckled. "All right, Miss Christenson." He glanced over her shoulder to the sidewalk beyond the curb. "Ready for me to walk you to your door?" he asked.

"Not really," she teased. "But I suppose we must." She sighed. "After all, tomorrow is a workday."

He looked at his watch as he replaced the glove he'd removed minutes before. "Which means I get to see your sweet face again in a little more than ten hours."

Magda sighed. "You say it like they're minutes." She pointed to her heart. "In here, they feel like months."

He laughed out loud as he opened the door. "Ah, Magda," he said. "What joy you've brought back to me." With that, he climbed out of the car and closed the door, sealing her own happiness.

Inga couldn't say she was shocked. She wasn't. By the middle of December, as storefronts displayed their Christmas cheer and the goods designed to entice children to write to a jolly man from up north, Inga's sense of desperation had given way to overwhelming gloom. Not even the tiny tree her roommates had managed to find—the one they'd strung with popcorn and cranberries and placed the little dime-store crèche in front of—could bring hope to her hopeless and miserable heart.

She was expecting a child, all right. And the time had come to tell the father.

And there he was. As soon as Inga and Henrietta arrived at the Los Angeles hotel, Inga spotted him, talking to a lovely creature. Smiling like the devil himself—a spider drawing a fly into his web.

"Look at him," Retta muttered as they crossed the polished floor toward the registration desk. "Papa Bear with innocent Goldilocks."

Inga tried to smile, but it didn't come as easily as she wished. "Only he doesn't know he's a Papa Bear. He still thinks he's a Baby Bear, all cuddly and adorable."

Retta grabbed Inga's arm, turning her so they faced each other. "Tell. Him. Tonight."

Inga nodded. "I promise, Retta. Tonight's the night." She pressed her hand against the flat of her stomach. "Besides, I can't wait much longer. We need to get married sooner rather than later."

Retta looped their arms together and pulled her toward registration. "I still say there's got to be a better way than marrying that . . . that . . ."

"Polecat," Inga said, then giggled. "I heard Evelyn use the term once."

Inga managed to avoid Frank in the lobby, but called the concierge desk as soon as they'd unpacked.

"I thought that was you," Frank said, his accent drawing a rush of memories to the surface. "I was—uh—a tad busy or I would have walked over."

"So I saw. Hey—um—how's this? I'd like to take you to dinner tonight. On me this time. There's something . . . something I need to discuss with you."

"Sounds ominous."

She pressed her lips together and squeezed her eyes shut. *Slow it down, girl.* "Nothing like that. Just thought we could talk."

"I'm not off until eight tonight," he stated as if it were a question.

She looked at her watch; that gave her three hours to prepare, if she wasn't ready enough. "That's fine," she said. "How about if I pick you up at your room at eight fifteen?"

"Excellent," he said. "See you then."

By the time eight o'clock had rolled around, Inga had talked herself into not telling him—no, telling him—not telling him—telling him—at least twenty times. Finally, dressed in a pair of tapered ankle-length black slacks topped with a black-and-white-striped long-sleeved sweater and a pair of black wedged slipper shoes, she told Retta good-bye and went to meet Frank.

He greeted her with a kiss, warm and familiar, as if nothing negative had transpired between them. When they broke apart, she turned from just inside the doorway. "Shall we?"

"You don't want to come in?" he asked—half-hopeful, she suspected.

Inga managed a smile. "Thank you, no. I'm ravenous. Aren't you?"

He gave her his best man-about-town look. "Only for you, my dear."

She raised a brow. "Me and half of Hollywood, I'd bet." She sashayed toward the elevator, glancing over her shoulder when she heard his door close. Frank rushed toward her, sliding his arms into his suit coat, flexing his shoulder muscles as he buttoned it over a green-and-red plaid vest. "Very festive, by the way," she said, pointing.

He grinned as he caught up to her and extended the crook of his arm. She took it and they rode the elevator down to the lobby in silence.

"Would you like to dine in the restaurant here or perhaps another, more intimate café down the street?" he asked as they passed through the doors when they slid open. "I've found the most amazing little place."

Inga looked toward the door. "Then let's try the café."

He leaned close to kiss her cheek. "Your wish is my command, milady."

"Such a white knight," she shot back, wondering how gallant he'd be once he heard her news.

They chatted lightly as they walked from the front door of the hotel to a small café around the block, one she'd not been in before. A blend of strong spices met them as they entered through the glass door, and a wave of nausea hit her. She brought a hand to her mouth, inhaled deeply through her nose, and then slowly released it between slightly parted lips.

Frank peered at her. "Are you all right, darling?"

She nodded, eyes filled with water. "The spices," she managed to eke out.

"Middle Easterners love good spices," he whispered. "The payoff is worth it, I promise. The food here is amazing. The best I've had since London."

"Good evening, Mr. Martindale," the handsome, olive-skinned host said.

Frank shook his hand. "Good evening, Gabir," Frank returned. "May I introduce you to my date, Miss Inga Christenson."

Gabir shook a finger at Frank as he chuckled, the light from the chandelier glistening in his black eyes. "Such a lovely lady," he said, followed by, "Please, please." He beckoned them to enter into the heart of the room, leading them past the few patrons who remained from the dinner hour, one or two who enjoyed smoking from a hookah.

Inga held her breath as they walked through a veil of fruity-scented tobacco smoke to a U-shaped booth angled into the back corner.

Once they were seated, she looked up at Gabir and asked, "Excuse me, Gabir, but do you have hot tea?"

Gabir smiled down at her. "We have a marvelous Moroccan green tea."

Green. Much like her face, she felt certain. If God were trying to further punish her for her bad decision from a few weeks back, he was doing a good job of it.

"Please," she said, then swallowed. "And the sooner the better."

Frank raised his hand. "Tell you what, Gabir, let me order for us now."

Inga closed her eyes and attempted to concentrate more on what she might say next than on the foods he rattled off as if he, himself, were Middle Eastern—grape lcaves, *harira*, and baked *kibbi*.

"Inga?"

Inga opened her eyes slowly, then blinked in an effort to force Frank into focus.

"Darling, are you sure you're all right? You look positively ill."

She shook her head quickly. Too quickly. Her hand gripped the edge of the table to keep herself from falling to the floor. "I'm not ill," she said. "I'm pregnant."

CHAPTER 31

Frank slid away from her, putting at least two feet between them. His lips parted as though he wanted to say something but had lost the ability to speak. Then he blinked. Once. Twice. And he swallowed. Hard.

Inga blinked as well, her nausea suddenly dissipating, replaced by the near humor associated with the shocked look on her baby's father's face. "Frank?"

A whoosh of air left his lungs. He cleared his throat, then looked up as an exotic creature approached carrying a tray cluttered by a hot tea service for two. They sat in strained silence as she placed the service on the table, then bowed slightly. "Your appetizers will be here soon," she said.

Inga waited for Frank to speak. When he didn't, she said, "Thank you." She set about pouring their tea into miniature cups, inhaling the relaxing fragrance of it.

"Here you go," she said, setting Frank's cup in front of him. "Although you look like you could use something stronger."

He took a long swallow before looking at her, his jaw flexing. "Why are you telling me this?"

She managed half a sip of the tea before returning the cup to the table. "I think you know why. The baby is yours."

He chuckled. "How would I know that, Inga?"

She stared at him as she took slow, shallow breaths. *In. Out. In. Out.* "Because you are the only man I've been with. You *know* that."

He poured another cup of tea, drinking it down. "I know no such thing," he said into the cup; then he turned his face toward hers. "And you can't prove it, you know."

The nausea returned. She took a slow sip of her tea, buying time. Finally, she giggled. "This isn't going at all the way I thought it would."

Her eyes found his; they were rock hard. Cruel and icy.

"I suppose you thought I would ask you to marry me. That we'd live happily ever after."

Of course she had. She'd not even considered the alternative—that he'd suspect she'd been with another man . . .

"I've only slept with one man, Frank, and that's you." She shrugged. "You're right, though. I have no way to prove it." She squared her shoulders, fighting the tears she knew would surface soon enough. "I'm also not well enough or mature enough to sit here another minute," she said, sliding out of the booth. "Make my excuses to Gabir—I'm sure his food is wonderful." Inga inhaled sharply. "And you know how to find me once you've had a chance to think this through. Once you come to your senses."

He looked toward the wall, and when she realized he would say nothing in response, she turned and walked away, feeling his eyes on her every step.

Magda's early morning routine now included watering the poinsettias Barry's mother-in-law had brought into the office. She suspected the gesture had been more about checking in on *her* than it was about making the office more festive. Not that Magda minded. When she and Barry were at work, they were nothing more than Miss Christenson and Mr. Cole. He had never, not once, closed his office door behind her, gathered her in his arms, and kissed her.

She wished he would at times, but he never had.

Even so, they both knew a time would soon come when they could no longer hide their feelings for each other, nor would they want to. Barry had made inquiries into openings in other offices throughout the building, but—as he told her during dinner one evening—the end of the year was not when people typically *quit* their jobs.

"Santa Claus must be paid off," he said with a wink.

Santa Claus and Harriet Nielson, Magda reflected now as she tipped the water spout into one of the gold-foiled pots in Barry's office. The woman had all but ignored her at every get-together in the past two weeks, encouraging little Deanne to do the same.

Douglas, on the other hand, let everyone know in full volume that he liked Magda. That he thought she was as pretty as a peach. Magda couldn't help but giggle at the memory of him giving his father a playful slug and saying, "Way to go, Daddy-O."

"Good morning." Barry's voice sounded from behind her.

Magda turned, bringing the chrome watering can to her midsection, resting it on the palm of one hand. "Good morning." She walked toward him. "You have a meeting with—"

Barry raised one hand as he set his briefcase on his desk. "I know." He released a long and heavy sigh as he unfastened the top button of his overcoat.

"What's wrong?" she asked, stopping in front of him. "You look awful." She jutted her thumb toward the opposite side of the room. "Would you like a cup of coffee?"

He shrugged out of the coat, smiling in appreciation. "I would *love* a cup of coffee. And pour one for yourself while you're at it. I have something to talk to you about."

Magda crossed the room to the bar, where she set down the watering can, then poured two cups of hot coffee.

"Here you go." She placed the cup directly in front of him, then took a seat and a long swallow from her own. "What's wrong? You look like you didn't sleep a wink last night. Is it something with the kids? Deanne?"

He grasped his coffee cup with the fingertips of both hands, then hunched his shoulders as he brought it to his lips. After swallowing, he looked up and said, "We've been found out."

Her cup rattled in its saucer and she immediately set both on the edge of the desk nearest her to keep it from spilling. *"How?"* she whispered. "We've been so careful." Barry shook his head. Magda noticed then the flame of anger in his eyes. "You're upset," she said.

"Wouldn't *you* be?" He blinked. "*Shouldn't* you be?"

Magda breathed out. "I don't suppose it's hit me yet. What . . . what does it mean? For us?"

"For *us*, nothing. For *you* . . ."

Realization hit like a wrecking ball. "My job . . ."

"I'm afraid so."

Her heart squeezed inside her chest. "When did you . . . when did you find out?"

"Last night. I got a visit from Mr. VanMichaels after you left."

Magda glanced over to the door between their offices, noting for the first time that he'd closed it. She hadn't noticed it earlicr—had he done it after walking in? When she was watering the poinsettia? Or later, when she'd walked across the room for coffee?

"And did he . . . did he say how he found out?"

"No. He just walked in and asked me, point blank, if you and

I were having . . ." His voice trailed before he took another long swallow of coffee.

"An *affair*?" Magda gripped the arms of the chair, squeezing them until she worried she'd done permanent damage to her hands. "I hope you set him straight."

Barry stood, walked around the desk and squatted in front of her, bringing both hands to her face. "Of course, darling. He asked if we were having an affair. I told him no. He asked then if we saw each other personally. Outside the office." He sighed. "I told him yes. I told him—"

Magda waited, and when it became obvious he would not finish his thoughts, she asked, "Told him what?"

But he waved the question away. "I *did* tell him that I'd tried to find you another position within the company, but—"

"There aren't any."

"No."

When he fell silent, Magda felt the room spin around, and her hands squeezed the thin leather cushion at her knees. "What am I going to do?" she asked, staring at them. "I have to have a job to stay here. In Chicago."

Barry crossed the room, sitting next to her. "I spent all night thinking about that. You remember Harlan Procter?"

Magda jerked around to face him. "What about him?"

"He's a full-time writer. I called him last night—"

"You *didn't*."

"Is there something wrong with that?"

Magda's breath caught in her throat. The last thing she wanted was for Barry to know she had dated Harlan. "No. No, of course not."

"I told him you have amazing talent."

"And what did he say to that?"

Barry smiled. "He said he'd be interested in reading some of your work." His hand rested on hers. "Mainly, darling, I talked to him about how we might find enough work for you in freelance to make a living." He shifted. "I can tell you now that I will personally see to it that at least one of your stories is published monthly. I can also put in a call to some friends of mine at other publications. *And* . . . I also want you to continue to work at weeding out some of the submissions that come across my desk. I think between all of that, you'll do fine."

Magda slid her hand out from under Barry's, placing it in her lap where she knew he wouldn't reach for it. "Is that all Har—Mr. Procter said?"

"No."

She cut her eyes to his.

"He said that if I believed in your talent, then you must be quite gifted."

"Did you . . . did you tell him about . . . us?"

"No. No, of course not."

Magda took in a breath through her nose, exhaling slowly. She forced a smile and turned to him more fully. "So, when do I start this new career of mine?"

"Today, I'm afraid. Right now." He stood, extending a hand, which she took, allowing him to help her stand. "But do you know what that means?"

She shook her head.

Barry wrapped his arms around her, bringing his lips to hers. "It means I can do this from now on, right here in this office, and it will be no one's business but our own."

"I wish the airline would stop with these fly-in-one-day, fly-out-early-the-next-morning schedules," Retta complained. She sat in one of the two hotel room chairs, pulling her nylons up one leg, checking the seam in the back. "The sun hasn't even come up yet, and here we are getting ready to hop in a cab for the airport."

Inga smiled across the room at her before clicking the locks on her Samsonite. "Personally, I couldn't be more ready to get out of here."

"Sorry, chum," Retta said, smoothing the nylon as she hooked it to the garter. "I know you wanted that phone to ring all night, but—"

"Or that he would at least knock on the door."

Retta stood, adjusting her uniform skirt over her legs. "At least you're not all alone in this."

"Meaning?"

"You have family who loves you, kiddo. They're not going to leave you to freeze in the cold."

Inga's heart pounded at the thought of how "loving" her father would be when she told him the news. "Come on," she said to Retta with a sigh. "The sooner we leave this hotel, the sooner we get home."

Shortly after lunch, Inga opened the front door of her apartment to find Magda sitting on the sofa, cross-legged, with a cereal bowl in one hand and a large spoon in the other. In the corner, "Elmer's Tune" crooned its way out of the Philco.

"What are you doing here in the middle of the day *this* time?" she asked. "Don't tell me you quit again." She closed the door behind her. "Is that oatmeal I smell?"

Magda nodded as she shoveled a spoonful into her mouth.

For as long as Inga could remember, Magda had reached for oatmeal when she needed comfort. She dropped her luggage at her feet and glanced into the kitchen. "Got any more in there?"

"Plenty," Magda said around the spoon.

Minutes later, Inga collapsed next to her sister on the sofa, crossing her legs and dipping her spoon into the cinnamon-sprinkled cereal. "So, tell me. What's it this time?"

Magda made a show of stirring her oatmeal before setting the half-eaten bowl of homemade goodness into the center of her crossed legs. "I got fired."

"What?" Inga kicked off her shoes, then drew her feet up under her, twisting ever so slightly. "How can you get fired? Aren't you dating the boss?"

Magda stabbed at the cereal with her spoon. "*That's* what got me fired." Her face brightened. "But never fear, Sister dear. I'm going to be a freelance writer." She raised a fist into the air, shaking it. "Top *that* if you can."

Inga took a bite of her cereal, inhaling the warmth of it, savoring the tasty lumps along her lips and tongue before swallowing. "Oh, don't think I can't," she drawled.

Magda crossed her arms and pouted. "Of course you can. No matter what I do, you think you can top me. Well, not this time." Her eyes wandered around the room, from the pitiful little Christmas tree all the way to the door where Christmas cards had been hung around the frame. "It's Christmas, my boyfriend just fired me, and, to top it off, he then informed me I'm to start working in the world of freelance. He even called my *old boyfriend* to tell him of my talent." Her shoulders slumped as she brought her face to her sister's. "Okay. Top that," she challenged.

"Sure thing," Inga said, rising to the dare. "*You're* going to be a freelance writer? Well, at least you have a future." She stabbed her chest with a finger. "Me? My future is over."

"Oh, the drama, Inga. What does *that* mean?"

"It means, dear Sister, that while *you're* going to be a freelance writer, *I'm* going to be a *mother*."

CHAPTER 32

"Did you exchange gifts with your roommates?" Pat asked Betty as they zoomed toward his family home.

"What?" Betty asked, turning to look at him. Until that moment, her attention had been on the landscape outside the window of Pat's car, focusing more on the fields blanketed by fresh snow, linen-white and sparkling under the midmorning sunlight, than on the man behind the steering wheel.

Pat chuckled. "I asked if you and the girls exchanged gifts today?"

"Oh. No." She shrugged. "That is to say, sort of."

Pat shook his head. "Dames," he teased.

She pointed a perfectly manicured, red-tipped finger at him. "Be careful." She smiled contentedly. "What I'm trying to say is that we drew names." Betty waved her hands around. "Sounds like we live at the office, doesn't it? But none of us can afford to buy gifts for *everyone*, so we decided to draw names." Betty slid across the seat, close enough that Pat could wrap his arm around her.

"Mmm," he said. "You smell delicious."

"It's called Joy," Betty said, nestling her head along the curve of his neck and shoulder. "An early Christmas gift from my father."

"Jean Patou? 'The costliest perfume in the world'?"

Betty sat straight. "You know it?"

"I'm in the advertisement game, Betts. Of course I know it." He grinned at her. "Hey," he whispered. "Put that head back where it belongs."

She smiled, complying without complaint.

"I was just thinking, though," Pat's voice rumbled.

"About?"

"How difficult it's going to be to top your father's gift."

Betty sat up long enough to kiss his cheek. "Don't you even think about trying to top my father, Pat Callahan. Just being with you is gift enough for me."

He chuckled. "Oh, good. That's quite a relief, actually."

Betty dug her finger into his side until he hollered. "By the way," she said when she'd settled again, "my parents want us to come by before the night is over."

"I'd already planned it," he said.

She sat up again. "Really? And you weren't going to tell me?"

Pat took his eyes from the road long enough to cross them at her. "What I'm going to tell you—and only one more time, young lady—is to get that head back over here so it can nuzzle with mine."

Betty worked to get her arms around him as she laid her head on his shoulder. "You bet, Mr. Callahan," she said. "In fact, we don't have to even stop at your parents' house. Just keep driving and I'll stay like this all day."

Today could be the day. Today could be the day.

The words played over and over in Evelyn's thoughts as George drove her to his family home that Christmas Day. At some point, she reasoned, before the blessed holiday came to a close, George Volbrecht *would* ask her to be his wife. She simply *knew* it.

After all, they'd dated now for over a year. Exclusively. And, while he hadn't told her he loved her—*yet*—she believed he did. And if, for some reason, he didn't love her—*yet*—there was absolutely no doubt in her mind that she could win that love from him once they were married. Once the wedding day had come and gone, once the wedding dress from Carson's had been dry-cleaned and sent back to Betty, George Volbrecht would be declared the luckiest man alive because no man in the history of the world would have ever known or would ever know such devotion as what she'd shower on him. And as for his family, whatever shortcomings they believed she possessed *now* would be eradicated when they witnessed her sheer adoration for their golden boy. Not to mention once she gave him children. A boy first. Followed by two girls.

Evelyn squeezed her eyes shut. *Please, dear God. Hear my prayer. I know you brought George into my life for a good reason. Surely I was brought into his for a good reason too.*

"Wake up, sleepyhead," George said from the driver's seat. Only when she opened her eyes did she realize they were parked in his parents' driveway.

"I wasn't asleep, George," she told him. "I was praying."

"Praying?" What began as a look of astonishment evolved into one of amusement.

"Do you pray, George?"

"I'm Catholic, Evelyn. I pray at Mass."

"But . . ." She turned to fully look at him. "What I mean is, in your own heart. Do you pray? Do you listen for God to speak to you? To direct you?"

He stared at her for a long minute before cupping her chin and squeezing it lightly. "Evelyn, it's Christmas. Today is not the day to have this conversation."

Evelyn raised her hands. "*Christmas* is the celebration of the Christ child coming to live among man, George. It's a perfect time to talk about him. For heaven's sake, if not *today*, when?"

George grabbed the door handle and jerked it open. His eyes focused on the steering wheel as he spoke. "Evelyn, you knew the kind of person I am when you started all this. If you expected me to change, then I'll repeat what I said to you before. *Run.*" His eyes found hers and she mentally reprimanded herself for the tears she knew formed there. "I'm ruthless, inside the office and out."

"I don't believe that," she said, forcing the words past the lump in her throat and into the chill that had seeped into the car. "When I look at you, I see a man who . . . who may want to believe he's ruthless, but who, deep down, is a good man. A *caring* man. After all, who but you would care enough to make sure some hayseed from Georgia learns how to dress. How to speak properly. Who but you would teach her proper etiquette for social functions. You've even made sure I've learned to speak another language. A *beautiful* language. You did all that, George, for *me*. And I believe only a good, decent man would do all those things."

George leaned over, cupped the back of her head with his hand, and brought her lips to his in a bruising kiss. One that left her shaken . . . and strangely hopeful. When he pulled back, his eyes—smoky and tender—searched hers as a thumb brushed a wayward tear from her cheek. "That's where you're wrong, Evelyn," he said. "I didn't do this for you. I did it for *me*."

Betty had to admit—even if only to herself, as Pat drove them from his family home to hers—that she could learn to love the concept of a large family. She'd never before experienced a Christmas Day so full of laughter. So jam-packed with joy, especially at the concept of *giving*, rather than receiving.

"You're over there thinking again," Pat said, resting his arm against the back of the seat. "Why don't you scoot over here and do your thinking."

Betty slid over, adjusting her coat in the process.

"Are you cold?" he asked, his arm coming over her so he could reset the temperature.

She grabbed his hand and put it where it had been, draped around her shoulder. "Don't you dare," she said, tilting her head back to get a better look at him. Even in the gray of the early evening, she found him handsome beyond words. "Say, why did you want to wait to open our gifts until after we see my parents? Don't you know females aren't good at waiting? Especially when presents are at stake."

He shrugged. "No reason, really." He kissed her forehead. "Is there something wrong with wanting a little alone time with my girl while I give her a gift I shopped long and hard for?"

Betty looked forward, noting that they'd turned into her neighborhood. "That street up there," she said, followed by, "Turn right. And no. There's nothing wrong with it."

In fact, everything that could be right about it *was* right about it.

Pat turned right onto the street where her parents lived. "Much farther?"

"No. Almost to the end of the block here. On the left." She sat straight. "There it is." She pointed. "The one with the large Christmas tree taking over the window."

"Nice," he said. He grinned at her after he turned into the drive. "Remind me to tell your mother how *lovely* her home is."

Betty socked his arm and he feigned injury. "That was my

gift-giving arm," he said, his voice playfully strained. "Now what will I do?" Pat brought the car to a stop and slipped the gear to Park. "Well, my sweet . . ."

"Yes, my sweeter?"

He kissed her briefly. "I only wanted to say two things."

"And number one would be?"

"That I love you."

"I love you too. And two?"

"I'd give you a more passionate kiss, but your mother is watching us from the living room window."

"I'm sure she is." Betty placed her hand on his neck and pulled him to her for a proper kiss.

He drew in a deep breath when the kiss was done. "My gracious, little girl. What was it Rhett Butler said? 'You should be kissed, and often'?"

"Hats off to Mr. Butler," Betty said with a giggle.

Pat glanced toward the window. "Your mother is gone. I guess that means I need to get you inside before your father comes out with a shotgun or something."

Betty straightened. "That would be Adela's job. One more thing . . ."

He opened his door before looking over his shoulder.

"When this night is over, don't say I didn't warn you."

Pat laughed then, bold and infectious. "Let's go," he said, placing one foot on the driveway, "and see what this night has in store."

Evelyn eased into the room she shared with Joan—at least for the next couple of weeks—hoping her roommate would be asleep.

She wasn't. Instead, Joan sat propped up under a mound of

bedcovers with an Agatha Christie novel in her hand—the one Betty had given her for Christmas. "Hi, there," she said, looking up from her reading.

"Is it good?" Evelyn asked, closing the door behind her. "The book?"

"Very good." Joan looked at the cover as if to remind herself of the title. "*Murder with Mirrors*," she said. "It's a Miss Marple detective story."

Evelyn dropped her purse onto the dresser. "I remember when we were pen pals . . . the way you always wrote about whatever book you were reading at the time. You made me wish I were more of a bookworm."

"Never mind that. What happened today with George?" Joan plopped the book onto the bed as she crisscrossed her legs and drew them up to her chest.

Evelyn sat on the edge of Joan's bed and pulled the sides of her hair back to reveal a pair of rose-shaped diamond-drop earrings. "They're Dior," she said.

Joan leaned in for a closer look. "They're *exquisite*, Evelyn."

Evelyn rested her hands in her lap and stared at them. "They're not a diamond *ring*, though."

Joan grabbed her hands. "Evelyn . . ."

Joan's face shimmered through the veil of tears in Evelyn's eyes. "I'm acting like a child. I know."

"Please tell me you acted like a big girl when George gave these to you."

Evelyn nodded. "Of course," she whispered, then forced a wobbly smile. "I gasped appropriately and said, *'Ils sont beaux,'* which made his mother's cousin—the one who lives in Paris—applaud lightly before declaring the same."

"And then?"

"And then I took off the little earrings I was wearing—you know, the ones that look like silver bells. Like the Christmas song?"

"I know."

"And I said—very sweetly—'George, would you put them on for me?'" She sighed at the memory. "Honestly, Joanie, it was one of the most intimate moments of our relationship."

Joan's eyes grew large. "Evelyn, you and George aren't—"

"Oh, no . . . No. One thing my mama and daddy taught me is that a man isn't going to buy a cow when the milk comes to the door every morning for free."

Joan blinked several times before bursting into laughter, forcing Evelyn to follow suit. And the laughter felt so good. Like all had righted itself within the world again, just by sharing a chuckle with her dearest friend.

"Well, no, I suppose not," Joan said, breathless.

"I'm not foolish enough to throw *that* away, even for George."

"I'm glad to hear it." Joan paused in an attempt to stop her giggles. "So, did George—did George like your gift to him?"

For weeks Evelyn had used all her spare time to shop until she found the perfect gift for George—replicas of Roman coins made into a pair of cuff links. She thought them smart and sophisticated and, fortunately for her, so had George.

"Yes, he did. He very gallantly asked me to replace the ones he had on with them." She smiled. "The whole thing was quite romantic."

Joan patted her hand. "I'm sure it was."

Evelyn scooted back farther onto the bed. "Were you horribly bored today?"

Joan shook her head. "Not in the least." She pointed at the book. "I've read mostly. Napped a little."

"Did you miss being with your family? Being in England during the Christmas holiday?"

"Sure. I guess so. But in all honesty, I don't think it's the same for me as it is for you. You're always talking about your traditions and—how does the song go? 'Chestnuts roasting on an open fire'? The Christmases of my childhood were a bit austere." Joan shrugged. "Not so much to miss."

"Because of the war?"

"Mmm-hmm. My parents didn't have enough money really to buy anything, and anything that *could* be bought was in such short supply." She smiled. "I have to say, though, if nothing else, my parents made certain we had a nice Christmas dinner. I did miss *that* today. And we *did* have stockings. Regular old stockings, mind you. Not some of these fancy things I've seen displayed about town."

"My mother made ours," Evelyn said. "Embroidered our names across the top. 'Homespun is always best,' she'd say."

"On Christmas morning," Joan continued, looking toward the door as though she'd returned to England for a short visit, "we'd rush to see what we'd gotten in our stockings."

"Which was?"

"Typically fruit. Maybe some candy and one needed item. Gloves. Socks. A pencil box." She looked at Evelyn. "Not *all* that, of course. *One* of those."

"Did you have a tree?"

"Oh, no, no, no. But sometimes my brothers and sisters and I made paper decorations out of colored paper that our mother hung around the house. And there were no Father Christmases, but the churches all had a crèche."

"No lights strung around the house?"

"Oh, goodness, no. There was a blackout so . . . no. No twinkling lights. No decorated store windows showing off their goods with red and green bulbs. *But* . . . the children still sang carols around the neighborhoods." She laughed lightly. "And the sweet souls with nothing to give always dropped a few coppers into outstretched palms."

"Coppers?"

"You know. Farthings. *Or pennies.*"

Evelyn's hand reached for Joan's. "I'm sorry, Joanie. Here I am complaining because I got diamond earrings instead of a diamond ring and here you were, spending the day alone, recalling farthings and pennies."

Joan shook her head. "Don't be sorry, Evelyn. The times were bleak but we didn't know any better. For us, they were . . . *normal.* What we were used to. And, for the most part, we were all very happy."

"For the most part . . ." Evelyn scooted off the bed. "My mother's last letter said Hank has been seeing someone. Did I tell you that? Dixie Monroe." She frowned. "The dumbest girl in school. Maybe in the whole world."

"So? What do you care?" Joan asked, pulling her Miss Marple book closer.

Evelyn stared at the earrings she now held cupped in her hand. "I love George," she said. "But I don't want Hank to end up with just any ole body." She reached into her purse for the black velvet jewelry box the earrings had come in. The one she had—momentarily—believed nestled a diamond ring. "I want him to be happy." She eased the box open. "You know, like me."

CHAPTER 33

As soon as Pat left the room with Betty's father on their way to see Mr. Estes's impressive stamp collection, Chloe Estes eased herself down to her favorite place on the living room sofa and said, "I admit he's charming, Betty."

Betty, in an unusual move, sat next to her mother, closest to the wide door leading to the foyer. "He really is something else, isn't he?"

"I take it you fancy yourself to be in love then."

"I *am* in love, Mother. No fancy to it. Pure and simple love."

Chloe sighed before reaching for the tiny bell perched on a nearby end table. A minute later, Adela entered carrying a silver tray topped with crystal cups of eggnog.

"Plenty of nutmeg, Adela?" Betty teased.

"Your mama said this year to serve it on the side," Adela answered with a nod. She set the tray on the coffee table. Straightening, she said, "I'll be back in a jiffy with it."

As soon as she left the room, Betty turned to her mother. "I can't believe you didn't give her the day off."

Chloe crossed her arms. "I told her not to bother coming in since you and Pat weren't due until so late in the day. But she insisted that she'd be here." Betty's mother visibly forced a smile. "That woman wouldn't miss meeting your special someone if the good Lord himself were coming to her house for the holiday."

Betty tried not to laugh but couldn't help herself. "Mother . . . such sacrilege."

Chloe straightened. "Never mind that. Let me ask you something now while I have the chance."

"All right."

"I take it that your relationship with George is *completely* over?"

"Mother, I never had a relationship with George to *be* over. I tried to tell you *all* that, but no one was listening. Least of all George."

"And what do you think of this little simpleton he's been seeing for a year now? His mother is nearly beside herself, I hope you know."

Betty forced the anger rising inside her to stay put, even if it meant not being able to eat one of Adela's scrumptious Christmas dinners, which—from the smells emanating from the kitchen—was a fat ham, mashed potatoes, and asparagus drizzled with hollandaise sauce.

"Mother, please. Evelyn is *not* a simpleton. My gracious, did you know George has her learning French? *French.*"

Adela returned then, carrying a silver shaker filled with reddish-brown granules. "That's a fine young man, little miss," she said. "I can hear him in there talking to your daddy about stamp collecting like he's the one doing it."

Betty laughed. "He's a fine young man for more reasons than that."

"Shall I serve the two of you now, Miz Estes?" Adela asked Betty's mother.

Chloe sat straighter—if that were possible—and said, "Let's see how much longer—" Her words were halted when the two men walked in, Betty's father clapping his hand on Pat's shoulder.

"Chloe," he boomed, "this young man of Betty's is going places."

"Do tell," Chloe responded through a smile Betty recognized as feigned. Her eyes followed her husband as he sat in a chair on the other side of the coffee table. Adela busied herself in serving everyone their festive drinks.

"Sit, boy, sit . . . ," Harrison Estes said, indicating a nearby chair.

"If it's all the same to you," Pat said as Adela served him his eggnog, "I'd like to continue our conversation from inside your study, Mr. Estes." He placed the crystal cup on the end table near Betty.

"Go ahead then."

Betty looked at her father. "What conversation would that be?"

"Don't look at me, Daughter," he answered, taking the shaker of nutmeg from Adela. "If you want your questions answered, you best look to the one who can answer them." He nodded toward Pat.

"Pat?" Betty blinked in confusion.

"Well," Pat said, shoving his hands into his suit-coat pockets. "As I was telling your father, I know you and I haven't known each other long, Betty."

"You're right about that."

"But," Pat continued, "I'm over thirty and you're getting close."

Betty pointed up at him. "Watch it." Even as the words left her mouth, a sense of understanding fell over her and she knew—she *knew*—where Pat's speech was headed. "Oh, goodness," she breathed.

"I told your father a minute ago that I've waited a long time to find someone like you, Betty Estes . . ."

"Pat . . ." She brought a hand to her lips where it lingered, trembling.

"Long enough to know what's what. I've got a good job—like your father said, I'm going places—and I believe that, in time, I'll be able to offer you the best life has to give."

Something like a whimper came from deep inside Betty. Time suspended and while she clearly saw his mouth moving, she could hear absolutely nothing. Not a word. Not even a syllable. Then, just as her ears began to clear, he pulled a small ring box from his right coat pocket and knelt down in front of her. "So, right here, right now . . . in front of the two people who brought you into the world, and of course Miss Adela over there." He glanced beyond her father. "Will you do me the honor, Miss Estes, of becoming my wife?"

Betty stared at the ring, a single round-cut diamond set high between six smaller diamonds, three along each side. It caught the light from overhead, sending prisms of color. "Oh, Pat," she said through her fingertips. "I don't know what to say . . ."

"Here's an idea," he whispered. "Say yes."

She looked into his eyes, so beautifully green, so filled with love. "Yes," she answered, extending her left hand.

"Oh, praise Jesus," Adela said from behind Betty's father. Betty looked over in time to see the woman's hands fly up into the air. "Baby girl has finally done it. She's found the right man."

"Adela, please," Chloe Estes admonished as she reached over to take her daughter's hand. She inspected the ring thoroughly before turning to her husband. "You knew about this, I presume?"

"Your future son-in-law asked permission while we were in the study."

Betty looked down at Pat, who still knelt in front of her. "You are a sneak, Mr. Callahan." She placed her hands on both his cheeks and kissed him sweetly. "And I love you."

Her forehead rested against his as he said, "I love you too."

"I suppose," her mother said, drawing her attention away from Pat, "that we'll need to talk dates. I'll want to meet with your mother, Mr. Callahan—"

"Please, call me Pat."

"And, Betty, we'll want to start thinking about your dress. Your trousseau."

Betty turned fully to her mother. "Actually, Mother . . . you don't have to worry about a dress. I've already purchased one."

Chloe Estes blanched. "What? Why would you already—?"

"The girls and I. We went in together and bought a wedding dress from Carson's."

Her mother sucked in her breath and her eyes grew large and rolled upward. "Please tell me you're kidding, Betty."

Pat stood, but not before taking Betty's left hand in his and holding it protectively. "The girls? You mean, your roommates?"

Betty nodded as she looked up at him. "It's beautiful."

"You'd be beautiful in a gunnysack."

Harrison Estes laughed heartily. "What'd you do, Betty? Each put money in?"

"Yes, sir. That's exactly what we did."

Adela hummed a little appreciation as Chloe shook her head. "Betty, this simply isn't done. I don't care if the dress *is* from Carson's."

"Leave her alone, Chloe," her father boomed. Then, to Pat, "Well, son, one thing I guess I can say is this: When we stopped paying her an allowance, she became thrifty. That'll work in your favor one day."

Pat smiled at her father, but his eyes turned serious when they returned to hers. "Don't worry, Mr. Estes. I'm going to see to it that Betty never has to count a penny." He squeezed her hand. "Merry Christmas, darling."

Though not her idea of a romantic New Year's Eve with the man she hoped to spend her life with, Magda nevertheless agreed to celebrate the holiday with Barry and his family: Douglas, Deanne, and—of course—Nana. Her only time alone with him would be during the late-afternoon drive from the little apartment on Greenleaf to his home in Evanston, and then back home again sometime after midnight.

"Are you nervous about being in the house?" he asked as they pulled into what she assumed was his neighborhood.

"Why do you ask?"

He shrugged. "You're awfully quiet and I figured . . . this being your first time in my home . . . you know . . ."

When his words faded and failed to return, she finished for him. "You mean because this was the home you lived in with Barbara?"

He swallowed. "Yeah."

In all honesty, she hadn't even thought of it until that moment. When she entered, she wondered now, would she hear the ghostly vestiges of footsteps from a woman who had made the house a home for so long? Would the scent of her perfume linger in the rooms? Would her hand rustle the drapes as if a gentle breeze had passed through the room, only to leave behind an unexplained chill?

"Not really," Magda finally said.

Barry smiled, relief passing across his handsome face. "That's good. I almost couldn't sleep last night thinking about it." He turned the steering wheel to make a sharp right, then straightened it and continued forward. "What's got your mind so far away then? Thinking about your next plot?"

Magda laughed lightly. "Maybe a little." She looked out at the street, past the bare limbs of trees that would, within a few months, sprout new leaves—green and glossy. Snow laid a six-inch blanket over the sloping lawns, pockmarked occasionally by the boot prints of children and paw prints of their best friends tagging behind. Magda smiled, remembering the way she and Inga had played in the snow, building "snowladies" instead of snowmen. Even then, Inga had exhibited a rebellious streak against the norm. "Mostly," she admitted, "I'm thinking about Inga." *And the mess she's gotten herself into.*

"Your sister?"

Magda nodded, keeping her face turned toward the frosty window.

"Is she working today?"

Magda turned her head ever so slightly. "Mmm-hmm." *She says she won't quit until she absolutely has to. Until she begins to show . . . or Frank comes to his senses.*

"Are you feeling bad because she has to work on the holiday?"

"No. That's not it." She slid closer. "How much farther?"

Barry pointed to the left of the car. "See that house there? The American Foursquare?"

Magda laughed. "They're *all* American Foursquare, Barry."

He laughed with her. "Okay. The gray-brick American Foursquare."

"You mean the one you're pulling into the driveway of?" she teased.

He stopped the car, shifting the Buick Special four-door into Park. He looked out the windshield. "This is it. Rambling in places. Plagued by pipes that rattle and rooms I can't seem to get warm enough in the winter or cool enough in the summer. But we like it."

"It's home," she spoke gently.

Barry looked at the house with its wide front porch and short columns. "It is." He took her hand in his. "Magda . . . one day . . . if you don't like it . . . we can move, you know."

Her breath caught in her throat, and, not knowing what else to say or do, she placed her hand on his and replied, "Let's just get through tonight, shall we, Mr. Cole?"

The house invited her in whether the female inhabitants would or not. Garland strung up the narrow staircase leading from the foyer to the first floor gave an instant reminder of the season. Framed photos of the children from birth to present traveled upward along its wall. Inside the living room, to the right of the foyer, a large tree—heavy with ornaments but devoid of gifts—dominated an entire corner of the dark-paneled room. Comfortable yet elegant furniture gave the place a homey feel, one that eased the tension from Magda's shoulders. On the coffee table, arrangements of serving dishes filled with appetizers greeted her, followed by the aroma of dinner cooking in the kitchen. She closed her eyes and breathed in, trying to imagine that this was, indeed, her home. That she was its mistress and these were her things.

"Nana!" Barry hollered, jolting Magda out of her reverie. She almost wished he wouldn't call the others in. That he would allow them to enter at their own pace. In their own time. But as she opened her eyes, Douglas ran in from the back room—the dining room—where a long lace-draped table already set with fine china stretched across its center.

"Hey, Miss Christenson," he said, throwing a hand up. He was dressed exactly as he was the night she first met him—as if he were headed to church—and she wondered if the child ever wore dungarees and play shirts.

Barry discreetly cleared his throat, followed by the boy extending the same hand to her and saying, "Welcome to our home."

Magda shook his hand and smiled. "Please, Douglas. Call me Magda."

"Only if you call me Rock."

"Rock?"

"My son wants to be the next Rock Hudson," Barry told her, his voice low and confidential.

Magda raised her brow. "Oh, I see."

"I saw him five times in *Bend of the River* at the movies. Did you see it, Miss—Magda?"

"Why, yes, Rock," Magda answered, raising her chin. "As a matter of fact I did. And I thought he was quite handsome."

"Handsome, nothing. Did you see the way he carried his gun?"

"Oh, here we go again," Deanne declared as she stepped into the room with her grandmother behind her carrying a large meat-topped platter.

"I hope you like ham, Miss Christenson," Harriet Nielson called toward her. "Because we have plenty of it."

"I love it," Magda answered. "Is there anything I can do to help?" But the woman had already left the room and returned to the kitchen. She looked down at Deanne, who had also dressed up for the occasion, leaving Magda to wonder if her choice of a simple skirt and sweater set—even with the rhinestone buttons—had been appropriate. "You look very pretty this evening," she said.

Deanne neither frowned nor smiled. "I'm to be on my best behavior or I'm on house arrest for a month. I won't even be allowed to watch television." She harrumphed and glared at her father, which forced Magda to bite her lip to keep from laughing. She placed her hand on Deanne's back, felt it flinch, and then removed it. "I'm sure your father was kidding."

"No, her father was not," Barry said, sliding out of his coat. "Let me take your coat, sweetheart," he offered, which called forth a sigh from Deanne. "Young lady, go help your grandmother."

Magda handed her coat to Barry, who handed them both to

Douglas. "Here, Rock," he said with a lilt in his voice. "Hang these up for the old sheriff in town, will ya?"

"Hang 'em up and hang 'em high," Douglas called out as he walked into the foyer.

Magda giggled. "He's something else," she said. Then, lowering her voice, "And I think he likes me."

Barry kissed her cheek before whispering into her ear. "Not nearly as much as the old sheriff."

In spite of her surroundings, Magda kissed him back. "Yee-haw."

CHAPTER 34

January 1953
Amsterdam

After seven days on a ship, Joan docked in Amsterdam midmorning on a Tuesday. The nearly twenty civilians on board with the US Forces had been notified the night before as to where to meet after disembarking. What papers to have in hand. Whom they should and should not interact with.

Joan made it her business to arrive early to the area of the platform where a uniformed soldier with a clipboard stood waiting. "Hallo," she greeted him. Like the young man in the office back in Chicago, Joan reckoned this chap couldn't be more than eighteen. Nineteen, tops.

"Name, ma'am," he said.

"Joan Shirley Hunt," she supplied. She leaned over to observe the forms on the clipboard. "Looks like I'm first."

The soldier checked the tiny box next to Joan's name just as another civilian scurried toward them, breathing heavily. "Is this where the civilians coming to work for the US Forces are to meet?" she asked, her voice barely audible.

"Yes, ma'am," the young officer replied. "Name, please."

"Ruby," she said, pushing thin strands of dark-blonde hair from her face. "Ruby Shaw."

Her eyes grew large as two or three others approached and the soldier asked their names.

Joan wrapped her hand around the young woman's arm and pulled her a few steps away. "Do you have your luggage ticket?" she asked.

"Oh, dear." She sighed, opened a small brown handbag, then pulled a red ticket from the satiny inside pocket. "This?"

"That's it," she said. "And your ID. Do you have that?"

Ruby raised a gloved left hand holding an envelope matching the one Joan had received the night before. "Right here. Do you think that's all we'll need?"

"Well," Joan said, "that's all they *said* we'll need, so I imagine so."

Joan allowed her gaze to roam across the platform. She stood on a dock in Amsterdam. *Amsterdam.* Beyond where the ship had docked and the water lapped in gentle waves, the city churned with life. Even from where she stood, she felt the beauty of it. The quiet majesty in the gray- and red-bricked buildings and the blacktop of the streets, where men and women whizzed by in squatty autos and atop bicycles. The scent of salt water blended with the aroma of fresh-baked goods and cooked meat.

"I'm Ruby," the girl next to Joan said. "Ruby Shaw."

"Yes, so you said," she answered. "I'm Joan Hunt."

"I'm from Michigan."

"Oh," Joan said quickly. She pointed to herself. "Chicago."

"*Chicago?* You sound—"

"I grew up in England," Joan told her. "But I've lived in Chicago for the last—"

"Listen up," the young man in uniform spoke to the small group. "I am Sergeant Daniel Martin. You may address me as Sergeant

Martin." He paused. "We're going to head over to where your luggage should be by now. We'll match you with your belongings and then walk to where the bus will pick us up. From there, we'll head to the train station. If anyone needs to use the facilities, please do so before we gather your luggage. Questions?"

A woman standing on the opposite side of Sergeant Martin raised her hand like a schoolgirl. "And then we get on the train to Heidelberg?"

"That is correct, ma'am." He looked around. "The train to Heidelberg will take about five hours with a brief stop in Düsseldorf. You will *not* leave the train. Questions?"

Joan shrugged, wondering if there should be questions. To her way of thinking, his instructions seemed so simple to follow.

Chicago

Pat insisted on a sooner-rather-than-later wedding, which gave Betty's mother precious little time to plan . . . and Betty a series of sleepless nights.

She stared at the clock by her bedside, happy that, at the very least, Inga wasn't there to be disturbed. "Two a.m.," she muttered, drawing herself up from the warm blankets and quilts. She pulled the chain of the bedside table lamp, reached for the steno pad and pen she kept at hand, and jotted a few notes about flowers.

Flowers. Of all things to worry about in the middle of a January night.

She threw the covers back, slid her feet into her slippers and arms into her robe as she walked to her closed bedroom door. As she stepped into the hallway, she noticed light creeping from beneath Evelyn's doorway. Betty wondered if she'd fallen asleep with the light on.

Once she got closer to the kitchen, however, she knew that Evelyn was awake. She found her, standing at the counter, pouring milk into an orange-juice glass. The only light in the room came from the open door of the Frigidaire.

"Can't sleep?" she asked, flipping on the overhead light.

Evelyn jumped. "You scared me," she whispered. She glanced toward Magda's closed door. "I was trying not to wake anyone. I'm sorry."

"You didn't wake me," Betty whispered back. "I have too much on my mind, I'm afraid."

Evelyn reached into the cabinet for another glass.

"Thank you," Betty said. "Let's go into the living room," she added after Evelyn handed her the filled glass.

A minute later they sat, side by side, their legs covered with the handmade throw Evelyn's mother had sent during the Christmas holiday, the muted street light shining through the curtains.

"Are you excited?" Evelyn asked. "Is that why you can't sleep?"

Betty nodded. "A little, I guess. Mostly, with Pat wanting such quick nuptials, I can't seem to relax on the details." She took a swallow of the cold milk. "And my mother is no help. She keeps making mountains out of every molehill."

"Still," Evelyn said, gripping her milk, "to be planning your wedding . . ."

Betty remained quiet, hoping to say the right thing. "Evelyn, I—"

"Don't feel bad for me, Betts."

She didn't. Not entirely, anyway. She'd warned Evelyn time and again about George, but the young woman refused to believe anything she said. Evelyn clung to the hope that George Volbrecht would change. That he would fall passionately in love with her. That he would ask her to marry him. But Betty knew George better than that. He was a spoiled little boy who liked getting his way. And on those few times when he didn't . . .

"Does George know, Evelyn? About Pat and me?"

Evelyn took a long swallow of her milk, her eyes focused on Betty's, and nodded. "But I wasn't the one who told him."

"I wonder who—never mind. I know who did. My mother called his mother, I'd bet." Betty shook her head. "What do you think, Evelyn? What's going to happen between you and George?"

Evelyn smiled. "In my wildest dreams? He'll ask me to marry him on Valentine's Day. And we'll live happily ever after in that lovely house up in Highland Park."

The one he'd purchased while banking on Betty's acceptance of his marriage proposal.

"But in my nightmares," Evelyn continued, "we'll still be dating ten years from now and I'll realize, finally, that I will never be good enough for him."

Betty turned to look at her. "Listen to me, Evelyn Alexander. You *are* good enough for him. In fact, you are *better* than him; do you hear me?"

Evelyn's eyes shimmered with tears.

"George Volbrecht—or any man, for that matter—would be blessed beyond measure to have you. You're smart. Funny. A godly woman who deserves a godly man. Seriously, Evelyn." Betty placed her hand on Evelyn's. "Think about that."

"I will," Evelyn promised.

Betty drained her milk. "So, what got you up?"

Evelyn swiped at the tears pooling under her eyes. "It's hard to sleep without Joanie."

Betty nodded. "I understand. About the time I get used to Inga being gone, she's home for a few days."

Evelyn's shoulders visibly sagged. "Inga . . . have you noticed lately . . . ? She's different somehow."

"I've noticed."

"Does she say anything to you?"

"We don't chat a lot. Inga is a fairly private person."

"Hmm . . . I guess, if we thought she was moody before, she sure has been this past month."

Betty stood, taking half the afghan with her. "Maybe she has love problems."

Evelyn stood too, taking the afghan from Betty and tossing it over the arm of the couch. "Who doesn't? Apparently even wedding planning can keep you up at night."

Heidelberg

The European countryside sped by in a sea of colors—green, yellow, red, and blue—with flatlands and hills rolling toward the jagged peaks of the Alps. Joan sat next to the window, drinking it all in, and Ruby occupied the seat next to hers. Occasionally, Joan glanced over to find her clutching the strap of her handbag with gloved hands.

They approached Heidelberg slowly, as Joan thought it should be. She leaned as far toward the window as possible, craning her neck, widening her eyes, waiting for the moment that Heidelberg Castle came into sight. When—at last—the jutting and ancient fortress arose from an ocean of lush foliage, she gasped. The structure stood exactly as she'd envisioned, either from photographs seen in library books or from her own imagination.

The train slowed as they neared the station, past narrow streets and alleyways where the devastation of war lingered like old bones—dry, brittle, and gasping for water. But even from her seat on the train, Joan recognized the efforts of rebuilding and starting anew. One more time.

By the time they disembarked and gathered for their next set of instructions, the slow rumblings of hunger percolated in the pit of her stomach. As if on cue, Ruby leaned close and whimpered, "Do you think they'll feed us soon?"

Joan smiled. "I certainly hope so."

Minutes later, Sergeant Martin guided them onto a bus covered in German words and advertisements, which drove them to what had once been a swank downtown hotel, but had since been commandeered for US Forces use.

The bus pulled in front of the building, whose face had grown gray and forlorn. Blank eyes for windows stared down at narrow cobblestone streets glistening with age. Joan exited the bus with the others, who shuffled inside without speaking. She gazed up, reverently observing the pockmarks of battle and the more recent attempt at painting over those injuries.

Ruby scurried close on her heels, taking two steps to each one of Joan's, until they'd all gathered in the lobby and the single door had clicked shut. Joan's luggage—one average-size case carried in each hand—seemed somehow heavier now than when she'd first carried it to the porter on the ship, and the small hat she'd worn since early that morning felt more like a vise than an accessory.

When they were told, "Wait here," Joan set the luggage at her feet and looked around.

The lobby—a large, dark square with high ceilings—showcased a wide carpeted staircase leading to a landing before curving upward to the second floor. Dark paneling surrounded her and thick, square supporting columns rose from the scarred marble floor to the faint remainder of a frescoed ceiling. She studied it closely—the light pinks of cherub faces, the blues of the sashes covering their nakedness—and wondered what it might have looked like in another time. A better day.

After receiving their room assignments, they were handed keys and told to return to the lobby "at eighteen-hundred hours. That gives you almost two hours to unpack, freshen up. *This*," Sergeant Martin said, glancing around, "is your home for the next two weeks."

The civilians trudged up the staircase, no one speaking. Instead, Joan noticed, they looked at their feet, at the worn, bloodred carpet. When they reached the first landing, the group gathered in front of the glass panes of a massive window, and they peered at the world outside and below where the maimed buildings served as fragments of another time. Clusters of children played in an alley, and uniformed soldiers marched to the beat of their own drum.

They continued to climb, inching their way around and up another flight until they reached their assigned floor to face the thick, dark-stained doors that would open to reveal their new homes.

For all of two weeks.

Joan wrote to Evelyn as soon as she could spare ten minutes.

On the one hand, life here is desolate and sad. On the other hand, the students have returned to Heidelberg University, bringing with them hope and renewed vigor. They don't look at what used to be nor seem to notice that it's been fragmented by the war. Rather, they see what can be in the future. Their futures.

They will rebuild fully here in Germany, just as England will rebuild, and one day we will all wonder if the horror that was World War II ever really existed.

Though I'm sure we'll know it did. How could we ever forget, really? How can we move forward successfully if we forget the degradation of this blight in mankind's history?

I must tell you of a mouse of a girl I met nearly the moment I got off the ship and onto the platform. Her name is Ruby. She is from Michigan. Evelyn, I am more amazed that she came to Germany—that she ever boarded a train, and a ship, and now dwells in a hotel used by US Forces in the heart of Old Town (German word is "Altstadt") Heidelberg—than I ever was that you left Georgia. She often seems too frightened to leave her tiny room in the morning for our day's planned activities, much less leave the safety of her mother and father's home. She must be bright—she is here, after all—but she sure is timid and she has attached herself to me.

We will be here for two weeks and the first is nearly over. By the time you receive this, I will have arrived at my first assignment, which will be in Munich. I've already been told that Ruby and I will be roommates there.

As soon as I'm settled, I will write again. Please share my letter with the others. I miss you all.

Fondly,
Joan

CHAPTER 35

Chicago

With only five weeks until the wedding, Betty wasn't sure if she wanted to go out the evening of Valentine's Day or not. "We have so much to do," she told Pat the previous weekend. "It seems we should concentrate on other things."

But he had reservations, he told her, at one of the swankiest restaurants in town. "And romantic," he mentioned as he nuzzled his nose against hers. "You like romantic, don't you?"

Betty shook her head in defeat. "Only on Valentine's Day, I'm afraid."

And so it was settled. On Tuesday, she managed to rush to Peck & Peck after work to find the perfect dusty-rose chiffon gown, one she intended to reuse as a part of her trousseau. Perhaps, she thought as she struggled to tug the back zipper into place on the night of the fourteenth, her father had been correct. Maybe she *had* become thrifty.

Betty worked her fingers into cream-colored elbow-length gloves, then leaned over her dresser for a final pat of her hair, which she'd swept behind her head and clamped into place with a rhinestone-and-pink-pearl comb. Her only other accessories were pink pearl earrings—tiny droplets of elegance—and her engagement ring.

The last thing to do was wait for Pat to arrive, which a look at the bedside table told her should be any moment.

Betty picked up her jewel-encrusted clutch and left her bedroom, her dress swishing with femininity as she made her way up the hallway and into the living room, where she found Magda standing over a sniffling Evelyn. "Oh, dear," she said, stopping. She frowned at robe-clad Evelyn before sending a smile to Magda, who had chosen a red formal gown of satin and netting for her date with Barry. "You look enchanting," she said.

Magda's eyes thanked Betty while her lips pouted. "Evelyn's sick."

Betty set her clutch on the nearby end table. "When did this start?"

"Earlier today." Evelyn's voice was scratchy and her nose so stuffed up that she sounded as though it had taken a recent punch. She brought a delicate handkerchief to her watery eyes and dabbed behind the lenses of her glasses. "I called George around three and told him I didn't think I could make it this evening." Her weepy eyes became floodgates. "He'd made reservations for us . . . somewhere."

"Oh, dear," Betty said again, this time sitting on the sofa next to her. "I fear those are real tears now."

"I'm so sorry," Evelyn squeaked. "It's just that . . . I had hoped that . . . George would . . ." She hiccupped softly. "Tonight would be the night he . . ." Her words faded into sobs.

Betty looked to Magda, who frowned as she said, "Evelyn? If he were indeed going to propose, then there's always another night." She glanced at the front door. "What I mean to say is, it may not be as romantic as if it were on Valentine's Day, but there couldn't possibly be anything worse than a marriage proposal received while deathly sick with the flu."

"Speaking of which," Betty said, "why aren't you in bed?"

Evelyn blew her nose. "I wanted to see what the two of you were wearing," she said, her eyes darting between Betty and Magda.

Betty patted her back. "Well, now you've seen us. Get up, little one."

Evelyn stood and reached for the afghan her mother had knitted.

"There's a good girl," Magda said, stepping back to allow her to pass.

Betty stood as well. "Go on with you, as Joan would say. I'll check on you when I get in."

"Me, too," Magda called to Evelyn's back.

They said nothing until the bedroom door closed. "What do you think?" Magda asked. "Would George have proposed tonight?"

Betty reached for her clutch. "Quite doubtful, but with him, one never knows." She looked around. "Is Inga in LA?"

Magda nodded as she readjusted her wrist-length gloves. "She is."

"Does she have anything spectacular planned with her Mr. Wonderful out there?"

Magda looked up sharply. "I think she's planning to talk with him, but . . ."

"*Talk?* Are they no longer—?"

"No." Magda turned toward the occasional chair where her own clutch waited. "But I think Inga is hopeful that perhaps *this* trip will change that."

"All I'm asking," Inga said into the pay phone at LAX, "is for fifteen minutes to discuss this. Logically. Like two adults."

The sigh Frank emitted was strong enough that she thought she felt his breath against her ear. "I don't see the point, Inga. You told me over a month ago—a month and a half ago—that you're expecting a child. Congratulations. I'm sure you and the father will be very blessed."

Inga pressed her forehead against the boxlike phone. "Frank. I've told you before and I'll say it again . . ." She righted herself, then turned her face toward the back of the phone booth when a man stepped into the one connected to hers. "Frank," she said, lowering her voice, "you *are* the father. Don't you care? Aren't you even *concerned* about the welfare of your child?"

Frank sighed again. "Look, love. I'm at work, as you bloody well know. I can't stand here and discuss this."

"Which is why I'm asking for time tonight. After I get to the hotel."

He paused before answering. "Where are you now, then?"

"LAX."

"Tell you what. I have a date tonight but I don't pick her up until eight." Inga's heart squeezed at the news, but released at the tone of his voice, which was hopeful. "Why don't we meet for cocktails at five thirty?"

Cocktails. The very notion . . . "All right. That's all I'm asking."

"Meet me in the hotel bar." A final sigh and he said, "Until then . . ." before the line went dead.

Betty would say one thing for her fiancé: he knew *romantic* when he reserved a table for two in the back corner of it. The restaurant he'd chosen reminded Betty of something out of an epic Roman novel. Large Corinthian columns wrapped in wide ribbons of pink silk stood like softened foot soldiers around the large marble-floored room. Fat silver urns spilling with flowers in shades of red and pink surrounded the base of each, giving the appearance of the columns bursting from the arrangements. On the bandstand, a string quartet accompanied a pianist performing a haunting version of Debussy's "Clair de Lune."

"Oh, Pat," Betty whispered as she slipped her arm into his. They followed behind the maître d', a classy, older man dressed fashionably in a navy-blue fitted tux. "I admit, this is worth a night away from thinking about flowers and bridesmaids' dresses." She turned slightly to peer down at one of the urns. "Although, I must say, these flowers—"

Pat tugged her back to attention. "Oh, no, you don't." He removed her hand from his arm as the maître d' presented a table glistening with white china and silver and sparkling crystal atop pink linen. A single red rose lay diagonally across Betty's plate.

"I've got this, my man," Pat said to the maître d', then helped Betty to her seat.

Betty picked up the rose and inhaled its sweetness. "Pat, this is lovely," she said as he sat across from her. "I'm nearly speechless."

He winked. "Nearly . . ."

The maître d' handed them each a menu, reported that "Maurice will be with you shortly," and stepped away.

The small orchestra's tune changed to a simple version of Beethoven's "Für Elise." "Listen," Betty said, her heart leaping in her chest. "I learned to play this song on the piano when I was—" She turned to look at the bandstand and came up short. Her smile fell and her eyes blinked for clarity. *Surely not . . .*

"What is it, sweetheart?" Pat asked, his hand reaching for hers.

Betty turned back to look at him. "That's George over there."

Pat's neck stretched as he strained to see over her to the other diners. "Where?"

Betty looked again, if for no other reason than to make sure . . . then turned to Pat again. "The weasel in the corner booth for two with his lips buried in that woman's neck."

"Ohhhh. Yes, yes, yes . . . They are definitely making use of the shadow from that column, aren't they?"

"How dare he?" Betty looked again. George had graduated from his date's neck to her earlobe. She, in turn, had thrown her head back. Luxurious blonde hair, swept over her ear and held back with a rhinestone comb, brushed along her bare shoulder. Together, they re-created a Renaissance painting of unbridled passion.

Betty stood, her gown twisting around her legs.

"Betts," Pat warned.

She looked at him.

"This is none of your business, sweetheart," he warned.

Betty straightened the gown and took a step away from the table. "Oh, but that's where you're wrong, Pat. This *is* most definitely my business." Seeing the troubled look on his face, she placed a gentle hand on his. "I won't be but a minute."

She waltzed to the opposite corner, pausing in front of the small U-shaped booth. The woman noticed her first, her eyes opening from her moment of rhapsody. She looked up slowly, as if she were waking from a dream; then her eyes widened as though the dream had become a nightmare.

"George," Betty announced her presence, her voice firm.

Only then did his nibbling cease. Only then did he look up, blinking. "Hmm?" he said. But when recognition finally hit him, his face visibly flushed. He pulled at his bow tie and cleared his throat. "Betty . . . Don't you look lovely this evening."

"Georgie?" The woman pouted, her voice both sugary-sweet and venomous.

"It's okay, dar—It's okay." He made an attempt to slide out of the booth. "This is an old friend—"

"Stop," Betty ordered, and he did. "An old friend, my eye." She crossed her arms. "How could you? How could you do this to Evelyn, who is at home right now, so upset over not getting to come out with you this evening she can't stop crying?"

"Who is Evelyn?" the woman asked, her shoulders flattening as her neck grew long.

George placed his hand over the woman's. "No one, sweetheart. Just—" He made another attempt to slide out of the booth, but Betty quickly blocked his path. He pointed beyond them. "Say, is *that* your fiancé?"

"Never mind him. When I *think* of the hours Evelyn spent trying to please you. Repeating over and over every little thing you taught her, setting it to memory like some puppy on a leash. And the *French*. Learning a foreign language *just* to impress your *mother's cousin*, George. With someone like Evelyn bowing at your feet, hoping for the moon, *how could you*?"

The blue in George's eye flashed and his jaw set as the orchestra's selection eased into the "Moonlight Sonata." He leaned back in the seat, drawing his date's hand into his. Even from where she stood, Betty could see that he caressed it as only a lover would.

"I warned her," George said, his eyes now locked with Betty's. "I told Evelyn more than once that she should run from me. What she chooses, she *chooses*. For herself." He leaned over and kissed the woman's cheek, murmuring something in her ear before returning attention to Betty. "As for the French, I'm sure it will come in handy at some point in her life." He shook his head and put on a snarl. "Amazing, isn't it, that she didn't learn another language down there in Podunk."

"Portal, George," Betty said, leaning over. She cocked a brow as she supported herself with her fingertips on the table. "A fine town full of good people. As for language, get this: *Vous me dégoûtez.*"

"What does *that* mean?" the woman asked, sounding more like a harlot than a socialite.

Betty straightened, smiling. Apparently George's date, the woman she suspected shared his bed, didn't know French either. Meaning, of course, that Evelyn—poor, sweet Evelyn—was one up on her.

"It means," Betty said, "that he has a long way to go to reach the qualities of Evelyn Alexander." She started to step away, then looked back to the pretty but startled face. "As for you—whoever you are—if you're planning on a future with this cad, I sincerely hope you've had your shots."

"Ginger ale over ice, please," Inga said to the waitress when asked for her drink order.

Frank stared at her without blinking, then turned to the petite woman who stood beside their table balancing a round tray against her hip. "I'll have my usual."

The woman gave him a sweet smile before saying, "You got it, Mr. Martindale."

She walked away, Frank watching her every wiggle to the bar.

"Does she know?" Inga asked, startling him back to her.

"Know what?"

"That you're going to be a father come July."

Frank leaned over, resting his arm on the table. "That hasn't exactly been proven, now has it? My being the father, I mean."

Inga pinched her arm as a reminder that her plan was to be nice. To speak reasonably. "I'm sorry. You're right, of course. We've already established that I can't prove that." She took a deep breath, preparing herself for the speech she'd rehearsed a dozen times that day alone. "Frank," she began, but stopped when the waitress returned with her ginger ale and Frank's Tom Collins glass filled with something pale amber in color, small cubes of ice swimming in it.

He took a sip, then looked up at the waitress, who had yet to leave. "Perfect," he said, then winked.

She smiled back before turning and leaving the two of them alone again.

"Friend of yours?" Inga asked, then pinched herself again.

"I'd like to think all women are my friends." He placed the glass on the table. "Just as you are my friend, Inga." He breathed out of his nostrils. "Look. Tell me what you have to say so I can say what I have to say and we can be on about our lives, okay?"

Inga pinched harder, then released. "Frank . . . as you said, I cannot prove that this baby is yours. I can only tell you, without hesitation, that it is. I'm looking you dead in the eye and I'm telling you. I've been with one man—*you*. That night . . . that night was my first . . ."

Frank took another sip of his drink. "That's just it, Inga. Yes, I know I was the first. But I have no way of knowing if I was the last."

Inga reached for the purse she'd kept in her lap, opened it, and removed a piece of folded paper. She straightened it, then slid it across the table.

"What's this?"

"My medical report. I'm due exactly nine months from our night together last October. I'm twenty-five years old and you were my first. How likely do you think it is that I suddenly went out and slept with some other man immediately after our night together?" She leaned over as tears burned her eyes. "You knew how much I loved you. I still—"

She stopped herself. Truth was, she didn't love Frank anymore. Her only reason for sitting here now was that marrying him was the right thing to do. To save her child from growing up without a father. Without a name. To save herself from the guilt her own father would lay on her shoulders, day after day. Year after year. "I'm only asking you to do the right thing. By *your* child."

Frank studied the report as if memorizing every detail. Inga could imagine him calculating the dates, adding together the weeks, thinking back to that night. That *one* night. That one time. Then he folded it, sighing. "Look, Inga," he said, bringing his eyes to hers. His voice held a tenderness she hadn't heard since October. One she'd hoped for. Dreamed of . . . "Look." He blinked, then looked down as he slid the paper back across the table, his eyelashes dark against the typical pallor of his skin. "I have big plans. You know that."

She left the paper where it lay. "I know. And I can be a part of those plans . . ."

"No. Not *my* plans."

"Think of it." She reached for his hand, but he pulled away. "Think of it," she continued. "We'll get a little place. A charming little place. And you'll come home every night to a home-cooked meal and a wife and child who love you. Adore you. Whatever star you reach for, we'll help you get it. I promise." She took a breath. "Just . . . *please* . . . Do the right thing by me. That's all I'm asking."

Frank stared at the paper. "Tell you what," he finally said. "We'll get the charming little place—" his eyes found hers as she sighed in relief—"and you'll cook the meals and take care of the baby. *But* . . . no marriage. At least not right away. Not until I can see . . . and know for sure." His jaw flexed. "And that may be a long time from now, just so you understand. No commitments beyond what I just said." He took a final, draining sip of his drink. "If you want to tell your family that we're married, fine." He looked around the room. "But no one here. Not in this town, understood?"

Inga released the breath she'd held since he began with *tell you what*. "You mean . . . no wedding?"

"No marriage. No mister and missus. No 'till death do us part.' Those are my terms." He brought the glass to his lips again, then realized it was empty of all but a few cubes of ice. He returned it to the table and checked his watch. "I have to go," he said. "I'll give you until tomorrow morning to make up your mind. After that, the deal is off. I'll be at my station by nine."

Inga didn't watch him leave. She couldn't. Her focus was on a curlicue pattern on the carpet. Round and round. Round and round, but never quite making it back to the beginning. She closed her eyes, reminded herself to breathe, then opened them just as quickly.

Somehow, within the darkness of that one moment, she imagined a striking wedding gown from Carson's. An indescribable dress. White and pure. One she had so desperately wanted to wear.

CHAPTER 36

It had to be true. Betty would never make up anything like this. A cruel thing like this.

George. With another woman. A woman he had clearly been more than just friends with.

George must have called the woman as soon as he heard that Evelyn was too sick to go out. The woman, whoever she was, was the fill-in. The substitute. Yes, yes . . . That was it. Why, he didn't want to lose his reservations. That's all it was. Surely.

But then . . . Betty had said . . . the way he held her hand. The way he nuzzled her neck and nibbled on her ear. *Oh, George!*

Evelyn rolled over in bed, burying her face in the pillow that had once been Joan's. She drew it close to her, holding it tightly, wishing Joan were there right then to tell her what to do. To help her reason things out.

But Joanie had left her. Left for Europe. For Germany. For something new and different. Maybe even better.

Evelyn pushed herself up in bed, reaching for the tissues on the bedside table. She pulled two, then two more, and blew her nose. This stupid cold. Stupid, stupid cold. If only she hadn't gotten sick. Too sick to go to church that morning. Too sick to go out on a date the night before.

She buried her face in her hands and cried until her head ached beyond measure. She rolled over again, laying her face against the cool fabric of Joan's pillowcase. She drew in a shaky breath, then blew it out. "Dear Jesus," she prayed, sounding for all the world like a little girl, "please tell me what to do. I thought you brought George into my life. I thought he was the one, but . . ."

What was it Betty had said that morning before leaving for Mass? Something she said a nun had told her a few weeks back—that they could make their plans, but God determined their steps.

What did that mean, exactly? Didn't that mean that God had brought George to her? Couldn't anyone else have answered the door that night when he came looking for Betty? But God had seen to it that *she* had. That she had relayed the message from Betty. He could have asked anyone else out, but he'd asked her. So, didn't that mean . . . ?

Maybe, though . . . maybe *she* had made her plans *and* determined her steps. Maybe she had taken the reins in her hands and decided to guide the horse without fully praying it through. What was it Aunt Dovalou used to say to her when she visited the old family home in Savannah? That we often pray to God, asking him to control our lives, but we never really hand the responsibility over to him.

Had she done that?

Aunt Dovalou. Her beautiful yet single aunt. Her mother's sister who had shunned love. Or had love shunned her? Evelyn wasn't sure. The story of her aunt's singleness was one of those things her mother never talked about, Mama being so private and all.

Evelyn pulled Joan's pillow over her head, blessed by the darkness it brought. If she could just sleep . . . if she could rest awhile longer . . . *Jesus,* she prayed again, *just tell me what to do.*

Magda sat over her typewriter, painstakingly pecking out character descriptions for a story that had come to her only the night before as she watched an older couple who sat at a table near hers and Barry's. Something about the way they looked at each other. Talked to each other. Magda imagined that they had been childhood sweethearts, torn apart by some unforeseen circumstance as they neared adulthood. They'd married others and had good marriages, but they'd both known there was something else. Something better. Some*one* better. And then, when their respective spouses had died, they had found each other again. At long last . . . love at its fullest.

She stopped typing when she heard the front door open, then close quietly. She knew by the footsteps that her sister had returned from LA, and she stood, pushing away from the tiny desk.

"Inga?" she called as she stepped into the kitchen. "Is that you?"

A moment later, Inga came through the opposite door, leaning her back against the frame.

"You look terrible." Magda moved toward her, reaching for her. "Come. Sit at the table. Let me get you a glass of milk."

Inga complied like a dutiful child, and Magda set about getting the milk from the Frigidaire, pulling a glass off the shelf, and filling it nearly to the top with the rich white liquid. "Here," she said, setting it in front of her sister, who, until then, kept her eyes closed.

Magda sat near her. "Tell me," she said.

Inga cut her eyes over. "I suppose I deserve this."

Magda took her sister's hand in her own. "No. No. Tell me."

Inga chuckled sadly. "He said we could live together but he won't marry me. At least, not yet. Not until he knows for sure . . ."

Magda's hand flew to her lips.

Inga sighed. "I was thinking—on the flight home—how I deserve this . . . this punishment. I've not always been the nicest person."

Magda wouldn't argue that. They both knew Inga could be hurtful when she became too full of herself. Still, Inga was her sister.

So she waited until Inga said more. "I was thinking," she finally continued, "how God must really hate me."

"No, Inga. That's not true."

Inga turned her face fully to Magda's. "I sinned against him. And now I have to pay the price."

Magda could hear their father then, speaking in one of the many assemblies at the college where he taught, telling the students that Jesus had paid the price for sin. That while people often had to endure the circumstances, the price had been paid, once and for all.

She opened her mouth to remind her sister, then closed it. Now was not the time. "What will you do now?" she finally asked.

"Well, I'm not going to live with Frank; that much is for sure." She reached for her glass of milk and drank from it. "I actually prayed last night, Magda."

"Praying is good."

"And I came to the conclusion that two wrongs don't make a right."

Oh, how many times had they heard Far say that? More than a dozen. More than two dozen. Maybe a hundred. "When will you tell Mor and Far, then? About the baby?"

Inga reached for one of the paper napkins in the chicken-shaped holder, which sat in the center of the table along with chicken-shaped salt and pepper shakers. She dabbed at the corners of her lips. "I'm nearly four months along," she said, staring at the wadded napkin in her hand. "Retta said her sister didn't show until she was nearly eight months and that she and I are built a lot alike. I figure if I'm careful with what I eat, I can continue to work until at least the end of my seventh month."

"But . . ."

Again, Inga's eyes found Magda's. "I'm going to have to figure out a way to support a baby on my own. I have to make as much money as I can. When I can no longer hide it, I'll tell them and . . . whatever happens, happens."

Magda felt the wind rush out of her. "Oh, my. I don't know what to say."

Inga stood. "Say nothing." She reached out, bracing herself by placing a hand against her sister's shoulder. "Promise me you'll say *nothing*."

She hated being put in such a position, but— "All right. I promise."

Long-distance calls were cheaper on Sunday afternoons.

Evelyn dragged herself out of bed, shuffled into the bathroom, where she washed her face and brushed her teeth, and then trudged down the hallway, through the living room, and into the building's main hallway where the pay phone hung on the wall.

She waited for the operator, then gave her aunt's name and address in Savannah and deposited the coins that would buy her three minutes.

"Hold for that number," the operator said, leaving Evelyn to wonder if one of the requirements of the job was to master a nasal voice.

When her aunt answered, the operator announced, "I have a long-distance call for Miss Dovalou Smith."

"I'm Dovalou Smith." Alarm rang in her voice.

"Aunt Dovalou?" Evelyn said quickly, not wanting her aunt to worry one second longer than she had to.

"Evelyn? Evelyn, is that you?"

The operator cleared her throat. "You may go ahead now," she said.

"I'm sorry, Operator," Evelyn apologized. "Aunt Dovalou?" She realized she nearly shouted the woman's name, as if screaming were the only way to be heard from Chicago to Savannah.

"Evelyn? You sound just awful. Have you been crying, sweetie?"

"I have a cold," she said. "A doozy of a cold."

"Oh. So glad to know you haven't been crying. Is it cold in Chicago? It's miserable cold here, so I imagine it's *very* cold up there. Your mama tells me she hasn't gotten a letter from you in nigh on two weeks."

Had it been that long? She supposed so. "I know, Aunt Dovalou. Listen, I only have three minutes. I'm . . . I'm calling from a pay phone outside my apartment."

"Well, darlin', what's the matter?"

"I was wondering, Aunt Dovalou, if I could come—you know—there?"

"For a vacation or something? Honey, why wouldn't you just go see your mama and them?"

"No, Aunt Dovalou. I mean to live. I want . . . I want to come home, but I don't think that, after living in Chicago for the last couple of years, I could move back to Portal." Not to mention that Hank would be there. And not just Hank. Hank and Dixie . . .

"Why, darlin', I wasn't expecting this."

"Aunt Dovalou, I really want to come home, and I'll only stay with you until I can find my own place. I won't put you out for long."

"Now, listen here. Don't be silly. I got this big ole rambling house all to myself. I'd love to have you live here with me. But, hon, have you talked to your mama about it? I don't want bad feelings between me 'n' her, you know."

"Mama will be fine," Evelyn said, hope springing inside her. This had gone easier than she'd anticipated. "She'll just be so happy to have me back in George—*Georgia*."

"Well, when are you thinking?"

The operator's voice chimed in. "You have one minute. Please insert five cents more or end your call in sixty seconds."

Evelyn desperately wanted to say "tomorrow," or, at the very least, "two weeks," which would be after she gave her notice at Hertz. But she was to be a bridesmaid in Betty's wedding, and it seemed silly to move to Georgia only to return a few weeks later. "The end of March," she said, speaking as quickly as possible. "My roommate gets married on the twenty-first. I can take the train down on the twenty-second. I'll start looking for a job as soon as I get there."

"Well, sugar, I look forward to it. I'll even put some feelers out to see about a job for you."

"Oh, thank you. And I'll write," Evelyn said, knowing her time was almost up. "I'll write this week. You and Mama. I love you, Aunt Dovalou."

"Love you back."

Evelyn disconnected the line, wiped her nose on the wadded handkerchief she'd stuffed into the sleeve of her robe, and smiled. She had done it. She had made a plan and carried it out. "Now, Lord," she whispered to the face of the pay phone, "if you'll be so kind as to direct my path."

CHAPTER 37

Munich

In mid-March, on a Saturday pretty much like any other, Joan sat curled in one corner of the sofa while her roommate sat cross-legged in a nearby chair. They both drank from their morning cups of coffee as they read the newspaper. "Fools Rush In" played from the American Forces Network radio program, warming the chill right out of the room while adding a sense of hearth and home.

After Joan had read the last page of her section of the paper, she stretched her legs beneath the warmth of a terry-cloth robe and pointed her slippered toes. "Why don't we go to Ludwig's castle today?" she asked Ruby.

Ruby looked up from her reading. She placed a hand on her hair, still in pin curls, and opened her mouth to form a perfectly shaped O. "But . . ."

"I know. How will we get there?" If Ruby had asked the question once, she'd asked it a dozen or more times.

"Last night at dinner, Jackson said he was going to stay in today. Remember? To try to nurse the cold that's been hounding him for the last week?"

Jackson. One of their fellow American civil servants stationed in Munich. A man from Tennessee whom Ruby clearly had her eyes on . . . and who, unfortunately, had his eyes on Joan. But besides all that, he had also been handy when it came to hailing cabs or borrowing cars to get places. "I know," Joan finally said.

"So that means we won't have him to escort us. Help us onto a bus or walk with us on the sidewalks and streets."

Joan knew that too. She had been sitting right there at the table in the out-of-the-way restaurant they'd chosen for dinner the night before. She'd heard the same words spoken over the warm sauerkraut and steaming-hot wurst served on large, round plates.

"Ruby, really. Why do you think we need Jackson to do the simplest of things? We didn't have him when we—either of us—got on the train for New York. Or the ship for Amsterdam. Surely you walked on sidewalks without a man to guide you when you lived back home." A look on her face—blank and fearful—stopped Joan from saying another word. "*Didn't* you?"

"My father or my older brother always made sure my mother or I got where we needed to go." She frowned. "I guess it would be different if we had a car or something."

Joan bit her lip to keep from smiling, then folded the paper into a neat pleat before walking toward the tiny bedroom they shared.

"Where are you going?" Ruby asked.

"I'm getting dressed," Joan answered, already at the foot of her unmade bed, peeling off her robe.

"For what?"

Joan walked to the bedroom door in her pajamas and, with one hand on the doorjamb, leaned her head into the living room. "I'm going out," she said matter-of-factly. She ducked back into the bedroom and called out over her shoulder. "To buy a car."

That very afternoon, as snow fairies danced in the air and in the glow of a car salesman's happy face, Joan purchased an Austin A30, four-door, with just enough room for a ladybug to get in and drive.

The price—the equivalent of six hundred American dollars—was not a problem. She made good money working for the government. She didn't have to pay rent, and she ate most of her meals on the government's dime, so she'd managed to save a few pence.

The problem—and indeed she had one—was simple enough.

She didn't know how to drive.

"I've never really been *in* a car," Joan told Jackson later that day as they stood outside of their apartment building with Ruby gawking nearby. "If I sit on the passenger side," she continued, "you can show me how."

Jackson bent at the waist, peering into the car's interior like he didn't know what to make of it, all the while wiping his nose with a handkerchief. "Land sakes, I cannot believe you did this. I can*not* believe you did this."

"Well," Joan asked Jackson, "can you?" Her words formed a puff of warm air that lingered between them.

Jackson sniffled. He pulled the collar of his coat closer to his chin, his hat lower over his ears. "Can I what?"

"Teach me to drive. Try to keep up, Jackson." Joan crossed her arms against the brutality of the air—so cold and intense it stole away the delectable aromas from the bakery and coffeehouse down the block.

"Ay-yai-yai. I don't know." He eyed it again.

"But you know *how* to drive, don't you?"

He eyed her, straightening. He pulled the woolen scarf wrapped twice around his neck up to his mouth. "Of course I know how to drive." His words were muffled. "Been driving since I was a pup."

"Then what's the problem?"

He wiped his nose one more time. "Can we at least go into the lobby to talk about this? My nose feels like a dog's and my head is threatening to pop off."

She put a hand on his coat sleeve and squeezed. "Jackson. I'm sorry," she said, feeling genuinely bad for the man. "Of course we can go inside. I only wanted . . . I wanted you to see, that's all."

His watery eyes met hers. "Now I have. Take me inside before I die right here on this frigid sidewalk."

The three found a corner in the lobby—a cluster of mismatched chairs positioned near a radiator—and tucked themselves into them. As always, Jackson sat between the two women. "The problem is," he said as he unwrapped and pulled the scarf from around his neck, "the Austin itself. The space between the steering wheel and the driver's seat."

"I don't follow you." Someone behind the front desk had a radio on; "Choo Choo Ch'Boogie" jitterbugged on the terrazzo floor of the cavernous lobby.

"I do," Ruby said. "Jackson is a tall man, Joan."

Joan looked from Ruby to gaze the length of Jackson's legs, bent at the knees and bouncing up and down in an effort to thaw out, his hands still shoved in his coat pockets. He removed one, wiped his still-red nose, and then returned it. "So I see," Joan said.

"Six foot two," Jackson supplied.

"Eyes of blue," Ruby added, then blushed like she'd just spent the last ten minutes standing on the beaches of Hawaii instead of the frozen sidewalks of Munich.

Jackson looked at her. Smiled easily. Winked.

Ruby looked as if she might stop breathing.

The man of my dreams . . . Joan heard the words of her old contest entry from somewhere deep down inside. *And it would be nice if he were six foot two, had blue eyes, and . . .*

"Lots of dark hair," she mumbled as the memory rolled back on her.

Jackson removed his hand again, this time to unbutton his coat and take it off. He pointed toward his temple. "Blond, I'm afraid."

The room spun and she blinked. "What?"

"You said, 'Lots of dark hair.'" He sniffled. "My hair is blond."

Joan willed herself back to the conversation at hand. "I'm sorry." She forced herself to laugh. "I was thinking about something else." She slid to the end of the chair and angled herself to face him better. "You were saying something about the space?"

"I'm over six feet tall, Joan. I'm not so sure I can fit my legs in the car if I'm sitting behind the steering wheel." He thought for a minute. "But I can probably sit in the passenger side and instruct you."

"And I could ride in the back," Ruby offered.

Jackson sighed so faintly Joan almost missed it. She could only hope Ruby did.

"Okay, then," she said. "I'll learn *behind* the wheel."

Jackson smiled. "When do you want to get started?" he asked.

"That's easy," she said, brightening. "Yesterday."

Chicago

"You look exhausted," Pat said to Betty from across the kitchen table where they, once again, went through the list of last-minute wedding details. A pot of coffee brewed on the stove, emitting its delicious scent across the room. Between them, two empty cups sat waiting to be filled, among a scattering of papers filled with lists and names.

Betty glanced up. "I *am* exhausted. I hate to disappoint you, but I may do nothing but sleep on our honeymoon."

Pat frowned, then brightened. "We'll have to remedy that," he said, leaning over for a kiss.

"By the way," she said as the coffee gurgled from the stove, "the mystery of where you're taking me has me wondering if I've packed appropriately. Don't you want to tell even *the bride*?"

Pat leaned his arms on the table. "Nope," he taunted. "I told you, pack for warm weather. At least one formal gown, but otherwise, shorts, short-sleeved tops, and—for the love of pete—your bathing suit."

Betty stood to get the coffee. "My mother is nearly beside herself," she said. "You know she doesn't like not knowing the details." She picked up the pot and brought it to the table. "And I'm afraid the apple hasn't fallen far from the maternal tree."

Pat chuckled as she poured. "There's something I'd like to talk to you about. I'm—ah—not 100 percent sure now is the best time."

Betty returned to her chair at the table, concern squeezing her throat. "What is it?"

He must have read the concern on her face because he quickly added, "Oh. Nothing bad. I was just thinking the other day . . . I know you told Ferguson that you'd be gone two weeks for the honeymoon, but have you thought further about . . . you know . . . after that?"

Betty prepared Pat's coffee and then her own, buying herself time to answer. She'd wondered when this might come up. He'd hinted several times about her not working after they married, but he'd never come right out and asked. "You're talking about me quitting my job." She slid his cup toward him with a push of her finger against the saucer.

"I'm an old-fashioned kind of guy, Betts. I'd like to think that I can provide well enough for us . . ."

Betty wrapped her fingers around her cup. "It's not that."

They'd already gone to the bank and opened an account in both their names, so she knew his financial status. For a young man fresh in business, it wasn't bad. In fact, it was downright impressive. But still . . . "What would I do with myself all day?"

Pat grinned. "If I say 'cook and clean,' will you drop-kick me out of the apartment and onto the street?"

Betty answered by raising her brow.

He laughed. "I don't know, sweetheart. Both of our mothers are involved in all sorts of social and civic activities. Clubs. That sort of thing. I want you to be able to do those things too."

A lovely picture, but Betty wasn't entirely sure *she* wanted to do those things. Did she really *want* to be a socialite, like her mother? Always looking down her nose at those who were not?

She reached across the table, over the pieces of paper with their dozens of details, and laid her hand on Pat's. "Is this something we can decide after we return?"

His eyes locked with hers, unblinking and yet so full of love. No matter what she asked of him, she knew he would provide for her. Today. Tomorrow. Forever. She sighed, contented even in the wait. Finally, crow's-feet crinkled near his temples and he said, "Of course. I only want you to be happy, Betts."

She leaned across the table for a kiss. "I am, Pat Callahan. More than you can begin to imagine."

He laid his hands flat against the table. "So, what's on the agenda for tomorrow?"

Betty shuffled a few pieces of paper together. "The girls and I have a late-afternoon appointment for the final fittings, and then we're going out to dinner."

"Sounds like fun," he commented.

It would be, Betty thought, *if only my mother weren't coming along.*

"Looks like someone has put on a pound or two," the seamstress said to Inga in the privacy of the dressing room.

"What?" Panic rose inside her. She looked at her reflection in the mirror, turning her back toward it to see that the zipper to the emerald-green, cocktail-length, full-skirted dress had refused to travel past the middle of her back. "There must be . . . some mistake," she said. "Maybe they ordered the size wrong."

The seamstress—a woman who appeared to be in her fifties—stood straight and blinked behind her cat-eye glasses. "When are you due, dear?" she asked, keeping her voice whisper-soft.

Inga's lips trembled. "What . . . what do you mean? I'm—"

"My dear," she began gently, "I've had eight children of my own and five of them were girls. Three of those girls have blessed me with grandchildren. I know what a thick waist means, and it doesn't mean you've been eating too many ice cream sodas down at the five-and-dime." She smiled weakly. "If it's any consolation, one of those daughters wasn't married when she first conceived." She glanced toward Inga's left hand. "I noticed you aren't wearing a wedding band." Her brow shot up. "Or an engagement ring."

Inga fought the tears forming in her eyes. If she cried, the girls would know. "No," she whispered, bringing her fingertips to her lips. "I thought—I hoped—I'd have more time before . . ."

The seamstress patted her shoulder and brought a handkerchief out from the light-blue sewing smock she wore. "Here you go. Dab at those eyes before your mascara runs."

Inga leaned toward the mirror, bringing the lavender-colored handkerchief to one eye and then the other. "What am I going to do?" she asked. "I mean, about the dress?"

The seamstress smiled. "That's easy. I can let out the waistline and no one will be the wiser." She put both hands on Inga's shoulders. "The bow in the waistline's center will hide whatever may be trying to pop out up front, but . . . I'd say within a week, you'll be rethinking nearly everything in your wardrobe." Kind eyes met hers in the reflection. "Does the father know?"

Inga nodded.

"But he doesn't take responsibility?"

Inga shook her head.

"Your parents? Do they know?"

"No. But my sister does."

"All right. Step out of the dress and let me see how much material we have on both sides."

Inga pulled the dress off, stepping out of it as the older woman continued. "Tell your mother first," she said. "Mothers have a way of dealing with fathers, I've found." She took the dress from Inga with a wink. "Your mother is a good woman?"

"Very much so."

"Then trust me. What you've done will hardly separate you from her love. Oh, she may be disappointed, but she won't stop loving you."

Inga reached for her street clothes hanging nearby. "I'll tell her," she said. "Thank you."

She waited until she was alone before collapsing in the frilly pink boudoir chair, clad only in her lingerie. Inga buried her head in the crook of her arm, weeping until she knew her face bore the telltale signs of her distress. She didn't care; she needed to cry it out in order to think it through.

By the time she dressed again, she had a plan. She had two weeks off with pay, so at least she had a little money coming in. On Sunday—the same day Evelyn was scheduled to leave for Georgia—she'd leave for Minnesota. She'd take the kind seamstress's advice. She'd tell Mor first. Then, together, they'd tell Far, a man who always listened to the will of God.

And if she lived past Monday, she'd try to do whatever God had in mind for her.

CHAPTER 38

March 21, 1953

Betty stared at herself in the oval-shaped, full-length mirror in the bride's room.

She'd worn plenty of lavish gowns in the past, but in the Carson's wedding gown—as the first of the five to wear it—she hardly recognized herself. She appeared . . . *delicate*. Like fine china.

Stunning. Like a bride.

Her bridesmaids and maid of honor—Colleen, her childhood friend—bustled about the room, practicing their march and how, exactly, to hold the tiny nosegays of magnolias she'd chosen for their bouquets. Betty glanced over her shoulder, watching.

"Up close to the bodice?" Evelyn asked. "Or down low near the hips?"

Betty turned back to the mirror, taking in a deep breath. In a little less than an hour, she would be Mrs. Betty Callahan. *Mrs. Pat Callahan,* her mother insisted. "We take the names of our husbands fully, Betty," she had said. "Trust me when I tell you that your husband's full name will come in handy one day."

Betty closed her eyes. Could she do this? She loved Pat. Of course she did. More than she had ever thought she could love anyone. Otherwise, she wouldn't be marrying him so soon after meeting him. But all week the thought of becoming her mother had plagued her, creeping in between the final plans and festivities before the wedding.

Leaving Hertz had been the last thing on her mind when Pat had proposed. She and Joan were a lot alike in that way—they both enjoyed the nine-to-five. Not like the others who, she knew, were putting in their time until their perfect mister came along.

Well, not Magda. But Magda could write while her children napped . . .

She felt her mother behind her and opened her eyes to see her reflection. "Wedding-day jitters?"

Betty nodded, although the answer wasn't complete. How could she say, "I'm concerned, Mother, that if I marry Pat, I'll become you"? That wouldn't be the right thing to do. Completely hurtful to a woman who seemed content to be only what she was. And, who knew, maybe Chloe, in her own way, had done a world more good than Betty realized.

Chloe rested her hands on Betty's shoulders. "Don't worry," she said into her ear. "No matter what happens, even if you trip and fall down the aisle, in an hour you'll be just as married as if you managed without a stumble."

Betty couldn't help but giggle. "Mother . . ."

"But for the love of all that's decent, please don't stumble *or* fall. I'll never hear the end of it at the club." Her fingertips lightly touched the traditional veil crowning Betty's head. "You are a good daughter, allowing your father the honor of drawing back the veil. I'm not supposed to mention it, but he's been rehearsing his one line since last week."

"'Her mother and I,'" Betty said, drawing in a shaky breath as the door leading into the wide hallway opened. Betty swung around as all her worries seemed to wash away. "Sister Brigit," she breathed.

"Ah, there she is," the old nun said, walking toward her. "The blushing bride."

"Who—?" Chloe began.

"Mother, this is my friend Sister Brigit," Betty answered as the sister crossed the room toward them. A keen sensation washed over her, and Betty knew that the sight of Sister Brigit had caused her to beam, partly out of admiration and partly out of relief.

Sister Brigit grabbed Betty's hands. "You are a lovely vision of love," she said, her Irish brogue thick on every word.

"Sister," Betty said, squeezing the nun's hands, "this is my mother, Chloe Estes."

The nun nodded.

"Sister? May I have a few private moments with you?" Betty glanced at her mother. "I want the sister to pray with me."

"Oh," Chloe said. "Of course, then." She corralled the bridesmaids into the hallway "for a minute or two."

Betty led Sister Brigit to a couple of Queen Anne armchairs, exquisite roses carved along the woodwork, both upholstered in chintz.

"Now what is this about needing a prayer?" the sister asked.

"Sister, what I need more than prayer is an answer."

"Prayer holds the answer, sweet one. All you have to do is be patient and listen."

Betty smiled weakly. "Sister, I wanted to meet with you earlier, but—this week has been . . . Sister, Pat has asked me to consider *not* working outside the home. To become socially and civically aware like . . ." She looked toward the door.

"Like your mother?"

Betty nodded.

"Ah, yes. I can see the prominence in that one." She moved her finger along the white of her wimple. "It's in the brow." She patted Betty's hand as she'd done the day they first met. "Why don't you compromise? You'll work until you decide to start a family. Then you can become as socially and civically minded as the rest of them."

"I hadn't thought of that." For an unmarried nun, she'd been quick with an answer.

"But there's more, isn't there?"

Betty swallowed past a small lump of emotion forming. "I love my mother, Sister, but I don't . . . I don't want to be *like* her. For all her *social work*, Chloe Estes is a bit of a snob. What if . . . what if by marrying Pat, I'm putting my foot on the road to becoming my mother?"

Sister Brigit laughed heartily. "You, my pet, have no worries there. What you are deep inside your heart," she said, pointing to the sweetheart neckline of the gown, "you will always be. Like my da used to say, 'Sweet old ladies come from sweet young ladies.' I foresee that you will be a sweet lady, no matter your age."

Betty released a pent-up sigh. Somehow, coming from Sister Brigit, she could believe the words. "Thank you." She leaned over to kiss the dry and wrinkled cheek of a woman she'd come to greatly admire. "I'd half thought to cancel this wedding *and* this marriage."

The door opened again and Chloe stuck her head in. "Betty. We must finish getting ready."

Betty stood. "Sure, Mother. Come back in." She smiled down at Sister Brigit. "I'm ready now."

Plymouth, Minnesota

A thick mantle of snow clung to the ground, even as the sun beamed down upon it, sending glints of light shooting from it like twinkling stars. Tree limbs, naked and achingly bare, reached upward to the sky like an old woman's fingers reaching for a hand up. Evergreen boughs hung beneath the weight of the snowstorm that had come in overnight—winter's last hurrah.

Inga hoped so, anyway. Although in Minnesota, one could never be quite sure.

She stood at the double-front windows in the living room of her childhood home, a drafty Victorian built in the late 1800s, peering out and waiting for her father to come home from work.

Waiting, as she had when she'd been a girl of about twelve, the day she'd been caught red-handed in a lie to her mother. Mor, aghast that her beloved daughter would do such a thing, declared that she would not punish her, but banished her to "wait for Far's arrival."

That wait had been the most excruciating of her young life, perhaps second only to the one she experienced now, as her mother sobbed upstairs in her bedroom.

Chilled by the cold creeping around the windowsill, Inga turned and walked into the kitchen to prepare a cup of hot tea. Something to warm her. To soothe her. Something to ease the queasiness in her stomach. A few minutes later, the whistle sent its shrill announcement into the room that the water had come to a boil, and Inga grabbed a dishcloth for the handle.

Her mother's footsteps caused her to pause. Inga looked up, crushed by the sight of swollen eyes, wet and red with tears, then went about her task. "Can I pour you a cup, Mor?"

"Yes," her mother said, barely above a whisper.

They prepared their tea in silence. Inga went to the old farm table, scarred by time yet highly polished, and sat. "Sit with me, Mor."

Her mother did, although she didn't sit close. "What I don't understand is . . ." Mor finally said, then paused as if waiting for Inga to finish the sentence.

"Mor, please just tell me that you still love me. That you won't kick me out of your life."

Her mother frowned, deep wrinkles creasing her forehead. "Don't be silly. Of course I still love you. You are my daughter and . . ." She looked away. "That baby . . . that baby is my grandchild."

Inga began to weep. "I'm so sorry. I never stopped to think . . . Mor, I promise you it happened only once. Only *once*. I'm not a harlot."

Mor stood, walked the length of the table to where her daughter sat, and drew her close. "There will be no more of that. I don't need the details to believe you. But you and I have to face your father when he gets home. It won't be easy, for either of us, but we'll face him together."

Savannah, Georgia

Although her plan had been to put her feet to the pavement of downtown Savannah by Monday afternoon, Aunt Dovalou insisted that she "do no such thing."

"I want you to take a day or two and just be," the petite redhead said on Tuesday afternoon as they sat together in the expansive living room of the grand house on Victory Drive. While her aunt busied herself with some needlepoint, Evelyn kept looking beyond the tied-back sheers at the large-paned, floor-to-ceiling windows to the wide front lawn where dogwood trees and azalea bushes boasted of springtime, and fat old live oaks formed a canopy over a row of palms in the median.

"Golly, Aunt Dovalou," she said, pushing up her glasses at the twang of her accent. "I didn't realize how much I missed the look of spring in the South until just now." She closed her eyes against the internal sound of George's voice, correcting her. Telling her to *"speak correctly."* To *"listen to the inflection of your words, Evelyn."*

Against her better judgment, she rephrased her statement. "The South is glorious in the spring, is it not?"

"Now listen, hon. Don't start trying to be something or somebody you're not. There's not a thing wrong with the way you said those words the first time. My gracious alive, what did that Yankee boy do to your self-esteem?"

Evelyn tried to laugh, but it came out more like a whimper.

"Oh, Evelyn . . ." her aunt exclaimed, stopped by the ringing of the doorbell. "Oh, good," she said, throwing her handwork into the crafts basket at her feet. "I bet I know who that is."

"Who?"

"Just hold on," she said, darting out of the ladies' parlor, her soft-soled shoes making whooshing noises against the wide-planked boards of the floor. "I'll be right back."

Evelyn's eyes roamed upward, traveling along the hand-carved Corinthian columns between the parlor and the expansive foyer. As the front door rattled in protest at being opened, she tilted her head back to study the crown molding, elegantly trimmed in gold, which matched the gilding above the fireplace mantel.

"Evelyn," her aunt said, bringing her attention back to the opening between the two columns and the handsome man standing there. "This is Brother Edwin Boland. He's the preacher at the First Baptist down on Habersham."

Evelyn started to rise, but quickly pushed herself back onto the settee. *"No, no, Evelyn. A lady never stands when approached. And you extend* your *hand first, not the other way around, darling."*

Darling . . .

Evelyn's breath caught in her throat as she held out her hand in greeting. "Nice to meet you, Brother—"

"Please," the young minister said, his amber-laced brown eyes smiling, "call me Ed." He took her hand in his. Unlike when she held George's hand—or he held hers—rough calluses pressed against her palm. This was more than a man of the cloth standing before her. This was a man's man, even with his blond hair worn long on top and swept fashionably back.

Aunt Dovalou stood proudly beside him. "Ed, why don't I get you something to drink? A Co-Cola?"

He smiled at her, his full lips parting over slightly uneven, but white teeth. "That'd be nice, Miss Dovalou."

She started to walk away, then paused. "Over crushed ice?" she asked.

The amber in his eyes twinkled. "Yes, ma'am."

After her aunt left the room, Ed took to one of the delicate armless chairs across from where Evelyn sat. A tall, broad-shouldered man, he appeared to be perching on doll's furniture. Evelyn couldn't help but smile. "Brother—Ed—would you prefer to go into the gentlemen's parlor? The chairs are much bigger over there."

Ed Boland pinked like a schoolboy. "That might be better," he said. They stood and made their way out of the room, across the foyer, and into a room much like the one they'd come from.

"Great thing about these old houses," he said, waiting for her to find a seat. She chose to sit on the overstuffed divan. He, in turn, sat in one of the more masculine chairs left over from her grandfather's era.

"You mean the two types of parlors?"

He crossed his legs as his arms draped easily along the armrests, looking as comfortable as George would have sitting among such elegance. "That's right. So, tell me more about yourself, Evelyn. Your aunt hasn't been able to stop talking about your coming."

Aunt Dovalou waltzed in about then, carrying a tray of Cokes and three glasses filled with chipped ice. Evelyn stood to take the tray. She set it down on a butler's table. Aunt Dovalou leaned over the table to pour the colas.

Ed smiled as her aunt handed him a glass. "Oh, this does look good." He took a long swallow—Evelyn could hear the liquid going down his throat from across the room—then smiled at them both. "I guess I was thirstier than I realized."

They all laughed, giving Evelyn a new sense of ease. One she hadn't felt since the doorbell had rung ten minutes earlier.

Evelyn took an offered glass from her aunt. "What brings you here today, Rev—Bro—Ed?" she asked. "Should I assume you are a friend of Aunt Dovalou's?"

The young reverend smiled broadly. "Your Aunt Dovalou allowed me to live here for a while when the Baptist pastorium was getting a fresh coat of paint in between the old pastor moving out and me moving in."

"Pastorium?" Evelyn wrinkled her nose. "Sounds like an institution."

Ed laughed again. "Parsonage."

"Oh." She paused to think for a moment before asking, "And there weren't any Baptist families who would house you?"

"Evelyn," her aunt quickly admonished. "I'm shocked." She looked across the room, wide-eyed. "Forgive her, dear Edwin. I fear she's been up north too long."

Evelyn's cheeks burned. "I'm sorry," she said, washing down her shame with a sip of the cold drink. "I didn't mean it like that . . ."

Ed threw back his head and bellowed with such vitality, his laughter echoed across the high ceiling. "Please, Evelyn," he said when he'd righted himself. "You are as delightful as your aunt insisted." He half rose from his seat to place the glass—empty but for the remaining ice—onto the butler's table. "Now, then . . . as to why I'm here." He braced his elbows on his knees and rubbed his hands together. "I understand you could use a job."

CHAPTER 39

Magda didn't have only one decision to make, but several.

What to eat for lunch was an easy one.

By eleven that morning, after worrying since breakfast, she went to the phone in the hallway, called Barry, and asked if he'd like to meet her for a bite.

"With my favorite girl? Absolutely," he said. She could see his smile through the wire. "How about a greasy burger at the Soda Shoppe?"

"Sounds yummy. Meet you there."

Magda applied a touch of lipstick and powder before dashing out the door wearing nothing more than pedal pushers, a springtime sweater, and a lightweight jacket. She arrived at the small L-shaped café to see that Barry had already gotten there and managed to wrangle a table for two.

"It sure is crowded," she said as he helped her remove her jacket.

"It's a Thursday at noon and this is downtown Chicago." He winked at her. "Or have you forgotten?"

"No. I haven't," she said, although she wasn't sure if her words had been said loud enough to be heard.

"I ordered for us both," he told her. "Burger and fries and a Coke. That okay?"

She nodded, momentarily remembering the grilled cheese and Harlan. "Perfect."

Barry studied her for all of five seconds before reaching across the table and taking her hand. "Hey. What's wrong?"

Magda blinked and the tears she'd hoped to keep at bay spilled down her cheeks.

He squeezed her hand, sending sweet comfort throughout her body. "Magda?"

"I haven't wanted to bother you with this," she said, then swallowed. "I need to find a new place to stay." She chuckled. "Or four new roommates by the end of the month, which doesn't really give me a lot of time."

"I don't understand." He released her hand when the waitress approached the table.

"Burger all the way, hold the onions, with fries for the lady," she said, setting the steaming-hot food in front of her. Magda used the diversion to swipe the tears from her cheeks. "The same for the gentleman and—" she reached for two tall glasses—"two colas." Her gum popped as she smiled at Barry, all but ignoring Magda. "Anything else? You got your ketchup and mustard right here." She pointed to the table.

"Thank you," Barry said. "I think we're fine for the time being."

When she'd walked away, he returned his attention to Magda. "Now, what's this all about? I know Joan and Betty are gone, but what about the others? Evelyn and Inga?"

"Evelyn left on Sunday for Savannah. She's moved back home." She grabbed the ketchup bottle and shook a good-size dollop onto her plate near the fries, then lifted the butter-greased bun and made a fat circle around the slice of tomato. "As for Inga . . ." Magda handed the bottle across the table. When Barry took it, she dropped her hands into her lap. "My sister has gone back to Minnesota."

Barry stopped halfway through a shake of the condiment bottle. "Why? What about her job?"

Magda looked at the napkin holder sitting between them. Somehow, she found it easier to say the words to paper and chrome than to her boyfriend. "She quit. She's . . . she's pregnant."

He brought the bottle back down on the table with a thud. "You're kidding." He paused. "How long have you known?"

"Since before Christmas." She looked up.

His eyes locked with hers, refusing her the consolation of looking away. "Why didn't you tell me?"

"It wasn't my place. Besides, it's a little—I mean—if *Nana* knew, she'd really hate me."

Barry remained silent for a moment, a clear indication that she was right. "What about the baby's father?"

"He doesn't believe the baby is his. He offered for them to live together, but . . ." She blinked. "Inga told Mor and Far on Monday. Far still hasn't spoken to her, other than to say he has to pray until God gives him an answer."

Barry sighed as though it were the end of a long week. "I don't understand some men . . ." He looked up. "Not your father—I understand *his* reaction—I'm talking about *the* father."

Magda let the words resonate within her, to bring warmth to the part of her soul that had ached since late December. "Just like you not to blame my sister. To not call her names, but to criticize the man." She tried to smile.

She dipped a fry into the ketchup before popping it into her mouth, then blew out. "Still hot," she said around it.

Barry picked up his burger. "Okay, well . . . I think this has pretty much made up my mind on things." He bit down on it, then made a show of chewing his food.

Fear crept along her spine, tickling the hair at the nape of her neck. "Meaning . . . ?" Would he end his relationship with her over her sister's sin?

He put the burger down. "I wanted to wait. I wanted to court you for at least a year . . ."

"Court? How beautifully antiquated."

He waved a hand in the air. "I wanted to give Deanne time . . . and my—Nana—"

"Time? For what?"

"To accept you. Us. You and me." His finger darted between the two of them.

Magda blinked. "Are you . . . are you proposing *marriage*, Barry Cole? In the middle of a greasy spoon, me in a pair of pedal pushers and sneakers, and you with burger grease on your chin?"

"Would you love me any more or any less if we were all dolled up, dining in the finest restaurant Chicago had to offer? I know firsthand, Magda. Marriage isn't always easy. It's not always rose petals and candlelight." Barry pulled a napkin from the holder and wiped his hands with it, leaving it nothing but a shredded ball. He reached for her hand again, which she readily gave to him. "But I know I love you. And I believe you love me."

"You know I do." She couldn't have put up with Harriet Nielson otherwise.

He grinned. "If you'd like, I'll get down on one knee, right here and now."

Magda coughed out a chuckle. "No. Please, no. But . . . you really *do* need to talk to Deanne and *Rock*." She sighed. "And Nana."

His face grew solemn. "My children don't run my life, Magda. The day I make them my friends will be the day they've grown up and no longer need me to be their father."

"Will that ever happen?"

"Sure it will. I consider my dad my best friend. But that didn't happen until I became a father myself."

"I see." She reached for her drink with her free hand, then raised the glass toward him. "Can we at least toast the occasion?"

Barry picked up his glass, laid the rim against hers, and said, "Miss Christenson, what will it be? To our marriage or to your finding a gloomy room for rent?"

Magda grinned as she tapped her glass against his. "To us."

Munich

Joan stood in the lobby and all but ripped open the envelope with the red, white, and blue stripes across one corner.

> *Dear Joanie,*
>
> *Greetings from Savannah. Yes, I have returned to the Southland. To the land of cotton where old times are not forgotten.*
>
> *That probably makes no sense to you, having lived in England so long and all.*

She was correct. It didn't.

> *I had hoped to get this to you sooner rather than later, but I suppose by the time it crosses the ocean, it's later no matter what. You know the old saying, "Nothing stays the same but change"? Well, it's true. As I write this, Magda is the only one of the five of us left in the apartment on Greenleaf. Inga moved back to Minnesota (I don't know why, but I will tell you she left her job too, so obviously something is up). You are in Germany. I am here. And Betty is, of course, on her honeymoon.*

Oh, Joan! The wedding was lovely. I admit I'd never been to a Catholic service, but it was so full of meaning. And the way Pat looked at Betty while they exchanged vows was something to behold, I tell you. You should pat yourself on the back, Joan, for bringing those two together.

I am adjusting to my new life here in Savannah, which is completely different from life in Portal. My aunt's home is on Victory Drive, which is lined with grand old homes of a bygone era. If George could see me in this house, he'd have to rethink my humble beginnings. Although my mother married a poor farmer, she came from good stock. But even though my aunt has inherited the family house, I don't think there's a lot of money left in the bank, if you get my meaning. She tells me that she is existing just fine but that, one day, she wants to turn the house over to the church so they can house the preacher and his family.

Speaking of which. My aunt did the most amazing thing. She arranged an interview with a Baptist preacher—who, I will tell you now, is entirely too young and too good-looking to be a man of the cloth—who was in need of a secretary. The Baptists don't hire their own when it comes to the books nor do the Methodists, so when he (his name is Edwin, but he likes to be called Ed) told Aunt Dovalou that he would need a new secretary soon, she told him I was coming and . . . well, I got the job. I start next week.

I'm a tad concerned about working with a single man, Joan. I don't want people to gossip. And there's nothing Southern women like more than a juicy tidbit.

Besides, it's going to take me a long time to get past George Volbrecht.

Oh. If you are wondering about Hank Shute, he and Dixie are engaged. So, any thoughts I might have had about coming back home and rekindling something with him are out.

Write soon.

Love,
Evelyn

Joan folded the letter, pondering. *Any thoughts . . . about . . . rekindling . . .* She sighed. "Poor Evelyn," she said, stuffing the paper back into the envelope. "I'm sure God knows best."

She darted up the staircase leading to the apartment she now shared with Ruby, excited to write back to America, and to include details of her weekend adventures of exploring old German castles.

Plymouth, Minnesota

Inga and Mor sat like bookends on the living room sofa, staring across the room to where Far stood, his back to the grand piano. The steely displeasure at his oldest daughter remained stamped on his face, his lips drawn more thin than Inga ever remembered seeing them, and his eyes like black coal, waiting to ignite into flame. Behind the piano, past the front windows, rain fell from the gray sky, pattering the lawn and cracked sidewalk—a sure sign they'd see more snow before morning.

Far brought his hands together in front of him, clasping them together. "I have prayed without ceasing these past many days," he said, finally. "I have told God that I need him to answer me in haste as my daughter would not be able to hide her condition very long."

Inga's stomach clenched. How could it be, she wondered, that she had allowed herself to come to this place? She could have easily gone away. Far away. Had her baby and put it up for adoption. Or moved in with Frank as he'd suggested. Anything. Anything would have been better than this . . . whatever her fate would be.

Mor shifted on the other end of the sofa. "And has God answered you, my dear?"

Far nodded once. "He has."

Inga wanted to ask just how the answer had come. Telegraph? Telegram? Had God written the answer in the snow across the back lawn?

But she dared not, not even today—April Fool's Day.

She'd taken the risk of coming here—coming *home*—in the hope that her sin could somehow be absolved by whatever punishment her father doled out. She'd have to sit and calmly listen now to what that entailed.

"I may have mentioned this before," Far began again. "There is a young man who graduated a year ago. Nearly a year ago. One of the brightest students to ever set foot into one of my classrooms or ever grace our college, and one of the few young men with whom I've allowed a personal bond to form."

Slowly—oh, so slowly—the blood eased from Inga's brain and she somehow managed to step outside of herself to hear the rest of her father's words.

"Since completing his vicarage, he has graduated and has stayed in contact with me. He is the minister of a small church, but he's hungry for more. He sees himself with a larger congregation to lead and, one day, a wife and children to warm his home.

"I have made all the necessary calls, Inga. He will marry you quietly. Here. And the two of you will then move to Indianapolis, where Axel will lead the flock at one of the moderate Lutheran churches there."

The words, heard through a veil of cotton-like tension, sat heavy in Inga's ears. "Axel," she said.

"Axel Johansson. He has agreed to this." Far's words were so firm, Inga wondered if he thought he was standing before a classroom, barking out the day's lesson. "And he has assured me he will be good to you *and* to your child."

Inga reached for her mother, but Mor's face had grown as distant as her father's. She turned back to her father, wildly wondering how she could have gone from independent woman to being ordered to such a barbaric fate. "I have no say in this?" she all but stormed.

"Daughter!" Far's voice boomed in the room and she jumped, aware now of the tension coming from the other end of the sofa.

Inga stood. "I'm sorry, Far, but . . . don't you think *I* should have the right and the time to pray about this? To decide what is best for me and my baby?"

"Your time for praying will come later," he said. "And I suggest you do so in a way that would have saved you, had you done it in the first place instead of lying down with some—" He caught himself as Mor gasped. "My apologies, dear." He looked again to Inga, who remained standing. "Axel will be here in the morning to meet you. You'll marry next Friday. I'll perform the service and your mother and Magda will stand in as witnesses."

"I need . . . I need to get my dress," Inga said, although it sounded foolish even coming from her own lips.

"Dress?" Mor said, clearly shocked at the notion.

Inga turned to look at her, to see that—for the first time—Mor now looked directly at her. "I have a dress, Mor. My roommates and I bought it at Carson's." The words spilled out of her. "Betty's only been back to work two days from her honeymoon, and I'm sure she hasn't had time to have it dry-cleaned and . . ." She took a long breath, shuddering during the intake. Was she really going along with this? Did the dress from Carson's truly matter? "I have a dress," she said.

"A dress," Mor sighed, as though the dress were hanging right there before them.

"There will be no need for that," Far said. "This isn't going to be the wedding you dreamed of, Inga. This will be the wedding of—"

"A sinner?"

"Inga, no," Mor said, standing.

Her father rested a hand on the curve of the piano's top board. She stood transfixed as it flexed, then relaxed. "Do not defy me, Inga." The instruction came from an eerily calm voice. "It will not go well for you."

She felt her cheeks go hollow and she bit on a tiny layer of flesh to keep from screaming. "All right, Far. I'll marry this man." After all, marrying him didn't mean *staying* married. As soon as the baby was born, as soon as it showed enough of its father's features, she'd return to LA. Even marriage to Frank had to be better than marriage to a perfect stranger, a man of her father's choosing. "But I'm wearing my dress. I paid my sixty dollars."

Her mother took her hand. "Is it . . . is it *white*, Inga?"

Inga nodded. "It is."

"That will never do," Far stated, then turned on his heel and spoke to his feet. "I'll expect you down here at ten in the morning, Inga. None of this staying in bed half the day. And you'll be on your best behavior." He walked across the room, stopping at the foyer entryway and turning to look at her once more. "After tomorrow, we will never speak of this again. You will marry, leave, and when you will return, it will be after the baby is born and old enough that no one will question who its father is. There will be *no* further comments. Ever. Do I make myself clear?"

She had said it, hadn't she? That she would accept whatever God handed to her? But as she stood before this punishment, she wasn't sure she really could. To pretend none of it had ever happened—that her love for Frank had not happened—was nearly more than she could bear.

And yet—"Yes, Far. You have made yourself clear."

Far's cold eyes left her, turning tender as they rested on her mother. "Come, dear."

Mor followed him out, and when their footsteps were nothing but muffled memory, Inga darted up the stairs to her bedroom, closing the door firmly behind her.

The next morning, before the man she would marry stood at their front door, she placed a call to Mr. Ferguson's office at Hertz in Chicago.

CHAPTER 40

If Far had searched the world over, he could not have found a man more physically different from Frank Martindale, even if he'd given the search everything he had. To Frank's dark hair, thick brow, and radiant blue eyes, Axel Johansson's was blond, the longer hair at the top conservatively combed back. His brows rose at the bridge of his nose, as if he were in perpetual question. And his eyes—the color of a blue glass marble—were filled with wonder and innocence.

But he was tall—Inga would give him that—and broad-shouldered. The top lip had a deep Cupid's bow, which gave him the appearance of always smiling. His boy-next-door charm, she thought before they'd even been properly introduced, would work in his favor before "the flock." But she wasn't sure how far it would go with her.

Far introduced them in the living room, as promised. Axel took her hand in his, shaking it as if they'd just met at a party. He glanced momentarily at the infinitesimal swell in her belly, then brought his eyes back up to hers, apologizing with them. Mor walked in then, carrying a tray boasting two cups from her best china. The aroma of coffee laced with fresh-ground cinnamon wafted around the room.

Axel smiled. "My *mormor* puts cinnamon in her coffee as well."

Mormor. Of course Far has found a Swede through and through.

"Dr. Christenson and I will take our coffee in our sitting room," Mor announced, setting the tray on the coffee table. She looked at Inga. "Inga, we'll leave you to do the honors." Mor slipped her arm into Far's and, for the craziest of moments, Inga thought she saw Mor forcing him from the room.

"How do you take your coffee, Mr. Johansson?" she asked when she'd found her voice.

"Black, one sugar," he said, surprising her. She'd expected he'd want cream. Lots and lots of cream.

Inga wore a high-neck, emerald-green twirling dress with bold stitching on the triangle-shaped pockets—one she'd purchased at David & DuRand one evening when Joan worked. She knew, as she prepared his coffee, that she appeared the picture of domesticity. And, perhaps, of purity—especially with the single strand of pearls at her neck and the triple strand at her right wrist.

She handed him the coffee, her fingers loosely gripping the fragile saucer. He took it, keeping his eyes on the cup rather than her. "Thank you," he said.

Inga walked to the nearest chair. "Would you like to sit down?"

He didn't answer her; he simply sat. Only then did she ease herself into her chair, making certain to cross her legs at the ankles. "Mr. Johansson—"

He cleared his throat as he took a sip of coffee. She noticed the length of his neck, and the way his Adam's apple bobbed as he swallowed. "Call me Axel," he said, then smiled with discomfort as he looked up. "After all, we're going to be married in a week."

Inga laced her fingers, saying nothing.

"Don't you want coffee?" he asked, his eyes cutting to the tray.

"No," Inga replied. "I'm afraid my mother has forgotten—lately coffee doesn't—I'd prefer tea."

Axel pinked. "Oh."

"Do you mind if I ask how old you are? Axel?"

"Twenty-three." He took a hurried sip of coffee. "Twenty-four next month."

Two years her junior . . . And so seemingly innocent. Indianapolis would eat him for lunch. "And do you have any questions you'd like to ask me?"

Axel set the cup and saucer on the octagon-shaped table next to his chair. "I—uh—your father said that we aren't to talk about it." He nodded toward her stomach. "About the father. The baby. We're only supposed to talk about it as if it's ours."

"And you don't want to rock the boat with my father, I take it."

His eyes widened. "I want—" he began, but then pushed his weight against the back of the chair.

Inga waited, but when he didn't continue, she finished for him. "You want the church in Indianapolis." *Which you are clearly not ready for.*

What had her father been thinking?

The line of his jaw grew firm. "Yes, I do. More than anything else."

She laughed lightly. "Even if you have to give your life away to get it?"

"I don't see it that way, Inga."

Inga startled, hearing her name from his lips for the first time, as if he'd been practicing the syllables over and over the night before. Whispering them. Saying them with authority. In laughter and through tears. "How *do* you see it?"

"I trust God with the direction of my life. 'The steps of a good man are ordered by the Lord,' the Good Book tells us, 'and he delighteth in his way.'" He paused. "But I've not been happy in my present position and so I prayed for three days that a new door would open or that—at the very least—I would find joy in my present position. At the end of the three days, your father called. It seems to me that God heard my prayer as well as your father's."

But has he heard mine? "I understand."

"Do you?"

No. "Yes, of course."

He brought his hand up to his mouth, cupping it and pinching his nose before saying, "But right now you are struggling with your faith."

Inga blinked. How sweet, his trying to play pastor. "I'll be honest with you, Axel. There's not a lot to struggle with."

"Well, I hope to be a part of the rectifying of that," he said. "If you'll allow me to try, I think I can bring you some happiness. I know that, with the new position, I can take care of you and the baby."

"With a marriage in name only," she blurted. Heat rushed across her face.

His blushed as well. "There will be no pressure from me, Inga."

She shifted, crossing one leg over the other. "All right then. I *do* feel it important we are up front with each other," she said. "From the start."

Axel stood—was he leaving?—and crossed the room to her.

Inga rose, waiting unsure until he offered his hand again, which she took. "Friends, then," he said, his handshake less introductory and more businesslike.

She smiled, amazed that she could. "Friends."

That night she wrote Frank a letter, letting him know the name of the man she would marry—unless he called to stop her—and where they would reside. *I will send you a photo of your child in due time,* she wrote. *So that you will, one day, know the truth.*

Evanston, Illinois

Barry found Magda a room for rent in a boardinghouse not far from where he lived with his children and their grandmother.

"I need to stop calling her my mother-in-law," he told Magda as he helped her move the last of her things to the Victorian where he wasn't allowed to go past the living room. Jessie Higgins—a spinster friend of Harriet's who owned the house—wouldn't hear of it. She already looked down her nose at Magda, and the notion of Barry carrying a large box up the stairs to Magda's bedroom went over like the proverbial balloon made of lead. "She can carry it just fine," the stout, graying woman declared that Saturday morning. "If it's too heavy, she can separate the contents and make two trips."

Later, as they sat on the front porch, their hands clasped between two rockers, Barry chuckled. "She's a tough old broad," he muttered into the cool night air.

"Shhh." Magda bit her lip until the desire to laugh subsided. "She'll hear you."

Barry turned his face toward her. "I have to get going soon," he said.

She laid her head back, resting it against the hard slats of the rocker. "I know. I wish you didn't." She grinned at him. "But if she won't let you take a box up, I guess the notion of you and me staying out here all night is out."

"Very out."

Magda stopped rocking, sat up, and slid to the end of the seat. "Barry? How *are* the kids doing with this? My moving so close and our getting married? You said they'd come around, but that doesn't really tell me anything."

Barry looked at her, his dark eyes becoming more imperceptible as the gray closed in around them. "You know how Douglas feels."

"Rock," Magda corrected.

"Rock." He grinned and she sighed, loving the moments he smiled at her as though she'd just said something to set the world right. "Not to worry. Deanne *will* come around. So will Nana. Although she did insist on bringing a silver-framed photograph of Barbara to the living room the other day."

"Where had it been?"

"In her room."

"Did she say why?"

"No, and I didn't ask."

"I think we are both smart enough to figure that one out." Magda returned to sitting fully in the chair, looking out across the lawn to the houses on the other side of the street. Yellow light glowed behind many of the windows. In the house directly before them—the one with the Priscilla curtains drawn away from the living room window—a family bustled about. A mother, a father, and two children—a boy and a girl. "It's like a Norman Rockwell painting," Magda whispered.

"Hmm?"

"Nothing," she said. A story had begun to form. The perfect family . . . from the outside looking in. And perhaps they sat in the warmth of their home, staring out the window at the man and woman holding hands on the front porch of a boardinghouse. Young lovers, they supposed, with a bright future in front of them.

But in real life, nothing was perfect and little was bright.

That would be her next story for the magazine.

She jumped up. "I have to go upstairs," she said quickly, reaching down to kiss him briefly. "I've got an idea."

Barry chuckled as if he understood—and maybe he did—but he shook his head as he stood. "I thought we were going to set a wedding date tonight."

Magda shook her head. "Let's wait a couple of months, okay?"

"Months?" His voice held the squeak of a prepubescent boy's.

"Let my parents get over this thing with Inga, and give Deanne time to get used to me being so close." She glanced from the front door to the house across the street. "I need to get upstairs," she said, kissing him again. "Give the kids my best."

"What about Nana?" he teased. She could see him plainly now, standing there in the light coming from a streetlamp that had just flickered on. She smiled contentedly—he looked all put together, even in casual pants and a simple short-sleeved shirt tucked loosely at the waist—and, soon enough, he would be hers for life. Her husband.

"I love you," she answered, then opened the door and dashed up the stairs without so much as a good night to Jessie Higgins.

Plymouth, Minnesota

The wedding would take place in the church—Inga's father had given her that much—but without music. Without a cake or punch or a receiving line. Far would officiate with Axel at his left and Inga at his right. Mor's place would be where it should be, the first seat behind the bride.

And Magda would walk before her down the aisle.

"Did you bring it?" Inga whispered to her on Thursday evening after Magda arrived at the family home and all the niceties had been spoken.

Magda nodded as they exchanged unspoken words of understanding.

Of course, Far had wondered why Magda had brought two suitcases for such a short visit. Magda only shrugged. "I brought some extra things," she said.

"What things?" Mor asked.

Again Magda shrugged. "This and that." Then she cuddled against their father, nuzzling him as only she would be allowed to do—at least for a while. "Far, *try* to be happy, all right? Your oldest daughter is getting married and, soon, you'll hear the pitter-patter of tiny feet in this house again. Won't that be lovely?"

Far smiled at the younger of his two girls, but the smile didn't quite reach his eyes. "We'll see," he said.

"Far," Magda said, squeezing his hands. "Can you imagine how Mary's parents must have felt when she came home from seeing Elizabeth and told them she was with child?" She waved a hand. "I'm not saying, of course, that we can compare her pregnancy to Inga's, but all babies are a blessing, are they not? And this one, Far, shall likely have traces of the Christenson spark in its eyes, the upturn of Mor's nose. Won't that be lovely?"

And with those words, Far's eyes regained some of the love he had for Inga. She felt it again as he looked across the room at her and at the roundness of her belly.

As soon as the sisters made it upstairs to their old bedroom, Magda tossed one of the suitcases onto her bed, popped open the latches, and threw back the top. The dress lay there, bodice up, in all its glory. "Oh, Magda," Inga breathed, pulling it from the case. "It's as gorgeous as I remember it."

Magda reached out. "Get undressed and let's try it on. Hopefully it will still fit."

Inga stripped out of her clothes as fast as her fingers would allow. She stood before her sister in nothing but a brassiere, slip, and her nylons as she ducked her head, allowing Magda to drape the luxury over her body. "I've tried hard not to eat too much," she whispered, dipping her arms into the sleeves. "Or only eat rabbit food."

Magda giggled. "Okay. Here goes. Let's see if these buttons will meet in the middle." She started at the bottom and then, when she'd reached the buttons closest to Inga's waist, she switched to those at the top, working her way down. Inga felt the tugging. The pulling. The lifting of fabric to reposition it around her. "Well?" she asked, knowing full well she still felt cool air against her lower back.

Magda walked around her, frowning. "There's about a two-inch gap."

Inga's shoulders slumped as her brow shot up. "Well, I guess Far has won." She hiked up the skirt of the dress, walked to the closet door, and opened it wide. "I'm sure there is *something* in here that will do."

Magda pushed her aside. "Go. Go stand over there in front of the mirror and get a good look at how beautiful you are. Let me look for an alternative."

If wearing the dress in her bedroom for these few minutes was all she'd get, then so be it. She stepped slowly toward the dresser, eyes on her face, imagining that the mirror was Frank, watching her march down the aisle. Eyes full of love. A face filled with wonder—*amazement*—that he had landed such a beautiful bride.

"Inga," Magda exclaimed.

Inga turned.

"Look." She held up a wide pink satin ribbon—the sash from a gown she'd worn to a high school dance. "Come, come."

Inga retraced her steps and threw her arms out wide. Magda

worked the middle of the sash across her waist, then wrapped it around, tying it off in a large, full bow. She walked back around her sister and brought her hand to her lips. "Perfect," she sighed, and bit her bottom lip.

Inga turned slowly until her eyes found the mirror and the reflection of a young bride, gowned in white and swathed in sassy pink. *Not quite Mary,* she thought wistfully.

But not Hosea's Gomer, either.

CHAPTER 41

April 3, 1953

The next morning, Magda readied herself for her father's wrath and her mother's disappointment. She'd experienced neither in her lifetime, but if it meant taking a little of the heat away from Inga, she was glad to do it. If Mor and Far asked, she would take full blame for the dress. And the sash.

As Inga spent a few final moments in the church's bridal room—truly no more than an oversize restroom—Magda went into the richly paneled sanctuary, where her mother had already found her seat and her father, dressed in his pastoral robes, stood near the altar with a suited someone who looked more overgrown boy than man. She stopped halfway down the aisle, swallowed, and then continued on. "You must be Axel," she said, smiling, extending her right hand as she reached him.

He took it, squeezing. "And you must be Magda."

She nodded once. "I am."

"Where is your sister?" Far demanded, and Magda noted that the gruffness in his voice had returned.

"A little powder on her nose, Far." She looked around at the stained-glass windows and the pipes rising from behind the organ.

"I don't see a fire. And aren't you the one who always says patience is a virtue?"

Mor stood. "I'll go see if I can be of assis—"

"Mor, no." Magda hoped she didn't sound too anxious. "I'll go." She patted her mother's shoulder. "You sit here and enjoy being the mother of the bride."

She hurried back up the aisle, almost colliding with Inga in the vestibule. They smiled at each other and Magda held up her hands. "Wait. Don't go in quite yet."

She reentered the sanctuary, stopping at the pew farthest in the back. She opened her deep, wide purse, pulled out a small book, and stepped back to where Inga waited, fluffing the skirt of the gown. "Here," she said, presenting a white leather Bible.

Inga took it, reverently holding it in her hands. "Where did you get this?"

"I bought it. I wanted you to have something to hold since I knew Far wouldn't allow you to carry flowers." She reached for Inga's hand. "Promise me, if that baby is a girl, you'll give it to her one day to carry at her own wedding."

Inga smiled softly. "I promise. And if it's a boy, I'll give it to *his* bride." But then she frowned. "Did you happen to notice—by chance—if a letter might have come for me in the mail?"

"Noooo. Why?" A sense of dread washed over her. "What have you done?"

Inga shrugged one shoulder. "Nothing. Obviously, nothing. I'd only hoped . . ." She glanced at the open doorway to the sanctuary. "Is Axel in there?"

Magda nodded.

"What do you think? Be honest."

Magda knew she could tell her exactly what she thought. That she could have done worse with a young man who'd made a bargain with their father. That he seemed nice enough and that kindness danced in his eyes. But she chose another route. "I feel quite sorry for him, actually."

Inga's brow furrowed. "For *him*? He's getting a wife and a baby and the church of his dreams. Why would you feel sorry for him?"

"Because," Magda answered slowly, "he has to live with *you* the rest of his life." She winked, then jerked her head toward the inner door of the sanctuary. "Give me one minute; then *glide* down the aisle. Make this moment everything you want it to be and then some, okay?"

Inga nodded, tears glistening in her eyes.

"Ready?" Magda asked.

Inga's chest rose and fell behind shimmering illusion. "As I'll ever be."

Eight months later
December 1953
Lake Forest, Illinois

Magda parked Barry's car in the diagonal space in front of the storefront café Betty had given her directions to.

"In the middle of downtown Lake Forest," she'd said. "You can't miss it."

Magda tugged at her wool gloves before exiting the car. Lake Michigan sent a bitter wind to slap at Magda's face before pushing her body against the car as she tried to walk around it to the snow-lined sidewalk.

A struggle ensued, but she eventually made it to the garland-trimmed door of the café—head down and face buried in her hand-knitted scarf. Once inside, she brushed snow flurries from the shoulders of her coat and looked around. Betty had already arrived and sat in a corner booth for two, her hands wrapped around a steaming cup of coffee, her painted-red lips blowing into it. When she spotted Magda, she set it on the table and waved.

Magda grinned, moving between the tables—each decorated with tiny evergreens. As she moved toward her old roommate, Betty slid out of her seat, extending her arms.

"Look at *you*," she exclaimed over the din of noise from the other diners. From somewhere way back in the kitchen, a radio played the controversial hit of the previous year, "I Saw Mommy Kissing Santa Claus."

"Me?" Magda grinned after their quick hug. "Look at *you*!" She reached out a hand to touch Betty's swollen abdomen, then stopped. "May I?"

Betty nodded. "Why not? Everyone else does."

Magda pulled her right glove off before placing her palm against the baby growing inside and, within the time it takes a baby to bat its eyelashes, felt a thump against her fingertips.

Both women laughed.

"Sit. Sit and tell me everything," Betty said.

Magda hung her coat and scarf on the booth's brass hook before sliding in and looking for their waitress. Spying the middle-aged woman holding a coffeepot and walking toward them, she pointed to the table and said, "Coffee, please." She removed her other glove and stuffed both into her purse. After she'd been served, she set about preparing the hot drink. "Can you believe Barry and I are *finally* getting married?"

Betty rested her chin on her hand. "What *took* you so long?"

"A lot of things. First, there was Inga . . ." Magda made a face, hoping to lighten the issue that—even so far in the past—still made her feel uneasy.

"How is she?"

"Good. She had a little girl back in July, you know. Seven pounds, six ounces." She sighed. "Born with lots of dark hair. You've never seen so much. I told Axel—her husband—to put all his money on shampoo stock."

The women laughed again, and Betty sobered first. "I'm sorry that happened to her, but . . . she's doing okay?"

Magda nodded. "She doesn't talk about her life much. She really . . . She's trying to be a good mother. Focus on the baby."

"What did she name her?" Betty's eyes grew large as she brought her cup of coffee to her lips. "And please don't tell me *Frances*." She drew in a sip.

"No. It took Far a month after the wedding to speak to either of us—what with Inga wearing the wedding dress and all. If she'd named the baby after *her* father, I think *our* father would have disowned us."

"Well, then?" Betty set the cup on the table.

"Emma. She named her Emma."

"Emma," Betty breathed out the name. "If we have a girl, we've decided to name her Patricia."

"For Pat."

"Yes."

"And if it's a boy?" Magda wrapped her hands around the coffee cup, allowing the heat to penetrate the cold in her bones.

Betty smiled. "After his father." She patted Magda on the arm. "Now tell me. Details. I want details. Other than Inga, why have you waited so long?"

"Okay." Magda took her first sip of coffee. "Yes, Inga. That was the first thing. But the biggest is that I keep hoping, somewhere along the way, Barry's daughter and the children's grandmother will come to accept me."

"Not yet, huh?"

"We're not even close to acceptance. In fact, sometimes I feel that things have gotten worse." She dipped her chin. "So, I put my nose to the old grindstone, keeping my focus on my work. Until Barry convinced me that if we wait until *they* come around, he and I will be too old to care." She laughed lightly. "By the way, where's the dress? You brought it, right?"

Betty's eyes traveled to the door of the café and she raised her chin. "Tucked away in the trunk of my car. Say, Pat read in the paper that you won an award recently."

Magda shrugged even as a smile crept from deep inside her. "I had this story idea one night while sitting on the porch with Barry. I wrote it, submitted it to a contest, and . . . voilà. But—wouldn't you know it—Harlan Procter was the one handing out the awards." She shook her head. "I could have done without his condescending attitude as he handed me the plaque."

"Does Barry know? About the two of you?"

"There's really nothing to know. We dated a few times and he gave me some pointers on how to be a better writer. That's it."

Betty raised a brow. "And you thought you were in love with him . . ."

"No. Well, maybe I did *then*, but since Barry I see things much differently. There's love . . . and then there's *love*."

Betty grinned. "I can't argue with that." She gave a half laugh, then said, "Sister Brigit says that even though we make our plans, the Lord orders our steps. No matter what we think we want, he's always got it under control."

"I agree with that." She placed both hands on the table. "So, Betts. What do you do with yourself all day now that you are a woman of leisure?"

Betty laid her hand across the top of her belly. "Mostly, I'm getting the house ready for this one. I'm doing a little charity work—organizations my mother and Pat's mother have gotten me involved in." She raised a finger. "Before you go thinking something—"

"I'm not thinking anything," Magda teased.

"Well, before you do, I am *not* becoming my mother." She sighed. "I do enjoy it, though. The work. Far more than I thought. Oh, and Sister Brigit has encouraged me to work with the St. Vincent de Paul charity."

Magda rested against the back of her seat. "That's good." She sighed. "*Good* for you."

"Do you ever hear from—" they said together and then laughed again.

Betty pointed across the table. "You first."

"I was going to ask if you ever heard from Evelyn or Joan. I assume you were about to ask the same."

Betty nodded. "I got a letter from Evelyn . . ." She trailed, biting her bottom lip as though she contemplated the date. "Gosh, I guess it was back in September. She's working at a Baptist church in Savannah."

Magda grinned. "I should go see Evelyn sometime. I think I should become immersed in the Southern culture so I can write the next great Southern novel."

"Move over, Samuel Clemens."

Magda chuckled. "Or maybe Flannery O'Connor. Hmm . . . then again, I *am* getting married in two months. Oh, well. I don't guess I'll be running down to Georgia anytime soon." She pursed her lips. "Unless I can talk Barry into taking me there on our honeymoon."

Betty waggled a finger. "No, no. The Caribbean is *definitely* all it's cracked up to be."

Magda twirled her coffee cup before taking another long sip.

"So, has Evelyn managed to get over George? Is she seeing anyone down there? What was the guy's name she left behind?"

"Hank. And, no. He married. And . . . she says she's not seeing anyone, but she went on for a page and a half about the preacher she's working for." Betty nodded. "She *did* ask about George. I didn't have the heart to tell her that we see him from time to time, a different girl on his arm every night, so when I wrote her back I just didn't mention him at all."

Magda sighed. "Poor Evelyn. She's so much better off without George."

"Aren't we all."

"So, then, what about Joan? Do you ever hear from her?"

Betty slid her coffee cup to the edge of the table, alerting the waitress of her need for another cup. "I do . . . about once a month." She twisted a little to open the purse sitting in the seat beside her and pulled out a letter. "I got this just this morning, actually." She pulled the letter from the envelope and unfolded the paper while the waitress poured another cup and walked away. "It says:

"Dear Betts,

"I have been relocated to Nuremberg, Germany, where I will soon begin work as the secretary of Major General Richard C. Partridge, US Army. I will work for the Special Activities Division, US Forces in the Palace of Justice. I believe I will be here for the duration of my time in Germany, which should be another year.

"When I arrived in Nuremberg, my heart sank. This onetime-beautiful medieval town still lies in ruins. But I will say the Germans are very smart; the first thing they did after the war was repair the transportation system and

the heart of their communities—restaurants, bakeries, bistros. However, there are still gutted buildings with only half their walls standing jagged against the backdrop of devastation. Even after such a long time, I find this to be depressing."

Betty paused to take a sip from her coffee, and Magda used the break to shake her head and interject. "Nuremberg and the Palace of Justice . . . What else does it say?"

"After arriving in the city, I went directly to the Palace of Justice, where I met with the major general. He is a kind man. Tall. Stout. Serious. Old enough to be my father, of course. I can see now that he and I are going to get along famously. I was given my housing address (see the front of the envelope for future correspondence), then taken on a tour of the offices (which are more than a little impressive. Posh actually). Ours, the one I will work in, looks over the center of the courtyard, which is also the parking area. Or, I should say, the general's office windows look over the center of the courtyard. Ha. Ha. When I sit at my desk, I will have a direct view of a line of dull office chairs for those who wait to see General Partridge and, if I turn to the right, I can spy down a long hallway leading to the mail room and other offices. Not that I care one whit about the view. I'm here to work, not to gaze out of windows."

"Same old Joan." Magda chuckled. "Work, work, work."

"It's part of her charm," Betty replied.

Magda nodded toward the letter. "Anything else?"

Betty returned her attention to the pages in her hand.

"I drove my trusty Austin to my new residence—fifteen minutes toward Old Nuremberg. It's a small, fully furnished cottage that is part of civilian housing where I will live alone. I've met my neighbor, a nice woman, who lives with her two oversize German shepherd dogs. Lucy Cole is her name, and while she is probably forty if she is a day, I can see where we'll get along.

"This is a first for me, living alone, as you know. I have come to a new place in my life. I live alone and I work for the US Forces in Europe. Don't pinch me. I'm afraid I might wake up. (In other words, I think coming to Germany was a good thing for me to do.)

"Fondly,
"Joan."

CHAPTER 42

Nuremberg, Germany

For her first day working for Major General Partridge, Joan chose a classic dress she'd purchased from Chicago's Peck & Peck. Long-sleeved charcoal gray bordered with pink gingham checks, a narrow belt, and hidden buttons from the hem to the neckline. She checked herself no fewer than three times in the vanity mirror before leaving her new home, which was, remarkably, smaller than the flat she'd shared with Ruby.

Joan arrived at the Palace of Justice precisely fifteen minutes early to better acclimate herself to her desk, the offices, the filing cabinets. Her shoulders squared, she entered through the main doors using her clearance badge. After passing through security, Joan rambled around the cavernous hallways for a good ten minutes in search of her new office.

The first part of the morning went smoothly. Then, sometime between her morning break and lunch, General Partridge called on the interoffice phone. "Can you come in for a moment, Joan?"

Joan entered the inner office, where the aroma of cigars filled the room, clinging to the oil paintings and hugging the draperies and the dark-brown leather sofas and chairs. "Yes, sir," she said, poised in front of the general's desk. She held a pad of paper in one hand and a number two pencil in the other, ready to take notes.

"Joan." He looked down, his attention on a file spread across his desk. "I need you to head down to the TWX office."

Her brow rose. "I'm sorry, sir. Did you say 'the twix office'?"

He looked up, his poker face in place. "*T-W-X.* Very important office. That's where all messages meant for me are deciphered and prepared."

She jotted the letters down—*TWX.*

"Three doors down, that way," he said, pointing with a pen toward Colonel Wooldridge's office. "Toward the mail room. You can't miss it; it's marked."

"Yes, sir. I remember the rooms now."

He smiled briefly. "I'll need you to go down there about this time every morning, and again around fourteen hundred hours, and once again before you leave for the day."

She recorded the instruction between the wide lines of the steno pad gripped between her fingers. "I'll do that now, sir."

Joan found the TWX office easily. Just as General Partridge had said, three doors down, clearly marked, and closed and decorated with a handmade Christmas wreath. She took in a deep breath, drew her shoulders back, and entered.

Out of the six desks in the room—three facing to the left, three facing to the right—only two held occupants. One of the enlisted men sat to the right, nearest the door. The other sat to the left nearest the frost-covered windows overlooking *Fürther Straße.* Both wore Army uniforms. Both—a cursory glance affirmed—were young.

Joan clasped her hands together and turned to the right, announcing with the utmost of poise, "I am here for General Partridge's messages."

"By golly," a voice drawled from the desk near the window, "that's a Southern girl if I ever heard one."

She turned—slowly—and stared open-mouthed at the enlisted man who rose from his seat, as if he were unfolding himself to stand tall. Taller.

"Excuse me?"

"I declare, I believe you're from South Carolina." His eyes—a delicious shade of blue—twinkled beneath dark brows and a wave of black hair.

"And *where* is South Carolina?"

And with that, he laughed, picked up a short stack of papers, and came around his desk. "I believe this is what you're looking for, ma'am," he said, extending the messages. "I'm Private Second Class Robert Zimmerman," he continued with a wink. "But you can call me Robert." He paused, then looked over to the officer who stood nearby. "That's *Unteroffizier* McCorkle over there . . ."

"Harry," the man said, grinning at Joan. "Sergeant Harry McCorkle."

"Sarge," the private said, his voice low. Teasing. "Leave the little lady alone. I'm working here. Ma'am?" Joan looked at him fully again. "When you need the general's messages, you just come on down here and ask for me."

Joan blinked, trying to ascertain whether Private Second Class Zimmerman—Robert—had just played her or if he was, by nature, genuinely kind. Either way, his voice had a lilt similar to Evelyn's and Jackson's, which brought an odd comfort. A sense of friendship. "Thank you," she said, tugging the papers from his grip.

His eyes never left hers, and Joan couldn't have broken contact if she'd tried. "You're welcome," he said. Then, leaning closer, he added, "I'd avoid Harry over there if I were you. He fancies himself a ladies' man. That pretty wreath you passed on your way in is from one of his local sweethearts."

She held tight to the papers with her left hand. "I see," she managed to get out, pointing toward the door with the thumb of her right. "I'll just take these down to General Partridge now."

"You do that, ma'am." He looked at his watch. "And we'll be seeing you here around fourteen hundred hours."

"Yes." Joan turned to leave, clutching General Partridge's messages close to her chest.

Savannah, Georgia

"Lunch in ten," Ed said.

Evelyn looked up to see her boss leaning against the doorframe of his private office, glaring down at his watch. "Already?" she asked. She looked at her own watch and frowned. "How did the morning go by so fast?"

Ed stepped closer to her desk and took a seat in one of the padded chairs near the floor-to-ceiling sheer-covered windows. "Surely the time doesn't pass any more quickly here than it does in Chicago?"

She busied herself with closing the ledgers spread out on her desk. "Oh . . . I don't know. I guess it's about the same."

When he didn't say anything, Evelyn looked up to see that he watched her intently. The amber in his eyes flashed, causing her to return her attention to stacking the books. "Do you miss it?" he finally asked. "Chicago?"

Evelyn gripped the ledgers until her knuckles turned white, then relaxed as she set them on the left side of her desk. "Not the winters." She laughed easily, which allowed her the courage to bring her eyes back up to his. "I'm looking forward to a nice Georgia Christmas."

He straightened one leg, slid his hand into his pants pocket, and brought out a pearl-handled pocketknife, which he opened, then ran the blade across his thumbnail. His eyes eased back to hers—watching him—then back to his hands. "I have a little hangnail," he said.

Evelyn brightened. "I have a file if you could use one. Right here in my purse."

But Ed had already replaced the knife. "No bother. It's gone."

A sweet memory fell over her. "My father—I remember my father doing that."

"Then he must be a good ole country boy like me."

She crossed her arms, resting them on the edge of her desk. "You know he is. Southern farmers really have to be, don't they?" She tilted her head. "Somehow you don't strike me as a country boy, Brother Ed."

He chuckled. "Trust me. Get me out of this suit and into a pair of dungarees and I'm at my happiest. I'd rather sit in a little fishing boat in the middle of a lake or get up way before the crack of dawn to sit in a deer stand than just about anything I can think to do." He grinned. "No matter *how* cold it is."

Evelyn tried to picture George sitting in a deer stand, rubbing his hands together in the freezing cold, or even in the middle of a fishing boat on a warm spring day, but couldn't. Maybe—if she had enough time and Magda's imagination—she could see him somewhere over in Africa in an organized big-game hunt, or standing at the bow of a chartered deep-sea fishing boat. Both, of course, would have cost him a hefty sum of money, and neither would be about the fun of the sport, but about declaring himself to be a part of something.

George Volbrecht, she realized, couldn't just *be* for no reason other than to enjoy the process. Everything George did, he did to *gain* something. Everything, including turning her into his protégé.

Melancholy threatened the mild happiness she'd managed to grab hold of over the past nine months. How could it be that *that man* still managed to dominate her thoughts daily, even after all this time?

"Evelyn?" Ed asked, startling her. "Did I lose you?"

She sighed as heat rushed across her cheeks. "Sorry. I was just thinking of someone I knew back in Chicago."

"A special someone?"

She started to say yes, but stopped herself. To answer affirmatively might entice Ed—who by profession assumed the role of pastoral counselor—to ask further questions. Questions she didn't want to answer. *Couldn't* answer.

"No," she said, her voice only a fraction above a whisper, knowing full well her tone exposed the lie. She took off her glasses and set about in an unneeded task of cleaning them with the hem of her sweater. "He was just a friend."

Nuremberg, Germany

The afternoon had turned unseasonably warm for December, and Joan planned to heat up a can of soup for dinner. But when she got home, she realized she'd eaten the last of it on Saturday. After checking the time, she decided to drive to the PX, a part of Nuremberg's military base—the *Kaserne*—about fifteen minutes past the Palace of Justice.

Evening had already fallen around the city, hiding her battle scars with Christmas lights and the gaiety of crowds dining out.

Sweethearts walked along the streets, hand in hand, in front of buildings both partially and fully restored. A deeper chill had also begun to descend, but only slightly. Not so much as to drive people into their homes, but enough that wearing something heavier than a sweater became necessary.

Joan arrived at the Army base, passed through security, and, as usual, flew over the narrow roads until she found a parking spot near the PX. She took a moment to collect her purse and adjust her gloves and jacket, then exited the car while straightening her skirt. American music played in the distance.

"Well, I'll be!"

Her head shot up.

"Hey, Joan." Robert walked toward her, wearing a military jacket over his uniform and carrying his hat in his hand.

"Robert Zimmerman," she said, looking up to gauge the kindness in his eyes.

He half turned toward the PX and the small coffee shop nestled in front of it. "My friends and I are just having a cup of coffee. Want to join us?"

She looked over. Three enlisted men sat at a small table outside the building where four cups of coffee sent steam curling into the night air. The three men waved, and Joan waved back.

"That's Bob McPherson sitting on the right there," Robert pointed out. "And that's Leo Poitras on the left and Harold Moss in the center." Robert smiled down at her. "Would you like to join us?"

"For a cup of coffee?"

"Yeah. For a cup of coffee. We're just hanging out. Enjoying this little bit of a warm snap we're having tonight. Supposed to get *really* cold tomorrow. The coffeehouse brought out the tables and chairs today, so . . ." He smiled. "We're taking advantage of it."

He took a step and Joan joined in beside him, feeling quite natural in doing so. "I'd not heard that," she told him. "About it getting colder."

"Oh, yeah," he said, guiding her to the outdoor tables and chairs. "Supposed to get cold and icy." He glanced over his shoulder. "Be careful on these streets in that little car."

The men stood as they arrived at the table, each of them extending their hands, which Joan shook one by one. "I can run inside and get you a cup of coffee," Robert said, already moving toward the small shop in front of the three-story, M-shaped building. "Have a seat and I'll be back in a minute."

Joan took a seat at the table in the courtyard of the PX. "So," she said, placing her handbag in her lap, "where are you gentlemen from?"

Bob pointed to himself. "Hope, Arkansas."

She then looked to Leo. "Boston, Massachusetts."

And then to Harold. "Kansas City, Missouri."

"Missouri? I would have thought Kansas City to be in Kansas. Much like Dorothy's farm."

The three men grinned and nodded. "It is," Harold said. "But it's also in Missouri."

"I had no idea," she told them. "I've only lived in Chicago in the States, and to tell you the truth, I haven't ventured out much from there."

"You don't sound like you're from Chicago," Harold said, wrapping a beefy hand around his coffee and easing it to his mouth.

Robert appeared then, Joan's coffee in hand, just in time to chime in with, "That's right. I suspect she's from South Carolina."

Joan reached for the cup. "I looked up this South Carolina," she said. "It's near Georgia. I have a friend in the States from Georgia."

Robert bent at the waist, his eyes capturing Joan's. "I wasn't sure how you like your coffee. I can run back in and add some cream and sugar for you, if you'd like."

"No, no," she mumbled. "That's all right. I drink it black."

"A real woman, Zimmerman," Bob said. "I said she was, didn't I?"

Robert sat next to her, picked up his coffee, and smiled. "So, where *are* you from, Joan? Because I've only been teasing about South Carolina."

Robert Zimmerman might have caused her brain to go fuzzy, but she at least knew *that* much. "Leigh, Lancashire. England. But I was born in Chicago and I returned there a couple of years back to work."

"Chicago?" Robert leaned forward. "I've done some work in Chicago."

"Really? You lived in Chicago before you joined up?"

Robert laughed. "No. I said I did some work there." He looked from one friend to another. "And as these guys know, I didn't *exactly* join up."

CHAPTER 43

"What do you mean?" Joan asked, taking a sip of the strong coffee. "If you didn't join up, then you were drafted, I take it?"

Robert chuckled. "Yes, ma'am. I managed to avoid the Army as long as I could, but I guess, eventually, my luck just plumb ran out."

"Well," Joan retorted, "I suppose that's all in how you look at it."

"Meaning?"

"If you weren't in the Army, you wouldn't be sitting here. In front of the PX. In Nuremberg, Germany. Having coffee with your friends." She looked at Robert's friends, then back to him. "Or me."

The men laughed as Joan took another swallow of coffee. "So, tell me. Where are *you* from and just how did you manage to avoid the draft for a while?"

"Greensboro."

"Is that in South Carolina?"

"Ah . . . no. North Carolina."

"I see."

"To answer your next question, I managed to avoid the draft because, after high school, I went to Guilford College for two years."

Joan's heartbeat raced at the notion of going to college. Of higher learning and growing intellectually—something two parents raising a houseful of children in the middle of a world war could never have afforded. "Is that in Greensboro?"

"It is."

"What did you study at this Guilford College?"

"Economics and business."

"And that kept you out of the draft?"

"Well," Robert said with a wink, "it tried, but not entirely. I worked at night and on the weekends for my father's business." He paused. "My father's business, you see, was significant for the farmers."

Joan didn't follow entirely, but the intrigue became too much to interrupt. She encouraged him to continue with a nod as she brought her cup of coffee to her lips.

"So," he continued, "I got drafted twice, but both times I was deferred."

"Only son," Leo supplied. "*And* the work he did with his father was important to the farmers. It served agriculture, you see?"

Not quite, but she wanted Robert to tell the rest of the story. "I see," she said. "And then the third time?"

Robert laughed. "Well, that's when my luck ran out."

And mine came in . . . The inner thoughts of Joan's heart caught her off guard.

Harold stood. "I'm going to go inside. Get more coffee. Anyone else?"

Bob shoved his chair back a foot or so. "I'll go in with you."

Leo did the same. "Right behind you."

Joan held up her cup. "I'm good," she said.

Robert nodded. "Me too."

They watched in silence as the three men walked into the

coffee shop before Joan turned back to Robert and said, "How did you get here? To Nuremberg, I mean."

Again he chuckled. "Funny story, really, if you've got time for it."

She had all the time in the world, her previous hunger forgotten. "I have nowhere special to be." After all, home meant alone, but being here with him, like this—in spite of the temperature dropping significantly—felt warm. Inviting.

"My good friend—my childhood buddy—and I were both drafted at the same time. Phal Hodgin is his name."

"Phal?"

"Yeah. Phal. Unusual name, great guy."

"So you and . . . Phal . . . were drafted at the same time."

"That's right." Robert glanced toward the door of the coffee shop, chuckled a little, and said, "I think my friends are giving us our space."

Joan looked over that way and, seeing nothing of them, agreed. She took another swallow of the now-cold coffee. "Go on . . ."

"Phal had been drafted a couple of times before as well, but he also had been deferred because he was a conscientious objector."

"A conscientious . . . ?"

"Objector. He's Quaker. His family is. They don't believe in war, I guess you could say."

"Oh."

Robert started to take a sip of coffee, then placed the cup on the table. "Cold," he said, his eyes twinkling. "Do you want me to go inside and get us another cup?"

"Not really," she said. "I'm fine."

"So, Phal's luck ran out and mine too, and we were both sent to Fort Jackson for basic."

"Where's that?"

"Columbia, South Carolina."

Joan laughed. "Ah, South Carolina. Where all the girls talk like Brits."

He chuckled, and his thick, dark brows shot up. "That's right."

"And then?"

"About halfway through basic training I came down with a severe case of pneumonia. I'm telling ya, Joan. I was a sick puppy."

"Were you in hospital?"

"Sure was. By the time I got out, the Army pulled me from basic and then, a couple months later, sent me back. By that time, Phal and all my new buddies had been deployed in different directions." He shook his head. "It's my last week of basic—the second go-round—and I'm wondering where in the world I'm going to end up. The whole company was lined up on the street one morning when the sergeant came by and said, 'Any of you men know how to type?'" Robert grinned. "My first thought was, 'I can.' I'd had two years of typing in high school. On a mechanical typewriter I could type about ninety words a minute."

"Impressive."

"My second thought was that if I could type, I would get an office job somewhere, maybe in the captain's office typing memos or something. And I figured this was just for *that* day. I knew the day was going to be a scorcher, and I figured anything was better than being out there in the hot sun, you know?" He laughed again and Joan laughed with him. "I hadn't heard yet that you *never* volunteer in the Army, so I raised my hand and said, 'I can type, sir.' So the sergeant looks at me and says, 'Report to the commander.' So I did."

"And then what happened?"

"I'll never forget it, Joan. I walked in and the captain said, 'I understand you can type.' I said, 'Yes, sir.' He says, 'Get your bags and go on over to headquarters.' I said, 'My bags, sir?' and he said, 'Zimmerman, get everything you own in your duffel bag and report to headquarters.' Well, sir . . . That's what I did. I went and packed everything I owned that was there in the barracks—including my boots—shoved it all into my duffel bag, and reported to headquarters. Next thing I know, twenty-four hours have passed and I'm in New York heading for Germany." He burst out laughing.

In spite of trying not to, Joan belly-laughed with him. "Did they ever give you a typing test?"

He leaned sideways in his mirth. *"No."*

Robert's three friends rejoined them in time to see them sobering from their laughter. "He must have told you about the typing," Harold said. He carried two cups of steaming coffee—one in each hand. He placed one in front of Joan; the other he kept for himself. "We figured you two could use another cup."

"And he really can type," Bob added. He handed Robert a fresh cup and then sat with his own.

Leo returned to his seat. "He has long fingers, you know."

Robert wiggled all ten of his fingers as Joan wrapped both gloved hands around the warm cup of fresh coffee, held it close to her chin, and breathed in the scent of it. "A delightful story," she said. "Imagine if none of that had happened. Imagine that you hadn't been deferred twice before or that you hadn't gotten sick. You wouldn't have been on the street with your company that morning. You wouldn't have heard the sergeant ask if anyone could type." She took a slow sip. "It's like me, I suppose. If I hadn't taken a walk one afternoon around the Loop in Chicago during my lunch break, I wouldn't have seen the sign about working in Europe. And, if I hadn't seen the sign, I wouldn't be here now. Talking to the lot of you. It's the way God leads us, don't you think?"

Robert clapped his hands together and looked upward. "By

golly, boys," he exclaimed, looking at his chums. "I believe I'm going to marry this girl!"

"Well," Joan shot back with a grin, "I'm not spoken for." She wondered, albeit briefly, if on a second meeting she should tame her usual spunk.

The four men, eyes bright with surprise, laughed.

"And," she added, deciding against it, "As it turns out, I happen to have a dress . . ."

Savannah, Georgia

Evelyn descended the left side of the split staircase leading to the wide foyer of her aunt's home. She grabbed the curve of the banister and swung herself toward the back of the house, where the aroma of homemade vegetable soup became more prominent. She peeked into the formal dining room on her way to the kitchen, pausing long enough to admire the elegance of a room never used.

Her breath caught in her throat and she entered the long, narrow room, momentarily imagining herself to be her grandmother, remembering the stories her mother had told her so long ago about the dinner parties given in that very room. Evelyn ran her fingertips along the arched and polished wood of one of the side chairs as she walked around the expansive table where—she couldn't help but notice—not a single fleck of dust had dared to land, not even along the intricate details of the antique porcelain vases her aunt used as centerpieces.

"Oh, there you are," Aunt Dovalou said from the doorway. "What in the world are you doing in here?"

Evelyn smiled. "Admiring." She pointed to one of the vases. "Did you buy the Limoges or did my grandmother?"

Aunt Dovalou crossed her arms. "Buy the what?"

"The Lim—" Evelyn reached across the table, grabbing one of the vases with both hands. "Wait a minute . . . in case I'm wrong." She carefully turned the heavy piece to look at the bottom of it. "Yeah, it's Limoges. In fact, look at this—it not only has the *J. P. L.* stamped on it, but the name of the artist as well. And the date, 1906."

Aunt Dovalou came around the table and peeked at the underside of the vase. "Gracious. I guess Mama bought that. I have no idea. I never cared for stuff like this, but I haven't dared get rid of it."

"I hope not. These are valuable, Aunt Dovalou."

Her aunt rested a narrow hip against one of the sturdy armchairs. "Now how do you know that? Because I know your mama didn't teach you . . ."

Evelyn shook her head. "My—*friend*—George. He was very knowledgeable about things like this and I . . . I guess I—" She chuckled. "I guess I picked up more than I realized." She studied her aunt for a minute. "Aunt Dovalou, why didn't you or Mama—?" She stopped herself from going any further.

Aunt Dovalou, however, oozed wisdom. "Why weren't your mama and I more like *our* mother?"

Evelyn nodded. "From all the stories I've heard, she was a woman of such graciousness and refinement."

"Mama always said that we girls took after her people." She jerked her head toward the wide doorway leading back into the hallway. "Come on to the kitchen with me so I can check on my corn bread."

They exited the room and entered the kitchen without a word. Evelyn sat on a backless stool as her aunt peeked inside the oven. "Looking good," she commented, then turned back to Evelyn. "Hop down from there and come with me a minute."

Evelyn followed her aunt up the back staircase leading to the second floor, then down a long hallway to the master bedroom, rich in white eyelet and chintz rose patterns. "Mama and Daddy's room," Aunt Dovalou announced, as if Evelyn were on a tour of old Southern homes. "I rarely come in here." She sighed. "I just tell Sarah Beth to dust it once a month." She crooked her finger. "Come look over here at this wall."

Evelyn stepped up to a display of family portraits of various sizes, all in gilded frames. "Now, this bearded old cuss was your great-grandfather Zachariah Doyle."

"The preacher."

"Mmm-hmm. Not two pennies to rub together but a fine man." Her finger slipped to the expressionless face of the woman sitting next to him. "His wife, Rebekah Matthews. Doesn't seem too happy, does she?"

Evelyn snickered. "Not really."

"Over here—" she pointed—"that's their daughter Eloise and her husband, Thomas Hinton."

"Your parents. Yours and Mama's."

"That's right."

Evelyn leaned in to examine the portrait. "She was magnificent, wasn't she?"

"My mother was one of a kind. As gracious as she was beautiful. She lit up every room she ever entered." The hint of reverence was unmistakable. "And Daddy—what a charmer."

Evelyn smiled. "I can see that. Look at the mischief in his eyes."

"Cutting-edge business savvy is what he had," Aunt Dovalou said with a nod.

"Which is why they lived in this grand house."

"Nearly killed Mama when your daddy came into our lives." She walked over to a boudoir chair and sat, crossing her legs. "Not that *I* didn't come to think the world of him, but Mama always wanted us to marry well. But—" she sighed— "Judith met Colton at a dance one Saturday while she was visiting some of the Doyles over in Portal."

"And they fell in love . . ."

"That they did," she said. "Poor Mama. Sometimes I think your parents' marriage is what sent her into an early grave, not that I would ever say that to Judith's face." She popped up, eyes wide open. "Gracious, get me back downstairs before the corn bread burns." They hurried together down the servants' staircase to the sweet fragrance of freshly baked corn bread. "Hon, set the table, will you?" she called over her shoulder as the front doorbell rang.

Evelyn whirled at the sound of it.

"Oh, and set it for three," Aunt Dovalou said with a sugary-sweet smile. "Brother Ed is coming for supper."

"Aunt Dovalou," Evelyn exclaimed quietly. "Don't think I don't know what you're doing."

With her hand shoved into a quilted mitt, Aunt Dovalou pulled the skillet corn bread from the oven. "I have no idea what you're talking about." The doorbell rang again. She waved her hand. "Go on, now."

Evelyn hurried up the hallway, muttering to herself the whole way. A Bible passage she'd memorized as a child tickled the back of her brain. *"I will go before thee, and make the crooked places straight."*

"Isaiah, chapter 45, verse 2," she whispered with a smile.

By the time she opened the door to the tall, well-dressed preacher, she knew her face had registered a new and gushing excitement.

"What is it?" Ed asked, stepping over the threshold. "Are you *that* happy to see me?"

"No," Evelyn answered as she closed the door, listening for

the familiar rattle the wood and opaque glass had made for nearly half a century. "I mean, yes." She rolled her eyes as Ed chuckled. "What I *mean* to say is, I didn't know you were coming until two seconds ago, but—" Evelyn reached for his hat and then, after he turned to remove his coat, stood on her tiptoes to help. "I just had a marvelous idea, and I—" He turned back to face her as she dropped to her heels. "I want to tell you *all* about it."

CHAPTER 44

Nuremberg, Germany

Joan stood just outside her small home, staring up at the gray sky and the black tree limbs clawing their way toward it. Hearing a door open behind her, she turned to see her new friend, Lucy Cole, walking out. She stopped beside her.

"Good morning," Joan said, buttoning her coat up to her neck against the bitter weather.

"Sure turned cold, didn't it." Lucy tugged at her gloves as she gazed around, then patted the light-brown hair curling around high cheekbones as if to warm her ears. "I guess this is winter's first hurrah." She looked at Joan.

They walked together toward their cars. "Lucy," Joan asked. "I'm beginning to discern certain accents. Can you tell me where you're from?"

"South Carolina. Born and reared."

Joan stopped short. "South Carolina? Forty-eight states under Eisenhower's presidential authority and I seem to be zeroing in on only one of them lately."

Lucy smiled as she opened her chocolate-brown handbag and withdrew a set of car keys. "Meaning?"

"I'll have to tell you later," Joan said. "Why don't you join me for a bite to eat after work?"

"Your place or mine?" She opened her car door.

"Mine," Joan said. "I'll run to the PX after work and get something for us to eat."

"Sounds wonderful. I'll bring dessert."

Later that morning, Joan marched to the TWX office and straight to Robert's desk.

"Are you here for the general's messages or have you been missing me?" he teased.

"I'm here for the general's messages," Joan said, somehow managing to keep herself straight-faced.

Robert clutched his chest. "My heart is nearly broken," he said. "I'm not sure it can be repaired."

But he handed her the messages anyway.

"Robert," she began, keeping her voice steady. "I'm just wondering . . . would you be interested in meeting a *real* Southern girl?"

His eyes narrowed and the square of his jaw became more pronounced. "What do you mean?"

"I mean, a girl who is *really* from South Carolina. I know one. A friend of mine who lives next to me in civilian housing." She tried to read his face, to see if he might be disappointed at the thought that she would set him up with another female, albeit one nearly twenty years his senior.

He remained stoic long enough to make her wonder if she'd made a mistake in her gesture. Then the ends of his lips curled, finally breaking apart to reveal a large grin as the blue in his eyes burst into a prism of light that paralyzed her breath in her throat. "I would *love* to meet a girl from South Carolina."

"Well, then," Joan said, taking a step back, "how about tomorrow evening? Since I have a car and you don't, I can pick you up at the *Kaserne*. The three of us can go out for a cup of coffee at a local coffeehouse. And what with it being Friday, we can stay out as late as we please."

His eyes never left hers. "All right. Say nineteen hundred hours?"

"All right."

"I'll wait just inside the gates. There's a place to the right near where the buildings start."

Joan nodded once. "I know it. See you then." She turned to walk out but made it only halfway to the door when Robert called her name.

"Yes?" she asked, turning back.

"What's her name?"

"Lucy," Joan answered. "Lucy Cole."

Savannah, Georgia

Evelyn nearly squirmed in the chair at her aunt's kitchen table.

Aunt Dovalou sat next to her. Ed sat directly across from her. Between the three of them they had eaten six bowls of soup and devoured nearly all of the butter-slathered corn bread.

"So? You've heard the preliminary idea. What do you think?" Evelyn asked them both.

"You're saying, use *this* house?" her aunt asked.

"The parlors and the dining room only. Maybe the carriage house out back but . . ." She adjusted her glasses by the temples. "I'll know more about that later."

"And we'll open this up to the young people—both boys and girls—of Savannah?" Ed asked. "Beginning with the Baptist and Methodist youth?"

"Just to see how it goes. If it goes well enough, we'll extend it to the other churches in the community. And maybe I can work with some of the home ec teachers at the schools."

Aunt Dovalou sighed. "Just think, Ed," she said, putting her older hand on his. "A school of etiquette for young people, right here in my mother's home." She looked at Evelyn, tears shimmering in her eyes. "Oh, darlin', Mama would be so proud to know it."

"And you really think you can teach this?" Ed asked.

"Well, I can teach the girls what the girls need to know and you can teach the boys what *they* need to know that a woman can't teach them. And I can address subjects like dining and social etiquette. I can even throw in some lessons in basic, conversational French." *Teach them to count . . .* "And how to discern nice china." She winked in her aunt's direction.

Ed perched his elbows on the table to rest his chin on his fists, then jerked them off. "Oops. No elbows on the table," he teased.

Evelyn waggled a finger at him. "Oh, no. After the meal, it's fine."

He looked at Aunt Dovalou. "I did not know that . . . ," he muttered as he casually returned to his original position. He looked across the table again. "I guess all that etiquette training you received while working at Hertz paid off."

Etiquette training for Hertz. The half-truth had rolled off her tongue so easily, but leaving it at that was better for now. Maybe forever. What did her aunt or her boss need to know about George Volbrecht and the hours she'd spent learning etiquette for everything from a dinner party to a casual business gathering by an outdoor pool?

"It's funny, isn't it?" Evelyn asked, standing. She set about gathering up the dishes, slapping at her aunt's hand as she attempted to help. "I've got this."

"What's funny?" Ed asked.

Evelyn straightened. "That we think we are learning something for one reason, but God has in mind that we use it for something else." She walked across the kitchen balancing plates and bowls in her hands.

"Not so funny," Ed called across the room. "That's the good Lord's way. He knows what's what long before we do."

Evelyn placed the dishes into the deep white porcelain sink, then stared down at them. "Indeed," she said quietly. "Even a crooked path."

Nuremberg, Germany

The cold front that had descended on the state of Bavaria had decided to sink in its talons. By the next day, the wind had picked up, the temperature had dropped considerably, and precipitation had fallen, leaving thin sheets of ice along the highways, rooftops, and tree branches.

Friday afternoon, as Joan drove home after work, her car hydroplaned on the street and nearly jumped the curb of the parking area. Once inside her flat, she made a cold sandwich and washed it down with a small glass of milk, then washed her face and reapplied what little bit of makeup she typically wore—pressed powder, lipstick, and a hint of rouge.

Joan didn't have to think long about what to wear. She changed into a scoop-neck, long-sleeved dress that cinched at the waist, then blossomed to a full skirt. Two narrow ribbons wrapping around the hips and tied off with bows made it the most fetching thing she owned, which made it all the more perfect for the evening.

Minutes later, she slipped into her winter coat before dashing over to Lucy's. Barking and thick nails scraping the woman's slatted wood flooring greeted her before Lucy opened her door, shrugging her arms into her coat sleeves and banishing the dogs.

"Go back to your beds," she said, laughing and closing the door behind her. "Those two are itching for a trip outside of this door, in spite of the weather."

Joan laughed with her. "So, are we ready for this?" she asked as they walked toward Joan's Austin.

"*I* am, but the question is, are you?"

"I am. Most definitely."

After settling into the car, Joan shoved it into reverse. "I warn you," she said. "I'm a terrible driver."

Lucy's face wore a knowing look. "I know. I've seen you tear out of here and practically fly back in. To my way of thinking, when it comes time to return to the States, you won't need a plane."

Joan laughed again as she shifted, turned on the radio, and pulled out at breakneck speed. Hitting *Fürther Straße*, the minuscule car glided over the icy street.

"Good heavens," Lucy shouted over the music, "I think you left my stomach back there near the last intersection."

Joan smiled, though her stomach had tied in knots; the car's speed had risen against her will. If she applied the brakes too suddenly, the car would slide into one of the storefronts. But if they kept going at this speed . . .

The car rounded the corner toward the *Kaserne*'s gates, which spread east to west between brick columns and stretched from the ground, high above car or man. The guardhouse, Joan knew from previous experience, would have no fewer than two soldiers in it. Possibly even four. Guards who would be armed with guns and would not take kindly to a car approaching as hers did.

"Joan," Lucy shouted, "I'm afraid you're—"

Joan slammed her left foot down on the clutch, her right foot on the brake. "I can't stop it," she shouted back as metal struck against metal and the Austin crashed through the gates with determination.

"Joan!"

"Hold on!"

The Austin slid over the ice, angling until it came to a stop directly in front of a tall man standing on the sidewalk. Joan gasped as she looked into the rearview mirror. Four guards, guns drawn, ran toward them as, inside the car, Eddie Fisher sang "O Mein Papa." Trumpets rose in serenade behind his smooth tenor; Lucy simply burst into laughter.

"Joan!" From outside the car, Robert shouted as he tried to wave off the guards who now surrounded the Austin.

"Get out of the car!" they bellowed. "Get out of the car!"

Joan looked at Lucy. "I suppose we should get out of the car."

"You first," she said.

Joan opened her door, stepping out as Robert's hand reached for her elbow.

"Are you all right?" he asked. His attention returned to the guards surrounding them. "I can explain," he gasped.

The last thing Joan needed was a man cleaning up her messes. "*I* can explain." Joan turned to the guards. "I lost control of the car."

"But not on purpose," Lucy interjected from the other side. "Although she is a *terrible* driver."

Joan shot her a look.

"She's here for me," Robert added. "Private Second Class Zimmerman."

Four guns lowered as one of the guards demanded, "Your ID, ma'am."

"It's in the car." When he didn't respond, Joan pointed in the driver's window. "May I get it?"

He nodded.

"I'm with General Partridge's office," she told him, her head buried within the small confines of the automobile, all the while digging around, looking for her purse. She found it on the passenger floorboard, then backed out of the car. "Here you go," she said, pulling her government identification badge from the purse.

The guard in charge took it, studied it, then returned it.

"Private Zimmerman, will you vouch for Miss Hunt?"

Robert nodded. "I will, sir."

"All right," he said. "You're free to go, but . . ." He looked from Joan to the other guards, then back. "Private Zimmerman, you are responsible to drive the car out of the *Kaserne* and back."

Joan opened her mouth to protest. If Jackson hadn't been able to fit behind the wheel, then Robert would surely have the same problem. The North Carolinian had at least two inches on the Tennessean, for sure.

"I can do that, sir," Joan heard him say just before his gaze slid through the open door toward the steering wheel. "I think."

The guards walked away, muttering between themselves about repairing the gate until one joked about *"der große Mann in dem Kinderwagen."*

Joan looked at Robert. "This is my friend Lucy," she said, deflated.

But Robert continued to stare inside the car.

"Nice to meet you, Robert," Lucy offered over the top of the Austin. "And obviously, this whole thing was to introduce two people with only one thing in common—we're both from the South."

Robert's brow furrowed as he looked at her.

"I'm old enough to be your mother," Lucy suggested.

"Oh," Robert finally said. "Oh."

Joan pointed to the car seat. "Um, Robert? Do you think you can wedge yourself in there?"

"I. Don't. Know."

She stepped closer to him, peering up at his face. "Are you all right?"

His brow inched up. "I think so." He took a breath. "Okay. Let's see how I can fold myself in here."

Robert pushed the car seat back as far as it would go, then put his left leg in, bending the knee almost to his ear as he slid the rest of his body into the car. With his back pressed hard against the seat, he adjusted his body weight. "I'm in," he said.

"But can you *drive* the car?"

He looked in the rearview mirror to where the guards worked on the gate. "I don't know that I have a choice, Joan," he said without looking at her.

Joan glanced at Lucy. "Climb in the back," she said, then closed the driver's door, feeling it give as it met Robert's knee.

"Ow," he said, throwing back his head.

"Sorry," she shouted, running around the front of the car to the passenger seat.

Once the three were tucked inside, Robert turned the key. "Is this what it's going to be like with you, Miss Hunt?"

Joan stared ahead and bit off a smile. "Pretty much, Private Zimmerman. Pretty much."

Correspondence came to Joan from the States the following day—a Christmas card all the way from Lake Forest, Illinois, its front boasting Betty's lovely penmanship.

Joan gasped with anticipation. The thickness of the envelope promised a letter along with the card. She tore into the content as soon as she'd shrugged out of her coat and gloves, and dropped them across one of her two dinette chairs. "'Merry Christmas, Joan,'" she read aloud from the folded, lineless paper, then giggled at what followed:

> *. . . or should I say Fröhliche Weihnachten! I bet you are wondering how I know this, aren't you? Well, I'll tell you—our next-door neighbor is from Germany. A woman of sixty who left the country with her husband and children as soon as things started getting "iffy" over there. "Iffy" is my word, not hers.*
>
> *Allow me to play "catch up" with you. I saw Magda recently; she came to Lake Forest to pick up the wedding dress. Didn't I tell you? She and her old boss, Barry Cole, will marry soon. She's number three, Joan, which reminds me, Inga had a girl. She named her Emma. I hope she and Axel will be able to make a go of it. Magda seems to think he's a nice man.*
>
> *Do you hear much from Evelyn? I received a letter recently in which she writes that there is no man in her life but she went on and on about a preacher named Ed. Or Edwin. Something like that.*
>
> *Life continues to grow inside of me, Joan, and during this season of the Blessed Child I feel closer to His mother than ever. I can barely make it to the end of the driveway most days and then I think of her trek from Nazareth to Bethlehem and sigh.*
>
> *Pat sends his love. He's sitting across the table from me now, my feet in his lap (so he can rub them), insisting I tell you how he will be forever indebted to you and your matchmaking skills. Ha. Ha. He also says to tell you to be*

sure to go to Munich to the Christkindlmarkt, a holiday tradition which began in the 1600s and continues to this day. How my husband knows these tiny bits of trivia is anyone's guess. When I ask, he only reminds me that he is a man of much brilliance.

I'll close in hopes of hearing from you soon. Tell me everything! I hunger for news!

Fondly,
Betty (Mrs. Pat Callahan)

PS: Pat just said for you to be careful of those soldier boys. Ha.

CHAPTER 45

Evanston, Illinois

Magda stood at the bottom of the staircase with a pad and pencil in her hand, her mind breezing over the list of things she had to accomplish that day. With less than two weeks before her wedding, each day's list grew extensively longer than the previous. She wondered, briefly, if at some point that would change. Would the lists for the days inching toward Saturday, February 13, begin to dwindle until, finally, on their wedding day, only one thing stood at the top of the page: *Get Married*?

She checked her watch. Harriet Nielson would arrive at any moment, not to see *her*, but to watch television—*The Brighter Day*; the new soap opera *The Secret Storm*; and *On Your Account*—with Jessie Higgins. And, although the children's grandmother rarely had a thing to say to Magda—at least not when they were out of Barry's earshot—the thought of running into her in the middle of the afternoon turned what was left of her lunch.

Magda stepped off the last step, her hand brushing over the Christian Dior mink Barry had given her for Christmas. She walked to the back of the house, her heels muffled on the wool runner, where she found her landlady preparing a percolator of coffee in the kitchen. "I'm going out for a while," Magda said.

Jessie Higgins peered over her shoulder. "Should I expect you home in time to eat?"

Magda pressed her lips together. "No. I'm going to meet Barry in Chicago. We have a few things to take care of this evening."

The woman turned back to her coffee preparations without another word.

Magda looked at her watch again. If she hurried, she could manage to get out of the house. She paused in front of the foyer mirror, readjusted her hat, slid her hands into the warm leather gloves she'd left next to her purse on the table, and reached for the fur.

The front door opened and Magda whirled around. "Hello, Mrs. Nielson," she said, keeping her voice firm and her chin up as the woman entered without so much as a courteous knock. Magda shoved her arms into the coat.

Harriet Nielson frowned at her. "And where are you off to? As if I didn't know."

Of course she knew, so then why did she insist on asking? Still, as Mor would tell her, treating your friends kindly is easy. To show the love of Christ, you must love those who are not so friendly. Magda forced a smile. "I'm meeting Barry in the city." She stepped past Harriet, reaching for her purse. "I hope you enjoy your soaps with Miss Higgins."

Harriet harrumphed before stomping to the back of the house. Magda pressed her lips together, turned for a final look in the mirror, and opened the front door. She had stepped over the threshold and had nearly closed the door behind her when she realized the pad with her list had been left behind.

She stepped back inside, her eyes glancing toward the base of the banister.

The pad wasn't there.

Magda frowned. She'd had it in her hand not five minutes earlier. Right there. Standing on the stair.

And then she had gone to the back of the house . . .

Closing the front door, she retraced her footsteps, quickly spying the pad on an occasional table between the foyer and the hallway leading to the kitchen. She sighed and shook her head. She'd obviously set it down on her way to say good-bye to Jessie Higgins.

I need a vacation. Or a honeymoon.

Magda picked up the pad.

"I don't know what else you *can* do." Her landlady's voice wafted through. Magda paused, listening unseen as the two women walked out of the kitchen and into the small den where Miss Higgins's television set sat warmed up and ready for an afternoon of entertainment. "You've told Barry how you feel. You've enlisted Deanne's help . . ."

"If *only* I could get Douglas to be a part of the pact," Harriet stated.

"Well, he's infatuated, obviously. She apparently has some power over the weaker sex."

The two women cackled and Magda held her breath.

"I had hoped when I went to see that Mr. VanMichaels and exposed their little tryst that she'd find herself in the unemployment lines and Barry would move on. *Why in the world* does he think he needs another woman in his life? Did you see *me* running after another husband when mine died? My daughter should be plenty enough for him and I *will not* have that girl erase Barbara's memory from that house or from the minds of those children!"

Magda gasped, grateful that the television volume seemed to have been increased. She stepped lightly toward the front door, making sure to keep her feet on the carpets. She peered over her shoulder when she arrived at the door, her chin tickled by the fur of Barry's gift. Her hand gripped the doorknob and turned it slowly. She inched it open, slid through the crack, and once again stepped onto the front porch, pulling the door closed without so much as a click.

She felt like a World War II spy, snow crunching under her shoes as she quietly made her way to Barry's car, which he left in her care daily. Once inside, she pulled the keys from her purse and started it, hoping the women inside the house were too enthralled with their daytime stories to notice the gap from the time she had apparently left the house.

Magda backed out of the driveway and drove to the first intersection before a loud puff of air escaped from deep within.

Mr. VanMichaels.

"Nana," she said, through gritted teeth. "*You* were the one."

Savannah, Georgia

Less than a month after she'd first conceived the idea, Evelyn had managed to write a business plan and syllabus for The Victory Drive School of Etiquette, which would begin classes in March.

"I already have the first five boys and the first five girls registered," she told Ed one day after work, which was when they often took time to discuss her progress. "And I have nearly that many—three girls and two boys—signed up for the second six-week program."

Ed sat behind his office desk, elbows resting on the arms of his chair, fingers laced at his chest. He smiled broadly. "Did you get the business license taken care of?"

Evelyn pretended to check off a box in midair. "Done. And I'm nearly done with the first draft of the notebooks for the girls." She pointed at him. "I still need your notes for the boys so I can type them up and—" she felt her cheeks grow warm— "add whatever might need to be added."

Ed chuckled. "I'll have that for you before Friday." He stood. "I think we've made excellent progress."

Evelyn stood as well, smiling. "We really have." She crossed her arms, hugging herself as he walked around the desk toward her.

"Is Miss Dovalou excited?" He directed her toward the open door, grabbing his coat from the nearby brass coat tree.

"She is," she answered, walking toward her outer office. "But not nearly as excited as some of the young teens are."

"You should hear the mothers going on and on to me about it on Sunday mornings." He smiled down at her, then took in a deep breath and released it. "I'm real glad you came up with this idea, Evelyn."

Evelyn picked up her purse and coat from where she'd left them on her desk earlier. "Me too."

They started for the door leading outside. "Hey," he said, almost as an afterthought. "This Saturday's weather is supposed to be right nice for February. I was thinking about going fishing."

Evelyn stared up at him as he helped her into her coat. "Will they be biting with the weather this cool?"

"Perfect time," he said, sounding more than a little sure of himself. He slid his arms into the casual all-weather coat he wore every day except, he'd told her, on Sundays.

"Oh. Okay. Well . . . sounds like a fun thing for you to do."

They stepped outside. The temperature had dipped considerably since lunch and, with the moisture from the Atlantic, Evelyn felt the effects in her bones. She peered up at her boss. "Are you sure the weather is going to warm up?" she asked with a chuckle.

Ed concentrated on locking the office door, but answered her with, "Yes ma'am, I'm sure." He turned and his eyes found hers. "When was the last time you went fishing, Evelyn?"

"Me?" They resumed walking to the parking lot where their

cars, parked side by side, were the lone automobiles. "Gosh. I guess probably a year or more before I left for Chicago."

"With your father?"

"With Daddy, yes." She peered down at her shoes, noting for the first time in a long while the way she walked. *Heel in front of toes . . . heel in front of toes . . . wiggle, wiggle, wiggle like Marilyn . . .*

"Ever miss it?" he asked, interrupting her recitation.

They arrived at her car and she fumbled around inside her purse for the key before opening the door. She shrugged a little. Did she miss it? *Did she?* Sitting out in the middle of a big lake with her father, sandwiches and soft drinks in the cooler between them, watching in silence for the cork to bob off a cane pole.

Did she?

"Yes," she finally answered with a laugh. "I believe I do."

His hand clasped her elbow, sending shivers up her spine. She gasped lightly. What had Daddy said? *"When the right one comes along, you'll feel your skin turn to gooseflesh."*

"Then go with me," Edwin said, startling her even further. "We'll make a day of it. It'll be fun."

"It might at that," she replied. "But, Ed? As friends, okay? I'm not . . . I'm not looking for anything more."

She thought his face registered a flicker of disappointment, but he appeared to recover well. "We'll be fishing buddies," he said, extending his hand so they could shake on it.

"Fishing buddies," she agreed, slipping her hand into his.

Chicago

"Are you *absolutely* sure that's what you heard?" Barry asked from across the small, round table shoved in the corner of an overcrowded restaurant—a new one for them. One Barry said had been suggested to him.

Cigarette smoke formed thin clouds around them, and conversation created a cacophony of sound, so much so that the sultry voice of the tight-dressed singer sitting on top of the upright piano and singing "La Vie en rose" could barely be heard.

Magda leaned forward, her arms crossed in her lap where her stomach sat heavy inside her and she wished she had not eaten so much. "I'm positive. *She* is the one who told Mr. VanMichaels."

Barry's jaw flexed and his eyes—already dark—became darker still. He swallowed hard, then sat back in a chair nearly too small for him. "Well, then." His arms flopped to the sides. "I guess I'll have to have a talk with her. I'll—" He reached for the demitasse coffee that had come with their dessert of crème brûlée, a delicacy they'd both declared the best they'd ever eaten. "I've already found another place for her to live, but I'll need to find a new sitter for the children—in the interim."

Magda reached across the table, past the tiny candle flickering between them. "Wait. No."

Barry placed the cup back into its saucer. "What?" he asked.

She wasn't sure if he'd asked *why* she wanted to wait or *what* she'd just said. "I said wait," she repeated, her voice now elevated. She looked around. "Honestly, Barry, did you think we could have a conversation about the wedding—much less anything else—in this place?"

His brow furrowed. "I didn't know. Harlan just said he thought you'd like this place." He looked around. "Although I don't know why. You don't strike me as the dark and moody kind."

Harlan . . . Magda pushed the thought of her first love away. "Once upon a time, I think I may have been," she said.

"What? Dark and moody?"

She looked into her coffee cup, drained of everything but a tiny ring at the bottom, then back up suddenly, as unsure of her next words as she'd ever been. "Did you know I dated Harlan Procter for a while?"

Barry's face, typically full of color, drained, leaving him looking like a leading man in an old black-and-white film. "When was that?" Then he ran a hand down the thigh of one leg and said, "Well, isn't this just a night for surprises?"

Magda shook her head. "Harlan gave me some pointers on how to be a better writer. It was more mentor and student than boyfriend and girlfriend."

"What was?"

Magda had to think, to try to decipher his question. "The relationship." She took a sip of the tepid water in the short glass near her empty coffee cup. "Harlan used to say that I dwelled so much on my inferiority to my sister that I couldn't write good characters. I could only write . . . well, dark and moody. And, I have to admit, that was true." She forced a smile. "But when Inga—when she told me her news—something inside of me . . . changed. Suddenly, I saw *her* as needing *me*. The one who had always placed me in a shadow would now live in the shadows of life." She shrugged one shoulder. "Which is why I don't want you to confront Harriet."

"I'm not following you," he said, crossing one leg over the other.

"A year or so ago, I would have sulked and felt sorry for myself. Now, I just feel sorry for *her*. For Nana. Her husband is dead, her daughter died entirely too young, and all she has left is you and the children. She's *scared*, Barry." She blinked, her eyes burning from the smoke. *Of course Harlan had suggested this place.* "I thought about it on the train all the way to the city. Let *me* handle her. Please. After all, she and I have to come to some middle ground sooner or later, don't we?"

Barry stared at her for what felt like an eternity. "La Vie en rose" had shifted seamlessly to "God Bless the Child" and then to "Till the End of Time." As the singer crooned the first measures of the song, Barry's eyes filled with tears. He blinked them back, moistened his lips with his tongue, and said, "Want to get out of here?"

"Yes."

They walked to the coat check girl without a word between them, then made themselves busy with putting on their hats, gloves, and coats. The silence remained until they got onto the train, Magda well aware of the number of times the man she was to marry in only a few days swallowed. Swallowed hard.

When they'd pulled away from the station, she slipped her arm into his and squeezed. Barry looked over at her, his eyes sad and lonely beneath the brim of his hat. Magda reached up, kissed the place where his jaw and ear met, and whispered, "That was your song, wasn't it? Yours and Barbara's?"

He nodded once, then squeezed his eyes shut and wept openly.

CHAPTER 46

"I know you were the one who called Mr. VanMichaels." Magda stood in the middle of Barry's living room—her own soon enough—and raised her chin toward the woman who stood facing her near the hearth. In it, a fire roared to life, sparking at times and sending blasts of heat into the room.

Harriet Nielson crossed her arms. "I have no idea what you're talking about," she said, but the red creeping up her throat told another story.

Magda took a few steps so that she stood behind one of the wingback chairs. She laid her hands along the curved, velvety top. "Please don't," she said, keeping her eyes locked with the older woman's. "Don't bother to deny it."

"Did Jessie tell you this?"

"No," Magda answered quietly. "I hadn't left the house yesterday when you were talking. I had to come back in to get my notepad."

"So you were eavesdropping?"

Magda nearly choked. "*No.* I live in that home, Mrs.—Harriet."

"Mrs. Nielson will do just fine," she said, walking to the sofa and sitting in such a way as to let Magda know that, as far as she was concerned, *this* would always be her daughter's home.

Magda took a breath. "I want us to be friends."

"Never. You *can*not and *will* not take the place of Barbara."

Magda walked around the chair and sat, crossing her legs and keeping her hands in her lap. She'd prayed all morning before this meeting, which had left her with a great sense that, no matter what, she *had* to stay calm.

"Of course not."

She glanced at the ornate buffet table standing near the dining room door. An elaborately hand-stitched runner lay across the center. Tall and slender brass lamps with fringed shades stood on both ends. Between them, a number of framed photos—including the one of Barbara—stared back at her.

Magda stood again, walked to the photo, and gingerly picked it up. "She was beautiful," she said without turning to look at Harriet.

"You could never begin to match her."

Magda replaced the photo and turned. "Nor do I want to." She leaned against the buffet, crossing her arms. "She is and always will be Deanne and Douglas's mother, and she will always be your daughter. But her . . . *passing* . . . ended her marriage to Barry. And as sorry as I am to say that, and as painful as it is to hear it, the fact of the matter is, Harriet—" she took a deep breath— "it's true."

Harriet stood suddenly, jolting Magda. "How *dare* you!"

"I'm not trying to be mean."

The woman's face turned such a deep shade of red, Magda thought her head might explode. "You are *vicious*," she said. "You have managed to kick me out of my home, but you will *not* remove me or my influence from my grandchildren."

Magda noted the fists at her side and wondered if Harriet might cross the room and sock her. But when thirty seconds had passed and neither of them had moved, Magda discreetly cleared her throat and took a step.

"Harriet," she said as calmly as her nerves would allow, "I am going to marry Barry on the thirteenth. And after our honeymoon, I am going to come to this house and make it my home. If you and I cannot meet in the middle between now and then, I can only pray we will at some point in the lives we *will* share together." She crossed to where she had left her purse, coat, and gloves. Her hands shook as she pushed her fingers into them. She wanted to stomp her feet, but instead focused on the task.

Magda didn't look up again until she had wrapped the coat around herself, methodically sliding one arm in and then the other. "I guess that's all I have to say." She started for the door, stopping only when she heard Harriet call her name.

She turned without reply.

"Marry my son-in-law and I'll make your life miserable."

The force of the words struck Magda like a jackhammer coming to life without warning in her heart. She swallowed. Nodded. And when she could finally catch her breath, she said, "I suppose I'll just have to take my chances."

That night, Magda dreamed she was an old woman, struggling to take her last breath. Her children and grandchildren stood around her deathbed. Deanne and Douglas were there as well. They were older—much older—but she recognized them immediately. They all told her how much they loved her and that she would soon be with Barry again.

And then, as dreams so often jump from one place to another, Magda found herself approaching the gates of heaven. She was young again, and when she realized the road she was on, she ran toward the gates. They opened slowly, revealing thick white fog as the song from a chorus of angels became louder, and louder still.

Magda wanted only two things—to see Jesus for the first time and to see Barry again. Then a form appeared. Kindness and loveliness radiated from it, drawing Magda closer. And when she could finally see—when all had become clear—she realized Barbara stood before her.

"I wanted to be the one," she said, though her lips didn't move. "Before anyone else. I wanted to thank you." And then she smiled. Slowly at first, until the smile became broad and infectious.

Magda woke with a start.

And new hope.

February 13, 1954
Plymouth, Minnesota

"How do I look?" Magda stood in front of her mother in the same room where she'd helped Inga dress almost a year earlier.

Mor placed a hand against her ample breast. "You are a vision."

Magda smiled. "Tell me the truth, Mor. Is Far excited to walk the bride down the aisle? He's so accustomed to officiating."

"I believe, yes." Her blush became fuller, more pronounced. "But your father hasn't fully . . ." Her words trailed and she shook her head.

How foolish she'd been in her question. "Gotten over Inga? Not yet, Mor?"

Mor sighed. "Let's not talk about it on this special day." It seemed to Magda that her mother's accent had become more pronounced with the occasion. Mor took her daughter's hands and pulled them to the sides so that Magda stood like a kite in a March wind. "How interesting that the very same dress looks different than when your sister wore it."

Magda laughed nervously. "I thought we weren't going to talk about Inga today." Although she missed her. Missed her terribly. More than she could have imagined she ever would.

She'd so wanted Inga to come, to be her only attendant, but Axel had been unable to get away from his duties at the church and Inga—for whatever reason—hadn't wanted to travel alone, with a baby. With that in mind, Magda made a decision that, other than her father, no one would walk the aisle with her. "Maybe," she added now to lighten the moment, "it's because I'm not wearing a pink sash."

"And no veil and no flowers." Mor waved both hands like windshield wipers in the middle of a thunderstorm. "I don't understand your decisions, but . . ." She walked across the room to the round Samsonite hatbox she'd brought in earlier. She opened it carefully, then reverently brought out a clump of white tissue paper. She pulled the tissue away to display an elegant hat that seemed to be nothing more than a skull-shaped cap made of net with clusters of red-and-pink silk flowers on top. "I wore this the day I married your father," she whispered to it.

Magda joined her mother, now bathed in a shaft of light from a nearby window. "Mor," she said, her voice soft. "This is beautiful." The light shimmered on the flowers—azaleas, she now realized.

"It's a Schiaparelli." She touched it lightly. "The most elegant thing . . ." She extended it. "I know you said you didn't want to wear a veil, but I thought . . ."

"I would *adore* wearing this." Magda smiled. "'Something old . . . ,' and it will be like carrying flowers after all." She bent her knees to allow her mother to properly position the hat. When her mother was done, Magda turned to look in the beveled wall mirror. Seeing herself for the first time as a bride, her stomach clenched as a vision of what Barbara might have looked like on her wedding day swam in the reflection next to hers. "Mor," she said. "I'm in a predicament."

Her mother stood behind her. She placed her hands on Magda's shoulders and said, "The children's grandmother."

Magda's eyes widened. "How did you know?"

"I put myself in her place—I am a grandmother now, you know—and I have thought how I might feel if . . . if Inga died and then another woman came in to raise little Emma."

Magda reached for her mother's hands and squeezed. "Am I—do you think I'm—making a mistake marrying Barry so soon, Mor? I love him and I want to be a good wife and I want to be a good mother to the children, but—maybe I'm being selfish not waiting a little longer."

Mor shook her head. "Love cannot be selfish, Magda. Love is about giving and giving until you think you cannot give any more. And, just when that happens, *boom*. You are giving some more."

Magda couldn't help but giggle.

"But my dearest," her mother added, "every marriage—no matter how complicated or simple—requires much patience. Much prayer. Much *love*."

Magda nodded. "So, I *should* go through with this? Forget the fears and march down the aisle?"

Mor shook her head. "No. If you have any doubt whatsoever that your love is enough, then, no."

Magda gasped, surprised by her mother's answer.

"But," she continued, "if you believe your love will weather any storm, then yes. Meet your Mr. Cole at the altar and begin your life together *now*. Not to say that Mrs. Nielson will ever see the light. She may not. And that's not the point."

"Then what is?"

"The love."

"Oh, Mor." Magda turned, throwing her arms around the older woman. She breathed in her scent, the hint of flowers she'd always drawn comfort from when this close to her mother. "I love him so much."

A tap at the door caused them to separate. "Who knocks?" Mor called out.

"It's time," Far's voice carried into the room. "I'm here to get my wife and daughter."

Magda winked at her mother. "I think I know why you married that man," she said. "In spite of the crusty exterior, he can be quite cute when he wants to be."

Mor winked back. "And one day if God blesses you so, your daughter will say the same to you."

Magda took a final look in the mirror before clasping her mother's hand. "Let's go, then," she said. "So I can become Mrs. Barry Cole."

April 1954
Nuremberg, Germany

Dear, dear Joan,

I am enclosing a photograph of the most amazing son a mother has ever brought into the world.

Look at me, Joanie! I am a mother. Pat is a father. We are a family. Because of you.

We love and miss you. Hurry back to the States, will you?

Fondly,
Sean Patrick Callahan Jr.'s doting mother

Being a member of General Partridge's staff meant organizing a USO show for the troops stationed in Germany, which brought

Joan information about Garmisch-Partenkirchen, a resort town in southern Germany near the Austrian border.

"It's near the Zugspitze," she told Robert one evening as he walked her to the Austin.

"The mountain?"

"Mmm-hmm." As they reached the car, Joan placed a hand on his coat sleeve to keep him from opening the door. She wanted to talk a few minutes longer, in spite of the unrelenting cold in the evening air. "There's a lake nearby called Eibsee. It looks beautiful in the pictures I saw today, not too far outside of Garmisch-Partenkirchen, and there's a hotel right on the lake."

"Eibsee Hotel?"

"How did you know?"

"The one commandeered as an officers' club for the Army?"

"Yes," she said, excited he already knew about the place.

"I don't know why you're so excited. It's for officers. I'm not an officer."

Joan gripped the lapels of her coat. "But as a civilian employee, I have officer's rank. And I can take guests."

He leaned against the car and she did the same, her shoulder resting next to Robert's upper arm. "That's right," he said, drawing out the last word, his mind obviously fluttering with ideas.

"I thought we could get a group of us—small, my car will only hold four—and head over this weekend. Take in some skiing."

He crossed his arms. "I warn you: I'm not a good skier."

"I ski about as well as I drive," Joan laughed. "But that's the fun of it, don't you think?"

He chewed on his lips, pondering. Then he clapped his hands and pushed away from the car. "Let's do it. See if Lucy wants to go. I'll see if maybe Bob or Leo wants to join us. We can get a couple of rooms . . ." He opened the car door and Joan slid behind the wheel.

"I'll talk to Lucy this evening," she said.

He leaned in and, as he always did, kissed her cheek. "Drive carefully."

In spite of being on board with the trip, Lucy woke on Friday morning with such a head cold that she bowed out of both work *and* the ski trip. When Joan went down to the TWX office for the general's messages, she told Robert the bad news.

"I may have a solution," he said. "Leo's been pouting. He really wants to go but I told him we already had a full car."

"Can three of you bunk down in one room?"

Robert grinned. "We're soldiers, Joan. Bunking three to one room at a resort hotel after a day of skiing isn't exactly a hardship."

Joan pointed at him playfully. "Got it."

Eibsee Hotel rose like a beacon, pushing its way through blankets of snow and lighting the way for those seeking comfort in its warmth. But beneath the shadows of the Zugspitze, it looked like no more than a pesky bug. The mountain, which lifted its rocky, snow-laden face nearly ten thousand feet toward the heavens, appeared a jagged anchor against a neon-blue sky.

"I can't wait," Joan said as the foursome stepped out of her car. She stared at the side of the mountain. "Let's hurry and get settled in."

"What are you in such a hurry for?" Robert teased. "I thought you weren't much of a skier."

Joan laughed. "I'm not. It just looks like such *fun*."

The day turned out better than she could have imagined. All fun and no broken bones. After gliding between the snow-dusted evergreens for hours, they decided they couldn't ski another slope without collapsing from sheer exhaustion.

"Let's go back to the hotel," Robert suggested to everyone. "We can change, grab something to eat . . ."

"I want to sit in front of that fireplace in the lobby," Joan announced as they turned toward the cable cars. "It may take a month before my toes fully thaw."

By the time they walked into the richly paneled lobby, dusk had settled over the Eibsee Hotel, turning the snow to the color of a baby boy's blanket and the lake beyond the windows a rich shade of indigo.

"Before it gets too dark," Robert said to Joan as they approached the lobby elevator, "how about you and I drive into Garmisch?"

"Whatever for?"

He grimaced. "Bandages and Mercurochrome."

Joan stopped and he did too. Leo and Bob continued on. "We'll meet you down here at nineteen hundred hours," Bob said, already pushing the elevator's call button.

"Why do you need medical supplies?" Joan asked.

"I hate to sound like a baby, but the ski boots rubbed blisters on my heels."

Joan bit her lip to keep from saying, "Poor baby . . . ," but she patted the side of his face anyway.

An hour later, Joan and Robert headed back from Garmisch-Partenkirchen with a small white bag of first aid supplies. Robert read the label on the Mercurochrome and moaned.

"It's certainly cold outside," Joan said to change the subject. "Colder than I thought it would be."

"I guess that makes it better for skiing, which I'm not so sure I'll be doing tomorrow."

"I'll probably be too sore to ski anyway. If the boys want to go back up, why don't you and I sit in the lobby and drink hot chocolate?" Joan smiled as she parked the car at the hotel. She reached for the key in the ignition just as Robert's hand reached for hers.

"Leave it on," he said, his voice coaxing.

She turned to face him. "Something wrong?"

"Not a thing," he said as he brought his lips to hers. Joan felt the softness, the deliciousness, and—despite the ice and snow outside—warmth slid down her spine, her legs, and settled sweetly in her toes.

A sudden tap on the driver's window forced them apart. Joan gripped the crank to roll it down and peer out.

A German guard stood over the car. Joan looked from him back to Robert, whose eyes were caught somewhere between mirth and frustration. "Is there a problem, sir?" Robert asked.

"This area is for parking only," he said, his English remarkably decent for a German.

Joan looked at Robert, whose brow shot up. "But, sir," he said, chuckling, "that's what we're doing. *Parking.*"

CHAPTER 47

Seventeen months later
September 1955

Joan had not come to Germany with the intention of finding her special someone. Of falling in love. And, in spite of the number of times Robert had proposed that they marry while in Germany, she'd certainly not come halfway around the world to walk down the aisle.

She had, however, come to Germany to work. To seek adventure.

She had somehow accomplished both of those things . . . *as well as* falling in love.

But they—she and Robert—could not live in Germany forever, working during the weekdays and driving from Nuremberg throughout Europe on the weekends. Playtime had come to an end. Soon, too soon, she would have to return to Chicago.

And Robert would go home to the South.

The day of Joan's departure from Europe loomed in the form of two weeks. Fourteen short days. Train tickets—Joan's a one-way and Robert's a round-trip—would take them to Amsterdam. Then the *SS Rotterdam* would take Joan back to the States.

Robert would return to Nuremberg for another few months.

Joan sold her car to Leo for four hundred dollars with the understanding he would take possession on the day she left Germany.

"What will you do with all that money?" Robert asked her.

"Add it to what I've already saved." With her consistent promotions within the General Schedule levels of pay, Joan had made good wages. Because most of her needs were taken care of by the government, she'd been able to save the surplus. "I'm not going home to a job, so I'm sure I'll need it to get settled back in Chicago."

They sat together at one of the outside tables of the PX coffee shop where they'd had their first "date." Unlike that night, moderate weather wrapped around them like a summer sweater and they were able to sip their coffee more out of enjoyment and less out of a recourse against hypothermia.

"Tell you what, Joan," Robert said. "You could eighty-six this notion of going back to the States. Stay here. Marry me." He grinned.

"One," Joan said, holding up her index finger, "over the past year, I've gotten to know your mother through her lovely and gracious letters to me. Not to mention your sister, Nancy. I would *never* start my future relationship with your family in such a way as to rob them of seeing their only boy getting married."

Robert groaned.

"Two," Joan added, holding up another finger, "I told you before . . . I have a dress in the States that I truly wish to wear on my wedding day. I paid good money for it."

"But you love me, right?" he asked.

"I do, Robert. But I'm not going to marry you. Not here." She held up the third finger. "And certainly not without knowing what my life will be like in North Carolina."

Robert held up his hand. "I give up then. As long as you promise to write."

Joan nodded. "At least once a week." She held up her entire hand as if taking an oath. "On my honor."

November 1955
Lake Forest, Illinois

"You're *here*," Betty Callahan all but shouted as she ran from the front door to the long driveway where a taxicab had, not thirty seconds earlier, pulled in.

Joan exited from the back passenger door, her face bright. She stood upright, throwing her arms out wide, and Betty rushed into them.

"I can't believe it." Betty held her friend at arm's length. "Look at you." She gave Joan's shoulders a light squeeze. "Love looks good on you."

Joan laughed, her eye gazing overhead to where tall trees swayed and shimmered in reds and golds. "Everyone looks good this time of year." She glanced at the ranch-style home as the cab driver opened the car's trunk. "Your home is lovely, Betty. Even from out here."

Betty looped their arms and pulled her toward the still-open front door. "Wait till you see the inside. Pat has given me carte blanche when it comes to decorating, and—"

"And you've taken him up on it, have you, Chloe Estes?"

Betty threw back her head and laughed, nonplussed by the remark tying her to her mother. "Yes!" She glanced over her shoulder; the cab driver followed behind them, carrying Joan's small piece of luggage. "That's all you brought? I wanted you to stay a month, not a weekend," she said just as her husband dashed from the door dressed in his usual Saturday attire—casual slacks, a long-sleeved shirt, and a V-neck sweater.

"Pat!" Joan squealed.

"Joan Hunt," he exclaimed, awkwardly wrapping them both in his arms.

"Pat, for goodness' sakes," Betty said, her voice muffled against his shoulder. "Pay the cab driver, dear."

"Of course," he said, reaching for his back pocket. "Go on in, girls. I'll be right there."

Betty hurried Joan over the threshold and into the warmth of the living room, where stylish furniture had been expertly placed, looking ready for a photo shoot for the cover of *Good Housekeeping* magazine.

"Oh, Betty," Joan breathed out, and Betty smiled in appreciation. "Look how far you've come." She grinned. "A roomful of furniture . . . *and it all matches*."

Betty grabbed her by the hand and pulled her toward a sliding-glass door leading to a kidney-shaped swimming pool, their laughter trailing behind them. "Pat will take care of your things," she said. "Come see the expanse of this backyard, will you?"

They stepped outside to the patio and pool, its water dotted by autumn leaves that had spiraled earlier from the sturdy trees. "Oh," Betty groaned. She'd so wanted everything to appear perfect. "Pat will have to get the net out again. I suppose he should go ahead and cover the pool, but I enjoy sitting out here in the afternoon when Sean Patrick naps."

Joan turned to her. "Where is he? I'm dying to get my hands on him."

"Napping, thank the good Lord," Betty said. "He's quite the Irish handful." She laid her hand against her stomach then. "But guess what. I'm expecting again, Joanie."

Joan's eyes grew wide. *"No."*

Betty nodded. "Yes."

Pat joined them then. "No, yes . . . what?" Then, as understanding crossed the handsome features of his face he said, "Ah. You told her." A light blush blended with the natural freckles dotting his cheeks. "What do you think, Joan Hunt?"

Joan hugged them both once more. "I couldn't be happier. And you?" she asked them both. "You're happy? Really and truly? I mean, not just about the baby, but . . . really and truly?"

"Ecstatic," Betty said, her eyes searching for Pat's. She felt the sheer joy shimmering within them. "But as for this baby," she said, turning back to Joan, "I've not even had a moment of morning sickness this time. Have I, Pat?"

Pat shook his head and, deepening his Irish brogue, said, "No, Joan Hunt, she has not. Glory hallelujah. Glory be."

February 1956
Savannah, Georgia

Evelyn had tried. She had told Edwin every which way she knew that she could not—would not—date him. In the nearly three years they had been working together, and had occasionally gone fishing together, they had become good friends. But Evelyn wasn't ready for more. Not yet. And maybe not ever. She'd come a long way since her departure from Chicago and George; she didn't want to take three steps backward when she'd barely made two forward.

Yet, here she was, holding the telephone to her ear, listening to Ed tell her about the high school sweetheart dance they'd been asked to chaperone. "I got the call from Dr. Forrest not five minutes ago. You've made such an impression on the board of education, Evelyn. Especially now that you're working within the school system."

Evelyn had taken her idea of blending instruction on etiquette with their required PE and health classes to the school the previous September. These classes were somewhat different from what the boys and girls who attended the Victory Drive School of Etiquette received, and, Evelyn hoped, they would prompt new business for the evenings. So far, the plan had worked, but it had also put extra work on her and Ed in addition to their roles at the church.

More than anything, she feared that people in town—and especially the people at Ed's church and most especially *Ed*—were starting to view them as a couple.

She sighed. "On one condition," she told him. "You and I will not arrive together and we will not leave together. We must exhibit the utmost in decorum, Ed."

A long pause met her statement. "All right, Miss Evelyn, if that's what you prefer."

"It is," she said, though she had to pinch her arm to keep from grinning at his light form of endearment.

She ended the call and turned to see Aunt Dovalou standing in the hallway behind her, arms crossed. "Let me guess," she said, slowly shaking her head. "He's asked you out *again* and you've turned him down *again*."

Evelyn smiled politely but walked past her and toward the kitchen. "Aunt Dovalou, I'm just *not* ready."

"Darlin'," she said, falling in on her heels. "Let me tell you a little secret. Once upon a time, I thought I wasn't ready too. And look where it got me."

Evelyn spun around, nearly colliding with her aunt. "What?"

Her aunt took her by the elbow, guiding her into the kitchen where an apple pie baked in the oven and filled the room with spices and warmth. "His name was Rood Whiting," she said, jerking an oven mitt from the hook by the oven.

"Rude?"

Aunt Dovalou frowned from across the room. "Get the cooling rack, will you? And it was *R-O-O-D*—a family name."

"It would have to be . . . ," she muttered, pulling the rack from the shelf where her aunt kept it.

"Evelyn Ruth Alexander . . ." Aunt Dovalou's voice was both firm and playful.

Evelyn swallowed as she placed the rack on the countertop near the oven. "Sorry." She stood back. "So, what happened?"

"My own stubbornness." She opened the oven; a whoosh of heat sped past them. "Whoo!" She pulled the golden-topped pie out, set it on the rack, and kicked the door shut in one smooth movement. "He loved me and I loved him—no two ways about it—but . . . well, he was much like your daddy in that he hardly had two plugged nickels to rub together." She went to the Frigidaire, opened it, and brought out a bottle of milk, then set about pouring a couple of glasses. "Let's sit out in the wicker room," she said. "Too warm in here."

Evelyn followed her aunt into the glassed-in room at the back of the house filled with old white wicker furniture. Aunt Dovalou handed her a glass of the cold milk before they sat together on the divan. "Now, Judith had just run off with that sweet daddy of yours and got married. Mama and Daddy were both beside themselves and . . ." She took a drink of her milk. It left a small moustache along her top lip, which she licked off. "I kept telling Rood that we only needed to wait awhile. Let my parents get over the shock of it. Then Mama died, and I told him we needed to wait until Daddy got through the mourning period." She paused, her eyes scanning the room as though a scene had unfolded in front of her.

After long moments passed, Evelyn found the courage to speak. "What happened?"

She looked into her glass of half-drunk milk. "He got tired of waiting, especially after this pretty little thing started batting her eyes at him."

"Where is he now? Still here?"

Aunt Dovalou nodded. "He goes over to the Episcopal church so I don't see him—well, hardly ever. But sometimes we run into each other at the Piggly Wiggly." She smiled through tears, forcing Evelyn to bite her bottom lip to keep from crying. "They had three children—all grown by now—and then his wife took off with a Fuller Brush salesman." She pressed her fingertips to her lips.

"When?"

"About five years ago."

Evelyn shifted on the little sofa. "Aunt Dovalou! You are—what? Fifty-one? Fifty-two?"

Aunt Dovalou feigned shock. "And your point?"

"You should tell him how you feel. Because I can tell you still feel something for him."

Her aunt pointed a perfectly shaped nail at her. "That's not the point. Now you listen to me, little missy. A good man is hard to find."

"You're telling me . . ."

"Is all this about that Hank boy back in Portal?"

"No." She shook her head. "No." Evelyn inhaled deeply. "Aunt Dovalou, that pie smells so good." She stood. "What's say we cut a slice and pour another glass of milk?"

Aunt Dovalou stood. "I can tell when you're dismissing me. I can only hope you heard me."

Evelyn leaned over to kiss her aunt's pretty face. "I was listening, Aunt Dovalou. *And* I heard you."

Chicago

Robert had been back in the States a month before he flew up to Chicago—because of a business meeting, but also to see Joan.

"I'll go to my meeting," he told her on the phone the week before. "Then I'll pick you up at your work."

Shortly after she'd gotten resettled back into life in the States—this time in Evanston, where she moved into the same boardinghouse that Magda had once resided in—she found a job at the National Industrial Recreation Association, a forward-thinking company that placed recreational equipment in businesses so as to get their employees "moving."

"We'll go out to dinner. Just the two of us," he continued. "Anywhere you want to go."

"I can hardly wait," she told him, and it was true.

"See you soon, then."

Joan couldn't be entirely sure how, but somehow on the day of their first meeting since leaving Germany she managed to complete the tasks in front of her. At the end of the day, she pulled the typewriter cover out of the drawer and placed it over the machine, then retrieved her purse and coat and dashed out of the office toward the elevator. She pulled on her gloves while waiting for the doors to open, pausing over the left hand, staring longingly at the ring finger, wondering—fleetingly, but wondering—if Robert had come to Chicago with a ring in tow. And, if he had, what it might look like.

A deep breath escaped her lungs. "Oh, dear," she said, placing a hand on the wall to steady herself. As much as she loved Robert, she couldn't say with all honesty that she was certain of a future with him. Joan had heard a lot about the South—from the news, from Lucy, and from Evelyn. She couldn't imagine someone like herself living there. Surviving and thriving there. *If* he proposed and *if* they married, would she be expected to become a full-time homemaker? Would she be expected to get up every morning to cook her husband's breakfast, tidy up behind him after he'd left for the office, wash and fold the laundry, and then prepare a dinner feast for when he came home?

Or would there be a maid for that, like she'd heard nearly every Southern woman had?

"Oh, no," she said to no one as the elevator doors slid open to reveal an empty lift. "Not me," she said, stepping in and pushing the button marked *L*.

She couldn't bear the thought of becoming one of *those* women who hired other women to clean their homes and then paid them meager salaries. Then again, she told herself, perhaps everything she'd read, everything she'd seen in the movies—all of it—was nothing more than propaganda for the purpose of drama.

"And besides," she said as the elevator rattled to a stop. "Maybe Robert has no intention of proposing." The doors slid open again, revealing highly polished, black-and-white faux marble linoleum . . . and a pair of highly polished men's shoes.

Her eyes traveled up the length of the man—all six feet, four inches of him, dressed in a dark-blue suit and a narrow navy-and-white tie—looking so remarkably handsome that her feet froze and her breath caught in her chest.

"Robert," she finally managed.

He smiled, deep dimples digging into his cheeks. "Joan."

She practically jumped out of the lift and into his arms, her feet leaving the floor by a good six inches. His lips, warm and moist, found hers. The kiss, tender and sweet, left her dizzy.

When her feet finally found the floor again, she tilted her head back and looked into his eyes. "Hi, there."

They both laughed. "I worried I'd never see you again," he said. "Hungry?"

"Starving."

CHAPTER 48

Savannah, Georgia

Evelyn stood in the entryway of her home, back against the door, eyes closed. Her fingertips continued to grip the doorknob, but only barely.

She sighed.

Unexpected, that's what it had been. Edwin had been the epitome of a gentleman during the entire evening, and while they'd danced together about a half-dozen times, he'd not said or done anything that made her feel uncomfortable.

Maybe it had been the sweetness of the event . . . of watching the students swaying under twisted crepe paper and twinkling lights . . . of being all dressed up . . . of feeling special. Or maybe it had been the way Edwin placed his hand on the small of her back and held her hand so she wouldn't slip on the icy patches of winter as he escorted her to her car. Whatever it had been, combined with the way he said her name as she started to get into her automobile, had enticed her to turn her face up to his and to allow him to kiss her. Sweetly at first, like a butterfly landing briefly on a spring flower. Then, after a smile and breathing an "okay?" against her lips, she nodded, wrapping her arms around his shoulders as his slid around her back.

"Make no mistake about it, Evelyn," he said after the kiss had ended but the moment continued to linger. "I'm in love with you. Whatever or whoever hurt you before, I'll wipe away the memory, if you'll give me a chance."

"I'll think about it," she'd said. But, standing here now, she knew . . . There was little to think about. Edwin Boland loved her. He *loved* her.

He loved *her*.

Greensboro, North Carolina

Before March came to its official windy close, Joan flew into Greensboro early on a Friday evening, slated to return to Chicago Sunday night following her official "meet-the-family" visit.

Robert met her at the airport, and, as it had in her office building's lobby, the greeting soared sweetly between them. If he had suggested they find a cozy table in one of the airport's new restaurants and remain there the entire weekend, it would have been fine with Joan. Instead, his hand dropped to the small of her back, and with gentle pressure, he guided her toward the exit.

"Are you nervous?" he asked.

She looked up at him, at the concern in his face. "Not really. Not too much." While they'd been in Germany, Robert's mother and sister Nancy had always included little notes to Joan in their correspondence to him. In many ways, she felt they already knew one another. That they were friends.

"My mother said you probably wouldn't want to meet them and then sit down to a meal—you know, eating in front of them.

I'm to take you to dinner and then to my sister Nancy's where you'll stay for the weekend."

Following a leisurely dinner, Robert drove to Nancy's modest but lovely home.

"So, this is Joan," she said after opening the front door wide and throwing out her arms in welcome. She stood in the middle of a small foyer, the overhead lamp shining on light-brown hair and porcelain skin, giving her an angelic appearance.

Robert clasped her elbow with one hand and her suitcase with the other and escorted her inside. "Joan," he said, keeping his voice low, "this is the sister who wrote you all those nice notes while we were in Germany."

Joan looked up and crossed her eyes. "Well, yes, Robert, I remember . . ."

Nancy, who stood nearly as tall as her brother, laughed. "Goodness, Robert, what do you think? She has a pea-sized brain? Of course she remembers." Nancy slid her arm around Joan's shoulder, drawing her close. "Come on in. The kids are already in bed, but my husband is waiting for us in the den. Put that suitcase in Margaret's room, will ya, little brother?"

With that, Robert disappeared down a dark hallway.

Joan and Nancy entered a family room where a console TV showing *Our Miss Brooks* stood angled in a corner. A scholarly looking man stood bent over the coffee table, where he had apparently just placed a tray filled with a pot of hot coffee and four cups stacked two by two.

He straightened, revealing yet another tall Southerner. "Hallo," Joan said, all the while wondering if she'd somehow managed to find her way to the pages of *Gulliver's Travels*.

In reverse.

"Robert Procter," he said, shaking Joan's hand. "Welcome."

"Another Robert?" Joan asked. "How will I keep you straight?"

"I'm the better-looking one." Behind her, Robert placed his hands on her shoulders. "Let me take your coat," he said.

She shirked out of it.

"You can call me Bob." Robert's brother-in-law smiled. "Goodness, you really do have a British accent, just like Robert said."

"Yes, of course I do," she said.

"We have some coffee here and . . ." He appeared to notice Nancy had disappeared. "I'm sure my wife has gone to get the cake she made earlier today."

Within seconds, Nancy returned, balancing a delicious-looking chocolate cake on a plate and four dessert dishes. "Joan, I hope you saved room."

"Joan isn't a big eater," Robert offered, "but I told her to save some space."

"I can see that you're not a big eater," Nancy said. "You are the tiniest thing." She laughed. "Oh, Bobby, turn that TV off, will you? Miss Brooks we know. Let's take time to get to know *our Miss Joan*."

The next morning, Nancy drove Joan to her childhood home.

"Tell me," Joan said along the way. "What is Frances like?"

"We're quite different," she said.

"In what way?"

"Well—" Nancy glanced at Joan, displaying round cheeks and a bright smile—"I'm more talkative, like our mother. Frances is more like Daddy." Her eyes widened. "Now listen. Daddy can be a little rough around the edges, but don't let him scare you any."

Joan chuckled. "I've never been scared by anyone." Besides, it wasn't like she was meeting the Queen of England or the Duke of Edinburgh.

"Deep down, Daddy is nothing but a teddy bear. He's set in his ways and if he says jump, you'd best ask how high. But if he's in your corner, you'll never need anyone else."

Joan liked the sound of that, but she didn't respond. Instead, she looked out the window to the sidewalk-lined houses standing stately and proud. The lawns, sloping toward the road, were changing from winter brown to the deepest shade of spring green. Leaves shimmered on skinny trees, and colors burst from flowers that seemed more than ready to pop.

"So, *this* is spring in the South," Joan said, smiling. "So lovely."

Nancy returned the smile. "I declare, I could listen to you talk all day. The way you put things. And you're right. Greensboro is a lovely town," she said. "I think you'll like it here."

Joan's very core flexed. *What does that mean?* Had Robert talked to his family about the possibility of marriage? Of her moving here?

Nancy swung her car into the driveway of a house Joan knew well, if only by photograph. "So Robert really does live here," she said.

Nancy shoved the gearshift into Park. "I'm sorry?"

"I told Robert once that I'd heard horror stories about British girls who married American GIs, believing they lived in nice homes, only to end up in some shack somewhere awful."

"That *would* be terrible." She glanced at the house. "But no. This is where we grew up."

Robert descended the front-porch steps. "Good morning," he said, opening the car door.

Joan placed her hand into his extended one and swung her legs out.

"You look wonderful," he added while Nancy gathered her children from the backseat.

"Do I?" she asked. She'd worn a pleated, worsted-flannel chocolate-brown skirt and matching long-sleeved jacket lined with white satin. She pressed her hand against the flat of her stomach.

Robert guided her toward the wide front porch. Nancy and her children had already made it halfway through the opened door, little Margaret squealing in delight at seeing her grandparents.

Within a moment, Joan and Robert stepped into the entryway, grand and open and filled with people.

"Joan." An exceptionally tall, white-haired, and perfectly put-together woman took her hand. "I'm Robert's mother."

Joan squeezed her hand. "So nice to meet you, Mrs. Zimmerman."

Next, a mostly bald, square-jawed man took her hand. "And I'm his father."

Joan shook his hand as well. "Mr. Zimmerman."

Robert inched Joan along the lineup of family members, stopping in front of a dark-haired beauty who, even in the early days of spring, appeared sun-kissed. "My sister," he said.

She smelled of a mixture of sweet tobacco and perfume. "Frances," she said, her voice deep. Two dark-haired children—a lanky boy of about eight who mirrored his mother's image, and a younger girl—circled Robert's sister. "My children, Rodney and Vicki."

Joan bent slightly and extended a hand. "Hallo . . ."

Rodney looked up at his mother and whispered, "She talks funny," which forced laughter from everyone.

"And this," Robert said, waving his arm toward a dark-skinned woman in uniform who stood with both hands clasped over a starched white apron, "is our housekeeper, Marie."

Joan extended her hand, and when Marie didn't take it, Joan grabbed hers anyway. "I'm so happy to meet you," Joan said exuberantly.

"Miss Hunt." Robert's father cleared his throat in an authoritative manner. "We do *not* shake the hands of the colored."

Joan turned slowly, stunned by the words. So, it was true . . . all that she had read.

Her eyes scanned every shocked face in the room, including Nancy's. "Well, Mr. Zimmerman," Joan said finally. "I'm sorry, sir. *But I do.*"

May 1956

For the second time in two months, Joan sat in a plane as it touched down at the tiny airport in Greensboro. Remarkably, she'd been invited back to town. Back to the Zimmermans' household. She may not have made it into the fold exactly, but she remained steady in the race.

Robert met her inside the lobby, and after a sweet kiss, rushed her outside where the air hung heavier than it had the month before. Joan had hardly gotten settled in the passenger side of the front car seat when Robert shot out into the street.

"How's work going?" he asked, his voice pitched high.

"Robert, are you all right?"

"I'm fine. Why?"

"Your voice sounds strange." A thought crossed her mind. "Are you *sure* your parents want me to come back to Greensboro?"

His head jerked, then his eyes returned to the narrow road stretching toward town. "Of course they want you to come back. Mother insisted. In fact, we're having a nice cookout tomorrow night in your honor."

"In *my* honor? Why? What have *I* done that's so special?"

Robert slowed the car and eased it to the side of the road, the tires sliding smoothly near the curb. He put the car in park before turning toward her.

"Joan," he said, and he leaned toward the glove compartment. "There's something I want you to be wearing when we get back to the house."

"Something you want me to wear?"

She looked at her lap, to the practical skirt and sweater she'd chosen to travel in. Then to Robert's tanned hand as he popped open the hidden compartment's rectangular door. He retrieved a small black velvet box, then used the heel of his hand to click the door shut.

He slid closer and opened the box, revealing a simple solitaire diamond. It shimmered in the late-afternoon sun streaming brilliantly between the roadside trees.

"Robert," Joan whispered.

"Look at me," he said, and she did. "Last call. Will you marry me?"

Tears stung her eyes, pooling along the edges. She nodded, speechless—maybe for once in her life—and extended her left hand, slightly raising the ring finger.

"It's not the biggest rock," he said, sliding the ring on, "but I thought it was as pretty as you."

Joan shook her head and tightened her hand into a fist. "It's the most beautiful ring I've—" She started to laugh, then pressed her fingers against her lips.

"What?"

"I've never *owned* a ring before," she said, brushing away the tears. "So of course it's the most beautiful ring I've ever owned. But even if I had—Even if my jewelry box rivaled Queen Elizabeth's, *this* would be the loveliest." She placed her hands on the sides of his face and kissed him tenderly. "Thank you," she whispered.

His thumb pads caught the escaping tears. "Do you think you can do this, Joan? Come down here to live?"

"I guess any notion of you moving to Chicago is out?"

Robert grimaced. "I'm afraid so. I'll go there from time to time, but the business is *here*."

Yes, the business, she thought. But more important, *Robert* was in North Carolina. "Then, I suppose I'll have to."

"You'll at least have to try," he said with a smile; then his expression sobered. "Look, I know it's different here than anywhere else you've ever lived. And I know you and my father didn't exactly get along at first, and I know that . . ." His voice trailed off.

"What?"

He shook his head as he slid back behind the steering wheel. "Nothing."

She touched the sleeve of his jacket. "No. Don't do that. What is it you were going to say?"

Robert pulled the gearshift to Drive and eased back onto the road. "Do you remember my friend Jack Coleman? You met him last time you were here."

She remembered him. The old school chum of Robert's had given her a sideward glance, not that she hadn't done the same to him. "Yes."

Robert chuckled. "He said I needed to watch out for you. You know, your being *foreign*, as he puts it."

Joan crossed, then uncrossed her arms, keeping her left hand palm down against her thigh so she could watch the light that skipped into the car catch and play with the diamond. "You are just as foreign to me as I am to you, you know."

Robert's index finger shot up. "Good point."

"And touché."

"And touché," he concurred.

Robert pulled into his parents' driveway, where a number of cars had already lined up like train cars heading down a track.

"Who's here?" Joan asked.

Robert opened his car door. "Mother and Dad, of course. My sisters and their husbands and the kids."

"Anyone else?"

Robert got out of the car and closed the door, walked between Nancy's Cadillac and his own, then opened the passenger door. "If you're asking if Marie is here, she is."

Joan stood to her full five feet, three inches, jutted her jaw, and straightened her simple pink felt hat. "Then, I'm ready."

"Easy . . ." Robert said, taking her by the elbow as they crossed the lawn to the narrow strip of cement leading to the front porch steps.

"Mmm-hmm," she said.

Before they were halfway up the steps, the main door opened and Rodney pushed the screen door open. "You're back, Uncle Robert."

Robert looked down at his nephew. "Where is everyone?"

"Back in the den." Rodney tilted back his head for a better look at his uncle. "Did you do it?" he whispered.

Joan held up her left hand and smiled. "You mean this?"

Rodney grinned. "I guess that means you'll be my aunt Joan now."

"Soon enough."

They entered the house and made their way through, following the sound of conversation and laughter.

"Joan," Mrs. Zimmerman exclaimed. She rose from her favorite chair nestled in the corner under the wide, open window. "You made it."

With a smile, she threw out her hand. "Is this what you've all come to see?"

The three women gathered around, showering both her and Robert with hugs before Robert's father gave Joan a swift kiss on the cheek, followed by Nancy's husband, and finally a dark-haired man who prefaced his hug with, "Hi, Joan. I'm Vic. Frances's husband. Welcome to the family."

When the frivolity had settled down, Joan glanced toward the door leading to the kitchen to see Marie wiping her hands on a small dishcloth. Her eyes searched first the crowd and then Joan's hand.

"What do you think, Marie?" Joan asked.

"That's right nice, Miss Joan," she said, her white teeth shining bright against the chocolate of her skin. "Right nice."

Quickly, before anyone had a chance to react, Joan hurried across the room, threw her arms around Marie, then drew back, resting her hands on her shoulders. "I'm so glad you think so," she whispered. "Because we're going to be great friends. I just *know* it."

CHAPTER 49

For their wedding date, Joan and Robert chose a Saturday in late September.

For Joan, *that* would prove to be the easiest part.

In June, after moving to Greensboro and renting a room in Mrs. Bennett's Boardinghouse down the same street where Robert's parents lived, Joan set out to find a job, accepting one at J. P. Stevens with a Mr. Charlie Baxter.

Or, rather, *they* accepted *her*.

"What I mean to say," Joan told Robert as they walked from his home to hers, "is that *I'm* going to make Mr. Baxter an offer."

"*You* are?"

"Mmm . . . what the South offers women in the workplace is sinful. So, I've decided to offer to work for a salary instead of hourly wages."

Robert chuckled. "I'm listening . . ."

"Three hundred a month." Joan paused at the walkway leading to Mrs. Bennett's front porch and door. "When you figure that the average person works two thousand hours per year or forty hours a week—give or take an hour—then multiply the three hundred by twelve . . . that means I'd work for around a dollar eighty an hour. Give or take a penny."

Robert wrapped his arm around Joan's shoulder and they ambled toward the porch steps. "Well, if Charlie Baxter isn't impressed by your math and reasoning, then I don't know."

Joan grinned up at him. "If he accepts my offer, I'll make over *double* minimum wage."

"I am *doubly* impressed."

"Plus," Joan added, "I can walk to work, they offer wonderful benefits to their employees, and there seems to be a great deal of opportunity for advancement, especially in the PR department." She linked her arm with his and continued up the concrete steps. "Not to mention they offer amazing deals to their employees for all the products they sell—sheets, pillowcases, towels, curtains. As an employee, I'll pay a third of the retail cost." Again she smiled. "For two young marrieds, that will come in handy, don't you think?"

"You are nothing if not practical."

"Growing up in England with eight brothers and sisters, I had to be." She poked him playfully in the chest. "And there's nothing wrong with that."

"No, ma'am," he said. "There surely isn't."

Charlie Baxter accepted Joan's offer.

Now settled in a new town and a new job, Joan's next assignment—given to her by her future mother-in-law—was to accompany her to see a Mrs. Blue, who would "direct" the wedding.

Having a wedding *directed* felt as foreign to Joan as the fried chicken and sweet iced tea she hadn't gotten used to—and thought she never would. But if she thought it odd—this directorship—Mrs. Cora Blue found Joan to be equally unusual.

"What do you mean, your parents won't be here?" Mrs. Blue

reminded Joan of a schoolmarm, and she wore a look of shock and dismay after Joan had explained that *she* would be the only member of her family in attendance the day of the wedding.

The three women sat in Mrs. Blue's parlor, Mrs. Zimmerman and Joan sharing a bloodred velvet settee while Mrs. Blue sat alone in a matching chair. Between them, a low coffee table boasted a silver tray and coffee service along with three china cups and saucers.

"My parents and siblings live in England." Joan took a sip of her coffee.

Mrs. Blue looked at Mrs. Zimmerman, her mouth forming an O, and then gazed back at Joan. "But . . . this can't . . ."

"Joan." Mrs. Zimmerman spoke softly as she returned the cup and saucer to the tray. "Isn't there *any* way your parents, at the very least, can make it?"

"Mrs. Zimmerman," Joan said respectfully, "I don't think you understand the condition of most of us in England after the war."

Her face showed both care and concern. "Of course. Of course." She looked at Mrs. Blue. "We'll just have to make do, Cora."

Mrs. Blue continued to appear aghast. "But *Margaret*, people will think Robert is marrying an orphan!"

Mrs. Zimmerman shifted in her seat. "Then we'll have to explain it in the newspaper."

"And how do you propose to do that?"

"Simple. We'll say it matter-of-factly and be done with it."

"Which brings us to another point." Mrs. Blue's fiery eyes widened with concern. "If neither her father nor her brothers are going to be here to walk her down the aisle, who will?"

"Perhaps one of her brothers-in-law . . . ," Mrs. Zimmerman replied.

Joan wondered if the women had all but forgotten she sat in the same room.

"Bob will play the organ, of course." Mrs. Blue brought her coffee cup to her lips and sipped its contents delicately.

Joan's brow shot up.

"Of course, Cora," Mrs. Zimmerman answered. "Why wouldn't he?"

"Excuse me," Joan interjected. "Do you mean Bob *Procter*?"

Mrs. Zimmerman smiled, then laid her hand on Joan's. "He's a wonderful organist."

"Is music . . . *necessary*?"

The two older women looked at her like she'd dropped in for a visit from another planet. Apparently, it was. A new thought came, one Joan hoped would set her in good standing again. "Perhaps Nancy would serve as my matron of honor?"

"Before we dash off to that subject," Mrs. Blue insisted, "*who* will walk her down the aisle? Vic?"

Mrs. Zimmerman opened her mouth to speak, but before she could, Joan answered. "Why don't I have Robert walk me down the aisle?" The idea seemed so practical.

Mrs. Blue shook her head. "That would never do."

"Joan, dear," Mrs. Zimmerman said, "that kind of thing is just not done in the South."

"Then," she said as diplomatically as she knew how, "can we decide this after I talk with Robert?"

"Of course we can," Mrs. Zimmerman said. "And how nice of you to think of asking Nancy."

Mrs. Blue dabbed at the corner of one eye. "Now, let's set a date when we are all available to shop for your dress, Joan."

"Oh, no worries there," Joan exclaimed. "*That* I already have."

Small birds, Joan thought later, could have made nests inside Mrs. Blue's mouth. No doubt about it.

While Robert set out to find a starter home for Joan and himself, Mrs. Jack Coleman declared it her mission to teach Joan to cook.

"But I know how to cook," Joan told Robert one evening.

"Southern food," Robert said out of the side of his mouth.

"Oh." Joan frowned. "I can hardly get used to eating it; now I have to learn to *cook* it?"

Robert laughed. "You'll do fine."

Betty mailed the dress in late August; it arrived the first day of September. When Joan walked through the Zimmermans' front door that evening for dinner, it was to see Nancy walking into the foyer with a tall, sweating glass of iced tea in her right hand. Joan's eyes immediately went to the long box taking up residence on the living room sofa. *"My dress,"* she exclaimed.

"I told Mother that's what it was. *Mother!*" Nancy's face shone with anticipation. "Joan is here."

Mrs. Zimmerman hurried from a back room, her pumps clomping softly on the carpet, her deep-blue housedress bringing out the color of her eyes. She held a crystal vase of fresh-cut flowers, which she placed on a table. "You're here," she said. "I had to positively force Nancy away from your parcel." She reached behind the package on the long, formal living room sofa and pulled out an envelope. "This also came for you."

Joan took it. "A letter from Evelyn." She placed it with her handbag. "Shall we take the dress upstairs for further inspection?"

"Let's take it up to my old room, Mother."

Joan hoisted the box into her arms and followed the two women to the airy bedroom that housed Nancy's childhood. In spite of her not having lived in the home for several years, the room continued to boast her personality—frilly Priscilla curtains at the windows and a four-poster bed draped in pale-pink chenille. In the corner, an overstuffed chair held a bunny of the same chenille as the spread. He appeared forlorn at the long stretch of Nancy's absence.

Nancy and her mother stood on the opposite side of the bed and gasped as Joan tugged off the box top—the one with the Carson Pirie Scott & Co. emblem—and pushed back the tissue paper, revealing a treasure of white lace. She lifted the dress by the shoulders and drew it out, laying it against her frame.

"Joan," Mrs. Zimmerman breathed out. "It's positively . . ."

"No *wonder* you don't mind sharing it with four other women," Nancy said. She set her glass of iced tea next to the princess lamp on the bedside table. Both women came around the bed to fondle the lace on the sleeves and skirt.

"We'll need to send this over to Macy's Dry Cleaners. Mr. Macy does the best work with bridal gown steaming," Mrs. Zimmerman said. "I wouldn't trust another living soul with something so elegant."

Nancy laid the point of one sleeve in the palm of her hand. "And three other women have worn this already?"

"That's right."

"And you don't get to keep it," she said matter-of-factly.

"No," Joan said. "That will go to Evelyn, I suppose." She returned the dress to the bed.

Nancy opened the closet door and brought out a padded hanger. "Here." She brought it to her nose and sniffed. "Oh, good. It still smells like roses. Let's hang the dress on this and maybe some of the creases will fall out."

They set about the task of hanging up the dress, all the while talking about getting a hoop for underneath and the right shoes for the length. "And for my son's height," Mrs. Zimmerman said.

"You are a foot shorter than he is, Joan. If you don't have a shoe with *some* heel, you'll look like a midget."

Joan smiled at the thought.

Mrs. Zimmerman continued to stare at the dress, which now hung high from the closet door. "It's certainly practical doing it this way, isn't it?" She turned to look at Joan. "Thrifty."

Joan loosely crossed her arms. "I just think of it as *fun*. We had such a good time that day. Very unusual, you understand, for us to even be together on a Saturday, much less to go shopping together. In fact, I'm not sure we'd ever done *anything* like that before. Certainly not after."

Nancy walked to the bedside table for her tea and took a long swallow. "It's trusting too. What if you had put in your share of the money, and let's say the third bride had torn the lace or something?"

"Oh, dear." Mrs. Zimmerman set about inspecting the dress more carefully.

"Nancy." Joan walked to the chair and picked up the bunny. "What would you say to being my matron of honor?"

Nancy swallowed midsip before placing the glass back on the table. "Seriously? Mother? Did you hear?"

Mrs. Zimmerman blinked behind her glasses. "I'm standing no more than six feet away, Nancy. Of course I heard."

"I would adore it, Joan. What will your colors be?" Nancy dropped to the arm of the chair, tucking her right foot behind her bent left knee.

"Colors?"

"Yes. You know, for the wedding. Mine were champagne pink and rose. The bridesmaids wore the champagne pink and Frances wore the rose. I still have her dress in the closet over there." She jumped up, went to the closet, and carefully opened the door to avoid disturbing the gown. She drew out a long zippered bag, which she then draped across the bed.

"Here we go," she said, opening the bag and lifting a taffeta dress that rustled in protest. "Hey, I've an idea. Why don't I wear this? Of course we'll have to have it dry-cleaned too."

"Nancy," Mrs. Zimmerman said, "don't you think you're taking over just a tiny bit here?"

Nancy looked at Joan, her eyes wide. "Oh, Joan. I'm so sorry . . ."

"No," Joan said. "I don't mind. I've never thought about colors or dresses or any of those things. This makes it all quite easy, doesn't it? Practical?"

"And you're sure you don't mind, Joan?" Mrs. Zimmerman placed her hands on her ample hips, not waiting for an answer. "Well, all right then. We need to start thinking about what Robert will wear. And his best man—whom I assume will be his daddy—and groomsmen and . . ."

Dizziness slid down Joan's spine, turning the blood in her veins to dishwater. She eased herself down to the chair as Mrs. Zimmerman's voice traveled down a long tunnel, then returned to the bedroom. Her heart hammered from deep within, ceased to beat altogether, then resumed beating with a flutter.

"Joan?" Nancy took her hand and viciously patted. "Are you okay? Mother, grab my tea over there."

The thought of taking a drink of sweet tea brought Joan around. "I'm fine." She raised her free hand. "For a moment there, I just . . ."

"Do you need me to get Robert?" Mrs. Zimmerman asked.

"Mother," Nancy answered for her. "We've got the dresses all over up here." She looked at Joan. "This is normal. I think I canceled my wedding three or four times before we actually got to the day."

Joan swallowed. "You did?"

Nancy squatted, her pretty face glowing with memory. "With the choosing of the flowers and the planning of the reception and the luncheons and teas and showers and brunches . . ."

Joan blinked furiously. "We have to—do *all* that?" She'd already been through such changes. Perhaps too many for such a short period of time. In five short years, she'd gone from British citizen to American, from living in Chicago to living in Germany and back again, from focusing solely on working and growing as an individual to falling in love and moving to soil more foreign than anything she'd experienced in Europe. And now . . . a wedding and all this too?

Mrs. Zimmerman walked to the door and opened it. "Nancy, you'll give the poor girl a heart attack. Joan, I'm going downstairs to percolate some coffee. Come on down when you can and have a cup with me." She nodded once. "Trust me, whatever is ailing you will vanish with a strong cup of coffee."

CHAPTER 50

Dear Joan,

I will keep this note short. I look forward to attending your wedding, to meeting Robert and to having you meet Edwin. We will arrive on Friday afternoon, check into our rooms at the hotel you suggested, and then go out for dinner. I know our time—yours and mine—will be brief on Saturday, but I wouldn't miss your special day.

Well, Joan, you may want to sit down for this one. I am officially in love. I couldn't be a hundred percent sure after the Valentine's dance, even with the tender kiss he gave me at the end of the evening, but now, after all these months, I think my fears have begun to dissipate.

That doesn't sound too sure, does it? But I actually said it out loud the other night. I said, "I love you too," and I meant it.

I know you will adore him. He is a good man. A patient man. And a godly man.

George Volbrecht has a lot to learn.

Fondly,
Evelyn

P.S. How are you surviving the South?

Dear Evelyn,

I look forward to seeing you as well, and to meeting your Edwin.

How am I surviving, you ask. Southern women, I have come to realize, are often portrayed as dolled-up and frail, ready to swoon at a moment's notice. They are shown as silently standing in their husband's shadow—unsure of what might happen next, incapable of making quick decisions, and almost too delicate for a decent day's work.

In reality, they are the leaders of the South. While Southern men sit in powerful places of business, it is their female secretaries who keep them in line, who make sure they get where they need to be, when they need to be there, who remind them what's next on the agenda and of its importance. This may be no different than in the North, but the Southern secretary—in the few times I have seen her at work—has a command one can read in her eyes. A wisdom that doesn't need a title or a promotion (although, if I have anything to do with it, that will end on my watch).

If a Southern man stands behind a podium and makes a speech, I guarantee you both his wife and secretary read and approved the words therein. His wife also picked out his suit, his tie, and his socks.

While the Southern man believes himself to be the absolute head of his household, it is the woman he pledged his eternal allegiance to who dictates more of what goes on within the four walls of the home. She may be quiet, but she is powerful. Her children both respect and fear her, and with that combination, she is able to keep order. Her husband, oblivious to what happens while he is away at the office, only knows that when he enters the home at the end of his busy day, supper is waiting on the table, the children have been fed and bathed, and while a housekeeper may have been at work behind the scenes, it is the wife and mother who dictated when, where, and how.

I have come to see, Evelyn, even in the short time I've been here, that the Southern woman standing silent in the shadows isn't doing so because she doesn't have a spine. Rather, she is there to make certain things are run the right way. The only way.

The Southern way.

As Mrs. Blue (my wedding conductor) and Mrs. Zimmerman discussed the ins and outs of my wedding, I came to realize that if I want to have any say over my special day, then I'm going to have to be as strong and as "loud." Not in voice but in character. And in my demand that Robert, and Robert only, be the one to walk me down the aisle. When you and Edwin sit as the only guests on the bride's side, you will see that I have, finally, arrived in the South.

Fondly,
Joan

September 22, 1956

Joan chose a fingertip veil attached to a tiara of pearls and sequins as the one thing that would set her wearing of the dress apart from the others'. For Nancy's bouquet, she chose hearty chrysanthemums. Nancy loaned her a prayer book marked only with an orchid for her to hold as she walked down the aisle.

The simplicity of it sent a flutter through Joan's heart.

"What time is it?" she asked her soon-to-be sister-in-law as they stood in the bride's room.

Nancy glanced at her delicate gold wristwatch. "Ten fifteen."

Fifteen minutes later, Mrs. Zimmerman and Mrs. Coleman dropped the dress from Carson's over Joan's head. When they were done, when the final button had been fastened into place, Frances adjusted Joan's headpiece and veil, draping the netting over her face.

Mrs. Blue—a woman truly in her element—breezed in and out of the room, directing each moment like the maestro of a fine orchestra. For a while, Joan stood at a window, looking out over the lush lawn of the church property, to the street beyond where cars slowed as they neared the parking lot. She sighed in contentment, knowing that one by one in the large sanctuary not far away, Robert's family and friends were taking their places.

Organ music filled the room with each opening and closing of the door. Joan focused on the grandness of it. Bob Procter was, indeed, a fine musician.

"Joan?"

Joan turned at the sound of Mrs. Blue's voice to see the older woman standing at the open door. "It's time."

Nancy snatched up her bouquet, then the prayer book and orchid, which she handed to Joan. "Just think," she said with a smile. "In less than an hour you'll be Mrs. Robert Zimmerman. Are you nervous?"

"No," she answered honestly. "As far as I'm concerned, there are only two people in this entire church—Robert and me."

Nancy's eyes smiled before the rest of her face did. "Good answer." She patted Joan's hand and then turned and walked purposefully toward the door.

Mrs. Blue stopped Joan, fluffed the gown's skirt, and mumbled, "Since you'll see your groom outside the sanctuary doors, let's make certain you're all put together."

After meeting her approval, Joan fell in step behind her, blinking furiously when she saw Robert, who stood elegant and dapper in his morning suit near the closed sanctuary doors.

He pressed his hand against his chest and smiled as he offered her the bend of his arm, which she took.

"By golly, boys," he said, his voice low and teasing. "I believe I'm going to marry this girl."

The bridal march swelled from the front of the church. As they started down the aisle—step-together, step-together—Joan heard her mother's voice speak across the miles, whispering her favorite saying into Joan's heart: *"As God made them, he matched them."*

Joan breathed slowly, relishing the moment. *This is so right,* she thought. *And I am so blessed. So very blessed.*

Robert glanced down at her and, in turn, Joan gazed up at him. They exchanged a smile before facing forward.

Forward.

This is the beginning of something amazing, her heart nearly shouted within her. *Mum, you've been right all along. From the moment we were born—Robert in North Carolina and me in Chicago—God set about sending me to Robert.*

And Robert to me.

EPILOGUE

June 2015
London, England

Rachel sat on the long, low-backed sofa in the middle of the elegant room, her feet tucked under her, listening as her mother recounted the tale, start to finish, ending with her grandfather's long pursuit of her grandmother and the magic of a kiss he gave her after the Valentine's dance. "I can't believe MiMi made Granddaddy work so hard and wait so long," she said with a laugh. "But I'm awful glad she did. That way she was the last to wear the dress and the one who got to keep it."

Behind her, beyond the wide windows, the majesty of old London rose in temples and spires on the opposite shore of the Thames. Between them on the low marble-topped coffee table, the box lay unopened, off-white-and-chocolate-brown striped, the Carson's signature three squares touting, *Carson Pirie Scott & Co.*

"Neither one of us would have been able to wear it." Julie chuckled. "But you're right. Miss Evelyn sure made Mr. Edwin work for it. After all, he was a *Baptist* preacher. But—as she used to tell me—on the pro side, he was a pretty good fisherman."

Rachel's eyes twinkled. "I guess you could say she made him

fish for her." When Julie sat motionless too long, she added, "You know . . . how when you go fishing you spend more time sitting and waiting, watching for the cork to bob, than you do actually catching the fish?"

Julie laughed then. "Good metaphor." She winked. "Although I'm not sure Miss Evelyn would want to be likened to a *fish*."

Rachel leaned forward, clasping her hands together. "I only wish . . . they could be here." Tears shimmered in her eyes. "I miss them both so much."

Julie reached for a nearby tissue box, then stood and took it to her daughter. "If it's any consolation, Joan and Robert RSVP'd. *They'll* be here for the wedding."

Rachel brightened, even as she blew her nose delicately—as she'd been taught during her own time at her grandmother's charm school.

Julie patted her shoulder, then gave it a squeeze. "She said the wedding gave her a good excuse to visit family." Julie eyed the box. "Okay, Miss Priss. Ready to peek inside? Try it on?"

Rachel nodded. "Yes, ma'am, but . . ." She held up the crumpled tissue. "Let me toss this and wash my face and hands first." She stood. "Be right back," she said before heading toward her bedroom.

Julie stood with her, arching to stretch her back, then walking toward the wide window. She peered out, her vision lingering on the sleek silver water of the Thames, then on the street below, where, she hoped, she'd see her husband stepping out of an English cab.

She didn't.

"Oh, Miss Evelyn," she whispered as the story of the five brides swirled again through her memory. Each of them, so different. All of them, the same. What was it Miss Evelyn had said? The verse of Scripture that tied them all together?

"I will go before thee, and make the crooked places straight."

And now, it was Miss Evelyn's only granddaughter's turn to carry on the tradition. Julie fought tears as she continued. "Wouldn't you and your fishing buddy be so proud?"

She no sooner spoke than a taxi—which to her way of thinking looked more like a Matchbox car—slowed to a stop along the front curb. A second later one of her husband's long legs exited from the back door followed by the rest of him. She felt her smile all the way to her stomach. "Rachel," she called out, turning. "Your daddy's here. I'm going to go meet him at the elevator." She was halfway to the door when Rachel stepped out from her room.

"Ma'am?"

"Your daddy," Julie said, this time quietly. "He's here. I'm going to go meet him. When we get back the three of us can take the gown out together."

Rachel nodded, smiling. She had the stories now; she understood.

Julie stepped out of the hotel room and into the hall, turning toward the elevator, listening as it rattled upward, bringing her own sweet husband back to her. Not wanting to appear anxious (Miss Evelyn would have a hissy fit from the Great Beyond if she did), she slowed, keeping her eyes on the coral-painted toenails that looked so chic in her designer sandals.

Now, as she neared the end of the hall, Julie walked in the precise way her mother-in-law had taught her so many years ago when she'd been one of her cotillion students.

Heel in front of toes . . . heel in front of toes . . . wiggle, wiggle, wiggle like Marilyn Monroe.

Discussion Questions

1. Joan leaves her home and her family at the age of nineteen, with only a small amount of money, to start a new life in a different country. Have you, or someone you know, made such a drastic change at a young age? Is it something you would have the courage to do? Why or why not? Do you think it was the right thing for her to do?

2. Joan feels like she's different from every other young woman she's met because marriage and children are not her highest or first goals for her life. Would she still feel that way in today's culture? Do you think young people are pressured in either direction today, or do they have complete freedom to choose the course of their lives?

3. Evelyn invests a lot of time and energy trying to please a man who doesn't think she's good enough for him. Have you ever been in a relationship like this? What advice would you have given Evelyn? If you were in her place, do you think you would have listened any better than she did?

4. Evelyn ends up being the last to marry, and thus she is the one to keep the wedding dress. As a result, her

daughter-in-law and then her granddaughter are able to wear it. Has a wedding dress or other special garment been passed down in your family? Is this a tradition you'd like to start with your children or grandchildren? In what ways can this be a valuable tradition?

5. Betty comes from a life of privilege, and her parents want to make sure she continues to enjoy its benefits. What do you think of their wishes for their daughter? Of the ways in which they try to manipulate her life? Assuming they are motivated by genuine concern for her well-being, how might they communicate it more effectively?

6. One of Betty's fears is that she will "become" her mother as she embarks on marriage and motherhood. What specifically is she afraid of? How likely is it that she will fall into these patterns? What qualities of your mother's do you hope to emulate in your own life, and in what ways do you hope your life is different from hers?

7. For a time, Magda believes she is in love with a man whose talent and connections she admires. Have you ever found yourself attracted to someone, either as a love interest or a friend, primarily because that person has something you want? How can we guard against this when making new friends?

8. When Magda and Barry begin dating, Magda faces challenges common to blended families. What is the motivation behind Harriet's animosity toward her? Does Magda handle it appropriately, in your opinion? Do you think Harriet will choose to change her behavior in order to remain a welcome part of the family?

9. Inga's story is a little more poignant than those of the other women. When she learns she is pregnant, and that marrying her baby's father is not an option, she turns to her parents for help. In the end, she feels she has no choice to but accept their solution: marriage to a stranger. Do you agree that this was her only choice? What advice would you have given Inga? How do you think her marriage will turn out?

10. Which of the characters in the book were you most able to relate to? Which did you have the hardest time relating to? Which one(s) would you be interested in reading more about?

A Note from the Author

Writers of fiction hear it all the time—"Boy, do I have a story for you." We listen as though we just may use the tale in one of our works. But the truth is, we already have such a number of stories forming and making havoc in our heads, we don't need one more—true or not.

Typically we hear a story on the news . . . or find an old photograph . . . or overhear someone talking in a restaurant or airport, and we think, *What if . . . ?* But every so often someone comes along and says, "Can I share something with you?" and we are swept away. Intrigued. *We have to have that story!*

Such is the case with the one you have just read. Several years ago, my dear friend Sharon Decker told me of a wedding dress that had been purchased by five roommates who'd met while working in post–World War II Chicago. One dress. Five near-strangers. Each one had worn the dress on her wedding day. Each one had a special love story.

"And," she added, "I know the fourth wearer of the dress."

I nearly begged for the story. Begged and waited years before I had the opportunity to meet Joan Hunt Zimmerman, who willingly allowed me to take what she told me and add to it. "After all," she said, "this is fiction, right?"

To that end, for the most part, this is a work of fiction.

While the names of Joan Hunt and Robert Zimmerman (as well as the gist of their story) have been unaltered, the stories of the other women are completely made up. I did my best with all things pertaining to the US Forces, the US Army, and their work in Germany post–World War II. Although Joan only spent two years in Germany, for the sake of the story, I extended her time there by several months.

I hope and pray I have portrayed the land I truly love, the South—or "Dixie"—and that beloved part of it, North Carolina, in its truest light. We Southerners are proud of much of our history, but we hang our heads at the rest of it. North Carolina is no exception to this fact.

About the Author

EVA MARIE EVERSON is a multiple-award-winning author and speaker. She is one of the original five members of the Orlando Word Weavers critique group, an international and national group of critique chapters, and now serves as president of Word Weavers International, Inc. Her novel *Waiting for Sunrise*, which boldly approaches the topic of mental illness, was a finalist for the 2013 Christy Award for excellence in Christian fiction.

Eva Marie is a popular presenter at writers' conferences nationwide and serves as codirector of the Florida Christian Writers Conference and contests director for the Blue Ridge Mountains Christian Writers Conference. During the 2010-2011 school year, she was an adjunct professor at Taylor University in Upland, Indiana. She describes it as one of the best times she ever had while working.

In 2002 and 2009, Eva Marie served as a journalist for the Israel Ministry of Tourism. Her article series, "Falling into the Bible," served as the inspiration for her book *Reflections of God's Holy Land: A Personal Journey through Israel*, coauthored with bestselling Israeli author Miriam Feinberg Vamosh. The book went on to become a finalist for the ECPA Gold Medallion award.

Born and reared in the low country of Georgia, Eva Marie is a wife, mother, and grandmother. She lives, works, and finds respite in her lakefront home in Florida. She enjoys reading, knitting, traveling, boating, and singing along with country music on the radio. She is pretty much owned by her dog, Poods.